Kate El was born and broug ... drama i Manchester. Keenly in ... archae logy, she lives in Cheshire with her family.

Kate has been twice nominated for the CWA Short Story Dagger and her novel, *The Plague Maiden*, was nominated for the Theakston's Old Peculier Crime Novel of the Year in 2005.

Visit Kate Ellis online:
www.kateellis.co.uk
www.twitter.com/kateellisauthor

Praise for Kate Ellis:

'A beguiling author who interweaves past and present'
The Times

'[Kate Ellis] gets better with each new book'
Bookseller

'Kept me on the edge of my seat'
Shots magazine

'Ellis skilfully interweaves ancient and contemporary crimes in an impeccably composed tale'
Publishers Weekly

By Kate Ellis

A Painted Doom

Kate Ellis

piatkus

PIATKUS

First published in Great Britain in 2002 by Piatkus Books

7 9 10 8

A CIP catalogue record for this book
is available from the British Library.

ISBN 978-0-7499-3756-0

Typeset in Times by Action Publishing Technology Ltd, Gloucester
Printed and bound in Great Britain by
Clays Ltd, St Ives plc

Papers used by Piatkus are from well-managed forests
and other responsible sources.

MIX
Paper from
responsible sources
FSC® C104740

Piatkus
An imprint of
Little, Brown Book Group
Carmelite House
50 Victoria Embankment
London EC4Y 0DZ

An Hachette UK Company
www.hachette.co.uk

www.piatkus.co.uk

For Roger

Angel

I left you there in paradise,
Now in dreams I see your eyes.
Sweet thing wearing white,
You weren't meant for the dark night.

(Chorus)

Angel, sweet angel,
How good it was before the devil came.
Angel, my angel,
You were just part of his game.

He broke your wings like a butterfly.
How I often wonder why.
We were just kids, how could I know
That you'd burn in the fire's glow?

(Chorus)

Now you're gone and I don't know how.
You don't hear or see me now.
He took you off into the night;
Crushed your wings and put out the light.

(Chorus)

Words and music by Jonny Shellmer

Prologue

August 1966

The girl knew they were staring at her, glowering out of the gloom with hideous red eyes. Eyes that knew all her secrets ... even the worst secret of all. She put her hand to her face and felt the tears on her cheek.

Then, after a few long minutes of silence, she stood up slowly, stiffly, trying not to catch the watchers' eyes. She looked down and saw the old metal box still lying there on the straw: the box he had told her about; the box that had put the evil thoughts into his mind. She pushed it away with her foot. She wanted nothing to do with it ... ever. Thick golden needles of straw had stuck to her flesh, leaving livid indentations behind. She brushed herself down with trembling hands, sobbing gently and praying that nobody would hear her.

She heard a sound, distant at first, then closer: someone was outside calling her name. Recognising the voice, she froze, not daring to move a muscle even when a large spider scampered over her bare, pale thigh, its eight fragile legs tickling her flesh. She watched the creature scurry away and waited, quite still, with shallow, silent breaths, until she was sure that she was alone.

She stumbled out into the sunshine and began to run towards the water's edge. Down and down the steep path she ran; through nettles, through soft cowpats, through overgrown thistles. Her feet were bare but she felt no sensation, no pain, no disgust. Down and down until the water appeared before her; she kept her eyes focused on the river; on the moving, shifting ripples and the dazzling sparks of sunlight which flashed and danced on the surface. As she moved forward she felt that the eyes were still on her, watching, knowing: those devils' eyes that had witnessed everything.

She reached the river. It was high tide; no time for fear or second thoughts on the drowned shingle beach. As she waded in, the salt tears and mucus rolled down her face to mingle with the blue-green waters of the River Trad. She waded in farther, the force of the river slowing her pace, until the waters reached her waist and the currents snatched at her legs, knocking her off balance. As she sank beneath the surface, she felt a sudden, unexpected urge to fight, to struggle, to choose life over the other option. She kicked against the current, taking greedy gasps of air as she surfaced. She didn't want it to end like this. But it was too late now.

It was almost over. And she knew that the demons were still watching her with greedy, mocking eyes, hungry for another lost soul.

Chapter One

Right worshipful husband,
I recommend me to you, desiring heartily to hear of your welfare. All is well on your lands and yet I am much afeared that your loyalty to the Earl will lead you into danger.

But I would write of matters that concern us here. Touching the marriage of your son, John, I heard while I was in Exeter there is a goodly young woman whose mother is friend to a kinsman of his mother's and she shall have two hundred pounds at her marriage. I spoke with the maid's kin and friends and have their good wills to have her married to John. I do hope that they will not hear of his misdeeds or my plans will come to nought.

I heard talk in Exeter that Queen Margaret is in France awaiting a passage to our shores and that the Earl's people are waiting to rise up in Devonshire at her call.

I pray the Lord to keep you from all harm and our daughter, Elizabeth, sends greeting.
Your loving wife
Marjory

Written at Derenham this fourth day of March 1471

March 2001

Terry Hoxworthy parked his battered Land Rover with its rusty trailer in front of the old barn and gave his son Lewis, who was slumped beside him in the passenger seat, a sharp nudge before climbing out.

Lewis Hoxworthy was fifteen years old with bright red hair and the plump, doughy figure of one who took too many hamburgers and not enough exercise. Slowly, resentfully, he pushed the Land Rover door open, jumped down onto the rough damp earth and complained about the cold.

His father raised his eyes to heaven. When he was Lewis's age he'd have received a clip around the ear for the mildest dissent. When Terry was young, a farmer's son helped out on the farm and that was that. But Lewis had led a softer life, a life which in times past would only have been enjoyed by the privileged sons of the aristocracy. He looked at the boy's scowling face, attempted an encouraging smile and wondered where he'd gone wrong.

'Come on, Lew. We need to clear this place out. The people from the planning department are coming tomorrow.'

Lewis looked unimpressed.

'And after they've been Mr Heygarth from the estate agent's is coming round to value the place.'

Lewis looked at the ramshackle old building, doubtful that anyone would pay good money for it.

'If we both pitch in, it won't take long. Many hands make light work,' Terry said with awkward jollity.

The boy pressed his lips together tightly and said nothing. He turned away from his father and placed an experimental toe into the puddle that had spread itself across the doorway of the barn like a defensive moat, then he pulled it out again quickly before the water could soak into the soft white leather of his new Nike trainer.

Terry jumped over the puddle and suggested nervously that Lewis might put some wood down to stop their feet getting wet. Lewis gave him a look of contempt and shrugged his shoulders, but Terry forced himself to stay calm and resisted the urge to yell at the boy, demanding instant obedience. Teenage years were difficult years, and parents had to tread carefully if good relationships were to be maintained – or so his wife had read in one of her magazines.

After a few moments spent staring at the problem, Lewis relented a little and made a half-hearted attempt to create a makeshift bridge from a couple of planks he had found propped up just inside the doorway: hardly the product of a great engineering mind, but Terry reckoned it would probably do the job and made appropriate noises of praise. Praise was important.

Then things looked up. Lewis, having decided that further resistance was futile, began to help, and the pair worked quickly with hardly a word exchangéd between father and son. Half an hour later the first trailer-load of detritus from the barn was ready to be whisked off for disposal.

Lewis turned down the chance to drive with his father to the local tip, choosing instead to stay at the old barn: he was unused to the hard physical labour of hauling and carrying and he told his father that he needed a rest to get his breath back. Terry Hoxworthy thought it best to say nothing.

As soon as the engine of Terry's Land Rover was out of earshot, Lewis began to mooch around the barn, in search of anything to relieve the paralysing boredom of an afternoon parted from his computer screen.

The ladder leading up to the hayloft caught his attention first. It would do no harm to explore, he told himself. Whatever secrets the barn held, they could hardly rival the attractions of *Death Horror III* – the latest pirated computer game acquired from his mate Yossa at school – but he was stuck there so he might as well make the best of it.

He climbed the ladder, testing each rung carefully before he trusted it with his weight. It was darker up in the loft, and the layer of ancient straw on the floor smelled musty in the damp March air. Normally the hay was stored up here, but it had been cleared out in preparation for the anticipated sale.

At first sight the empty loft seemed as boring as the rest of the barn; nothing to be seen apart from a few sticks of broken furniture and a thick layer of dusty, mildewed straw. A scattering of rusty nails and a corroded horseshoe had inexplicably made their way up here at some time in the place's long history and, strangest of all, a pair of woman's low-heeled shoes – size four or five – lay dusty and unclaimed on top of a pile of deeper straw by the left-hand wall. Perhaps a bit of what his father called 'hanky-panky' had gone on in the barn at one time or another, and this thought set Lewis's hormones racing and his loins tingling for a few turbulent seconds. Girls were as yet uncharted territory for Lewis, but the barn would be an ideal place for That Sort of Thing should the chance ever arise. He felt a first small pang of regret that his father was having to sell the place.

The exposed rafters looked massive from Lewis's elevated position: tree trunk thick, the cross-beams would have made a tempting assault course for the adventurous. But Lewis wasn't tempted. Climbing was for kids.

At the end of the loft, by the great gable end, was a large filthy wooden panel leaning against the wall. The bottom jutted out slightly to form a lean-to hiding-place normally hidden from view behind bales of hay – an undiscovered, secret place. Lewis approached it slowly, and when he reached the narrow triangular entrance he bent to look inside.

He fumbled in his pocket for the torch on his key-ring – a cheap plastic affair that he'd bought last year while staying with his aunt in Cornwall – and pressed the switch, which sent a weak beam of light out into the darkness.

A rusty metal box lay on the floor at the farthest end: it looked interesting, mysterious, and Lewis resolved to crawl

6

in and retrieve it. Then the feeble beam swept over the wooden partition and he heard himself gasp. Perhaps he had been playing too many computer games, or watching too many of those horror films his mates got out of the video shop in Tradmouth. Perhaps his eyes were playing tricks.

He shone the light on the wood again, holding his hand as steady as he could. He could just make out the naked writhing figures being dragged by monstrous apparitions towards unspeakable torment. The beam settled on the face of a plump naked woman who anticipated her fate with the lost, despairing eyes of the damned. Then it shifted to her tormentor, a twisted, red-faced creature holding some instrument of exquisite torture aloft as it anticipated with evil delight the agony of another victim.

Lewis's heart pounded and his hands began to shake. All the electronic visions of horror he had witnessed on the flickering screen didn't compare with this dimly lit scene of abject terror. He grabbed the old metal box and backed out quickly, desperate to get away; to put as much distance as he could between him and that portrait of untamed evil.

He climbed down the ladder, almost missing his footing in his haste, and ran outside. A fine misty rain was falling in horizontal gossamer sheets across the rolling hills, but Lewis had no intention of returning to the barn to take shelter. He tucked the box inside the Adidas coat he had been given last Christmas and waited for his father outside, striding to and fro to keep warm.

Lewis Hoxworthy's mind was still filled with the horrors he had seen inside the barn when he heard the sound of a shot echoing in the dank, misty air.

The next day Paul Heygarth – of Heygarth and Proudfoot, estate agents – halted his car at the junction of two narrow country lanes and looked at his watch before checking that the road was clear. Ten-thirty. The appointment with Mr Hoxworthy to give a valuation on his barn was at 11.15, so he'd just have time to call at the Old Vicarage on the edge of the village of Derenham to check that everything had been left as it should be.

Paul set off again, steering the BMW with one hand as he dialled the number of the office. The firm's surveyor, Jim Flowers, was out on a job, so Nicola was on her own. Paul felt he should inform her of his whereabouts in case anything urgent cropped up. Not that anything urgent ever had – and Nicola had his mobile number in case of emergencies – but Paul Heygarth liked to be prepared for every eventuality. And to feel that he was indispensable.

It never occurred to Paul that Nicola might resent not being trusted to hold the mighty fort of Heygarth and Proudfoot for an hour while he and Jim Flowers were out. It would never have crossed his mind that Nicola had any feelings on the matter whatsoever.

The gates of the Old Vicarage appeared on his right, guarded by a pretty thatched cottage which had once served as a lodge but now, in more egalitarian times, had severed its connections with the big house and reinvented itself as a holiday home. He swung the car into the drive without indicating and drove too fast down the narrow roadway. The Old Vicarage wouldn't come into view until he was almost at the front door, shrouded as it was by trees and mature evergreen shrubs. The winding drive was lined with thick, healthy-looking laurel bushes that could have hidden a couple of commando units in their shiny green foliage.

Suddenly the building emerged before him. The Old Vicarage had been home to the vicars of All Saints, Derenham, during the eighteenth and nineteenth centuries. But back in the 1960s the place had been considered far too grand for Derenham's parish priest, so he had been moved to humbler and more practical accommodation nearer the church.

The name, however, had stuck, which was particularly fortuitous, given the current housing market. The Old Vicarage conjured images of solidity, of status; of old maids cycling to church and peasants doffing their caps to the lord of the manor. The Old Vicarage was exactly the sort of place that attracted those who wished to buy into the rural idyll – if only at weekends. Just the sort of place to pull in the punters from London with their well-laden wallets. With their fat City bonuses, times might have been very good indeed for Paul Heygarth – if it hadn't been for his problems.

Paul stopped the car and jerked up the handbrake. He sat there for a few minutes, reluctant to exchange the sealed, heated comfort of the BMW for the chill, damp air outside.

He looked in his driving mirror to check his appearance, and the pasty face of a man who took too many business lunches and far too little exercise looked back at him. There was no client to meet but he did this swift sartorial inspection out of habit, just as he checked his receding hairline and the balding crown of his head in the bathroom mirror each morning, wishing that he could turn back the tide of time.

Taking the key to the Old Vicarage from his inside pocket, he climbed out of the car. The sudden rush of cold air made him sneeze as the door shut with a satisfyingly expensive clunk. He wore a smart dark suit with a striped shirt and bright blue silk tie, but no overcoat: he wasn't one to spend any more time than was necessary out of doors. He fastened a button on his suit jacket and hurried towards the house.

Before the Old Vicarage had been used to house the local clergy and their dull and blameless families, it was rumoured that the house had had an interesting history. According to Heygarth and Proudfoot's brochure, there was a chance that parts of the place might date back to the fifteenth century, and that it might once have been home to the Merrivale family, who had links with the Earls of Devon and who, way back in the fifteenth century, had been loyal supporters of the House of Lancaster in the Wars of the Roses. Of course, the house had been knocked about, extended and modernised in the last couple of centuries so that no trace of that far-off age remained.

And there was the uncomfortable possibility that the Merrivales' home could have been somewhere else entirely. At the other side of the village some archaeologists were digging up a field next door to his colleague Jim Flowers' house. According to Jim, the workmen digging the foundations for the proposed new village hall had discovered the remains of a large building as well as a human skull grinning up at them from the soil. The experts seemed to think that the building was the Merrivales' old manor house, but there was no need to dwell on the facts. Who was to say that those archaeologists weren't digging up some boring old outbuildings?

The Old Vicarage was a far more suitable abode for the Merrivales of old: and there was nothing like a bit of history for pushing the price up, Paul thought with a smile of satisfaction. Knights of old, mad monks, visits by Queen Elizabeth I: they were all grist to the property mill. The punters loved a bit of romance. Paul reckoned he could easily push the price of the Old Vicarage over the million mark the way the market was going. And a quick sale would put an end to all his troubles.

As he reached the front door something caught his eye; a flash of shiny yellow to his left, screened by the ubiquitous laurels. He walked towards it slowly, and when he rounded the bushes he saw it. A shiny yellow sports car. He stared at it for a few seconds then turned and walked back to the front door, pausing to listen for any telltale sounds. But he heard nothing except birdsong and the distant hum of farm machinery.

Paul unlocked the great oak front door and marched straight into the hallway – oak panelled and deceptively spacious, with radiator and telephone point – where he stood for a few moments in the expensively carpeted silence. He stared at the closed drawing-room door, then turned the great ring of black iron which served as a handle and pushed. The door opened a little but there was something behind it, blocking the way. He pushed again, harder this time, but whatever it was wouldn't budge.

He took a deep breath before deciding to try the other way into the room, via the kitchen and the dining room.

As he walked slowly across the lush ruby-red hall carpet towards the back of the house, he felt a sudden chill in the air. Paul Heygarth was an unimaginative soul – never one to succumb to tales of hauntings, even in properties with strange grisly pasts – but standing there in the entrance hall of Derenham's Old Vicarage he had an uneasy, creeping feeling that he was in the presence of death.

Terry Hoxworthy greeted his visitors with a shotgun over his arm.

Neil Watson looked at his companion, a short young man wearing a thick grey anorak which had fallen open to reveal a tie crawling with Disney cartoon characters. 'Er ... are you sure this is okay, Mark?' he whispered out of the corner of his mouth.

Mark Telston, Assistant Planning Officer, ignored Neil's apparent cowardice and approached the farmer with a confident outstretched hand. 'Pleased to meet you, Mr Hoxworthy. I'd like to introduce Neil Watson from the County Archaeological Unit. He's in charge of the excavation that's going on near the church, on the site of the proposed new village hall. They've discovered the remains of a large medieval building up there. Have you heard about it?' he asked brightly.

Terry Hoxworthy nodded, his face expressionless.

'I thought Neil's department should be aware of your application for planning permission. There was an archaeological excavation on your land in the 1950s, I believe.' He looked at the farmer for confirmation.

Hoxworthy shifted the shotgun a little, and Neil noticed a pale, shiny scar across the palm of his right hand. He averted his eyes. It was rude to stare.

'Aye. That were when my dad had the farm. Bit before

11

my time. He were interested in history, all that sort of thing. Used to buy a load of rubbish at auctions and say it was antiques.' He looked Neil up and down suspiciously, noting the long straggly hair and tattered old jeans. 'What's it got to do with my barn?'

Neil glanced at Mark and then at the shotgun. He had an uneasy feeling that it was his turn to speak. He shifted his weight from foot to foot. He was used to dealing with academic matters, and facing a potentially irate member of the public like this really wasn't his sort of thing.

'The thing is, Mr Hoxworthy,' he began, trying to sound enthusiastic, 'it's very possible that your barn here is of considerable historical interest. The excavation in the 1950s found evidence of medieval field systems and various written records mention a fifteenth-century tithe barn connected with Derenham church. It's just possible that your barn may be, er ...' His voice trailed off. From the glazed look that had come into Hoxworthy's eyes, he suspected that either he was getting too technical or that he was saying things the man didn't want to hear.

'So what's that got to do with me selling it?'

To Neil's relief it was Mark who spoke. 'Well, if it does turn out to be a medieval tithe barn, it means you can't just do what you like with it. It may be appropriate to list it, and that means that all sorts of planning restrictions come into force, I'm afraid.' Mark Telston tried his best to look apologetic, but Neil thought he could detect a hint of triumph in his voice.

'So you're saying I can't do what I like with my own barn?' The shotgun shifted again. Neil took a step back as if to emphasise that he was only there in an advisory capacity.

'Not necessarily, Mr Hoxworthy. It might turn out that your barn was built much later than we suspect. It's just that with your application for planning permission to convert the barn into a luxury dwelling we have to be sure. Now if Neil here could just have a quick look at the barn ...'

'Okay, okay,' said the farmer impatiently. 'But don't be long 'cause I've got an estate agent coming to value the place soon. Bloody bureaucrats,' he added under his breath, scratching his head. Neil was beginning to feel sorry for the man.

After a few seconds Hoxworthy spoke again, more quietly this time, with an undercurrent of desperation. 'I've got to sell this place. I ain't got no choice. Do you know how far the income from this farm has dropped in the past few years?'

He looked at Neil challengingly, having selected him as potentially the most sympathetic of the pair. 'Bloody politicians are always on at us farmers to diversify, to think of new ways to make a bit extra. I do like they say. I try to sell one of me old barns for conversion and this is what happens ... bloody red tape tying me up again. It never bloody stops. If it's not Brussels playing silly buggers it's inspectors with their rules and regulations about BSE and ...' He shook his head. Then he looked Neil in the eye. 'Do you think I want to sell this barn? Do you think I want a load of yuppies living at the end of the bloody lane complaining every time my cock crows or the slurry doesn't smell of French perfume. Do you?'

'I'm sorry. I, er, see your point, Mr Hoxworthy, but ...'

'You're only doing your job. That's what they always say.'

Neil, who had never considered himself a natural member of the forces of oppression, feared that he was being cast as the lowest form of obstructive petty bureaucrat, and he could think of no reply that would convince the farmer otherwise.

He was rescued from an embarrassed guilty silence by Mark's timely intervention: he had clearly had more practice in these situations. 'If Neil could just have a look at your barn ...'

'Do what the hell you like,' Terry Hoxworthy said

before marching off towards the house.

Mark Telston watched him go with some amusement. Neil didn't feel like laughing.

He said nothing to Mark as he conducted the preliminary survey of the barn which, as he had predicted, didn't take very long. Keen to examine the construction of the roof, he climbed up to the hayloft while the assistant planning officer waited below with his feet firmly on the ground.

It was a few minutes later when Mark heard a gasp followed by an ominous silence. He put a tentative foot on the rickety ladder and called Neil's name. When there was no reply he climbed up slowly and called again.

Again the only answer was a brooding silence. Mark climbed farther up so that he could just see into the hayloft. He called Neil's name again, looking around. His heart started to beat faster and his mouth felt dry. Either the archaeologist had an infantile sense of humour or something was wrong.

Standing there on the ladder, his hands gripping tightly until the knuckles were bone white, he scanned the loft, registering the condition of the place, the evidence of neglect ... and the fact that Neil Watson was nowhere to be seen.

Paul Heygarth stared at the door which led from the rather grand dining room to the drawing room. It was shut, as all the doors should be. The owners, Colonel and Mrs Porter, had been quite particular on that point. Whoever showed potential buyers around had to make sure all the doors were shut. As the house wasn't alarmed, Paul thought this was probably a minor eccentricity on the part of the elderly couple – unless they knew something that he didn't. As the vendors – as he habitually thought of the colonel and his good lady – were away settling into their new property in the south of France, he supposed that if all the doors were left wide open they wouldn't have been any the wiser, but he had half-heartedly acceded to their wishes. They were

14

going to pay him handsomely when the place was sold. And he needed the money. Needed it soon.

He looked at his watch. There was plenty of time before his appointment at Mr Hoxworthy's barn. He opened the door and stepped into the drawing room, his feet sinking into the thick Persian carpet. The room was gloomy – north facing – and it seemed smaller than he remembered.

From his vantage point by the dining-room door he couldn't see the thing blocking the other doorway as a floppy dark red sofa of huge proportions was obscuring his view. He walked around the edge of the room, his estate agent's eye taking in every detail of the décor, which might push the asking price up a few hundred pounds.

When he saw the shape on the floor he stopped and stared. If Paul Heygarth had been a religious man, and if he had known the identity of the patron saint of estate agents, he might have sent up a swift prayer beseeching that the unfortunate soul lying on the carpet before him be taken up bodily into the next world and vanish from mortal sight without a trace.

There was nothing like a violent death on the premises for bringing down the value of a property.

Chapter Two

My well beloved wife,
I beseech you not to concern yourself overmuch with my
welfare. I have orders from the Earl of Devonshire to
ride speedily to Tradmouth to raise men for Queen
Margaret's cause. So fear not, good wife, I shall be with
you at Derenham presently.

As to the other matter, my son John was ever a wilful
and disobedient child (having inherited the nature of my
first wife, his mother). I think it best to advance the cause
of this young woman of Exeter as marriage will steady
the lad.

Is there no young man suitable as husband for
Elizabeth? She is a good girl and will have two hundred
and fifty pounds in money at her marriage. Look to the
matter if you will, and find her a young man with a good
fortune. As to Edmund, he does well in the Earl's house-
hold and will soon have need of a good wife. But all this
we will talk of on my return.
Your loving and faithful husband
Richard

Written at London this twenty-fifth day of March 1471

Nicola Tarnley sat at her desk in the front office of Heygarth
and Proudfoot typing house details into her flickering

computer. The office was empty for once; that was good. It meant she could get on with some of her paperwork instead of being charming to well-heeled house-hunters and sympathetic to the sheepish young local couples who watched the area's mounting house prices with a mixture of open-mouthed disbelief and resentful bitterness. But just as Nicola was anticipating half an hour of peace, the telephone on her desk began to ring.

She picked it up. 'Heygarth and Proudfoot, Nicola Tarnley speaking. How may I help you?' The words were second nature. She was sure she mumbled them in her sleep.

'Nicola.' The voice on the other end of the line was low, conspiratorial, and at first she didn't recognise it as Paul's. 'I've got a problem here. Can you come down to Derenham? The Old Vicarage.'

'But there's nobody else in the office. Jim won't be back for an hour or so.'

'Just lock up and get here quick. It's an emergency.'

'Okay,' she said, pressing the Save key on the computer. 'What kind of emergency? A burst pipe? Do you want me to call a plumber or anything?' She could hear Paul breathing heavily on the other end of the line. 'A doctor?' she suggested anxiously.

'Just get down here as quick as you can.'

Without another word Nicola switched off her computer and turned on the office answering machine. She locked the door of Heygarth and Proudfoot behind her and marched down Tradmouth High Street, heading for the carpark near the waterfront. Parking, like most of life's mundane tasks, was easier out of the tourist season. The river was a deep shade of battleship grey, and a pale mist was beginning to creep into the town off the water. Nicola shivered. It was cold, but at least the drizzle had stopped.

Nicola drove, a little too fast, out of the town and down the winding lanes leading to the village of Derenham – a pretty place about three miles upstream from Tradmouth with a wealth of desirable country properties – wondering what Paul's emergency could be.

Neil Watson looked stunned as he wandered out of the great barn doors. Terry Hoxworthy had returned for the verdict, and now he stood staring at the archaeologist, waiting for him to speak. Mark Telston hovered behind, fidgeting with his Disney tie, also awaiting the expert's verdict.

'Do you want the good news or the bad news?' Neil asked, not quite sure how to break either.

'Let's start with the bad, eh?' said Hoxworthy. He still had the shotgun over his arm, and Neil eyed it warily.

'The bad news is that the barn certainly seems to be a medieval structure, so it's probably going to have to be listed. Various other experts will be consulted, of course, and I'll arrange to have samples of wood from the beams taken for dating. Then we'll have to await the verdict. I won't be making the final decision.' He mentally added the words 'so don't blame me'. 'But in view of the field systems found in the course of the previous excavations I do feel . . .'

'Is there a chance you could be wrong?' the farmer asked, shifting the shotgun a little.

Neil shrugged. 'I'm not infallible,' he admitted modestly.

Hoxworthy was staring at him as if he were something one of his prize herd of cows might have deposited on the ground of the meadow next door. Neil sensed that what he had to say was as unwelcome as a fresh batch of forms from the Ministry of Agriculture.

'So what's the good news?' said Hoxworthy under his breath.

Neil pulled his old khaki coat tightly around him against the damp, chilly air and tried to look cheerful, which was difficult in the circumstances. 'Well, I think there's a chance that you might have something very exciting in there,' he said.

18

Terry Hoxworthy looked anything but excited. 'So what is it, then?'

'I think I've found a piece of medieval art up in the loft. I can't be certain, of course, but . . .'

Hoxworthy's eyes lit up. Art: that meant money, lots of it. He'd heard of people finding priceless art treasures in their attics: perhaps not getting planning permission for the barn wouldn't be such a disaster after all.

'What kind of art? How much do you reckon it's worth?'

'I really can't say.'

'What is it? A painting?' It must have been a small one, Terry thought, or he'd have noticed it. Perhaps it was something his dad had picked up at one of those auctions he was always going to. One of those Madonna-and-Child pictures perhaps, by some famous Italian painter. Worth a fortune. Millions. His heart began to beat faster. His troubles might be over.

'Sort of,' said Neil non-committally. 'It's in the hayloft.' He looked at Terry Hoxworthy, feeling a little more confident now that the farmer was obviously so keen on the subject of medieval art. 'Are you coming up to see it, then?'

'Just try and stop me,' Terry replied, propping his shotgun against the wall of the barn.

Two hours later Terry Hoxworthy strolled across the steep field which tumbled down almost to the riverbank, and stared into the distance, a disappointed man.

He could see that Neil Watson's yellow Mini was still parked by the old barn. The archaeologist was hanging about, apparently excited about the 'art' in the hayloft, which had turned out to be no desirable Madonna-and-Child but a great ugly sick thing that anybody in their right mind would put straight on a bonfire. Watson either had a warped sense of humour or he was a fool.

The planning officer and the estate agent had left long since. Heygarth, the estate agent – whose mind hadn't seemed to be on the job – had brought the good news that the barn was a desirable property, ripe for conversion, and should fetch a decent price, which was what Terry wanted to hear. Prices of livestock and produce had plummeted and red tape had spread like foot-and-mouth disease. Times were hard.

The barn's sale would put the farm on a sounder financial footing. He knew that another local farmer had sold a redundant barn for a pretty price, and now it was used by a lawyer from London as a holiday home. You had to do what you could these days.

Terry trudged on through the field, his Border collie, Bess, walking patiently at his heels. The cows spotted him with their great, calm eyes and began to amble slowly towards him. Terry looked at them and smiled. His girls. Early that morning he had thought one of them might be going lame and he had come to have a look at her. He spotted her and watched her for a while. She seemed to be walking normally now. Nothing to worry about. No need to go to the expense of calling the vet out.

Bess had bounded off towards the hedge that divided the meadow from the narrow lane beyond. Terry called to her but, unusually, she didn't come to him. She had more important things to concern her. More important, even, than obeying a much-loved master with whom she'd worked for seven contented years.

Terry Hoxworthy was no longer a young man; his round face had been beaten by fifty winters and browned by as many Devon summers. But there was nothing wrong with his eyesight, and one glance towards the hedgerow told him that the dog had found something. Something big. The cows watched, disappointed, as he walked away from them and headed down the field towards the gate that opened onto the lane.

A few yards to the side of the gate something lay against the towering hedge. Part of it looked black and shiny. A bin-bag? Had someone been dumping their garden rubbish

20

in the field? People from the town who hadn't a clue about the countryside? He quickened his steps, anger rising within him.

'Leave it, Bess,' he called.

But when he drew closer he saw that the object of Bess's attention wasn't a sack of rubbish. It was a man lying on his side, his face turned towards the foot of the hedge. A man wearing tight denim jeans and a black leather jacket. Terry shouted sharply to Bess again. This time she gave him a reproachful look and slunk to his side.

Terry's first thought was that it was some drunk, sleeping it off in his field. But the man's clothes looked expensive, the black leather jacket soft and well cut, hardly the attire of a vagrant. He stepped forward and gave the man an experimental tap with his muddy wellington boot. But there was no groan, no drunken stirring.

Patting Bess reassuringly on the head, Terry bent down, leaning over to see the face. The man did look as though he was asleep; the lined face was strangely peaceful, as though he would wake up refreshed at any moment.

But then Terry saw the mark on his forehead. A small round mark. Neat and black.

Bess gazed up at her master adoringly as he drew a tiny mobile phone from the deep pocket of his well-worn coat and punched out 999, keeping a wary eye on the cows, who were edging forward, curious to see the still and silent newcomer to their domain.

As the police car sped along the lane, the young man sitting in the back seat spotted Neil Watson in the doorway of Terry Hoxworthy's old barn. He couldn't be sure it was Neil, of course, as he had only glimpsed him for a second. The police don't have time to slow down and admire the scenery when a suspicious death is reported.

Detective Inspector Wesley Peterson turned to his companion. 'I'm sure that was Neil back there. He's working on the other side of Derenham, near the church.

21

Do you remember that workman who came into the station about a month ago – he was working on this new village hall they're building in Derenham. He had a human skull in a carrier bag and he dumped it on the front desk. It gave poor Bob Naseby the shock of his life?'

'Oh, aye. I remember,' said Detective Chief Inspector Heffernan absently, his mind on other things.

'As well as the skull they'd uncovered a section of medieval wall. I told Neil about it and he rushed down to Derenham and halted the building work. The site's being excavated properly now.'

Heffernan grunted. 'I haven't seen him lurking around making the place look untidy for a while. So what's he found in Derenham, then?'

'He reckons it's a high-status domestic building, probably a manor house. He's quite excited about it.'

Detective Chief Inspector Gerry Heffernan slumped in his seat. He was a big man with unkempt hair and a pronounced Liverpool accent. His shirt strained open at his midriff, exposing a patch of bare, hairy flesh which he scratched absent-mindedly from time to time. 'I've come across your mate Neil when he's excited – not a pretty sight.'

Wesley Peterson, in his late twenties, black, good looking and positively dapper in comparison to his boss, smiled philosophically and said nothing. They turned into a narrow lane where several police cars were parked.

The thoroughfare – two cars wide, which was rare for this part of Devon – was completely blocked, and a young uniformed constable guarded the junction, his face serious as he contemplated the awesome responsibility of his allotted task.

About twenty yards down the lane, behind the barrier of police vehicles, was an area cordoned off with the constabulary's customary blue-and-white tape. Wesley and Heffernan climbed out of their car and began to walk towards the action.

White-overalled men and women swarmed over the field, absorbed in various tasks. Some knelt on the muddy ground as though in prayer: a fingertip search. Wesley took a deep breath. The death must be more than suspicious. More than just a tramp's demise in a hedgerow or a hit-and-run.

They stood staring at this hive of industry for a few seconds before Heffernan asked to see the body. A young policewoman, barely out of the school netball team, led them a little farther up the lane to a wooden gate. The cows in the field beyond, a fine body of Jersey milkers, stood some way off, watching the activity with their great curious eyes.

Heffernan asked a constable stationed at the gate whether Dr Bowman had arrived. Colin Bowman, the genial pathologist who attended whenever they encountered a suspicious death, was the man to provide the answers to their questions. But the enquiry was greeted by the shake of a constable's head.

'Dr Bowman's not here, sir. It's a Dr Kruger. She's examining the body now. She's just over there by the hedge, sir,' the constable added reassuringly.

'She?'

Wesley detected a wariness in his boss's voice.

'Dr Kruger's a lady, sir,' replied the constable, a little nervous.

Gerry Heffernan snorted in disgust, in Wesley's opinion unreasonably. 'I don't care if she's a member of the royal family, I want Colin Bowman. Get someone to call him, will you? And don't take no for an answer.'

'Dr Bowman's on holiday, sir. Someone said he's in France.' The constable who had hopes of joining CID, was glad to be able to show off his aptitude for detection.

Gerry Heffernan muttered something incomprehensible which Wesley thought it best to ignore.

'We'd better have a word with Dr Kruger, then,' said Wesley firmly. He followed the young constable through the gate. A few yards to the right, up against the thick hedgerow, the product of centuries of nature's work, the police photographer's flashbulbs knifed through the gloom like lightning. Wesley could almost feel the waves of disapproval emanating from Gerry Heffernan, who was shambling along behind him. He just hoped that he wouldn't take his disappointment out on the unsuspecting Dr Kruger.

It seemed they had timed their arrival well. Dr Kruger, a tall young woman with dark curly hair and a face which, although not pretty, was pleasantly attractive, stood a few feet away from the body, removing her plastic gloves which, Wesley guessed, meant that she had finished her initial examination. She wore jeans, a dark-coloured fleece and, sensibly, a pair of sturdy green wellingtons. Wesley noted approvingly that she had come prepared.

He introduced himself and Heffernan. The doctor rewarded them with a friendly but businesslike smile.

'Single gunshot wound to the head at fairly close range,' she announced matter-of-factly. 'Death would have been instantaneous.'

Wesley studied the body lying on the ground a few feet away. The dead man lay on his side facing the hedge. His slim form was clad in black leather and faded denim; on his feet he wore clean blue suede trainers. His clothes weren't brand new but something about them told Wesley that they were expensive. The man's hair was dark and fairly long; he couldn't see the face from where he was standing, and he was glad of this as he stared down at the shell that had once been a human being. He hated looking into the faces of those who had suffered violent deaths.

The doctor squatted down beside the body and heaved gently at the dead man's shoulder until the face was revealed: an old face, far more furrowed with age and experience than the clothes and hairstyle suggested.

Wesley stared for a few moments at the neat black hole in the forehead, then he turned away. When he looked back he was relieved to see that the face was hidden again.

'Could it have been suicide?' he asked hopefully.

'No gun's been found near by,' said Dr Kruger. 'I should think that rules out suicide or accident.'

'Anything else you can tell us, love?' Heffernan growled. 'Time of death, for instance?'

Dr Kruger gave the chief inspector a warning look. 'I'd say he's been dead approximately twenty-four hours – give or take a few hours. That means he probably died some time on Wednesday afternoon.'

Heffernan grunted and walked away towards a group of scenes-of-crime officers; familiar faces. Wesley stood by Dr Kruger and watched him go.

'Is he always that rude?' she asked.

Wesley found himself feeling apologetic. 'Sorry about that,' he mumbled.

'And does he call all women "love"?'

'Usually.'

She looked Wesley up and down. 'Is he racist as well as sexist? I bet he gives you a hard time, does he?'

'No. We get on quite well, actually. You've just caught him at a bad time,' said Wesley, wondering why he was feeling so protective of his boss's reputation. 'He was expecting to see Colin and . . . well, DCI Heffernan likes what he knows.'

Dr Kruger nodded. 'Doesn't everyone? I'll forgive him this once.' She gave Wesley a wide smile, and he noticed that it had transformed her face from merely attractive to beautiful. 'My name's Laura, by the way.' She held out an ungloved hand and Wesley shook it firmly.

'Wesley Peterson,' he said.

'And what shall I call the chief inspector?'

'He'll answer to the name of Gerry.'

'Oh, I might just call him "love",' said Laura Kruger with a mischievous glint in her eye.

'Has the body been moved?' asked Wesley, returning to police matters.

'Yes. I don't think it's been here long. It was drizzling

until about ten this morning. The ground's fairly damp but the body's dry. I think he was kept somewhere else then he was dumped here within the past few hours. And if you want any more evidence for my theory, look at those shoes; they're far too clean for someone who's been tramping round fields, don't you think?'

Wesley looked down at his own shoes, now in need of a good polish, and nodded in agreement.

'We'll have to see what forensics come up with,' she continued. 'And I'll do the post-mortem tomorrow morning. Is that all right?'

Wesley said that was fine, then he looked down at the body again, willing it to give up its secrets. 'Any clues to his identity?'

Laura Kruger shook her head. 'There was a set of keys in his trouser pocket and some money. Nothing else.'

'Who found him?'

'The farmer who owns this land, a Mr Hoxworthy. It gave him a bit of a shock. He was in this field first thing this morning fetching the cows in for milking, and he's certain the body wasn't there then. He's gone back home if you want a word, but I don't think he'll be able to tell you anything. He said he didn't recognise the dead man.'

'Where does he live?'

Laura pointed into the distance. In the rolling landscape one green hill folded into another, but the long stone farmhouse was built on rising ground, easily visible from the field.

'That's the house over there. You get to it down the lane. You pass a big old barn and then go down a track to the left. I reckon that you can see this field from there, but Mr Hoxworthy said he hadn't seen anything suspicious. His theory is that someone dumped the body here from a passing car, and I reckon he could be right.' She gave Wesley a shy smile. 'I'm doing your job for you.'

Wesley returned the smile. 'A lot of my colleagues could do with your observational skills.' He paused and stared down at the body.

26

'That jacket didn't come cheap,' Laura observed. 'Could he have been a drug dealer; gangland killing come to rural Devon?'

'He was still a human being,' said Wesley quietly, almost in a whisper.

Neither spoke for a while as they contemplated the unfortunate man who had ended his earthly existence at the foot of a hedgerow like some medieval vagrant. It was a sad end, thought Wesley, to leave this world violently with only a field of cows for company.

The mortuary van had arrived. Its occupants, discreet as trusted butlers, moved swiftly as they prepared to transfer the mortal remains of the man in the leather jacket to their unobtrusive black van.

Gerry Heffernan wandered over to watch, standing silently as the sad little procession passed. The body was carried on a trolley, packed inside a zip-up bag which reminded Wesley inappropriately of the bags used by pizza delivery-men to insulate their wares. Heffernan stepped forward, stopping the trolley's progress, and unzipped the bag so that he could have a last look at the dead man's face.

Everyone stopped what they were doing, frozen until the DCI delivered his verdict.

'I've seen him somewhere before,' he pronounced with a confident jollity that Wesley considered inappropriate for the occasion. 'I know his face. Hang on, it'll come to me.' He screwed his chubby face up as he mined his memory.

Wesley watched him expectantly. If the dead man had been a customer of the local constabulary in the past, dredging up his details would be a piece of cake once the DCI provided them with a name.

'I know,' Heffernan pronounced to all who cared to hear. 'He looks just like that pop singer. Back in the late sixties, early seventies. What was his name?'

The faces around him were blank. The majority of the officers there hadn't even been born at the time he

27

mentioned. Wesley, numbered among the young, assumed an expression of polite interest, like a child whose grandparents were reminiscing about the Second World War.

'He was in the local paper the other day. He's moving down here and he gave some money for a new village hall in Derenham. I'm sure it's him. He was quite well known – lead singer. What was his name?'

The young officers standing around shook their heads. Laura Kruger shrugged her shoulders. It was before her time.

'It'll come to me.' Heffernan wrinkled his brow in concentration.

Wesley waited, willing him to remember: a name for their corpse would save a lot of time. But the boss shook his head. It had been on the tip of his tongue but the more he thought, the more the name retreated into the mists.

'Come on, Wes,' Heffernan said suddenly. 'Let's get Rach and Steve over and start interviewing the neighbours, see if they heard anything suspicious. Someone's bound to have heard a gunshot.'

'This is farming country,' said Laura, stepping forward. 'Every farmer has a shotgun.'

'But he wasn't killed with a shotgun, was he?' said Heffernan, looking down at the body impatiently, still searching his memory for the name to fit the face.

'No. Probably some small handgun, but . . .'

'So the noise might have been different. Someone could have noticed an unusual shot.'

Laura nodded. She hated to admit it but the DCI had a point.

Suddenly Heffernan's face lit up. He grinned at the others triumphantly, like a man who had just made a great discovery: something on a par with Archimedes' bath water or Newton's apple. 'Jonny Shellmer.'

All eyes were on him. Most looked puzzled. It was Wesley who asked the question everyone below forty was longing to ask. 'Who's Jonny Shellmer?'

'Lead singer of Rock Boat,' Heffernan answered, as though this were obvious. 'Ruddy heck, it's like working in a flaming kindergarten. Have none of you heard of 'em?'

Among the blank faces, a middle-aged uniformed sergeant at the back of the group put up a tentative hand. 'Whatever happened to Rock Boat, sir?' he asked.

Heffernan looked relieved that he wasn't the only one who recalled the heady days of the sixties. 'Search me. Where do flies go in wintertime and where do rock groups go when they're past their sell-by date?' he asked rhetorically. 'Wonder how Jonny Shellmer ended up shot dead lying in a field full of cows.'

'If it is Jonny Shellmer,' said Wesley, wondering if his boss's fit of nostalgia was affecting his judgement.

'Well, it doesn't half look like that picture of him I saw in the paper the other day. I noticed it specially.' Heffernan shuffled his feet. 'I used to be a bit of a fan in the old days.'

Wesley smiled but made no comment. At least they had a name, a starting point; although he'd keep an open mind about the dead man's identity. But he was the right age and he was wearing what Wesley, in his limited experience of such matters, would expect an ageing rock star to wear. But it was possible Heffernan might be on the wrong track completely, and it would be up to him, as usual, to steer him back onto the steep and narrow path of known facts and common sense.

Heffernan nodded to the undertakers and they zipped up the bag: the next time they would see the body, it would be lying on the mortuary slab. Wesley shuddered at the thought.

'Right, then, love. See you at the post-mortem,' Heffernan said to Laura, narrowly avoiding a large soft cowpat as he made for the gate.

'I'll look forward to it ... love,' Laura answered, giving Wesley a most unprofessional wink.

*

Lewis Hoxworthy could see the field next to the lane from his bedroom window. He sat on his bed and watched the activity.

It had started about an hour ago when his dad had returned to the house in a rare old panic. Of course, nobody had thought to tell Lewis what was going on, but he knew that, whatever it was, it was big. Police cars passed along the lane, more and more of them, blocking the way.

They had found something. And Lewis felt uneasy.

He could have gone right up to the window to get a better view, but he stayed on the bed out of sight as some survival instinct told him to make himself inconspicuous, invisible. This wasn't difficult for Lewis: there had been times when he had felt that he was the most invisible boy in his year at school; the one nobody noticed and everybody ignored. But things would be different now.

He surveyed the posters on his bedroom walls. Knights in full armour and glossy cut-away sections of medieval castles. Above his bed, a knight on his charger rode into battle; an image so vivid that as he gazed at it he could almost hear the snorting of the great warhorse and the clattering of the shining metal armour.

Yesterday Lewis had won his spurs. And when he returned to school on Monday they wouldn't laugh at him – they wouldn't dare. He wouldn't feel invisible any more.

He wondered how his father had got on with the man from the planning department. Had they seen what he had seen in the old barn? He shuddered. Surely they would take the thing away and burn it. Unless it wasn't there: unless those terrible horrors had crawled into his mind when he had swallowed those pills Yossa had dared him to take. Unless he was going mad.

He wouldn't watch any longer. The thought of what the police might be doing in the meadow was making him jumpy, and he had to see if there was an answer to the e-mail he had sent earlier. Surely somebody would be interested in what he had to sell.

He sat on his computer chair and wheeled himself over to the flickering screen. There were three e-mails: one from Yossa ordering him to do his school history project for him; one from Mary-Jo, the American girl to whom he had written that he was twenty-one, ran his own software business and drove a Porsche; and another which said simply that he should bring the merchandise to a boat moored at Tradmouth. Lewis stared at this last one for a while, wondering what to do.

He looked at the window, at the grey sky laden with early spring showers. It looked like rain: hardly the weather to cycle all the way into Tradmouth. Unless he took the ferry from Derenham. That would probably be best: he would take the ferry to Tradmouth tomorrow morning, taking an example of the merchandise with him to whet his customer's appetite.

As he began to type a reply to the e-mail, he heard a thunderous knocking on the farmhouse front door. He sat very still and listened as the door was opened, and when he heard the word 'police' he froze, contemplating flight.

But he would keep his head. Lie low. There was no reason the police should suspect him. No reason at all.

Chapter Three

Right worshipful husband,
There is much talk in Tradmouth that Queen Margaret
will reach these shores presently. She is assured of a
loyal following here and the townsfolk await her arrival.
It may be that the Queen will honour us by dining at our
house, therefore I will have need of a new gown and
jewels for I durst not for shame go with an old gown
among the Queen's ladies.

I had words with your son, John, a day since concern-
ing his misdeeds. It is said that on Lady Day even last he
did come upon a servant of the Earl's and did rob him of
some money and did smite him with a sword. It seems,
husband, that your son has fallen in with certain wild
fellows who, in drink, do much mischief. Good husband,
he is in sore need of a father's chastisement for he pays
no heed to my requests. And Elizabeth spends much time
in his company which worries me greatly. I await news of
the young woman of Exeter I told you of but I fear her kin
have learned of John's ill reputation.

I send this by a servant of Master Hollers who travels
in the service of his master, and I pray God in His mercy
to defend you from all danger for I never heard tell of so
much robbery and manslaughter in this county as is now.
Your loving wife
Marjory

Written at Derenham this ninth day of April 1471

Gerry Heffernan was a man with a mission.

He sat in the passenger seat as Wesley drove the unmarked police car through the back lanes to Tradmouth. The high hedges of the damp green lanes glistened with recent raindrops, and Wesley drove slowly. The lanes were narrow, one car wide with the occasional passing place. Wesley sometimes had nightmares where he was hurtling too fast down these Devon lanes – shady green Cresta runs where the fields either side were hidden behind towering hedgerows, and slow-moving farm vehicles or idiots in sports cars might lurk around every blind bend. Not for the nervous or the learner driver. The locals – like Rachel Tracey – didn't seem bothered by these fearful thoroughfares. But Wesley still navigated them with extreme caution.

Heffernan tapped his foot impatiently. Although he never drove on dry land – saving his navigational skills for the water – he wasn't slow to offer a few words of advice now and again.

'Hurry up, Wes. Put your foot down.'

'Where are we going exactly?'

'The *Tradmouth Echo* offices in Market Street. I want to track down that picture of Jonny Shellmer and talk to whoever did the story – they ask a lot of questions, these journalists.' He grinned. 'Almost as bad as us lot. Someone must know what Jonny Shellmer was doing down here.'

They drove in amicable silence towards the town. Wesley was relieved to reach the main road, and changed gear to slow the car on the steep incline down to the town and the harbour. They passed the imposing bulk of the Naval College on their left and drove along the waterfront until they arrived in the ancient heart of Tradmouth with its narrow streets and overhanging shops and houses. The damp pavements glistened and a thin mist rolled in off the river.

Wesley parked by the police station and, by unspoken agreement, the two men walked the short distance to their destination, a large building in the middle of the main street that had once served as the town's main gentlemen's outfitters but whose modern plate-glass window now proclaimed it to be the offices of the Tradmouth Echo Group of Companies. Impressive – if you were impressed by that sort of thing.

But not much impressed Gerry Heffernan. Without ceremony he barged the glass door open. A thin young girl with a blond ponytail was sitting at a pale wooden desk in the reception area. She looked the newcomers up and down suspiciously, as if fearing a sudden robbery or attack. 'Can I help you?' she asked with a nervous squeak.

Gerry Heffernan muttered their names and flashed his warrant card. The girl still looked nervous, but in a different way.

'Is Ray Davenport about, love?'

The once large shop had been partitioned off into offices when the *Echo* took over the building. The girl pressed the intercom button and passed on the information that the police wanted a word – a phrase guaranteed to strike fear into a fair proportion of the population. After that she turned her back on them and pretended to do some filing. Something told Wesley that the girl didn't like the forces of law and order much, and he wondered fleetingly why.

It wasn't long before a door burst open and a voice boomed out, 'Gerry. Good to see you.'

Wesley swung round. A middle-aged man with receding hair and the face of an innocent weasel was bearing down on them.

'Hello, Ray.' Gerry Heffernan drew himself up to his full height. 'Wesley, I don't think you've met Ray Davenport of the *Tradmouth Echo*.' He grinned. 'How are you, Ray? Long time no see.'

'I'm fine, Gerry. Apart from the ulcer, of course, but these things are sent to try us, eh? Aren't you going to introduce your colleague?' he asked, looking at Wesley greedily, sensing a human interest story.

34

'This is DI Peterson. He's been with us about eighteen months now, but your paths haven't crossed.'

'Pleased to meet you, DI Peterson. I have heard of you, of course – word gets round. Actually I've been meaning to get in touch: I was wondering if you'd be interested in helping with a little piece I was planning about the difficulties faced by ethnic minorities in the ...'

'Sorry, Mr Davenport, but I think I'm going to be rather tied up with ...'

'Unlike some, we've got work to do,' Heffernan interrupted bluntly.

'Haven't we all, Gerry. Now what can I do for you?'

'There was a piece in the *Echo* last week. An ageing rock star donated money to some village hall project. There was the usual photo of him handing over a cheque and shaking hands with some local bigwig. Remember it?'

''Course I remember. I went over to Derenham and did the story myself. It was Jonny Shellmer of Rock Boat. I used to be a bit of a fan in my younger days. Things have been busy over in Derenham recently. We've run a couple of features on the homes of local celebrities – we did Jeremy Sedley's house last week ... you know, the actor. And we're due to do a piece on Jack Cromer's place – you know, the TV interviewer?'

Heffernan nodded. He'd heard of Jack Cromer all right. His TV show was watched by millions.

'And we're planning to do a piece about these archaeologists who are digging something up over there – the punters like a bit of local history from time to time.'

'Have you got a copy of Jonny Shellmer's photo handy?'

'Why?' The journalist's nose twitched. Something was going on. Something he wanted to know about.

'Can I just see the photo?' Gerry Heffernan knew full well that if it had been in the *Tradmouth Echo* at any time over the past thirty years, Ray Davenport would know exactly where to lay his hands on it.

Ray led the two policemen down a hessian-lined corridor

into the spacious but cluttered back office which was his personal domain. Somehow Wesley had expected a newspaper office to be more lively. But then a local weekly paper wouldn't be run with the same frantic urgency as a national daily. He watched as Ray Davenport opened the top drawer of a metal filing cabinet, rooted in a file and drew out a glossy black-and-white photograph.

'Here are you. "Rock star makes a hit in Derenham." He gave a cheque for ten thousand pounds to the village hall appeal.'

'Very generous of him,' said Wesley. 'But why?'

'He's intending to move to the village. Probably trying to curry favour with the natives.' Davenport passed the photograph to Gerry, who in turn passed it to Wesley with an almost imperceptible nod. It was the dead man all right. Even down to the leather jacket. Gerry Heffernan's misspent youth had had its advantages.

The photograph showed Jonny Shellmer smiling at the camera while presenting a cheque to a middle-aged woman who was named in the caption beneath as Maggie Flowers, treasurer of Derenham's village hall committee. She too was smiling gratefully at the camera. Happy faces all round.

'Where's Shellmer living at the moment?' asked Wesley. They might as well get all the information they could out of Ray Davenport before the news broke and his opinions were coloured by thoughts of murder.

'He's rented a cottage in Whitely while he's house-hunting. Why?'

'And you actually interviewed him yourself?'

Davenport nodded.

'What's he like?' asked Heffernan with an innocent grin. 'I was a bit of a fan myself once upon a time.'

'He seemed okay. Quite happy to chat – not like some of them. He's been keeping busy in the music business since Rock Boat broke up, but now he's decided to move to the country for the quiet life. He's thinking of buying somewhere in Derenham. He said he was interested in a place called the Old Vicarage – he'd been to see it a few times and was considering making an offer.' Ray looked Gerry Heffernan in the eye. 'Correct me if I'm wrong, Gerry, but a little bird tells me there's been a lot of police activity up near Derenham today. And here you are asking questions about Jonny Shellmer. Could the two things be related, by any chance?'

Wesley decided to let his superior do the talking.

'It'll all come out soon, Ray, so I might as well tell you now. There's been a suspicious death.'

Ray Davenport became suddenly alert, like a dog that had smelt an obliging rabbit. The term 'newshound' now seemed strangely appropriate as Wesley observed the journalist sniffing the air like a bloodhound on the scent.

'I reckon you've found Jonny Shellmer dead. That's why you want chapter and verse on him,' said Davenport, wheedling.

'We'll make a statement to the press in due course. You know the form, Ray.'

'Go on, Gerry. What's the cause of death? Was it suicide? I can't say he seemed depressed when I spoke to him.'

'You know I can't tell you that yet, Ray. Anyway, what makes you think Shellmer might be dead?'

Davenport touched the side of his long, narrow nose. 'Come on, Gerry. You scratch my back, et cetera. Was it suicide? Rock star's lonely agony?'

'Sorry, Ray, you'll have to make do with the formal statements just like everyone else,' said Heffernan. 'But of course, if you know anything else about Shellmer that we might be interested in, I could make sure you got anything juicy before the opposition, if you see what I mean. Maybe something the nationals would be interested in,' he added tantalisingly.

'I get the picture, Gerry. But there's nothing more I can tell you.'

37

'Nothing he mentioned in passing while you were having this cosy chat? Something you might not have thought was important at the time?'

Ray sighed. 'I'll see if I've still got the interview on tape.'

Gerry Heffernan slapped the reporter heartily on the back. 'See, that wasn't so difficult, was it? And for that DI Peterson here might even consider helping you with your piece on ethnic minorities. Won't you, Inspector? But now you can find that little tape machine of yours and we'll see if there's anything juicy on it.' He beamed at Wesley, who had the nagging feeling he had been a pawn in one of the boss's little games. He felt mildly annoyed, but he had no option but to nod in agreement.

'There we are. Everyone's happy,' Heffernan said as he sat down in the only comfortable chair in the office. 'Any chance of a cup of tea, Ray? I'm spitting feathers 'ere.'

It was eight o'clock when Wesley Peterson headed home. Gerry Heffernan had kept him talking, making plans for the investigation and indulging in his usual wild speculations about the case, as he always did before the full facts were known.

They had listened to Ray Davenport's taped interview with Jonny Shellmer, which could hardly have been classed as 'in depth' – more a pleasant chat than an interrogation. There had been the usual questions about Rock Boat and Shellmer's plans for the future. Shellmer's answers were measured, thoughtful; his muted Liverpool accent quiet. As Ray had said, Shellmer hadn't seemed depressed, and yet he sounded like a man with a lot on his mind.

Eventually Wesley managed to get away. Gerry Heffernan was a widower with nobody waiting for him in his cottage overlooking the river on Baynard's Quay. But Wesley had a wife and son waiting for him – and he was hungry.

When Pam Peterson heard her husband's key in the door,

she wandered out into the hall to greet him. Her face looked pale and drawn as she stifled a yawn. 'You're late,' she said, without reproach. 'I haven't eaten yet. I started writing up my lesson plans for next week and I lost track of time.'

'How was school?' Wesley asked dutifully. The Easter holidays had been an oasis of peace in their otherwise hectic domestic lives. Pam had read the books she had received for Christmas, played with baby Michael and made the arrangements for his first birthday party; she had had a home-cooked dinner on the table every night, caught up with friends. But two days ago term had started again and Michael had returned to his childminder. Things were back to normal, thought Wesley with regret.

'Two days back and it feels like I've never been away. Some schools aren't back till next Monday,' she said with a touch of envy. 'And it's my turn to do an assembly: I'm getting the little darlings to sing a couple of French songs – "Frère Jacques" and "Sur le Pont d'Avignon" – should impress the parents if nothing else. What about you?'

Wesley put his arm around her and kissed the top of her head. 'Someone's been shot dead at Derenham. Found in a field of cows. That's why I'm late.'

'Accident?' Mishaps with shotguns weren't unknown in the countryside.

'Doesn't look like it. But we'll know more tomorrow. Have you heard of a singer called Jonny Shellmer?'

'Of course I have. My mother had all Rock Boat's records – she was a big fan. Why do you ask?'

'There's been no formal identification yet but it's possible that Jonny Shellmer might have been the victim of this shooting.'

This got Pam's attention. 'You mean he shot himself?'

Wesley shrugged his shoulders. 'Well, there was no gun found by the body so that usually rules out suicide. What do you know about him?' he asked tentatively. 'What kind of rock star was he? Was he the wild, drug-crazed variety smashing up hotel rooms? Or was he the caring type, saving the rainforest and visiting African villages?'

Pam began to laugh. 'You sound as if you've never heard of him.'

Wesley smiled sheepishly. 'Jonny Shellmer was way before my time. And even if he had been around when I was of an age to be interested in that sort of thing, you know what my parents are like: an unhealthy interest in pop stars wasn't encouraged in our house.'

'You poor, deprived child,' she said with a grin, planting a kiss on his cheek.

Wesley's parents, having come over from Trinidad to study medicine in London, had been determined that their children should succeed in their adopted country and had sent them to the best private schools and ensured that their musical experiences were more in the line of piano lessons and church choirs than an enthusiasm for rock stars. Pam, raised by an ineffectual father and a giddy mother blown by the winds of fashion, had a sneaking admiration for the Petersons' dedication.

She thought for a moment, trying to sort Jonny Shellmer in her mind from her mother's other enthusiasms. Wesley noticed how pale she looked, the dark rings standing out beneath her eyes. She didn't look well.

'I don't really know much about him. To me he was just some pop singer my mum liked in her youth.'

'Gerry Heffernan reckoned he came from Liverpool,' Wesley said, steering her towards the kitchen. They would make the supper together – it would be quicker.

'Gerry would, wouldn't he,' she said, making for the refrigerator. As she pulled out a packet of sausages she remembered that she had something to tell Wesley. 'I almost forgot – your mother rang. She's coming down to Morbay on Saturday for a weekend conference. I think she said it was some kind of drug company do when they get a load of doctors down to a posh hotel and try and push the latest wonder drug. I said we'd meet her for lunch on Sunday. Is that okay?'

'Yes, of course,' he said quickly, hoping that Shellmer's death wouldn't put paid to the family reunion.

The fact that he hadn't seen his parents since Christmas was nagging on his conscience. They lived in London, where his father was a consultant surgeon in one of the great teaching hospitals and his mother a family doctor. But the recent lack of contact wasn't through choice: they all lived busy lives and time passed so quickly. It was the way of the modern world.

'I just hope this shooting doesn't muck up our plans,' he said, frowning. Things had been quiet recently: only a couple of break-ins and some thefts from boats moored on the Trad. A few days back, Gerry Heffernan had joked that the villains were taking their holidays before the tourist season started. Wesley had known it was too good to last.

A mournful wail drifted through the living room, and Pam thrust the sausages into Wesley's hand. 'I left Michael in his playpen. You see to these.'

He could hear her singing softly to the baby: 'Frère Jacques'. The tune must have been to Michael's taste because the wailing stopped immediately.

He looked down at the cold, unappetising things in his hand and wrinkled his nose. 'I spotted Neil today,' he called through. 'He was standing outside some old barn, but I didn't have a chance to stop and see what he was up to.'

There was no reply. Either Pam hadn't heard or her silence indicated disapproval. Perhaps it was best that he hadn't had time to stop. Neil had a habit of drawing him into the puzzles of his profession, and Wesley had problems enough of his own to be going on with.

But as he sat on the sofa that night drinking red wine and watching Pam's eyelids close as her favourite TV detective, Inspector Morgan, sprang via a series of impenetrable clues to some brilliant conclusion that left Wesley's sleepy brain way behind, he found himself looking at the telephone and willing Neil to call and tell him just what he had been doing at that old barn in Derenham.

Neil Watson sat in the Red Bull at Derenham and thought about phoning his old friend. But then, he thought, if there had been some major incident at that place near Terry Hoxworthy's farm, Wesley would probably be busy interviewing suspects with the aid of a few electrodes or whatever it was the police did down in those cells. Neil had held a dim view of policing ever since a small incident involving a cannabis plant when he was a student.

He had been shaken when Wesley – the brightest student of his year on the archaeology course at Exeter University – had chosen to join the police force rather than pursue an academic archaeological career. A less likely member of the forces of oppression Neil couldn't imagine. But Wesley had always claimed that he relished the challenge of detection rather than the chore of everyday law enforcement. And he had risen rapidly in the Met's CID, his special talents propelling him into the Arts and Antique squad before he opted for a posting to the supposedly calmer waters of Tradmouth.

Neil, meanwhile, had settled into his own niche in the County Archaeological Unit. And now that he had almost completed his PhD he would soon be able to call himself 'Dr Watson'. That would tickle Wesley, he thought as he raised a glass of beer to his lips – his friend had always been a great fan of Sherlock Holmes and his medical side-kick.

He glanced around the pub, low beamed and cosy with a roaring fire in the hearth. The locals he had talked to while working on his excavations had told him that several celebrities had places in Derenham. A couple of television presenters, three actors, including Jeremy Sedley – quite a household name – a TV chef, a bestselling author, Michael Burrows the weatherman, and feared TV interviewer Jack Cromer all featured in the latest roll-call of famous inhabitants. But if these august personages were resident in the village, they hadn't chosen to drink in its pub tonight, although the place was filling up nicely.

Neil looked at his watch. He had limited himself to one pint of bitter. He had to drive back to Exeter, so hanging around for another drink might not be the wisest of options.

He resented the fact that he had to attend a meeting at his Exeter office first thing in the morning. He wanted to stay in Derenham. The aerial photographs he had seen, the geophysics results and the finds they had already unearthed, all pointed to something really exciting in Manor Field: something he was impatient to uncover.

Everything found so far dated from the fourteenth and fifteenth centuries, and evidence of scorching on the low stone walls suggested a building which had been destroyed by fire.

The skull – the village hall contractors' original grisly find – was still a mystery. No other human bones had been found, as yet, among the medieval foundations. Just the skull – a head buried on its own. Some sort of ritual, perhaps. Were the inhabitants of the big house back in the Middle Ages involved in black magic?

Neil had already begun to delve in archives and consult local historians. Some deeds he had discovered in Tradmouth Museum suggested that the foundations belonged to a lost manor house, the home of a family called Merrivale. All mention of the house had ceased at the start of the sixteenth century, and later Tudor records made no mention of a family called Merrivale in the village at all. Old tithe maps named the site of the excavation as Manor Field but gave no hint of any sort of building there. In fact the field, although in a prime position in the village, hadn't been built on since the Middle Ages, as far as he could see.

But the skull and the sudden disappearance of the manor house weren't the only secrets kept by the pretty riverside village. There was the strange painting in the old barn: a huge semicircular wooden panel covered with bizarre

43

painted scenes which seemed tantalisingly old. At some point in its existence it had been shoved up in the old hayloft, face to the wall and out of sight behind the hay bales – but then it wasn't the sort of thing anyone would keep around for decoration. Neil had seen medieval wall paintings in a similar style, but he hardly liked to speculate about what it could be until it had been examined by experts.

He had the uneasy feeling that perhaps he had let his enthusiasm run away with him and raised Terry Hoxworthy's hopes too much; that it might be some lurid and worthless nineteenth-century daub after all, a gross fantasy in oils produced by some sexually repressed Victorian amateur artist. But the thing did look old – and Neil was an optimist by nature.

Just as he was thinking of Terry Hoxworthy, the man himself appeared in the doorway of the long, low-beamed pub. Now was his opportunity to convince the farmer that bringing in experts to examine his barn and his strange painting would bring no end of nameless benefits.

He was about to call Hoxworthy over and offer him a drink to oil the wheels of co-operation, but he saw that the farmer looked secretive, preoccupied, and sensed that it wouldn't be a good time to broach the subject of history. Terry Hoxworthy obviously had other things on his mind.

A woman walked into the bar. She wore a long, hooded black coat which billowed behind her as she moved. She looked around, searching for a face among the drinkers. Neil watched as she removed the coat to reveal a shapeless black dress which covered a small skinny body. Her shoulder-length dark hair was peppered with grey, and it was obvious to Neil that she had been pretty once, maybe even beautiful. But now her movements were mouselike, quick and anxious to avoid attention. Her great dark eyes looked from left to right, scanning each face in the bar. She caught Neil's eye and quickly looked away.

At last she spotted her quarry, and Neil watched as she

scurried over to the corner of the bar and sat down next to Terry Hoxworthy, who looked about him as though afraid that someone would overhear.

Neil drained his glass and walked quickly out of the pub and into the damp night air. His instincts told him that it wasn't a good idea to hang around. From the woman's obvious unease and Hoxworthy's furtive manner, he guessed that he had unwittingly stumbled on an extramarital affair. Terry Hoxworthy, he thought to himself with an inward smile, was a man with something to hide.

Detective Sergeant Rachel Tracey was still relishing her brand-new rank. Men, she thought as she strolled through Derenham village early the next morning, weren't worth it: she would concentrate on her career from now on. She had to put up with her mother's worried looks and the jibes of her three brothers about her continued single status, but she didn't let them worry her. She was making plans to move away from her family's farm and into a flat of her own anyway. She would put the past and all its associated pain and embarrassment behind her and begin again, start afresh.

She looked at her companion, a good-looking dark-haired man in his twenties; a snappy dresser with a brown leather jacket that must have cost him a couple of weeks' salary. Detective Constable Steve Carstairs walked beside her, hands in pockets. They didn't make conversation. It was hard to think of anything to say to Steve Carstairs that wouldn't be twisted and taken the wrong way. It was best to stick to professional matters.

'What's next on the list?' she asked.

Steve consulted the sheet of paper in his hand. 'The boss wants us to visit the houses along the lane. There's a big place called the Old Vicarage, but I don't think the vicar lives there – and there's a cottage near its gates. Someone called yesterday but there was no answer. Then he wants us to go to Hoxworthy's farm again. The uniforms talked to

45

Mrs Hoxworthy yesterday but the boss wants us to pay another visit. You can see the field from their farmhouse, so someone might have spotted something suspicious.' He looked at Rachel, slightly wary. 'Okay, er . . . Sarge?'

Rachel smiled. She knew the title 'Sarge' stuck in Steve's throat. For one thing they had joined CID at around the same time and he remained a detective constable – and for another thing, she was female. But Steve, she told herself, had only himself to blame: he hadn't even attempted his sergeant's exam, so what did he expect? In this life you reaped what you sowed.

'Fine,' she said, feeling suddenly charitable. 'I know the Hoxworthys – or rather my mother does – so I'll do the talking when we're there.' Rachel's mother, Stella, a woman of indomitable energy, was a local farmer's wife and an authority on the successes, failures and scandals of the area's farming community.

Steve didn't answer, and they walked on in silence to the outskirts of the village, until they reached the Red Bull, a long, low, whitewashed establishment with a thatched roof: a certainty for a picture postcard.

'Looks like a good place for lunch,' Rachel said, holding out the olive branch. 'If we get time for lunch, that is.'

Steve grunted in the affirmative.

'What did you make of the boss's briefing this morning? Do you think the victim could be this pop singer, Jonny Shellmer?'

Steve shrugged. 'The boss seemed pretty certain. But then he always does.'

'Do you know anything about Shellmer?' Rachel asked as they reached the lane that led out of the village. The narrow roadway was overhung with budding plum trees which promised a good late-summer crop.

'Bit before my time,' said Steve thoughtfully. 'But he was very big in the late sixties and seventies. One of the bad boys of rock – drug convictions, smashed-up hotel rooms: the usual. He's just sold a big place in London and

46

rented a place around here – in Whitely, I think. I read that he'd decided to stay here permanently and was looking for a place around Derenham. It was in the paper the other day. He'd given some money to some village hall appeal in Derenham because he wanted to move there.'

'I presume the boss knows about all this?' she asked, impressed by Steve's encyclopaedic knowledge of the doings of ageing rock stars.

'He's been to the *Tradmouth Echo* offices so he'll know about the Whitely place and the Derenham money. And as for the rest, I suppose he'll have found out for himself by now.'

Rachel admitted to herself reluctantly that Steve was probably right. But all the same, she'd mention it to Wesley when she got the chance. She seized every opportunity to speak to Wesley.

'Actually . . .' Steve hesitated.

Rachel looked at him impatiently. 'What is it?'

'This, er, girl I'm seeing is a big fan of some of these old rock groups. I'll, er, ask her what she knows about Jonny Shellmer.'

Rachel looked at him, stifling a grin. So Steve's love life had taken a turn for the better. Although he boasted of his conquests in the clubs of Morbay, Rachel suspected that his success rate wasn't high. 'You do that, Steve. What's her name?'

'Melissa,' he replied with a mixture of affection and pride. Maybe it was the real thing, Rachel thought, reflecting on some women's odd taste in men.

They had arrived at the gates of the Old Vicarage. Through the local grapevine Rachel had heard that the place was up for sale. If Jonny Shellmer was looking for a place around Derenham, the Old Vicarage would certainly fit the bill. The gates were rustic and rusty rather than impressive, but if Shellmer had bought the place, all that might have changed: electronic gates with elaborate security devices would probably be *de rigueur* for a former rock star's hideaway.

On the lane beside the gates was a small cob cottage, pink washed and thatched, with a neatly painted sign announcing that it was called 'Vicarage Lodge'. Pretty to look at but probably dark and cramped inside, Rachel thought. She had lived in the countryside too long to take a romantic view of such places – that sort of thing was for townies.

She turned to Steve. 'We'll do the cottage first. All right?'

Before he could answer, she marched up to the smartly painted front door and let the grand lion's-head knocker fall three times. After a few moments the door opened an inch and a woman's voice asked, 'Who is it?'

Rachel poked her warrant card around the door. 'I'm DS Tracey and this is DC Carstairs. Tradmouth CID. We'd just like to ask a few questions about the incident near here yesterday. May we come in?' She spoke with confident efficiency and her no-nonsense approach seemed to work. The door opened wider to reveal a woman in late middle age. She wore tight black leggings and a huge, silky blouse; her silver hair was stiff and elaborately coiffed, the sort that required regular shampoos and sets.

'You'd better come in,' she said with a hint of reluctance. 'But I never saw nothing until all them police cars arrived with their sirens blazing. Shouldn't be allowed in a place like this. People come here for peace and quiet, you know.'

Rachel refrained from saying that the area wasn't some sort of theme park, that people had to conduct their everyday lives and businesses there. She also noted that the woman showed no curiosity as to why the police cars were causing a disturbance in the first place. They were led into a small, low-beamed living room decorated in an unexpectedly modern way; bare floorboards, stark white walls, panels of snowy voile at the windows, and angular modern furniture. Somehow Rachel had expected chintz – and lots of it.

It was clear from the outset that Rachel and Steve wouldn't be invited to make themselves at home. The woman made no move to sit on the white linen sofa but stood there, arms folded in front of her brightly patterned chest.

'Do you live here, madam, or are you here on holiday?' Rachel began, sensing that the woman wasn't going to make it easy for her.

'Neither,' was the non-committal reply. Her accent wasn't local: somewhere near London, Rachel guessed.

Steve, not setting much store by etiquette, sat himself down on what appeared to be a modern take on the traditional director's chair. The woman shot him a hostile glance but said nothing.

Rachel rephrased the question. 'Is this your house?'

'No.' There was a pause. The woman's silky blouse undulated around her ample bosom as she shifted her stance.

'Well, can you explain what you're doing here?' asked Rachel with a touch of impatience in her voice. She was tired of guessing games. Steve looked across at her and grinned. It wasn't often Rachel lost her cool.

'We're house-sitting. Me and my Alec. Answered an advert, we did. We look after people's places when they're away.'

'So the owners employ you to look after this cottage?' The woman nodded impatiently. 'And how long have you been here?'

'Since October. They just come here for the summer, you see. They live in London most of the time, but they're in Tuscany at the moment.'

'All right for some,' mumbled Steve automatically. Rachel turned and gave him a withering look.

She asked the woman's name, and was told reluctantly that it was Gloria Treadly. Rachel, like the heroine in the story of Rumpelstiltskin who gained the upper hand over her tormentor once she knew his name, at last felt she was getting somewhere. 'And do you know the owners of the

Old Vicarage?' she continued more confidently.

Gloria Treadly shook her head. 'Some old colonel and his la-di-da lady. Never talked to the likes of us unless they wanted something. Up for sale now, it is. They've gone off to the south of France,' she added bitterly. Rachel diagnosed a bad case of social envy here. She wondered whether looking after the holiday homes of the rich was really the right job for Gloria Treadly.

She returned to the matter in hand. 'A body was discovered in a field near here yesterday and we're treating the death as suspicious. Have you noticed anything unusual at all? Or seen any strange vehicles parked in the lane?'

Steve took out his notebook and sat on the edge of the uncomfortable-looking modern chair expectantly.

'There's been all sorts of comings and goings what with the Old Vicarage being up for sale. All them car engines ... it's like living on a main road. There's been this big BMW going into the drive at all sorts of times and other cars racing up and down. Not that I have time to stand and watch, of course,' she added righteously.

Steve and Rachel exchanged looks. For someone who claimed to have seen nothing, Gloria Treadly was surprisingly well informed.

'And did you see any cars around on Wednesday afternoon or evening?'

Rachel, tired of standing, sank down into a nearby chair, a blue plastic specimen that hadn't been designed with the human posterior in mind.

Gloria too sat herself down on the hard white sofa, her large bright blouse spreading around her like a parachute. After a shaky start she was just getting into her stride.

'Let's see, what day is it today? Friday.' She wrinkled her brow in an impressive display of thought. 'I reckon that BMW was up at the Old Vicarage a couple of times on Wednesday and I saw a yellow sports car going up there in the late afternoon. And then the BMW was there yesterday in the middle of the morning. There was a little red car there too, and after that had gone a yellow one shot out of the drive – it might have been the sports car but I didn't see clearly. Then later on all hell broke loose and the police started dashing up and down the lane, so I wouldn't have been able to hear anything going down the drive for all the commotion,' she finished disapprovingly.

Rachel stood up, unable to trust the seating any longer. 'Thank you, Mrs Treadly, you've been very helpful. We might have to come back some time and talk to your husband as well.'

Gloria Treadly looked mildly affronted. 'Alec's not my husband. He's my son.'

'I'm sorry. But we'd still like a word with him.'

Gloria pressed her lips together and nodded warily. Rachel guessed that at some point in Gloria's past the police had not been welcome visitors.

'Just one last thing,' Rachel said casually as Steve was putting his notebook away. 'Have you or your son ever been up to the Old Vicarage?'

'No. Never,' was the sharp reply as Gloria opened the front door wide to let them out, avoiding any eye contact and anxious to see the back of them.

When they were a few yards down the road, Rachel turned to Steve. 'Do you think she was telling the truth when she said she'd never been up to the Old Vicarage?'

'No way,' Steve answered with an unpleasant grin. 'She was lying through her teeth – and they're probably false and all.'

Rachel nodded. It would be worth keeping an eye on Gloria and Alec Treadly.

Lewis Hoxworthy could hear his mother in the kitchen. The clattering of plates and pans told him that she was washing up. It would never have occurred to Lewis to offer to help: washing up was her job and he had better things to do.

He glanced at the poster above his bed, at the mounted knight in his gleaming armour riding off to some unnamed medieval battle. Then he closed his eyes and the sights and sounds of battle swirled in his head; the clash of steel, the panicked whinnies of the horses, the terrified cries and rough oaths of desperate men facing death or mutilation.

He could almost smell the fear. Fear was something he knew well. He had experienced it many times when they had picked on him at school.

But not any more. Everything would change now.

He checked the pocket of his coat. He was only taking one: just a sample to whet the appetite of the man he was to meet. He looked at his wristwatch, a sleek, black, expensive birthday present. The ferry was due to leave Derenham for Tradmouth in fourteen minutes. It was time to go.

He crept downstairs, the soles of his soft white trainers making no sound on the brightly patterned carpet, and when he left the house, he shut the front door softly behind him. As he trudged down the lane towards the river the old barn loomed up on his right and he averted his eyes, trying not to look at the place. He hadn't been near it since that day when he had made his discovery; when he had seen that vision of hell itself.

A couple of vehicles passed him on the road: a battered yellow Mini that had seen better days and a gleaming Range Rover. He glanced back as they came to a halt by the old barn. Something was going on: probably those archaeologists his dad was talking about last night before he went out to the Red Bull.

But Lewis hurried on. Digging up the past interested him – although he would never dream of admitting this to Yossa and his mates. But at that moment money interested him more.

And with any luck he'd soon have money – and lots of it. Money made you somebody. Money bought respect and friendship. Everything would be different when he had money.

Rachel Tracey marched slightly ahead of Steve, heading for Hoxworthy's Farm.

'Shouldn't we have called at the Old Vicarage?'

'It's for sale. There's nobody living there. It can wait till later,' she answered sharply.

'She said there's been cars up there.'

'Probably the estate agent showing people around,' she said smugly. Sometimes Steve didn't think.

'I still think we should have a look at the place.'

'Thinking of buying it, are you?'

He fell into sullen silence as he tried to keep up with her. 'What's the hurry?' he said breathlessly, smarting from her words.

'We've got a lot of work to get through, that's all,' she said pointedly, not slowing her pace. 'You should get more exercise, Steve,' she added with a grin he couldn't see.

The old barn was looming up on her left. Not far now. There was a car parked outside the barn, a car she recognised; a battered yellow Mini. She slowed down as a familiar figure emerged from the great barn doors.

'Well, if it isn't the lovely Rachel. Hello, stranger. Long time no see.' Neil Watson stepped forward, a wide grin on his face. 'Is Wesley about?'

'Hello, Mr Watson. I thought I recognised the car.' She looked at the vehicle with distaste, wondering, not for the first time, whether the thing had a valid MOT. 'Inspector Peterson's gone over to Whitely with Chief Inspector Heffernan.'

Neil's grin widened. 'Ooh, we are being formal today, Constable.'

'Sergeant, actually,' she said coolly.

She had always been a little wary of Wesley's scruffy friend. There was something anarchic about the man, a disregard for appearance and authority, that made her instinctively suspicious. But Wesley seemed to like him so, she told herself, he couldn't be that bad. Perhaps she just felt uneasy with someone so passionate about uncovering the past that he put it above the conventional concerns of the modern world.

'Congratulations.' Neil did his best to look impressed, but the ends of his lips twitched upward, amused at the young woman's pomposity. 'So what's been happening?'

'What do you mean?' she asked defensively.

'Well, I presume you don't call out half the local force to look for a couple of missing hens. What's been going on? And when will Wes be back?'

Rachel noticed that Steve was scowling by her side, his usual reaction when Wesley's name was mentioned.

'I thought everyone would have known by now. There's been a suspicious death. A man's body was found in a field near here yesterday, so I'm afraid Inspector Peterson will be tied up for quite a while.'

'Well, if you see him, tell him I've got something to show him. Something he'll be interested in.'

As Neil spoke two men and a woman emerged from the barn doors, staggering under the weight of what looked like half of some gigantic round table-top, big enough to accommodate King Arthur and a fair number of his knights. They shouted to Neil to give them a hand, and he trotted over and took hold of a corner. Carefully, with great concentration, they manoeuvred the great awkward thing and propped it up against the barn wall.

Steve, who was quite content to see other people work, folded his arms and watched. Then, when the huge board was standing against the rough stone wall, his mouth gaped open. 'What's that?' he muttered, looking at Rachel. 'Looks like something that would interest the Vice Squad.'

He edged a little closer, staring at the painted images on the wood. Rachel glared at him disapprovingly. She didn't want to waste valuable time while Steve salivated over a filthy old painting of naked, writhing figures.

Neil and his companions stood back to look at the thing they had brought out into the light. Unlike Steve's, their excitement didn't seem salacious; in fact their eyes were alight with wonder, as though they had uncovered some great treasure.

Rachel tried to sound casual. 'What is it?' It was time to move on, to conduct more interviews, but her curiosity was conquering her sense of duty.

Neil's female companion answered. She was in her thirties, slim and unadorned with make-up. She wore old jeans and a shapeless brown jumper. Her hair was flyaway brown tied back in a makeshift ponytail. She looked at Rachel with keen blue eyes. 'If I'm not mistaken, this is an important piece of late-medieval art. It's better painted than most examples I've seen before – almost reminds me of the work of Hieronymus Bosch. Extremely rare.'

Steve mumbled something incomprehensible, then asked how much it was worth. The woman ignored his question.

'So what is it exactly?' asked Rachel, hoping she wasn't displaying undue ignorance.

'In the medieval period it would have been displayed at the front of a church above the chancel arch to remind the congregation just what was in store for them if they didn't behave themselves in this life. It was commonly known as a Last Judgement or a Doom.'

'Bloody hell,' was Steve's only comment.

'Exactly,' said the woman with a smile of triumph.

'This is it.' Wesley Peterson stood at the garden gate, staring at the thatched, whitewashed cottage.

It had been easy to find the place. A ring around the local estate agents who dealt with rented property had produced quick results. A Tradmouth estate agent called Jones and Carlton in Lower Quay Street had admitted to renting Warwick Cottage in the village of Whitely, three miles inland from Derenham, to Mr Shellmer on a three-month lease. All dealings with Mr Shellmer had gone smoothly, the young woman had assured the constable who rang, and now he was looking for a permanent home in the area.

The keys to Warwick Cottage were obtained and the secrets of Jonny Shellmer's life would, Wesley hoped, soon be revealed. If the body did indeed belong to Jonny

Shellmer – until he was properly identified they couldn't be a hundred per cent sure. And experience told Wesley that it wasn't always wise to jump the gun.

First thing that morning they had replayed the tape of Ray Davenport's interview with Shellmer. According to the singer, the motive for his move was a desire to get out of London and live life at a slower pace. He was concentrating on composing and his solo career, but a Rock Boat reunion tour couldn't be ruled out. He had chosen Devon because he liked it, he stated in a Liverpool accent watered down by years of exile. There had been no hint of any past connection with the area: like many others he had simply fallen in love with the place.

Wesley was still going over Shellmer's words in his head as Gerry Heffernan pushed the gate open and strode up the crazy-paved path. They had already spoken to the next-door neighbours – two elderly ladies, one with cropped white hair wearing manly tweeds and the other a fluffy, doll-like creature – and the pair had seemed quite happy to share their knowledge of Jonny Shellmer's comings and goings.

Shellmer had lived in the cottage for about three weeks and had led a life, according to the ladies, of quiet contemplation. As for visitors, they had seen a small blue car parked outside on more than one occasion. And at weekends they had observed an attractive blonde female arriving in a red hatchback and then driving off in the passenger seat of Shellmer's yellow sports car. They had a key to the cottage next door, but they would only use it in case of emergencies, they assured him earnestly. They never pried. Wesley wasn't sure whether to believe them.

The interior of Jonny Shellmer's cottage was dark in the gloom of the dull spring day. Wesley flicked a switch and the long, low room was immediately bathed in light. There was a faint whiff of cigarette smoke in the air, and a full ashtray stood on the dark wooden coffee table in the middle of the room.

'It's not really what I expected,' Wesley said, looking around.

Heffernan stood, arms folded, in the centre of the room. 'I don't know why but I thought all pop stars lived in pads covered in leopard skin with sunken Jacuzzis and wall-to-wall blondes.'

Wesley could tell that his boss was mildly disappointed in Shellmer's whitewashed walls and velvet curtains. The pair of plain claret-coloured sofas and the Victorian cast-iron fireplace hardly shrieked out drug-induced decadence. But it was a rented place, a temporary stop hardly worth stamping the personality on. And Shellmer had probably left his wild days behind. Like most people, he had, no doubt, mellowed with age.

The only clues to Shellmer's past were four framed gold discs propped up on the mantelpiece and an electric guitar resting against the arm of one of the sofas. If Wesley's parents had been less inclined to keep him on the straight and narrow path of worthy education and classical music, he might have recognised it as a Gibson Les Paul. Gerry Heffernan, who hadn't had Wesley's advantages in life, picked the instrument up lovingly, like a mother with a new baby.

'Beautiful,' he purred. 'What I wouldn't have given for one of these little beauties when I was in my group.'

'You were in a group?' Wesley had a sudden mental picture of the overweight chief inspector in studded vest and skin-tight leather trousers caressing the neck of a gleaming electric guitar as he cavorted across a spotlit stage.

'Don't sound so surprised, Wes. I've had me moments, you know.'

Wesley smiled to himself. 'We'd better search the place, I suppose,' he said, focusing his mind on the task in hand. 'Let's face it, we don't know much about Jonny Shellmer. We don't even know where to find his next of kin.'

'The old dears next door mentioned a blonde woman who

appeared at weekends and another visitor who had a small blue car. Do we assume that Shellmer didn't have a wife or – what do they call it these days – a partner in tow?'

'There doesn't seem to be any sign of one.' Wesley thought for a moment. 'Pam's mother used to be a fan of his at one time.'

'How is your mother-in-law, by the way?'

Wesley raised his eyes to heaven. 'No change, unfortunately.' He looked around the room, planning his campaign: he liked to be well organised. 'We'd better make a start. If you do in here, I'll take the bedrooms.'

Heffernan nodded. It seemed that Wesley had everything under control. A good education was a wonderful thing. So was delegation.

The perfunctory search didn't tell them a lot about the dead man. There wasn't much in the way of personal possessions in his rented cottage, just the bare basics needed for a comfortable existence. Wesley strongly suspected the furniture wasn't Shellmer's style, and deduced that most of his stuff might be in storage somewhere.

There were two bedrooms. The smaller was obviously used as a spare and had the neat, empty look of a hotel room. The larger, the one occupied by Shellmer, contained the usual assortment of personal items – clothes, toiletries, a couple of paperback thrillers, passport, credit cards, the stuff of everyday life.

Wesley opened the top drawer of the dressing table and found a card lying on top of a collection of snowy-white T-shirts: on the front was a picture of an angel painted in delicate medieval colours. For a few seconds Wesley stared at the picture's unearthly beauty, then he turned it over to discover that the artist was Botticelli. He opened the card. Written inside in gold pen were the words 'To Jonny from Angel. Thank you.'

Wesley put it back in the drawer. It was probably from a girlfriend of his . . . or even from a fan. He resumed his search and discovered two photographs nestling underneath a pair of neatly folded black boxer shorts.

Wesley took them out and examined them. In the first a pretty, fair-haired young woman holding a bonny-looking baby smiled out at the camera. Wesley turned it over and found the words 'to my darling Jonny with love from your Liz and William' written in neat square handwriting on the back.

He returned it to the drawer and studied the second: a group of young teenagers on the cusp of adulthood. The scenery looked local. He recognised the shore at Derenham with a huddle of cottages in the background. The children, three boys and a girl, were frozen there in the fuzzy, anaemic hues of the early colour photograph, enjoying a perpetual summer.

A holiday snap. Happy times. His parents had similar photographs featuring him and his sister, Maritia, now a junior hospital doctor in Oxford. It was the sort of photograph found in the forgotten drawers of most houses in the land. Somehow Wesley had never thought of rock stars as having happy, innocent childhoods, but here was the evidence. He assumed that one of the boys in the picture must be Jonny, probably the dark, lanky lad at the end of the group. For a split second he experienced a deep sadness that a carefree, innocent young boy sitting with friends on a Devon beach could, years later, end up lying in a damp field against a hedgerow with a bullet through his brain.

But his boss's voice distracted him from these thoughts of mortality. 'Come on, Wes. I've not found anything out of the ordinary, but we'll get someone to give the place a good going-over later. I found some estate agent's details – that place called the Old Vicarage in Derenham; Ray Davenport mentioned it.'

'Well, he was house-hunting. Anything else?'

'I couldn't see an address book and there's nothing to say if he was married or if he had any kids or other family.'

'I found a picture of a young woman with a baby in his

drawer – could be his wife and kid, I suppose.'

'But there's no sign of them round here, and we need a positive identification of the body. How about the two old dears next door?'

'Good idea,' said Wesley. 'We'll pay them a call on our way out.' He thought for a moment. 'Where's his car?' he said rhetorically. 'It isn't here and it wasn't parked near where he was found. The neighbours said he drove a yellow sports car: not easy to miss. Where is it?'

'It's bound to turn up eventually – unless it's been nicked.' Heffernan looked at his watch. 'We'll call next door, then we'd better get back to Tradmouth. The post-mortem's in an hour. You wouldn't think an attractive young lass like that Dr Kruger would want to go round cutting up dead bodies, would you?' he mused. 'You'd think she'd want to be a GP like your mum or work in baby clinics or something.'

Wesley smiled and said nothing. As many female officers at Tradmouth police station had discovered, Gerry Heffernan wasn't the most politically correct of creatures. But Wesley knew that there was no malice behind his unfashionable opinions. And, unlike many colleagues Wesley had come across in the course of his career, Gerry had never treated him any differently because of the colour of his skin and came down hard on any that did: he'd had sharp words with Steve Carstairs on more than one occasion. But Wesley feared he might find it difficult to convince Laura Kruger of his virtues, especially if they were late.

He began to make for the door, looking around to make sure that everything was as they had found it.

'What the hell's that?' Gerry Heffernan's urgent question made him jump.

Wesley looked round. The small leaded window near the fireplace was blocked by a dark shape, a human face. Someone was watching them through the window, a blur of a face shadowed by some sort of hood. It was Heffernan

60

who reached the door first. He was a big man, a little over-weight – or so his doctor kept telling him – but he moved swiftly. He flung the door open and ran outside. Wesley, slimmer and theoretically faster, followed him. But when they reached the garden gate they could see nobody about.

Wesley opened the wooden gate and ran into the lane. Then he saw her. A small figure swathed in a hooded black coat was disappearing round the corner. Wesley began to follow, cursing his lack of fitness and the fact that he'd used the car too much over the winter months. He caught sight of her again, but when she reached the main village street she flitted off down a tiny side lane.

Wesley reached the lane and stopped. The village was deserted: those who worked were out; it was too cold and damp for the elderly to venture forth; and the holidaymakers wouldn't be arriving for another month at least. In the stillness the only sign of life was a ginger cat strolling arrogantly across the road. The woman had gone. He walked down the lane slowly, getting his breath back, looking into gardens and through gates.

Gerry Heffernan caught up with him. 'Any sign?'

Wesley shook his head. Then he saw her likely escape route, a tiny footpath which appeared to lead back to the main street. But as they turned into it and began to jog along, avoiding the small brown deposits left by the local dogs, they heard the urgent revving of a car engine and the squeal of tyres coming from the direction of Shellmer's cottage. She'd got away.

They ran back down the footpath and stood helpless, staring after a small blue car that was disappearing down the road at considerable speed.

'Now I wonder who that was,' said Gerry Heffernan.

'Your guess is as good as mine,' said Wesley, scratching his head.

Chapter Four

My well beloved wife,
I hear grievous news from the Earl's messengers that the
Earl of Warwick is dead, killed in battle at Barnet with
Lord Montague and many other knights, esquires and
noblemen, and that our rightful sovereign, King Henry
VI, is captured and held in the Tower of London while
the usurper who calls himself Edward IV rules.

There is word that Queen Margaret and her son have
landed, not at Tradmouth as we expected, but at
Weymouth along the coast, after spending a long time at
sea for lack of good winds.

I travel to join the Earl of Devon at Cerne Abbas, and
daily the ranks of the Queen's army are swelled as there
are many in the West who favour King Henry's cause
above all others.

Do not worry overmuch about my son, John, and his
influence upon Elizabeth. He is young and headstrong as
was I at his age. I will have words with him on my
return. And, dear wife, do not concern yourself for my
safety but pray always that our just cause doth prosper.
Your most loving husband
Richard

Written at Dorchester this eighteenth day of April 1471

Lewis Hoxworthy walked to the end of the jetty. There were rows of boats tied up, gyrating wildly on the dark, rough water. They looked dangerous, out of control, as if they could slip their moorings at any moment. He shivered and pulled his coat closer around him. The journey on the ferry had been bad enough; his stomach had churned with the waves as the fine spray froze his face.

The sky was dark grey and there was fine drizzle in the air. Lewis shivered again and thrust his hands into his pockets. Was this wise? Should he have told someone where he was going?

Audentes fortuna iuvat. Fortune favours the brave. It was his school motto, embroidered onto the pocket of his blazer. Not that he and his friends studied Latin at school but, when Yossa and his mates weren't about, he had asked his history teacher what it meant and she had told him willingly, glad that someone was taking an interest. He took a deep breath of salty air.

Audentes fortuna iuvat. It seemed rather appropriate now.

He checked the inside pocket of his coat. It was still there. Walking slowly back along the wooden jetty, he looked at each boat in turn, searching for the name on the stern.

Then he saw it. The *Henry of Lancaster*. It was a substantial yacht, its gleaming white hull immaculate and its deck spotless. Someone looked after this vessel, probably loved it. It reminded Lewis of a toy yacht that had been his pride and joy when he was young. So perfect, the sails so tightly and neatly furled. But this was no toy. Near the top of the mast he could see the discreet bulge of an expensive radar system and GPS. This craft could probably cross the Atlantic if its skipper felt so inclined.

There was no sign of life on board and Lewis hesitated, uncertain what to do next. There was something final about stepping aboard a boat. To board a boat was to trust its skipper, and Lewis wasn't sure whether he was willing to leave dry land and fall hostage to the whim of ... who?

H. Lancaster. *Henry of Lancaster*. He had used the boat's name, not his own. Lewis, suddenly fearful, began to back away. It had seemed a good idea in the cosy security of his bedroom. But now it was beginning to rain. And he wanted to go home.

He turned to face the town. There were people walking along the quayside; people hurrying in and out of the shops; people standing around talking; boat owners walking back to their craft with carrier bags full of victuals; a small fishing boat tying up, laden with crab baskets. Normality. He touched the package in his pocket and started to walk back towards the worn stone steps that led upward to safety.

'Lewis. Is it Lewis?'

It was a man's voice, deep and resonant. Lewis turned round.

'I've been waiting for you, Lewis. Come aboard. Have you got it?'

Lewis swallowed hard and nodded.

'Well, what are you waiting for? Come on. Come aboard.'

Lewis Hoxworthy turned and walked slowly back towards the boat.

The man lay there, pale and naked, on the stainless-steel table. Wesley Peterson took a deep breath, but this was a mistake. As he inhaled, the stench of blood, death and air freshener made him feel slightly sick. He glanced at Gerry Heffernan, who was standing beside him watching the procedure keenly, arms folded, seemingly without a care in the world.

The fact that most of Wesley's immediate family were doctors made no difference. He was squeamish and he wasn't afraid to admit it. He must be a throwback, he thought: the medical gene must have passed him by.

The same couldn't be said of Dr Laura Kruger, who

64

conducted the post-mortem with effortless efficiency, but without Colin Bowman's habitual social chitchat. Wesley looked away, thinking with some regret that he would miss Colin's gourmet refreshments and pleasant small talk afterwards. The luxurious little indulgences that Colin happily shared in his well-appointed office somehow made the whole unpleasant business easier to bear.

'Well, I think I can safely say the cause of death was a gunshot wound to the head, fired at close range; very neat hole in the forehead. The bullet went straight through. Want to see the exit wound?' Laura Kruger was about to turn the corpse when Wesley shook his head.

Gerry Heffernan looked a little disappointed. 'Any idea what kind of gun it came from? Time of death?'

'I estimate he died some time on Wednesday, late afternoon or evening. Sorry I can't be more accurate. And as for the gun I'd say a smallish pistol. The bullet would tell us more.'

'They've done a fingertip search of the field and nothing's been found. Anything else interesting?'

Laura stood back and looked at the body. Lying there, Shellmer seemed older than he had done when they first found him. Without the youthful clothing he looked lined and haggard. 'His hair's dyed,' Laura added helpfully. 'I reckon it's completely grey.'

'We all have our little vanities,' said Wesley, thinking she was being a little hard on the dead man.

'And he wasn't a healthy specimen. He was definitely a smoker. His heart and lungs were in a bit of a state.'

'Too much sex, drugs and rock and roll,' said Heffernan cheerfully.

'I shouldn't be at all surprised,' said Laura, smiling at the chief inspector for the first time. 'But they weren't what killed him.'

'Is there anything else we ought to know?' asked Wesley as Laura began to sew the body back up with neat precision.

'The body was definitely moved some time after death, possibly not long before it was found; that's probably why you haven't found the bullet. I examined the clothing. Apart from traces of grass, mud and pollen where he'd come into contact with the ground, there are fibres adhering to the trousers which look like red wool. Probably from a carpet, but that's just a guess. We'll have to see what forensics come up with, but I think he was lying on a carpet for some time before he was moved. Interesting.'

Wesley and Heffernan exchanged looks. 'Very interesting,' said Wesley. 'So if we can find this carpet . . .'

'You'll have found the scene of the murder. There were some fibres of other colours too, which means the carpet was probably patterned but predominantly red. And it was a pure wool rug or carpet, good quality I should think.'

Gerry Heffernan looked at the young woman, obviously impressed. 'You've done a good job there, love.' Credit where credit was due.

Laura looked up from her stitching. 'Thanks, Gerry,' she said with a grin.

Neil Watson pulled up outside the Petersons' modern detached house above Tradmouth and checked his handbrake. The road was steep, as were most of the roads in the town, and he wondered whether he could trust the little yellow Mini to stay put. He saw Pam's VW Golf in the driveway and decided to take the risk.

She looked harassed as she opened the front door, as if she were expecting an unwanted call from a doorstep salesman. Her expression softened a little when she recognised Neil, and she stood aside to let him in.

'Wes not about?'

She led the way into the kitchen and glanced up at the clock on the wall. 'You'll be lucky. There's been a murder out at Derenham and I'm not expecting him back till late. In fact I'm not usually back this soon, but we got back early from a school trip and I didn't feel too well so I came home.' She looked at a mountain of files on the kitchen table. 'But I've still got an evening's work ahead of me. And I've got to pick Michael up in an hour from his child-minder, so I can't be long.' She rubbed her eyes.

'You don't look too good,' was Neil's only comment.

'Thanks a lot,' Pam replied, sinking into a chair. 'I'll be okay. But I've got to keep an eye on the time.'

Neil, oblivious to the urgencies of the Petersons' family life, sat down at the table and made himself comfortable. 'I saw Wes flashing past in a cop car yesterday. Don't know if he saw me. I left a message for him with that Rachel this morning.'

Pam nodded. She'd met the cool, blonde Rachel a few times, briefly, and hadn't quite made up her mind whether she approved of her or not. Wesley spoke well, even fondly, of her. This was enough to make Pam reserve her judgement.

'I've not seen my husband since he went out this morning.'

'Well, that's the price you pay for being a copper's wife.' Neil grinned mischievously and Pam avoided his eyes.

'Maybe,' she muttered. 'What did you want to see him about?'

Neil looked at her sheepishly. 'Actually it was you I really wanted to see. We're doing a dig down at Derenham. Some workmen were digging the foundations for a new village hall in a field near the church and they found the remains of an old building with a skull buried next to it.'

Pam raised her eyebrows. She had heard this story before from Wesley.

'One of the men took the skull down to the cop shop in a carrier bag, and when Wes went to see where it had been found he had a look at the stonework the digger had uncov-ered and he gave me a call. I arranged a geophysics survey, and now we think there could be a whole medieval manorial complex there – a real high-status site. And it looks like the skull's medieval and all, but we've not found the rest of the body yet.'

His eyes glowed with enthusiasm. Pam's head was swimming, but she didn't like to interrupt. 'And then at the other end of the village there's this huge painting in a medieval barn. The experts are as sure as they can be that it's late medieval, probably a Doom from a church.'

'A what?'

'A Doom. A big lurid picture of hell and the Last Judgement that was put at the front of the church to terrify the peasants.'

Pam shuddered. 'I think it'd terrify me. Where did it come from?'

'We don't know yet.' He paused, looking Pam in the eye. 'Have you heard of the Paston Letters? A load of gossipy letters written by a well-to-do Norfolk family in the fifteenth century, all about their everyday life?'

Pam nodded. 'I read something about them once. Why?'

'When I was in Exeter someone mentioned some letters written in the fifteenth century by a family called Merrivale who were lords of the manor of Derenham. Apparently a Victorian vicar of Derenham who fancied himself as a bit of an antiquary discovered them and had them published, but nobody seems to know what happened to the originals. He died suddenly at what was then the vicarage, and I suppose a lot of his things got lost or thrown out.'

'So you're trying to track them down?' said Pam, wishing he'd get to the point.

'If we could get hold of the Victorian edition of the letters they might give us some clues about this manor house we're digging up. It's likely that it belonged to the Merrivales and ...'

Pam nodded, her eyes on her watch. Neil lived life at his own slow pace and she lived another, more pressured existence. She was sure he hadn't just come round to tell her about his latest project. He must want something, and she wished he'd get to the point.

'I thought you might be interested in tracking down these Merrivale letters. You made a great job of translating that old Anglo-Saxon document . . . remember?' he said, trying flattery.

'I was still on maternity leave then. I wasn't working.'

Neil didn't pick up the reproach in her words. He continued, 'Do you still see that friend of yours who works in the library? Anne, isn't it?'

'I don't get much time for a social life these days.'

She detected a brief glimmer of disappointment in Neil's eyes. In more leisured times she had once tried a spot of matchmaking between her widowed friend, Anne, and Neil, but nothing had come of it. If only she hadn't been quite so exhausted, she would have been pleased he was taking an interest.

'I was wondering whether there's still an edition of the Merrivale letters somewhere in the library system. I could ask Anne myself, I suppose.'

Pam forced herself to smile. 'Good idea, Neil. You do that. I'll give you her phone number.'

'Yeah.' He gave a shy grin. 'But I think it'd be better coming from you. Er, these things might not be easy to track down, and asking a favour's always better coming from a friend. Don't you think? And she probably won't even remember me.'

He looked at her like a pleading puppy. They had gone out together in their first year at university but it hadn't lasted long. She had soon tired of Neil's single-minded passion for his work. Through Wesley, she had come to know of many policemen 'married to their job', but Neil proved that the phenomenon wasn't confined to the police force.

'Okay. I'll give her a ring tonight.' Pam felt mildly exasperated.

'By the way, I'm on the last leg of my PhD. I'll be Dr Watson in the not too distant future.' Neil looked down at the kitchen table modestly. He was never one to boast of his achievements.

Pam summoned up a weak smile. 'Congratulations. I'll tell Sherlock when he gets in.'

'Yeah. And if you're not doing anything tonight there'll be a few of us from the dig in the Tradmouth Arms if you and Wes fancy coming down.'

Pam looked at Neil's eager face and forced herself to smile again. He really had no idea how the other half lived.

It was 4.30 when Gerry Heffernan put his feet up on his desk and looked across at Wesley, who was sitting with his notebook open.

He looked at his watch. 'Mustn't be too late tonight, Wes. Choir rehearsal at eight. What have we got so far, eh?'

Wesley cleared his throat. Gerry Heffernan's nimble fingers were beating out a rhythm on the desktop; probably something the church choir were rehearsing. It was always like this after a certain time on a Friday afternoon.

'Jonny Shellmer's next-door neighbours have identified him.'

'Good.'

'Unfortunately there was no sign of an address book among his belongings.'

'It shouldn't be that hard to track down his next of kin and associates. What else have you come up with?'

'That woman we saw in Whitely. The neighbours said they've seen someone answering the same description visiting Shellmer on a couple of occasions, possibly driving a small blue car.'

'So the blonde in the red car wasn't the only one. Some blokes have all the luck.'

Wesley smiled to himself. Heffernan had mentioned that Susan Green – a widowed American lady with whom he'd been conducting a decorous semi-courtship for just under a year – was up in Scotland visiting her daughter, who'd just presented her with her first grandchild. Perhaps he was missing her.

70

Heffernan was a gregarious man, always ready with a joke and a slice of canteen gossip. But since his wife's death over four years ago, and the departure of his two children for distant universities, he had led a solitary existence to which Wesley suspected he wasn't altogether suited.

Wesley returned his thoughts to police matters. 'We've done checks on Terry Hoxworthy, the farmer who found the body. There's nothing known about him, and I reckon it was just bad luck that the body was dumped in that particular place. Rachel and Steve have done a house-to-house in the immediate area but they haven't found anyone who saw anything.'

'Anything else?'

'The Old Vicarage. It's empty at the moment and we know Shellmer was taking an interest in the place. According to a mother and son who are house-sitting, or whatever they call it, in the cottage near the gates, there have been quite a few people up there, probably prospective buyers. I thought I might go over there now and have a look around, seeing as there's a connection with our victim. I'll take Rachel with me.'

'Good idea.' The chief inspector scratched his tousled head and leaned back. 'I'll stop here and have a think. See what I can dredge up from my memory about Jonny Shellmer. And I'll get someone on to tracking down his next of kin.'

'You do that,' said Wesley as he left the office in search of Rachel Tracey.

Rachel, as usual, showed a remarkable degree of organisation. She flicked through her notebook and made her announcement. 'Heygarth and Proudfoot are dealing with the sale of the Old Vicarage,' she said, looking at her watch. 'If we're quick we'll get there before they close.'

The estate agent's office was only a few minutes' walk from the police station. Wesley and Rachel marched quickly, side by side, each fearing that the place would shut early on a Friday.

But their fears were groundless. Behind the large window filled with coloured photographs and tempting details of myriad local properties, the electric spotlights blazed and a woman in her late twenties sat behind a computer at a sleek beech-wood desk. A young couple wearing anoraks and denim jeans sat at the other side of her desk. Their faces were solemn, as though they had just been told bad news.

As Wesley and Rachel entered the office, the couple rose to leave and ambled out silently.

Wesley walked up to the young woman, showed her his warrant card and introduced himself and Rachel before explaining what they were there for.

The young woman, who said her name was Nicola, wore a dark suit, and her straight brown hair was cut in a businesslike bob. She had the svelte look of a single woman with no one to care for but herself, a woman who was no stranger to the exercise bikes and rowing machines in her local gym. Pam, Wesley thought, with her hectic teaching career and young baby, would have regarded her with envy.

Nicola handed over the keys to the Old Vicarage without a word, her face an expressionless mask. Then she seemed to rouse herself from her reverie and asked unenthusiastically whether they wanted her to go with them. Wesley assured her that there was no need as they only wanted a quick look, then he thanked her and promised to return the keys as soon as they had finished.

'Strange,' said Rachel when they were halfway back to the police station.

'What is?'

'That Nicola never asked us why we wanted to look inside the Old Vicarage. You said it was in connection with a suspicious death in the area, but she never asked any questions. Don't you think that's odd . . . sir?'

She added the 'sir' as an afterthought. Wesley smiled. He was still getting used to the title himself, and it sounded odd coming from Rachel whom he knew so well – and with whom he'd shared so much.

'Perhaps she knew we wouldn't tell her much so she didn't bother asking.'

'I still think it's a bit odd.'

'Perhaps she doesn't possess your natural inquisitiveness,' replied Wesley. 'In which case she'd make a lousy policewoman. Good job she chose to sell houses for a living.'

Paul Heygarth emerged from the back office. 'Is Jim Flowers about?' he asked.

Nicola Tarnley looked up. 'He's doing a survey on that property on Newpen Road. He said he'd go straight home.'

'He's not coming back?'

'No.'

Paul muttered something under his breath that she couldn't quite hear, but she guessed it wasn't complimentary.

'What is it between you and Jim? You've been at each other's throats for the past week or so.'

'It's none of your bloody business. Come into my office, will you. I want a word.'

The words were spoken casually but somewhere, buried beneath the calm, was a gritty edge. Nicola rose from her desk and took a deep breath. Whatever was coming, she could deal with it. She walked slowly towards Paul's office, each step on the thick grey carpet taking her closer to her nemesis. She entered the office and closed the door behind her.

'What did the police want?' Paul stood up, glowering down at her. There was the hint of a threat in his voice but she stood her ground.

'The keys to the Old Vicarage.' She held her head up confidently.

'And you just handed them over?' He started to move,

stalking round the desk towards her.

'I hadn't much choice, had I? I offered to go with them but they said it wasn't necessary.'

'You should have insisted.'

She could sense the pent-up violence in his words and she took a step backward. 'The police are hardly going to damage anything. And they said they'd return the keys as soon as they'd finished. Anyway, what could I have done to stop them looking round?'

He was getting closer, his hands clenched in tight fists.

'You should have used your fucking brains, you stupid cow. You should have stalled them.' He hissed the words with suppressed anger.

Nicola backed away. 'Don't you ever talk to me like that. I'm handing in my notice as of now.' Her heart was thumping in her chest. He was still coming towards her. She backed towards the door. 'There's nothing for them to find. I don't know why you're so worried.'

He was near her now. She could smell garlic on his breath, a souvenir of a good lunch. He raised his right hand and struck her hard across the face.

She stared at him for a few moments, wondering how she could have been so stupid. How could she have wanted him? How could she have put up with his arrogant fumblings and the unsatisfactory couplings in the back of his car? How could she have deluded herself all those months?

His mood had changed. He was looking at her now, a slight smile on his thick lips. With a sudden movement, he grabbed her round the waist and pulled her towards him, forcing his mouth onto hers.

'Come on, Nicky, what's the matter?'

Nicola gave him a hefty push which took him by surprise. He staggered backward then, taking her rejection as a challenge, stepped forward again and put his arms around her shoulders. 'What's the matter? You've never objected before.'

'You've never hit me before,' she replied, wriggling out of his grasp.

'I'm sorry, Nicky. I really am. It's just that I've got a lot riding on that particular property; a big commission. My ex has taken me for every penny I've got and I'm in a spot of bother – just cash flow. But I've got a few people interested, so if the sale goes through quickly all my problems are solved.' His voice softened as he did his best to sound contrite. 'Sorry I lost my temper, Nicky. Can I take you to dinner tonight to make up for it?' He looked at her appealingly, stroking her hair.

'I've got choir practice.'

Paul Heygarth smirked. 'I can't imagine you singing in a church choir. Give it a miss, eh?'

'I'll go where I want.' She pushed his caressing hands away from her hair. 'And I'm handing in my notice. I'm not putting up with this.' She put her fingers to her cheek, which smarted under her touch. 'I've given you too many chances, Paul. I won't be back.'

Nicola rushed from the office, her hand shielding her stinging cheek. She grabbed her handbag and her jacket from the coatstand in the corner and ran out into the street.

Even if Paul apologised again, even if he got down on his knees and begged her, she was never going back there. Never.

Wesley let Rachel drive to Derenham as she was better at negotiating the narrow Devon lanes than he was. They meandered up the Old Vicarage's winding drive and she brought the car to a stately halt by the front door.

Wesley climbed out of the car and studied the building. 'Nice,' he said. 'What do they call this style? Strawberry Hill Gothic, isn't it?'

'Don't ask me. But whatever it is I bet it's on the market for quite a bit. Not many locals'd be able to afford it,' she added disapprovingly.

'Neither would police inspectors – unfortunately,'

75

Wesley observed as he approached the front door, keys at the ready. He and Pam lived in a modern house with all the character of a cereal packet. Pam would have liked something a little more interesting – and so would he, one day. 'The woman at the estate agent's didn't mention an alarm, did she?'

'No, and there's no sign of one. If a burglar came here, he'd think it was his lucky day.'

Wesley placed the key in the lock and turned it. The door opened and they stepped onto thick ruby-red carpet.

'Nice,' Rachel muttered, looking around the hallway.

'Bit gloomy. You take upstairs, I'll stay down here,' said Wesley, displaying his powers of leadership.

'What are we looking for exactly, er, sir?'

He saw a smile playing on Rachel's lips. That was a good sign, he thought. Since the traumatic events of last September when she had almost met her death at the hands of someone she'd trusted, she'd lost her natural ebullience. And mental scars, he knew, took time to heal.

'I haven't a clue what we're looking for,' he said. 'But no doubt we'll know when we find it. If we find it.'

Rachel gave him another shy smile before disappearing up the rather grand oak staircase. Wesley stood in the hall, wondering where to begin. He chose the drawing room first. After pushing open the heavy oak door, a monumental example of Victorian domestic interior design, he stepped into the room and looked around.

The drawing room had a comfortable, lived-in feeling, and the traditional furnishings, though worn and not particularly fashionable, looked expensively solid. It was the taste of the older upper-middle class, the retired judge or military man. Effortless class without ostentation or unnecessary expense. Even though the walls were pale cream, the room seemed gloomy. North facing, Wesley thought as he searched for the light switch which, when he found it, turned out to be a solid piece of pre-war engineering. The place probably needed rewiring.

76

He looked down at the rich Persian rug which covered most of the floor. It was almost a shame to walk on such a work of art but he stepped onto it and surveyed the room, his sharp eyes looking for something – anything – out of the ordinary. But there was nothing. The place was spotless apart from a faded brown splash mark on the wall near the door. A spilt cup of coffee perhaps. Accidents happened in the best-run homes.

He wandered through the dining room, crammed with heavy oak furniture, and into the kitchen. Dark oak again. The owners obviously had a taste for it. He looked around and saw nothing out of place.

Then his eyes caught the telltale glint of glass on the floor by the back door. Sharp daggers of glass from a window pane. It was the oldest trick in the burglar's book: smash the glass, turn the key that's been left conveniently in the lock, and in. He drew a pair of plastic gloves from his pocket and put them on before trying the door. It opened smoothly. The place was unlocked and anyone could have walked in.

This changed things. He went into the hall and called up the stairs to Rachel. She came running down, her footsteps silent on the stair carpet's thick red pile.

'There's been a break-in. Someone's smashed a pane in the back door and the place has been unlocked. Has anything been disturbed upstairs?'

'Not that I can see. Everything's shipshape, as the boss would say. But that doesn't mean that nothing's been taken. They might just be very tidy thieves.'

Wesley thought for a moment. 'There's something I want to have a look at. Come with me and tell me what you think.'

Rachel followed him into the drawing room, pleased that her opinion was appreciated. There were some in the job who didn't think that a young policewoman had any opinions worth listening to at all.

Wesley stood by the huge sofa and pointed at the rug. 'Remind you of anything?'

While Rachel was thinking, Wesley walked over to the door, and squatted down to examine what he had assumed to be a coffee stain on the wall. The cream paint had rubbed off slightly, revealing a former coat of greyish white beneath. Someone had scrubbed this area. And coffee didn't leave a stain quite that shade of pale rusty brown. There had been a bloodstain here, a large one. Scrubbing had removed most of it, but there was still a telltale watery brown mark.

Rachel walked over to join him. 'It could be blood,' she said. 'And the rug. Pure wool, predominantly red – just like in the forensic report.'

Wesley said nothing. He was looking intently at the wall. Just beside the stain a large bookcase stood on the strip of polished parquet flooring which edged the room. He looked at the other side of the bookcase and, about three feet away, saw a slight indentation in the wood where the thing had once stood.

'I thought this bookcase looked wrong. It's too close to the door. It should be more to the centre of the wall.'

'Perfectionist,' Rachel murmured with the ghost of a grin.

'I reckon it's been moved. Can you give us a hand to move it back?'

Fortunately the bookcase only housed one row of books, mostly lavish coffee-table editions. The other shelves were taken up with knick-knacks and souvenirs of foreign travel. It wasn't too heavy to move.

They stood back and looked. The bookcase had concealed more stains, washed-out rusty patches that hadn't been removed as effectively as the others. And Wesley could see a small hole in the plaster at around head height. He moved closer to examine it.

'It's a bullet hole. And it looks like the bullet's still embedded in the wall.'

Rachel stayed silent for a few moments. Then she spoke quietly. 'This is where it happened, isn't it? The break-in.

78

The bullet. The carpet fibres. This is where Jonny Shellmer was shot. But who moved him?'

'His murderer presumably.' Wesley took his mobile phone from his pocket. 'I'll ring the boss and get forensics round. Will you let the estate agents know we'll be sealing the place off? We don't want any eager house buyers coming to view and trampling all over the evidence, do we?'

Rachel tried the number of Heygarth and Proudfoot but there was no reply. 'Looks like they've gone home,' she said, putting her phone back in her jacket pocket. 'We'll have to inform them first thing in the morning. What about the owners?'

'Abroad, apparently. Went to live in the south of France back in January.'

'Well, that lets them out, then.'

'Do you know what my first guvnor at the Met told me when I was an innocent DC?'

'No,' said Rachel. 'What did he tell you?'

'Never jump to conclusions.' He paused, watching Rachel's face. 'And by the way, the guvnor was a she.'

For the first time in six months Wesley heard Rachel Tracey laugh.

Lewis Hoxworthy did his best not to make a sound as he climbed the farmhouse stairs. It was all arranged. The man would make his way upstream to meet him. All Lewis had to do was show him the rest of what he had to offer.

He reached his bedroom and listened. He could hear his mother downstairs, clattering pans in the kitchen. Dinner would soon be ready, but Lewis had more important things to do than eat, even though hunger was starting to gnaw at his stomach. If everything went well he could go out to eat anywhere he liked. McDonald's, Kentucky Fried Chicken, Burger King. The whole world of fast food would be his oyster. He could take Yossa and his mates – that would impress them.

He checked his e-mails. Nothing, not even from Yossa. He pressed a few keys on his computer and switched the machine off before rummaging in his wardrobe, searching for the packet concealed at the back where his mother wouldn't dream of looking. Apart from brief visits to deposit clean clothes and complain about the mess, she rarely ventured in here these days. The room was Lewis's domain, his kingdom. He just hoped that nobody had interfered with the merchandise – or with the other thing.

As his fingers touched the packet, he smiled. He had been reasonably sure that it was safe there but he hadn't been certain. He remembered hearing how the mum of one of his classmates had found a mucky magazine hidden under his mattress: mothers had a nasty habit of stumbling across the best-kept secrets.

He stuffed the packet into the inside pocket of his coat. It would be safe and dry there: his customer had made it quite plain that he didn't want damaged goods. He shut the bedroom door behind him and made for the stairs.

'Lewis, is that you?'

Lewis froze. She had heard him. Another thing to remember about mothers was that they had sharp ears.

'Lewis?'

'What is it, Mum? I'm just on my way round to Yossa's.'

'But your dinner's nearly ready.'

He could visualise the hurt indignation on his mother's face. Why did she always have to fuss about food? 'I'll get something at Yossa's.'

'But . . .'

'I have to go. He's expecting me.'

Before she could emerge from the kitchen he flew down the stairs and out of the front door, hoping he wouldn't meet his father on the way in. Terry Hoxworthy had seemed quiet, preoccupied, since the discovery of the body in the field. Lewis thought that the event had probably upset him. But to Lewis it was something else to boast to

Yossa and his mates about; something to earn their acceptance: a murder on the premises.

The coast was clear. He ran out of the farm drive and down the lane, speeding up as he passed the old barn. There were cars outside which probably belonged to those museum people who'd been hanging about. His dad had said that they had come about the sick painting he'd seen. He shuddered, trying to banish its gruesome images from his head.

Lewis felt his chest tightening, but he didn't slow down until he was well past the barn. Since he'd seen that thing he didn't want to go near the place. His father had said that various experts reckoned it was medieval and might be worth a bit. But Lewis thought it was sick. Any art gallery was welcome to it. The sooner someone took it away the better.

He had to stop for breath, taking his blue-and-grey inhaler from his pocket and pressing it to his lips. His asthma didn't usually bother him, but the damp air and the exertion, coupled with nervousness about his forthcoming meeting, had made his airways tighten uncomfortably. The inhaler worked like magic, and soon he was walking on briskly down the path that led down to the river.

The relentless drizzle had stopped, and Lewis gazed across the wide grey waters. There were boats moored here and there bobbing on the tide. He stood on the long wooden jetty which protruded into the river from Derenham's picturesque quayside, studying the names of the yachts moored along its length. He saw that the *Henry of Lancaster* was tied up right at the end, brighter and more gleaming than her fellows.

As Lewis walked along the jetty, the wooden planking seemed hollow and unsteady beneath his feet. But he felt in his inside pocket again and breathed deeply, trying to stop his heart from thumping and his hands from shaking. There was no turning back now. It was time to make the delivery.

*

Wesley's discoveries at Derenham's Old Vicarage had made Gerry Heffernan ten minutes late for choir practice. He'd rushed back to his silent home, shovelled down a hastily prepared meal of beans on toast, and dashed out again to St Margaret's church, where he took his place in the richly carved oak choirstalls and sang out, his rich baritone voice providing a booming bass beneath the tenors' and sopranos' flights of musical fancy.

Gloria in excelsis Deo. Et in terra pax, hominibus bonae voluntatis.

Thomas Tallis's great Gloria echoed around the ancient church, the soaring harmonies of sixteenth-century praise drifting to the lofty roof with its great carved beams. When it was over, in those few seconds of charged silence which followed the final chord, Gerry Heffernan felt a tingle of satisfaction. It had been good – each note spot on.

The rehearsal continued for another half-hour or so as they went over the medieval carol they were to sing as they processed down the aisle. Learning all this Latin for the coming history evening to be held in aid of Derenham's new village hall was making Gerry's head spin. At his Liverpool grammar school, he had dropped Latin at the very first opportunity, and now he couldn't remember even the basics. And at work he usually left the intellectual stuff to Wesley, who seemed to like that sort of thing.

When the rehearsal was over one of the more adventurous tenors suggested a visit to the Star for a well-deserved pint. Gerry Heffernan, his mouth dry from singing and with only an empty house to return to, took him up on the offer, glad of the prospect of some company. He was just donning the scruffy grey anorak which had served him well for several years when he heard a soft voice behind him.

'Er, Gerry, could I have a word?'

He swung round to see one of the sopranos standing there. Her slender body was encased in a neat grey jumper and black trousers, not jeans. Even in her most casual moments Nicola Tarnley looked businesslike.

''Course you can, love. What can I do you for, eh?'

Nicola looked faintly embarrassed. What she had to tell him was no joke. 'Can I speak to you in private? Can we go for a drink?'

Gerry could sense that the young woman was worried about something, and he was in no mood for exercising his non-existent counselling skills. He glanced longingly at the party who'd shortly be heading for the Star, a cosy inn next to the church. Perhaps he could join them later.

'Okay, love. How about the Angel? That okay with you?' He looked at his watch, hoping that they would get a seat given that it was Friday night.

They slipped out of the church before the others, Gerry Heffernan feeling a little self-conscious. He wondered whether he should attempt to make conversation, but every time he hit on a suitable subject he rejected it as inappropriate. Until he knew what was bothering the girl it was probably best to keep his mouth shut in case he put his foot in it. Nicola walked silently by his side through the dark, narrow streets until they were almost at the pub, then she suddenly spoke.

'I'm sorry for dragging you away like this. I'm sure you'd rather be going to the Star with ...'

Gerry made the appropriate noises of denial: a few small white lies never came amiss.

'The thing is somebody told me you were a detective chief inspector and I wanted some advice.'

Gerry had suspected something like this. When he had met his wife Kathy he had been first officer aboard a cargo ship, twenty-five years younger, considerably slimmer and quite a catch. But since Kathy's death he knew that he had let himself go, and he hadn't the heart to do anything about it. Nowadays women confided in him because of his occupation, not because of his dashing good looks and suave charm ... more's the pity, he thought to himself.

'That's okay, love,' he said, trying to put her at ease. 'All part of the job.' He forced himself to sound enthusiastic, but work was the last thing he wanted to think about right now.

They had reached the Angel on Tradmouth High Street, reputedly the oldest pub in town; black and white, higgledy-piggledy, and renowned for the quality of its bar food. He led the way inside and saw that the place was full. The Angel attracted a well-heeled clientèle; local professionals and officers from the naval college up the hill. Gerry Heffernan took in his surroundings and felt very out of place.

Fortunately, a few seconds after they walked in, a well-dressed middle-aged couple vacated a seat near the window. When Heffernan had bought the drinks – a pint of best bitter for him and a mineral water for his companion – he sat down beside Nicola and looked her in the eye. 'Right, love. Fire away. What's bothering you?'

She took a sip of her mineral water but looked as though she needed something stronger. 'The thing is, Gerry, I've got a confession to make.'

He felt curiously relieved. An unpaid parking fine, an unreturned library book, forgetting to pay for some trivial item in a supermarket. This one, he thought, was going to be easy. He'd make it back to the Star well before closing time.

'Oh, aye. And what have you got to confess?'

He took a sip of his beer and there were a few seconds of awkward silence.

'I helped to dispose of a body,' she said, as if it were the most normal thing in the world.

Heffernan sat forward, puzzled. 'Say that again, love.' Perhaps he'd heard wrong.

'Someone was murdered and I helped to move the body.'

Gerry Heffernan took another drink, a few large gulps that left his glass three-quarters empty.

'I think you should tell me all about it,' he heard himself

saying. 'Just start at the beginning, eh?'

'I had a phone call from my boss yesterday. He told me to meet him at the Old Vicarage in Derenham. Two of your officers asked for the keys this afternoon. I don't know whether they found ...'

'Yeah, they found something all right. The place has been sealed off.' To Heffernan's surprise, Nicola looked relieved. 'What's your boss's name, love?'

She hesitated for a moment. 'Paul Heygarth. Of Heygarth and Proudfoot.'

Heffernan stared at his glass for a few moments. Nicola thought he'd turned rather pale. 'Is anything the matter?' she asked, concerned. She knew that middle-aged men of a certain weight with stressful jobs were prone to no end of ills, and she hoped there wouldn't be another emergency to deal with: she'd had enough excitement for one week.

'No, love. I'm fine.' To Nicola's relief the colour was returning to his cheeks. He took a long drink which emptied the glass. 'Go on, then. Tell us exactly what happened.'

As Nicola Tarnley told her story, Gerry Heffernan listened carefully.

Chapter Five

Right worshipful husband,
I send this by a servant of Master Paltrow who has heard
news that you are with the Earl's party at Exeter.

Touching on your son John's marriage, I fear his
behaviour of late hath discouraged the family of the
young lady of Exeter. There is, however, a widow of
Tradmouth who was wife to one More, a merchant there,
and worth seven hundred pounds. I have spoken with her
at a pretty leisure and, blessed be God, she is willing to
consider the match.

John is in sore need of a wife's steadying hand. There
is talk that friends of his did come to the church of Saint
John in the parish of Neston and assaulted the priest
there who was preparing for Mass and took the offerings
and carried them away. I am uneasy that our daughter,
Elizabeth, spends much time in John's presence and I
seek most urgently a suitable husband for her but have
found none as yet. If our son, Edmund, were here I think
John would not behave so.

I pray, dear husband, that God grant victory to Queen
Margaret and that He grant you a safe homecoming.
Your most loving wife, Marjory

Written at Derenham this twenty-sixth day of April 1471

Heffernan had walked Nicola home. It was the least he felt he could do in the circumstances. He had taken her to the police station, where she had made a full statement, and now he felt wide awake and impatient to act on what she had told him. But Heygarth could wait till the morning. They would pull him in first thing.

When he'd seen Nicola to the front door of her small terraced house on a steep narrow street just outside the town centre, he realised that he wasn't far from Wesley's house. He looked at his watch, wondering whether it was too late for a quick visit to inform his colleague of this latest development. It was twenty to eleven, and when he reached the house the downstairs lights were on. He decided to risk it.

To his relief Wesley and Pam were still up. Although Pam had dark rings beneath her eyes and looked exhausted by her day in the classroom, she still went through the motions of hospitality, offering a beer which Wesley fetched obediently from the kitchen.

It wasn't long before she disappeared upstairs, leaving the two men alone. Wesley sat back in the armchair and looked at his visitor expectantly. Heffernan had never before turned up at this time of night on a social call. But if it was police business, why hadn't he come straight to the point?

After a few moments Heffernan spoke. 'I think we've found our murderer.'

Wesley sat forward. This was sudden. 'Who is it?'

'A man called Paul Heygarth – he's the estate agent selling the Old Vicarage. I've just been down at the station taking a statement from the accomplice who helped him move the body out of the place. I'm having him brought in first thing in the morning.'

'This accomplice, is he trustworthy?'

'It's a she. And I'd say she was trustworthy. She's in the church choir,' he added, as though this rendered her incapable of even the smallest misdemeanour.

'And she's said he actually killed Shellmer?'

'As good as.'

'Well, did she?'

'He shifted the body and got rid of the evidence. You wouldn't do that unless you had something to hide.'

Wesley wasn't going to argue. Gerry Heffernan obviously accepted that the case was solved, that this Paul Heygarth had shot Shellmer for some reason and then moved the body to cover his tracks. It was probably safe to assume that his deductions were correct. And besides, Wesley was too tired to pick any holes in the theory now. All he wanted was a good night's sleep: they had a busy day ahead of them tying up the case.

Heffernan knew better than to overstay his welcome. The streets of Tradmouth were silent as he made his way back to his lonely whitewashed house at the end of Baynard's Quay.

He stared straight ahead as he walked down the steep narrow streets that led to the waterfront, thinking that Justice sometimes wielded her avenging sword when you least expected it.

The two uniformed officers whose task it was to give Paul Heygarth his early-morning call at 7 am arrived quietly at the luxury apartment (two beds, one en suite, with stunning views of Tradmouth harbour), where he'd lived since his wife had decided she'd had enough of his philandering with female colleagues and grateful house buyers, and had left him to set up home with her hairdresser.

The policemen rang the doorbell and spoke into the Entryphone, careful not to give too much away. A minute later Heygarth appeared wearing a thick towelling dressing gown, pristine white with no tea or coffee stains. PC Paul Johnson observed this fact and reckoned that it said a lot about Heygarth's lifestyle.

It was too cold for doorstep conversations in what Johnson assumed was night attire, so he suggested they talk inside. Heygarth shot him a resentful look but acquiesced, leading the way up the wide, sweeping staircase to his first-floor apartment. It was then that Johnson, unable to think of anything more original at that hour of the morning, uttered the time-honoured lines about accompanying him to the station. Heygarth made no comment. He went off into the master bedroom to get dressed and came with them without complaint. Almost as though he'd been expecting it.

Half an hour later, when Johnson was leading him down the corridor to the interview room, Heygarth stopped suddenly. 'Who's in charge of this case?' he asked. He hadn't shown any sign of nerves before, but Johnson noticed that his shoulders had tensed and that he had begun to chew at a fingernail.

'Chief Inspector Heffernan's in charge of the investigation. If you'd just go into the interview room, sir.'

But Paul Heygarth swung round. 'I'm not going anywhere until my solicitor arrives.'

'He's on his way, sir.'

Somehow this didn't make Paul Heygarth feel any better.

Wesley Peterson yawned.

'Keeping you awake, are we?'

Wesley didn't answer but carried on walking down the corridor towards the station foyer. Heffernan seemed to be in a strange mood; not his usual self.

'What did you make of Heygarth?' Wesley asked, watching his boss's expression, which was giving nothing away.

'He did all right. All that rubbish about just happening to find the body lying there and moving it so that he could sell the house quickly 'cause he needed the commission. Load of bloody crap. Does he think we came in on the last ferry boat?'

Wesley raised his eyebrows. Heffernan rarely swore in the conventional sense.

'So we hold him for further questioning?'

'Too right we do. We'll apply for an extension if necessary, but we'll have him.'

'It's always possible that he's telling the truth. He seems like a bit of a shark, businesswise, and I reckon that he would bend the rules a bit if he was desperate for cash. He said he was having financial difficulties. His ex-wife's trying to take him for every penny he's got and . . .'

Heffernan stopped and looked his companion in the eye. 'Wesley Peterson. The voice of bloody reason. Look, Wes, you don't go around shifting murdered corpses unless you're trying to cover your tracks and throw us off the scent. If Nicola Tarnley hadn't grassed on him we'd never have known he was involved. She admitted they'd been having what is known nowadays as a relationship, in other words a bit of how's your father behind the filing cabinet: he was probably cocky enough to think he could trust her to keep quiet.'

'But he was wrong.'

'They had some sort of row and she decided to come clean. And he's admitted that he knew Jonny Shellmer. He'd shown him around the Old Vicarage a few times, including the day he was killed.'

'So he'd met him professionally. What's the motive?'

'How should I know? Perhaps he let him down over the house sale. Perhaps he'd known him before and there was some bad blood between them. He'll tell us eventually if we keep the pressure up.'

'And what about the gun?'

'Anyone can get hold of a gun these days if they know which pub to go to and who to ask.'

Wesley sighed. Heffernan was worrying at this case like a terrier. He'd obviously decided Paul Heygarth was guilty, but Wesley preferred to keep an open mind at this stage.

As they reached the foyer, Heffernan pushed open the swing-doors with a dramatic flourish. Rachel Tracey was standing by the reception desk with a middle-aged woman. They both turned to look at the newcomers.

Rachel spoke first. 'Sir, this is Mrs Jill Hoxworthy. She's come to report that her son, Lewis, has gone missing.

From Hoxworthy's farm ... Derenham ...' The words 'next door to the murder scene' were left unsaid.

Wesley looked at the woman sympathetically. She was in her forties and showed every sign of having been stunning in her youth. She was still attractive, even in an old waxed jacket and worn jeans, but her face was drawn with worry. Her child was missing. Every mother's nightmare.

Rachel took Jill Hoxworthy's arm gently. 'Come on, I'll take all the details and get you a nice cup of tea.' Rachel was always good in this sort of situation.

As she led the woman away to one of the interview rooms, Wesley walked up to the front desk where Bob Naseby greeted him with a knowing grin.

'How are things, Inspector? Has that mate of yours turned up any more skulls at Derenham, eh? It didn't half give me a start when the bloke came in here and produced it out of that carrier bag.'

'Glad to see you've recovered from the shock, Bob.'

Bob Naseby leaned forward. 'The season's nearly upon us. Can we persuade you to join the team, then? You were good that time you played.' He winked at Wesley. He was a man who followed the game of cricket as the devout follow religious teachings.

'Beginner's luck.'

'Nonsense. Your great-uncle played for the West Indies: it's in the blood. You're a natural. Can I put your name down? Nets start this week.'

'Sorry, Bob. I'm too busy with this case right now.' Wesley turned to seek support from Gerry Heffernan, who was standing behind him, lost in thought.

Wesley decided it was best to change the subject. 'When did the Hoxworthy boy go missing?'

Bob leaned on the desk. 'He went out yesterday teatime and didn't come home. I told her it's too early to report him missing. She's fussing about nothing if you ask me,' he said confidentially. 'She says it's not the sort of thing he usually does, but the lad's fifteen. If I had a pound for every fifteen-year-old lad that takes it into his head to take off for a day or two, I'd be able to retire and spend my remaining years watching Test matches at Lord's. He'll turn up with his tail between his legs in the next few days, you mark my words.'

'I hope you're right, Bob.'

Somehow Wesley didn't share Bob Naseby's confidence. Teenagers did go missing, but they were usually the ones with a history of running off. If it was out of character, then it was worrying. Before he became a father, Wesley might have shared Bob's casual attitude. But Michael's arrival in the world had changed all that. If, in fourteen years' time, young Michael Peterson disappeared without a word, Wesley knew that he and Pam would be frantic with worry.

'Come on, Wes. Rachel's dealing with it. Let's leave it in her capable hands, eh?' Gerry Heffernan was anxious to be off, to interview some potential witnesses who might have seen Paul Heygarth's car at the scene of the murder.

Wesley turned and followed him out of the station. He was right. Rachel was quite capable of dealing with a missing-person report. But the fact that Lewis Hoxworthy lived so close to the scene of Jonny Shellmer's murder made him uneasy.

If there was some sort of link, he wanted to find it.

WPC Trish Walton had been posted outside Jonny Shellmer's cottage, charged with the unenviable task of keeping away the curious and the ghoulish. There might be a lot of press interest, the chief inspector had said. It would be as well to have a police presence to make sure things didn't get out of hand.

It hadn't been too bad. The journalists who had turned up had gone away with only a photograph of the cottage and a 'no comment' from the neighbours for consolation. Two elderly ladies next door had plied Trish with regular mugs of tea, and a spot of local gossip had provided a welcome diversion, if not much information about the dead man. Surprisingly for a small place like Whitely, nobody seemed to have much to say about him.

Trish shifted from foot to foot and tried to stifle a sneeze. Police presences couldn't be seen to sneeze. As she fumbled in her uniform pocket for a tissue, a car drew up outside the cottage, a bright red hatchback, sporty and practical. Trish abandoned her search and drew herself up to her full height. The itch in her nose seemed to have vanished now that more important things demanded her attention. If this was another reporter, she was ready.

The woman who emerged from the car had a toned, slender body and long blond hair, but telltale lines around her mouth and beneath her eyes told Trish that she wasn't as young as she first appeared. Trish noted the pair of long and shapely legs, barely hidden by a small denim skirt, with envy. Why, she wondered, were some women given more than their fair share of assets?

As the woman opened the gate and walked towards her, Trish saw that she looked puzzled.

'Can I help you, madam?' she asked formally.

'What's going on? Has something happened?'

Trish looked at the woman's face and decided that her anxiety was genuine. 'Could you tell me your name, madam?'

'Sherry Smyth. Why? What's happened?'

'And you're a friend of Mr Shellmer's?'

'His girlfriend. Why? Where's Jonny. What's happened? Has something happened to him? Is he all right?' Sherry Smyth was becoming quite agitated.

Trish wondered what to do for the best. The woman obviously hadn't heard that Jonny Shellmer was dead. Should she tell her there and then or should it wait until she was down at the station sitting in an interview room with a nice cup of hot sweet tea? She decided that it would be kinder in the long run to get it over with. She put on her best sympathetic expression and broke the news as gently as she could.

Sherry Smyth said she had been staying at a health farm

for the past few days – a place mercifully free of television and newspapers – so she hadn't been aware of the news coverage. The shock on her sun-bronzed face was undoubtedly genuine. Trish judged that she needed a cup of tea, if not something stronger, so she knocked at the cottage next door. She knew she could rely on them to look after Sherry while she called the station.

Twenty minutes later, as Rachel Tracey and Steve Carstairs arrived in the patrol car to question Jonny Shellmer's girlfriend, Trish spotted a small blue car draw up a little way down the road. She couldn't see the driver clearly as he or she was wearing a hood that disguised both gender and features. It was strange, Trish thought, to wear a hood inside a car, especially on a bright spring day.

As the car drove off slowly, Trish took her notebook from her pocket and wrote down the registration number. The boss was always telling them to use their initiative.

'So what's she told us so far?' Gerry Heffernan sat back in the passenger seat while Wesley concentrated on the road ahead.

'Rachel and Steve have spoken to her and she's given them chapter and verse on Shellmer's private life and all his associates, past and present.'

'Has Paul Heygarth's name been mentioned?'

Wesley took his eyes off the road for a split second and glanced at his boss. 'Not that I've heard.' He paused while he concentrated on overtaking a tractor. 'Poor woman,' he said. 'Comes down expecting to spend the weekend with her boyfriend and finds he's been murdered.'

'Any chance she might be responsible?'

'No. She's been at a health farm in Surrey all week. She's a dancer and she's been working in a West End Show, so when she got the chance of a break she gave herself a week on the carrot juice as a treat. Her story's been checked out: she's telling the truth.'

'How long has she known Shellmer?'

'Eighteen months, she says. She couldn't tell us much about his early life, except that he grew up in Liverpool, so we still don't know if he has any local connections. She says he didn't talk much about his childhood, but he told her that his parents split up when he was young. He was married when he was still in his teens to a girl named Liz, and they had a son, now grown up, of course. I found a photo of them in the cottage, apparently the marriage didn't last long.'

He thought for a moment. 'He might have come down here on holiday. I found another old snap in his cottage; it was of a group of kids and it was certainly taken locally. I'm certain that one of the kids was Shellmer but the photo was fuzzy so it wasn't easy to tell.'

'Well, keep digging. We need to track down the ex-wife and son. What about his work, his music? Anything there?'

'Not really. She said he's been writing a lot of songs since Rock Boat broke up. He's made some solo albums and other artists have recorded his songs. According to her he wasn't doing too badly. And she's certain he had no enemies. Her exact words were "everyone liked Jonny".'

'Somebody didn't. Anything else?'

'Yes. Jonny told her there was someone very special he wanted her to meet. He said he was going to introduce her to this person this weekend.'

'Who was it?'

'He never said ... just someone special.'

'That woman who was looking through the cottage window? Long-lost illegitimate child?'

'Anything's possible.' Wesley thought for a few moments. 'If that woman was hanging around here, I'm just wondering if she was a stalker, some crazed fan who might have followed him the day he was killed. In which case she'd be a vital witness.'

Heffernan grunted. 'Bit far fetched, isn't it? The phantom stalker.'

'A lot of celebrities are stalked. Occupational hazard.' Wesley grinned. 'Almost makes you glad you're a humble copper, doesn't it.' Heffernan grunted again. 'Anyway, I think it's worth tracking the woman down and having a word . . . whoever she is.'

'You could be right. Did Sherry Smyth say anything else?'

'Apparently his things didn't go into storage. He sold his last place fully furnished and had a big clear-out. He wanted to make a new start, she said. She's been very helpful in compiling a list of Shellmer's associates, including the ex-members of Rock Boat and their manager. She mentioned that the manager's a keen sailor, so if we need to interview him I'll leave it to you, shall I?' Wesley grinned. 'She also said that he's been trying to get the group together again for a tour.'

Gerry Heffernan shook his head. 'I would have thought they'd be a bit past their sell-by date. Mind you, nostalgia's big business. Was Jonny Shellmer keen on the idea?'

'Sherry says he was quite happy with the way his solo and songwriting career was going and he wanted to lead a quieter life. The last thing he wanted to do was to start touring again on a regular basis, but she said if it was a one-off reunion tour he would have considered it. Another thing that might interest you is that, as far as Sherry knows, the ex-wife lives in Liverpool. The son must be in his thirties now, but she didn't know much about him. Shellmer hadn't seen them for years, apparently, but Sherry doesn't think there was any ill feeling there – just a teenage marriage that didn't work out.'

'They'll still have to be told.'

'We can get Merseyside police to track 'em down and break the news – if they haven't already heard it by now.'

Gerry Heffernan gave an almost imperceptible half-smile which told Wesley that he had other ideas.

When they reached Derenham, Wesley took the road leading to the Old Vicarage. Hoxworthy's barn loomed up on their right and he changed gear to turn into the farm drive. 'I'd like a quick word with the Hoxworthys before we talk to these people in the Old Vicarage lodge.'

'Why?' Gerry Heffernan sounded mildly exasperated.

'Well, Terry Hoxworthy found the body and . . .'

'We know who shot Shellmer. I don't know why you're making such heavy weather of this case, Wes, I really don't.'

Wesley decided to ignore his boss's last comment. 'I think young Lewis's disappearance just after a body's found near by is too much of a coincidence.' He stared at the farmhouse ahead of them in the distance. 'I reckon you can see the field where Shellmer's body was found from the upstairs windows of Hoxworthy's place. If Lewis's room happens to overlook . . .'

'You think he might have seen something?' Heffernan latched on quick.

'It's possible.'

They left the car near the drive gates. Wesley wanted to walk the half-mile up to the house, to kill two birds with one stone. This way they had to pass the barn where the painting he'd heard so much about had been found, and Wesley was hoping for a glimpse of the thing.

The huge barn doors were wide open: now was his chance. Without a word to the boss, he took a detour. Heffernan followed.

'What is it? What are you looking in here for? Do you think Lewis might be playing hide-and-seek in this old place?'

'Neil told Pam they'd found some sort of huge medieval painting in the barn. I want to see if it's still here.'

He walked on ahead, across the straw-covered floor of the great barn. He soon saw what he was looking for. Propped up against the far wall was a massive semicircular painting, at least fifteen feet high, its figures standing out clearly in the watery sunlight that streamed through the barn doors. One side heaven and one side hell.

In the centre, the Almighty, bearded and robed in white, sat in judgement on the assembled sinners, aided and abetted by helpful saints armed with scales and large books, presumably containing records of good and bad deeds. The virtuous to the right wore smug expressions as they enjoyed an everlasting bliss with sumptuous clouds and soaring angels. But it was the fate of the damned on the left which caught Wesley's eye. The artists hadn't backed off from depicting any torture or depravity, however horrific. Lewd, leering devils committed serious sexual assaults on naked women and men alike, while their colleagues inflicted various agonising tortures with hot irons, racks and chains on vulnerable white bodies.

'Whoever painted that was sick,' Heffernan stated bluntly.

Wesley stared at it in silence. The thing made him uncomfortable, but somehow he couldn't take his eyes off it.

Then a soft female voice made him turn round. It belonged to a slim woman in her late thirties with an untidy ponytail. 'It's a Doom,' she said quietly. 'They used to have them in churches, often over the chancel arch at the front so everyone could see what was in store for them.'

Wesley nodded. 'It's very, er ... powerful.'

The woman looked pleasantly surprised. 'You're interested in medieval art?'

'I'm no expert but I suppose I know the basics.' He held out his hand. 'I'm Detective Inspector Peterson and this is DCI Heffernan. Tradmouth CID.'

The woman shook his hand firmly. 'I'm Emma Fawley from the county museum. You're not the Wesley Peterson Neil Watson was telling me about? The one who was at university with him and worked in the Arts and Antique squad at the Met?'

Wesley shuffled his feet modestly. 'That's me.'

'It was Neil who discovered the Doom when he was examining the barn. I'm really pleased to meet you. I suppose you're here because of that murder. Terrible business. Some ageing rock star, wasn't it?'

'That's right,' Wesley replied quickly, anxious to change the subject. 'Have you any idea yet where the Doom came from?' At that moment he felt more inclined to discuss art than Jonny Shellmer's death. He glanced round at Heffernan and saw that he was still staring at the painting, his mouth gaping open.

'It must have come from one of the churches around here. I'd guess at Derenham; probably rescued from destruction in the Reformation. You'd hardly move a thing that size very far. Have you been up to see Neil's dig yet? At the other side of the village near the church.'

'I went there when a skull was found by builders digging the foundations for the new village hall, but I've not been since Neil began work there,' he said with genuine regret.

'It's possible that the manor house they've discovered had connections with a family called Merrivale who owned most of this land in the Middle Ages. They'd probably have been major benefactors of the church – maybe even had this Doom painted. I'm told that some Victorian vicar of Derenham found a pile of well-preserved medieval letters relating to the Merrivales and published them. Neil's hoping to track down an edition – there's always a chance the letters might tell us something about the origins of the Doom.'

'What happened to the original letters? Are they in some museum or archive?'

'Nobody knows what became of them. The church sold the Old Vicarage to private buyers back in the early sixties. If they were still there they might have been lost or sold off in some job lot at an auction of the contents. Shame.'

Gerry Heffernan nudged Wesley's arm. Wesley could sense the boss was anxious to be away.

'I'm sorry, Emma, we'd better get a move on. It was very good to meet you.'

'I hope we'll see you around here again.'

Wesley stood for a moment, staring at the great painting, reluctant to move. 'It seems to be in very good condition,' he said.

'Yes, it is . . . considering.'

'Where will it end up?'

'I've really no idea. We'll have to discover a bit about its history first. I've been contacted by a Maggie Flowers, who's organising a history evening at Derenham church. She asked if it could be put on display there and I said it seemed like a good idea. That's where it probably came from, after all.'

Maggie Flowers, the woman photographed in the *Tradmouth Echo* with Jonny Shellmer. She was another person Wesley wanted to talk to. He made a mental note to pay her a visit at the first opportunity.

Heffernan nudged Wesley. 'Sorry, love,' he said to Emma. 'I'll have to drag him away. Much as I've enjoyed our little art appreciation class, we've got a murder to investigate, you know.'

Wesley smiled at Emma apologetically and said goodbye.

'I wouldn't put that thing in a church,' Heffernan mumbled as they walked down the track to the farmhouse. 'It's obscene. All those naked bodies and them devils doing, er, whatever it is they were doing.'

'I suppose it was to illustrate the consequences of sin,' Wesley answered, trying not to smile.

Gerry Heffernan grunted. 'Perhaps we should ask the Chief Constable to put one up outside every nick – that should cut our crime figures.'

The two men walked the rest of the way to the farmhouse in silence. Wesley stared in the direction of the church tower that peeped through the budding trees. The church – and Neil's dig – seemed far away at the moment. But perhaps that was for the best. The last thing he needed now was a distraction.

Jill Hoxworthy answered the door. She looked as though she hadn't slept, which, Wesley thought, was hardly surprising. She watched their faces keenly, hopefully, as though she expected them to be bearing news of Lewis, and Wesley felt guilty that he had nothing to tell her which would put her mind at rest. She stood aside to let them in, then she led them into the living room and sank down on the sofa – an ancient construction in dark red moquette inherited from her parents shortly after her marriage and never replaced – before pulling a tissue from a box on the floor. She dabbed her eyes with it and screwed it up in her hand absent-mindedly.

'I'm terribly sorry, Mrs Hoxworthy, I'm afraid there's no news yet,' said Wesley. 'But his description's been circulated and all patrols are on the lookout for him.' He didn't mention that this sudden police interest was connected with the murder on their land. He didn't want to worry her unduly.

'We're doing our best, love,' Heffernan assured her gruffly. 'Is your husband not here with you?'

'Terry's down seeing to the ewes in the bottom field. It's lambing. Lewis used to love helping with the lambs when he was little,' she added quietly, her lip trembling slightly. 'A farm doesn't run itself,' she went on before taking a deep breath. 'And Terry says it helps, keeping busy.'

'Yes,' said Wesley softly. 'I wonder if I might ask you a few more questions.'

Jill Hoxworthy nodded. Anything that would help find Lewis.

'Has Lewis had anything on his mind recently? Has he done anything out of character, mentioned any new people? Been anywhere you didn't know about?'

'He's fifteen. You can't watch them at that age like you can when they're five. He never told us much about who he was seeing. He'd just go out and not say, even when I asked him.'

'What about his friends? I presume you've been in touch with them all to check if they've seen him?'

Jill thought for a few seconds. Wesley sensed the subject

of the company Lewis kept wasn't a comfortable one for her.

'He never used to have a lot of friends,' she began. 'He was always interested in history and things like that; seemed quite happy with his own company.' She swallowed hard. 'But he's changed recently. He's gone very sulky and secretive. And he spends a lot of time on his computer. I'd ask him how he'd got on at school and he'd just storm off or tell me to mind my own business. Terry says it's just his age but ...' She hesitated, her brow wrinkled with worry. 'He's mentioned some boys at school ...'

Wesley sensed that she was leaving something unsaid. 'Did you sense he was unhappy? Do you think it's possible that he was being bullied?' It was a question he had to ask.

'He never said anything but ...' She shook her head, near to tears.

'The boys he mentioned, what were their names?'

'I know one's called Yossa. That's where he said he was going – Yossa's. It's the school holidays – they're not back till next week – but I rang the headmaster and he was really sympathetic: he got the phone number for me. I rang this Yossa and he said that Lewis had never been there and he hadn't been expecting him. He lives on the Winterham estate in Morbay.'

Wesley and Heffernan looked at each other. Winterham was a council estate well known to the local force ... and not for the quiet and law-abiding nature of its inhabitants.

'We'll check him out, love,' Heffernan assured her earnestly. 'And try not to worry too much, eh? Most lads who go missing like this turn up safe and sound after a couple of days.'

'It's just not like Lewis. He's never done anything like this before.'

Wesley could see tears welling up in her eyes, and as she rubbed at them with the sleeve of her cream jumper he noticed that the cuff was grubby, stained with what looked like tomato sauce: laundry was probably the last thing on her mind.

He spoke to her gently. 'Do you mind if we have a look at Lewis's room?'

Mrs Hoxworthy gave a weak smile. 'Of course not. Anything that helps.'

She led them upstairs. Lewis's room, as Wesley had guessed, was at the front of the house with a perfect view over to the field where Jonny Shellmer's body had been found. The Old Vicarage gates and the lodge were clearly visible, although most of the drive was obscured by trees and bushes.

Lewis's room was untidy; dirty too, probably, as nobody could have penetrated the layers of papers, CDs and clothes on the floor in order to clean it. It clearly hadn't been touched since Lewis's departure, and Wesley suspected that searching it would be a Herculean task, but perhaps a necessary one if the boy didn't turn up soon. There might be some clue to his whereabouts amidst the chaos. He hoped Lewis would appear safe and sound before a detailed excavation of his room was necessary.

The two policemen glanced at each other. It was time to go. As Wesley left the Hoxworthys' farmhouse, he offered up a silent prayer that Lewis would be found alive and well ... and soon.

Neil Watson stood in the largest trench, breathing in the scent of newly dug soil and listening to the soft scraping of trowels on earth. He watched as the team of students around him worked away at the emerging wall foundations. It was all appearing too quickly, the outline of the great hall of a medieval manor house, complete with central hearth. What they had found before today was a mere crumb of the cake. Now they were getting great slices of it ... plus the icing.

His colleague, Matt, a man a little older than himself who wore a ponytail and a permanently worried expression, took a breath from his labours and strolled over.

'From the geophysics outline we got a clear picture of a large house buried under here, a medieval manor house

103

judging by the layout. But from the state of these stone foundations, I'd say the place was demolished after some sort of fire.'

Neil scratched his head. 'It's strange that this site's in a prime location, near the church and the village centre, and it's never been built on again over all those centuries. Don't you think that's odd?'

'There must have been a reason.'

Neil shrugged, squatted down again, and began to scrape away the fine reddish-coloured earth from a charred lump of carved stone.

Wesley knew there was no time to seek out Neil to find out what the digging had turned up so far. And besides, the boss was looking preoccupied and impatient. He drove the short distance to the lodge of the Old Vicarage, and parked in the narrow lane.

He climbed out of the car. His eyes were drawn to the field near by where Jonny Shellmer's body had been found. Peace had returned to the spot, but the police tape remained and the cows had been moved to another field to recover from their few hours of excitement.

Most police attention now focused on the Old Vicarage. The forensic team had been examining the place minutely.

As they walked towards the lodge, Wesley noticed that Gerry Heffernan had fallen uncharacteristically silent, as though he had something on his mind. But he didn't have a chance to ask what was wrong because as soon as Wesley's hand had touched the lodge's lion's-head knocker the front door opened wide. Gloria Treadly had watched them walking up the lane from behind the voile curtains, and she was ready for them.

She stood blocking the doorway, looking Wesley up and down with barely disguised contempt as he displayed his warrant card.

'I've had two of your lot here already,' she said. 'I told them I didn't know anything.'

Gerry Heffernan pushed forward. 'Can we have a word, love?'

She didn't budge. 'I'm busy.'

Gerry Heffernan didn't have Wesley's good manners. He took another step forward and Gloria Treadly instinctively moved back. 'Cup of tea'd be nice, love,' he said as he crossed the threshold. Wesley had no alternative but to follow him.

They were soon perched on the uncomfortable seating in the living room. Gloria glowered at them both from the white sofa. There was no sign of tea.

Wesley felt Heffernan's elbow gently nudge his ribs. He knew that it was up to him to do the talking.

'You told our colleagues you saw some vehicles driving up to the Old Vicarage last week.'

Gloria nodded impatiently. 'I told them everything I know.'

Gerry Heffernan took out his notebook and squinted at it. 'You said you saw a BMW driving up there on Wednesday afternoon. What time would that be?'

'I can't remember. I've got better things to do than look out of the window all day,' she added self-righteously.

'What colour was this BMW?'

'Black,' she replied, glancing at Wesley.

'And you said you saw a yellow sports car. Was that before or after you saw the BMW arrive?'

Gloria Treadly shook her head. The stiff lacquer on her grey hair ensured that each hair stayed in its appointed place. 'I don't remember. After, maybe. I can't be sure. If I'd known it was going to be important I would have written it all down,' she said with a hint of sarcasm.

The door opened and a well-built man appeared. He was probably thirty or older, with longish, greasy hair, and he wore a checked shirt tucked into jeans stretched tight around an expanding waist.

'Who's this, Ma?'

London, definitely, Wesley thought. Or possibly Essex

or Kent. He watched the man as he came into the room. He looked familiar. But then he'd come across so many men – honest and dishonest – in the Met. And the name Alec Treadly didn't ring any bells – unless he'd changed it.

'Old Bill,' said Gloria warily. 'They've come about that body in the field. Want to know if we'd seen any cars going up to the big house.'

'Well, Mr Treadly,' said Wesley. 'Did you see any cars going up to the Old Vicarage on Wednesday?'

Alec Treadly stared at him vacantly for a few seconds. 'That's Ma's department. She keeps an eye on all the comings and goings. I was out.'

'Do you mind telling us where you were on Wednesday afternoon, sir?'

'Wednesday I was at the bookie's in Tradmouth. I didn't see nothing. Got home about ... what time was it, Ma?'

'After half four – twenty to five maybe.' She began to beam at her son with maternal devotion.

'I saw a big black BMW turning into the Old Vicarage drive when I was walking home.'

Gerry Heffernan sat forward. 'Did you see who was driving it?'

'Yeah. I'd seen him before. Middle-aged man, balding. I thought he was the estate agent selling the place. He'd been in and out like a fiddler's elbow.'

'Did you see any other vehicles after that?'

'Yeah. I went out just before five to empty the kitchen bin and I heard something that sounded like a sports car going up the drive – powerful engine, like. Didn't see it, mind.'

'How can you be sure it was going up the drive and not just going down the lane?' Wesley asked.

'It had to change gear. You can tell by the sound of the engine. It had turned into the Old Vicarage drive all right.'

'And you didn't see it? Or the driver?' Wesley asked hopefully.

'Nah. Why?'

'And did you see or hear the BMW leave before the sports car arrived?'

Treadly shook his head.

'This man driving the BMW. Could you identify him?' Heffernan sounded positively excited.

'Yeah. I suppose I could.'

Wesley saw that his boss was starting to look triumphant, like an athlete who realised that he was about to be first past the finishing line. 'And he was going up to the Old Vicarage around half past four on Wednesday?' Alec nodded.

Wesley turned to Gloria Treadly. 'You told my colleagues that you saw a yellow sports car late on Wednesday afternoon. Is that right, Mrs Treadly?'

'I think so. But I can't be sure of the time. I was busy. I had things to do,' she added.

'Could the yellow sports car have been the sports car your son heard when he was outside just before five o'clock?'

Gloria shrugged. 'Could be.'

'We think that yellow car might have belonged to the dead man,' said Wesley. 'Did you happen to see who was driving it?'

She shook her head. Then Wesley saw a glance exchanged between mother and son. There was something they were holding back.

'Anything else you can tell us?' he asked hopefully.

Another shake of the head.

There was a short, awkward silence which was broken by Gerry Heffernan. 'We might need you to identify the driver of the BMW.' He stood up. 'You've been a great help. Thanks.'

The chief inspector strutted out of the tiny cottage looking very pleased with himself. Wesley followed quietly, suppressing his annoyance. He was certain the Treadlys were hiding something, and if the boss hadn't been so heavy handed he might have got more out of them.

But he bit his lip and said nothing.

He didn't know what had got into Gerry Heffernan recently. He wasn't his usual self at all.

WPC Trish Walton sat down in front of the computer and typed in the registration number of the blue car she had spotted in Whitely, telling herself that it was probably the vehicle of some innocent law-abiding person. Wearing a hood inside a parked car could hardly be construed as an offence. Perhaps the person had earache. Perhaps they were parked there waiting for someone. Trish watched as the details came up on her screen.

Angela Simms of 7 Cawston Street, Neston was the proud owner of a 1994 blue Ford Fiesta. No driving offences had been recorded. To Trish it all sounded very mundane.

She printed out Angela Simms's details and made for Gerry Heffernan's office.

Neil Watson looked down at his newest trench, the one which, hopefully, straddled the corner of the great hall. It looked as though the initial diagnosis had been correct. The building had been burned, then demolished, and the good stones carted away by the locals to be used as building materials. What remained of the foundations were charred black. It had been some conflagration that had brought this place, a substantial manor house, to ruin.

He looked around. The field was full of men and women digging, drawing and operating strange instruments that penetrated the ground with radar to show what lay beneath. A small yellow digger was scraping off the top layer of earth on the other side of the field.

It was Neil's intention that the whole of Manor Field should be excavated thoroughly and that the layout of the buildings beneath the grass should be exposed, examined and recorded before the site was built on.

Jim and Maggie Flowers in the house next door to the field seemed almost as keen as Neil to unearth Derenham's secret past. They had even allowed a couple of trenches to be opened in their immaculate garden, and Maggie was helping with the digging, chivvying on the other volunteers. She was a great organiser.

Neil's mind began to wander as he scraped away at the masonry. He licked his lips; he was thirsty, and began to think longingly of the beer in the Red Bull. But the sight of a shard of medieval pottery lying in the soil brought his thoughts back swiftly to archaeology.

The quiet, preoccupied hum of archaeological conversation was suddenly interrupted by a shout of astonishment. Neil looked up and saw Maggie Flowers standing quite still, a look of shock on her face. The people digging near her, an assortment of students and locals supervised by Matt, had stopped what they were doing and turned to stare.

Neil watched as Matt put down his trowel and walked carefully along the trench towards Maggie, whose face was drained of colour. 'Down there.' She pointed at the ground. 'I think it's bones.' She began to play with her wedding ring nervously, twisting it round and round.

Neil began to make his way over slowly, hoping it was nothing that would hold up the dig. Then he thought of the solitary skull; the rest of the body must be buried somewhere.

'Don't worry,' he heard Matt saying. 'Most bones found in excavations of domestic buildings belong to animals; parts of meat carcasses thrown into middens.'

It was possible that Maggie had never seen buried bones before and was jumping to conclusions. But Neil knew that Matt was trying to look on the bright side.

Maggie stood silently, staring at the ground as Neil squatted beside Matt and began to work away, watched by the rest of the diggers. 'Well?' she asked anxiously after a few minutes.

Neil stood up and attempted a smile which turned out to be more of a snarl. He told himself it wasn't this poor woman's fault. If she hadn't found it, someone else would have ... maybe himself. But somehow he couldn't help wishing that it hadn't turned up now and that they'd all been left in blissful ignorance for a few more days.

'The bones look human,' he said, trying to sound positive. 'I'm afraid we'll have to inform the authorities.' He looked at Matt. 'We'd better stop work on this trench for now and concentrate on the other side of the field. I'll do the necessary,' he said quietly.

Matt nodded and began to shepherd the assembled diggers away to the opposite side of the field. A few stragglers, a group of third-year archaeology students, loitered around the edge of the trench, hoping to see something exciting. But as Neil pulled his mobile phone from his pocket he looked up at them impatiently. They took the hint and scattered like nervous sheep.

The necessary phone calls made, Neil knelt down and began to scrape away the reddish earth. One thing was certain, he thought with some relief – the remains couldn't possibly be those of Terry Hoxworthy's missing son. Things could be a lot worse.

Terry Hoxworthy looked up before pushing the shop door open. The name 'Angela's Angels' was painted on the fascia board above in large Gothic lettering, and ethereal winged beings in shades of blue and silver weaved between the letters.

The shop window was crammed with more angels. Angel figurines, angel books, angel jewellery. Angels like St Michael, warlike but kindly – or firm but fair, as Angela preferred. Angels like Gabriel, glorious and shining. And lesser angels, the heavenly host, their gossamer wings shimmering.

And there were guardian angels beautiful and benign, protecting their charges through thick and thin. Angela stocked a selection of books about guardian angels and said that they sold well in a New Agey place like Neston, where a high proportion of townsfolk seemed to be on some spiritual quest.

In fact Angela's Angels, along with the crystal healing shop next door, made an adequate living from the inhabitants of the pretty medieval town which nestled in a valley eight miles upstream from Tradmouth. But Terry couldn't see the appeal himself.

A tinkling bell announced his arrival and Angela hurried out from the back of the shop. When she saw him she gave a weak smile. 'Come through. I'll make some tea.'

She floated out into the back of the shop and Terry followed, walking slowly past the rows of watching angels, careful not to bump into anything. Angela always made him feel clumsy, earthbound; a clodhopping mortal who lived on a lower plane of existence.

When they reached the back kitchen she turned to him, her eyes anxious. 'Have the police asked you anything? How much do you think they know?'

Terry shook his head. 'Sorry, I don't know. With Lewis going off I've had other things on my mind.'

'If they start to ask questions, don't mention me, please.' Her small, heart-shaped face turned towards him and her large eyes pleaded, childlike.

'I promise,' Terry whispered, touching her thin, blue-veined hand. 'I promise.'

She took his hand and ran her finger gently across the ugly scar on the palm, tracing its shape. The tears began to trickle down her face, and Terry hoped that her guardian angel was looking after her. She was going to need all the help she could get.

Chapter Six

My well beloved wife,
We made our way to Wells where the common soldiers,
to their disgrace, did loot the Bishop's palace and broke
open his gaol. Then we marched on to Bristol to seek
both men and guns and we join soon with Jasper Tudor
and his Welshmen but I fear that King Edward's army is
close by.

Our son Edmund has leave from the Earl to march
with us. Knowing your concern, I tried to dissuade him
but he is sixteen years, barely younger than Queen
Margaret's son, Prince Edward, who fights now for the
crown of his poor imprisoned father. My good wife, be
not anxious for Edmund, I beg you, but pray for our
safety and victory.

By all means pursue John's alliance with the widow
More as I mislike his closeness to Elizabeth. Who knows
what thoughts he could put into an innocent girl's head?
I would he were here to fight like his half-brother.

I send this by a carrier of Bristol who has business in
Tradmouth and I will send word of our fortunes as soon
as I am able.
Pray for myself and Edmund.
Your devoted and loving husband, Richard

Written at Bristol this first day of May 1471

Paul Heygarth sat in the interview room clutching a plastic cup filled with a brown liquid which somebody had told him was tea.

Gerry Heffernan leaned forward. 'Why did you really move Jonny Shellmer's body? Was it to cover your tracks? You've got the key to the Old Vicarage. Neighbours saw you coming and going. We've got witnesses.'

Heygarth took a sip from the cup and wrinkled his nose in disgust. Then he leaned back. He looked tired, drawn. Wesley Peterson watched him closely and thought that maybe the man had had enough.

'I've told you already. I've been having cash-flow problems and I wanted a quick sale on the Old Vicarage.' Heygarth sounded weary, sick of the whole thing. 'I had a few potential buyers lined up, including Jonny Shellmer. I knew that if the place was a murder scene, it would be ages before things were back to normal and ... well, nobody would want to buy a house where someone's just been murdered, would they? And why would I want to kill Shellmer anyway? He was keen on buying the place and that would have solved all my problems. And even if he'd pulled out, I had a couple of other interested parties lined up. And I hardly knew the man.' He looked Heffernan in the eye. 'I'm bloody sick of this. I keep on telling you, I didn't kill him.'

The young woman solicitor sitting by Heygarth's side spoke firmly. 'I think my client's had enough for now, Chief Inspector.' She looked at her watch.

Gerry Heffernan was well aware of the time limits for the detention of suspects. He tried again. 'What did you do with the gun?'

'What gun? I've never handled a gun in my life,' Heygarth answered with quiet desperation. 'Honestly. I've never ever touched a gun, let alone fired one.'

Wesley looked at the man's face, at his eyes. Something made him believe what Heygarth was saying. Everything they had learned so far suggested that Shellmer had only met Heygarth professionally when he had started looking for a house in the area. There was no evidence that they had known each other before, and certainly no evidence of bad blood between them.

Heygarth had admitted to meeting Shellmer late on Wednesday afternoon to show him around the Old Vicarage for a third time, but he swore that he had driven off just after five o'clock, leaving Shellmer alone in the house because he'd said he wanted to look round on his own and get a feel of the place. When someone's paying that much money, you tend to go along with their whims; and he knew Jonny Shellmer by reputation and trusted him not to nick the fixtures and fittings. Jonny had been alive and well when he'd last seen him, and he had promised to make sure all the doors were firmly shut when he left.

When he had finished, Heffernan stared at him for a few moments and announced in no uncertain terms that he didn't believe him, that there was no way that he'd left Shellmer alive in the empty house. Wesley glanced at his boss and noticed his chin jutting out with determination. He was convinced of Heygarth's guilt. But Wesley wasn't.

'Perhaps we should take a break,' he said with what he hoped sounded like authority.

To his surprise, the boss nodded. He was probably as desperate for a decent cup of tea as Wesley was.

There was a loud scraping of chairs as the two officers stood up. 'We'll be wanting another word later,' Heffernan said brusquely before marching from the stark interview room, Wesley following behind, trying to keep up.

A few minutes later they were in Heffernan's office awaiting the cups of hot, steaming tea promised them by a harassed Trish Walton.

Wesley looked through the window at the scene of bubbling activity in the office beyond. Officers spoke on telephones or typed busily into computers. Others were out interviewing witnesses. Photographs of Jonny Shellmer, in life and death, together with a list of his movements and all his known associates, were pinned to a large notice-board on the wall at the end of the room, focusing their minds on the matter in hand.

An easel stood near it, bearing Lewis Hoxworthy's photograph and details. Wesley hoped that soon this would be an unnecessary addition to the room, that soon Lewis would be found safe. But experience had taught him to be pessimistic. If the two cases were linked, as he suspected they were, then Lewis might already be dead. But he would never have shared these thoughts with Lewis's mother. She, at least, should have hope.

Steve Carstairs knocked on the office door and let himself in, glancing at Wesley with a hint of hostility.

'How's it going?' Wesley asked.

Steve looked nonplussed. 'Er, we've been tracking down the members of Rock Boat, er, sir.'

'Well, come on,' said Gerry Heffernan, wearily. 'What are they up to? Still enjoying a life of sex, drugs and rock and roll, are they?'

'Not exactly, sir. Mickey Charles, the rhythm guitarist, has got a big place up in the Highlands of Scotland and runs a thriving salmon-farming business. He's not been away from home in the past year. Peter Davies, bass guitar, lives in the south of France, lucky sod. He's not visited the UK for at least six months. But Chris Pauling, the drummer, doesn't live far away He's got a smallholding in Gloucestershire. It seems that when the group split up he sank all his money into some leisure complex that went bankrupt and now he's broke.'

'Do you know if this Pauling has had any contact with Jonny Shellmer?'

'He says he hasn't seen him for over two years. But I wouldn't take that as gospel.' Steve grinned unpleasantly, showing the gap between his even front teeth.

'Thanks, Steve.' Wesley forced himself to smile approvingly. 'It might be a good idea to have a word with this Chris Pauling. See if you can find out where he was when

Shellmer was killed, will you? And if he's got anyone who can confirm it.'

'What else is there?' asked Heffernan, scratching his head.

'Rock Boat's manager, Hal Lancaster, has a big place in Surrey. They say he was the man who discovered Rock Boat. He's from New York originally but he moved here back in the sixties,' Steve added, showing off his knowledge of pop trivia. 'I spoke to his housekeeper and she told me he's away. He's a big collector, she said.'

'What does he collect?' asked Wesley.

Steve felt a little silly for not having asked. 'I don't know. She just said a collector.'

Heffernan grunted. 'That could cover anything from stamps to guns.'

'And if it's guns ...' Wesley didn't finish the sentence. He watched Heffernan's face. Normally his eyes would have lit up at the mention of a new line of enquiry, but there was no reaction.

'I've got hold of Jonny Shellmer's biography,' said Steve eagerly, trying to impress. 'I was reading it last night.'

'Did you discover anything interesting?' Wesley asked.

Steve shrugged. 'Not much we don't know already. He came from Liverpool and he got married to a woman named Liz and had a son. It didn't last long and he never married again. It mainly goes on about Rock Boat's wild tours and ...'

'Any mention of him having any connections with this area?'

Steve shook his head. 'No, but I've not finished it yet.'

'Well, let us know if you find anything relevant, won't you. And perhaps DCI Heffernan would like to read it after you.'

Before Heffernan could say anything, Trish Walton appeared with two large mugs of tea.

'There's been a call from Merseyside police, sir. They haven't been able to track down Jonny Shellmer's ex-wife yet. If she's married again and changed her name they might have a difficult job ... she might not even be living there now.' She looked at Gerry Heffernan expectantly, thinking he might just jump at the chance of a visit to his native city to try to succeed where their Merseyside colleagues had failed.

'Thanks, Trish. We'll have to make further enquiries,' said Wesley. He too glanced at his boss but saw no reaction.

'And that address I left on your desk earlier, sir – Angela Simms. She was sitting in a small blue car opposite Shellmer's cottage. The neighbours said someone in a blue car visited Shellmer and ...'

'Oh, aye, thanks, love. It might be worth having a word with Ms Simms some time.'

'Well done, Trish. Thanks,' said Wesley. A bit of encouragement never went amiss.

As Trish left the office, Wesley saw that Steve was watching her long shapely legs.

'Could this Angela Simms be the woman we saw hanging around Shellmer's place in Whitely?' Wesley asked when Trish had closed the door.

'Jonny Shellmer was a rock star,' said Steve. 'Do you reckon he might have had crazed fans who followed him around – or a stalker?'

'It's always a possibility,' Wesley answered. 'But I found a card in Shellmer's bedroom drawer. It was from someone called "Angel". Angela – Angel?'

'Very nice. Wish some angel'd send me a card,' Heffernan said wistfully. He put his feet up on the desk and sighed. 'I think we'll have to put Ms Angela Simms on our visiting list.'

After a late lunch of a single cheese sandwich, eaten rapidly at his desk, Wesley Peterson answered his telephone. He mumbled an absent-minded 'hello' into the receiver, only to be answered by a voice enquiring whether he was busy. He took a deep breath. He'd recognise Neil Watson's voice anywhere.

'Of course I'm busy, Neil. What is it?'

'I thought you'd like to get down here. The coroner's on his way.'

Wesley took a deep breath. This was all he needed. 'Is it a body?' he asked, thinking with dread of Lewis Hoxworthy.

'It's a skeleton, buried on our site. Headless – I think we've found the rest of the body to go with that skull.'

Wesley hesitated. 'Any indication of how old it is?' He hoped that it was old, the more ancient the better, so it wouldn't add to his workload.

'An Elizabethan coin was found in the soil above it and the ground hadn't been disturbed. I'd say it was very old. From the context I'd say it was medieval, contemporary with the building we're excavating.'

Wesley sighed. 'In that case it's not my problem. But I'll call the pathologist out to have a look at it ... just to make absolutely sure it belongs to the head and it's not some modern murder victim.'

'Aren't you coming to see it yourself?' Neil sounded disappointed.

'No time, Neil. We're rushed off our feet here. We've got a major murder investigation and a missing boy.'

'Terry Hoxworthy's lad? I heard. What do you reckon's happened to him?'

'It's possible that he's got in with a bad crowd at school, so he might be off somewhere getting up to no good. That's what we're hoping anyway.'

'Yeah. When I was down at the old barn again having a word with Emma from the museum I saw Terry Hoxworthy wandering around like a lost soul. He saw me but he didn't say anything. Poor sod.'

Wesley smiled to himself. It wasn't often Neil noticed what was going on around him. Normally during a dig his mind would be focused on what he was uncovering. Terry

Hoxworthy's problems had obviously made an impact, and he was sure that Pam would consider Neil's new-found sensitivity a change for the better.

'Look, Neil, if I'm down that way I'll come and have a look at your skeleton. Okay?'

'Don't leave it too long if you want to see it *in situ*,' Neil warned.

Wesley put the phone down. Perhaps he'd nip over to Derenham and pay Jill Hoxworthy another visit. Kill two birds with one stone.

From the details provided by Jill Hoxworthy they managed to track down Lewis's friend Yossa, also known as Joseph Lang.

Rachel decided to take PC Paul Johnson with her to see him. When she had found Wesley unavailable she had considered taking Steve, but she was afraid that his macho attitude might cause tension. Then she had thought of Trish but, although it went against her feminist principles, she knew she'd feel far safer with a six-foot-tall man on the Winterham estate.

She'd looked Lang up on the police computer. At fifteen he had climbed the first few rungs of the criminal ladder. Joy-riding, theft from a motor vehicle. And two months ago he'd branched out into breaking and entering. No wonder he didn't have much time for his schoolwork, she thought. And based on what she knew of Lewis Hoxworthy, she wondered what the two boys had in common. But then who knew what power the likes of Yossa could wield over a vulnerable boy from a sheltered background – or what fascination he held? Something made her think of rabbits and snakes.

There was no twitching of curtains as the patrol car drew up outside 5 Carter Gardens. The neighbours probably regarded visits from the police with the same nonchalance as more law-abiding neighbourhoods regarded visits from the postman.

Number five was at the end of a terrace of pebbledashed, flat-roofed houses, built in the sixties when urban planners had been a little carried away by what they considered to be their own revolutionary brilliance. The results were depressing. Nothing ages faster than modernity.

The cars and vans parked in the street and the garishly painted front doors provided the only splashes of colour among the dirty grey pebbledashed walls and the matching grey of the littered pavements. Rachel and Paul Johnson opened the rickety wooden gate. The house looked empty.

A grubby sticking plaster stuck over the doorbell indicated that it might be better to knock. Johnson rapped on the door glass five times with his knuckles. Then another five. At his third attempt the door was answered by Yossa himself. He looked them up and down with distaste then, when Rachel told him why they were there, he stood aside reluctantly to let them in.

Yossa was short on the social graces. He led them into the lounge, then stood there staring at them. Rachel moved aside a pile of tabloid newspapers, turning brown with age, and sat on the edge of the stained settee.

'Are your parents in?' she began, aware of the rules on interviewing minors.

He shook his head.

'We've come about Lewis Hoxworthy.'

He stared at her and folded his arms. He was five feet seven, skinny with close-cropped hair and a slightly bulbous nose, and Rachel might have taken him for a little angel if she hadn't been told otherwise.

'I don't know nothing about Lew. Haven't seen him since school broke up.'

'His family are very worried. Have you any idea where he might have gone?'

'Nah. I told his mum when she rang. I've not seen him. He never came here.'

'Is there anywhere he might have gone, anywhere he talked about?'

120

Yossa shook his head, smirking unpleasantly. 'He was into castles and battles and that. Kid's stuff. And he was always going on about his computer: how good it was; how much it cost; all the people he'd talked to on the Internet. Always bragging, trying to impress us. We took the piss but he still hung around us. Couldn't get rid of him. We had a laugh, though.'

'What do you mean?'

Yossa shrugged. 'He'd fall for anything – do anything we told him.'

'And you found that funny?'

Yossa grinned. 'Yeah.'

Rachel noted the casual cruelty in Yossa's manner. She found herself feeling desperately sorry for Lewis Hoxworthy.

'Did you see Lewis on the day he disappeared?'

'Nah. Like I said, I've not seen him since school broke up.'

'So you haven't seen him over the Easter holidays?'

'I got better things to do.'

She looked into his eyes. 'There's something you're not telling me, Yossa.' She hesitated, glancing at Johnson. 'Look, if it's something that's against the law maybe we can use our discretion, eh? At the moment all we want to do is to find Lewis.'

Yossa hesitated, weighing up the options, and decided that it wouldn't do any harm to give them something. And it'd get them off his back. 'He sent me an e-mail: he was bragging that he had something that was worth a lot of money – something he was going to sell. He reckoned he was going to be rich.' He looked at Rachel, watching her reaction. 'And he said he had a gun.'

'Did he tell you anything about this gun? Where he got it? How long he'd had it?'

Yossa smirked and shook his head. 'Nah. He was bullshitting. He said he found it. But his dad's a farmer so I reckon he was talking about his shotgun. It was all bullshit.

121

He was always trying to impress us, like I said.'

'Can you remember anything else he said?'

'He said a load of stuff. All bullshit. Look, we didn't want him around but he kept trying to get in with us.'

'I bet you teased him,' said Johnson, who was young enough to remember the cruelties of adolescence. 'I bet you played some tricks on him, made him do some daft things,' he added with a conspiratorial grin.

Yossa grinned back unpleasantly but said nothing.

'Did you have anything planned for him the day he disappeared?'

The grin disappeared as Yossa realised the implications of Johnson's question. 'Nah. I told you, I've not seen him since school finished.'

'That was a couple of weeks ago?'

'Yeah, but I've not seen him, honest. He's sent me e-mails but I've not seen him.'

'Can you get us a print-out of these e-mails?' asked Rachel sweetly.

Yossa thought for a moment. 'Don't see why not. Wait there.'

He disappeared and returned a few minutes later with some sheets of paper. Rachel suspected that he hadn't wanted them to see his computer equipment. It was bound to have fallen off the back of some lorry or other, she thought uncharitably.

She took the sheets of paper from him. 'Thank you, Yossa. You've been very helpful,' she said formally. There was no way anyone was going to accuse her of browbeating a defenceless minor. Not that she'd ever class the likes of Yossa Lang as defenceless.

In view of what Rachel had learned from Yossa Lang, Wesley thought it might be worth seeing what other e-mails they could find on Lewis Hoxworthy's computer. The world of high technology was a mystery to many parents, so it was possible that Terry and Jill hadn't thought to look.

122

The e-mails Lewis had sent to Yossa had been intended to impress. He boasted of finding something which he intended to sell for a lot of money. He also boasted that he had a gun in his possession which he offered to show to Yossa and his mates once they were back at school. He didn't specify the type of gun. Perhaps, Wesley thought sadly, it was all a fantasy to attract Yossa's friendship. A lonely boy desperate to be accepted by those who would bully and tease him if the mood took them.

Wesley's heart went out to Lewis Hoxworthy; the odd one out. As the only black boy in his form at school, Wesley had sometimes felt isolated. But then he had always possessed a more sociable disposition than he imagined Lewis to have, and his natural amiability had ensured a steady supply of friends to render any racists and bullies powerless. And whereas at Wesley's academic private school a keen interest in history was considered quite acceptable, at Caraton Comprehensive, Lewis's alma mater, it probably marked an odd, sensitive boy out as different . . . as a potential victim.

The overwhelming feeling of pity for the missing fifteen-year-old worried Wesley slightly. He was getting too involved, losing his professional detachment. But perhaps it just meant he was human, he told himself by way of comfort.

Wesley knew the basics of computers, but if Lewis had deleted anything he wasn't confident that he could retrieve it. But there was someone in forensics, a young man called Tom who looked no more than sixteen, who was reputed to know all there was to know about the things. Wesley could consult him if all else failed.

While Gerry Heffernan took Steve Carstairs with him to the interview room to have another go at Paul Heygarth, Wesley and Rachel drove out to Hoxworthy's Farm.

Wesley felt a little uneasy on the journey. Heffernan, normally affable and easy going, seemed to be stepping up his efforts to prove Heygarth's guilt, and Wesley was beginning to wonder whether his boss knew something about Heygarth that he wasn't sharing with his colleagues.

He'd looked Heygarth up on the police computer and found that only a trio of speeding offences blotted an otherwise pristine record. Perhaps Heygarth had let the boss down badly on a house sale. But then Wesley knew that he had lived in his house on Baynard's Quay since he had married about twenty-five years ago. A long time to bear a grudge against an estate agent, and it was very doubtful that Heygarth was in business all that time ago. Gerry Heffernan was not normally one to harbour resentment, so perhaps he genuinely believed that Heygarth was the murderer. Perhaps Wesley was reading too much into it.

Rachel was quiet during the journey, concentrating on driving.

'How are things at the farm?' he asked, breaking the silence. 'Still looking for a place of your own?'

'Perhaps. But the holiday season's coming up soon. The apartments need to be cleaned and I don't like to leave Mum with all the work at the moment. Maybe in September.'

Wesley smiled. She had talked about moving away from the family farm ever since he had known her. But there was always something to keep her at home – and no sign of any knights in shining armour riding down the track to Little Barton Farm to whisk her away. But then her last foray into romance had ended in disaster and she had been extra cautious ever since.

He watched as she brushed her shoulder-length fair hair away from her face. She was an attractive young woman, and if Wesley hadn't been a married man he might have allowed himself to be interested. But he knew that anything other than friendship would end in tears. He had seen it so many times among his police colleagues, and it always led to grief for all concerned. However, sometimes a little devil on his shoulder whispered that Rachel might be interested – but it was a little devil he knew he must ignore.

'Turn right and head towards the church,' he said.

Rachel signalled, and they were soon driving through the village of Derenham; steep and picture-postcard pretty. Many of its houses were thatched and painted in pastel colours, and the narrow main thoroughfares led down to the waterfront where yachts bobbed steadily on the high tide.

'It's a nice village. Very pretty,' he commented as the ancient stone church came into view.

'Famous for its plums ... and its house prices.' Rachel smiled. 'They reckon that more celebrities have second homes in Derenham than in any other village around here.'

'And Jonny Shellmer was planning to join them.'

Rachel didn't reply. The Red Bull loomed on their left – the quintessential country pub. It was open, and a blackboard displaying a mouth-watering menu was propped up outside the door to tempt in the hungry. Wesley made a mental note that he should try it one lunch-time.

A few doors down from the pub stood a large ivy-clad house. Wesley stared out of the car window as the front door opened and a man stepped out. He was tall with snow-white hair, probably in his fifties.

'See who that is?' Rachel whispered.

'It looks like Jeremy Sedley.'

'I read in one of my mum's magazines that he's got a place here.'

They drove on, Rachel taking her eyes off the road to look at the strolling celebrity. It wasn't every day they saw an actor whose face was well known from television dramas and films. Rachel made a mental note to tell her mother about it: Stella Tracey was impressed by that sort of thing.

Just past the church a police patrol car and a new-looking Japanese four-wheel-drive were parked at the entrance to a field. Wesley told Rachel to pull up behind them.

'Shouldn't we be seeing the Hoxworthys?' Rachel asked, mildly annoyed. She'd spotted Neil Watson in the field and thought it her duty to stop Wesley being sidetracked.

'Neil said they've found a body. A skeleton. He's called

the coroner and I think that's Laura Kruger's car parked in front of us.'

'The new pathologist?'

Wesley didn't answer. He was already out of the car and climbing the gate. Rachel took one look at the gate and decided to wait in the car. That way she'd preserve her dignity.

When Wesley reached the middle of the field he found Neil and Laura squatting in a deep trench, watched by a motley crowd of students and local volunteers. Neil greeted him with a grin. Some of the locals stared.

'Come down and have a look at this, Wes.'

Wesley scrambled down into the trench, thankful that the rain had held off for a couple of days and the ground wasn't a mudbath.

Laura looked at him and smiled. 'Nice to see you again, Wesley. Found who killed Jonny Shellmer yet?'

'We're still working on it,' he answered. 'I take it the police needn't be involved with this one.'

He looked down at the bones. Apart from the obvious absence of a head, the skeleton seemed to be complete. And, as far as Wesley could see, it seemed to be lying face down.

'We'll have to be careful lifting this one,' said Neil. 'Laura here reckons it met a violent death. The head's missing ...'

'The skull was found over near the gate, I believe,' said Laura. 'I've still got it down at the mortuary. From the look of the neck vertebrae somebody took the head clean off – with a sharp sword at a guess.' She bent down and gently picked up the skeleton's left forearm, which had just been released from the earth by Neil's trowel. 'And I think he tried to protect himself from the attack. Look at these cuts on the arm bones – classic defensive wounds.'

'So he was killed in some sort of fight?' Wesley felt mildly disappointed that there didn't seem to be much of a mystery surrounding this particular skeleton. He – or she –

was the unfortunate victim of violence.

'Yes,' said Neil hesitantly. Wesley sensed there was a 'but'. 'But if that was the case why was he buried just here outside the walls of the building? Someone went to the trouble of bringing the body outside and burying it. And burying the head some way away. But why there? Everything points to a medieval date, but in those days it would have been considered terrible not to be buried in the churchyard ... in consecrated ground. Criminals and outcasts from society might be buried at crossroads or boundaries but this sort of casual burial strikes me as very strange.'

'Medieval skeletons are found buried on or near battle-fields – I read in the paper that some were found at Towton in Yorkshire, thrown into a pit after the battle during the Wars of the Roses. Perhaps there was some kind of skirmish here and the losers were chucked into shallow graves. Maybe more bodies will turn up.'

Neil frowned and shook his head. 'There's no record of anything like that round here and there's no sign of any other bones. I think the body's been buried secretly ... like a murder victim.'

'Bit of a mystery, eh?' said Laura. 'I'll get these bones down the mortuary when you've lifted them and have a better look.'

But Neil's mind was still on the past. 'I'm trying to find out about the people who lived here. This field belonged to a family called Merrivale. They owned a lot of land in the village and made gifts to the church, according to some documents I've found. I'm going to Exeter on Monday to look for any relevant wills and parish records.' His eyes lit up with the excitement of the chase. 'I've been told that some of their fifteenth-century letters were collected and published by a local vicar about a hundred years ago so I'm trying to track them down. I asked Pam yesterday if she could find out from her friend Anne whether there are any copies of the Merrivale letters about in the library system.'

Wesley smiled. 'Yes. I heard. She rang Anne last night and she says she'll see what she can do. She also said that the Merrivale letters have been popular recently – I don't know what she meant by that. And Pam says that you should ask Anne yourself if you want anything finding in future.' Giving Neil a little push in the right direction wouldn't do any harm.

'Is Pam okay, Wes?' said Neil unexpectedly. 'She didn't look too good when I saw her.'

Wesley was surprised. It wasn't often that Neil noticed anything that hadn't been buried in the ground for centuries. 'She's just a bit tired. I think work's getting her down.'

He climbed out of the trench carefully. Neil climbed out after him and led him over to a plastic sheet laid on the ground on which the afternoon's finds were displayed. Pottery fragments galore, sections of fine masonry; roof tiles; coins; an almost complete medieval bowl; and fragments of window glass. Glass windows meant wealth in the Middle Ages, the equivalent of a private indoor swimming pool today. The Merrivales hadn't been short of a groat or two.

A woman was standing at a trestle table near by, washing the finds. She wore rubber gloves on hands that were immersed in a plastic washing-up bowl full of dirty water. He had seen her somewhere before and quite recently. He closed his eyes for a few seconds, trying to remember.

Then it came to him. Maggie Flowers, the woman who had accepted the cheque for the village hall fund from Jonny Shellmer. He had been intending to pay her a visit at some point to see what she knew about the dead man.

'Mrs Flowers, isn't it? I saw your picture in the *Tradmouth Echo*. You were receiving a cheque from Jonny Shellmer.'

The woman flushed and began to dry her hands on a greying white towel. She was around fifty, Wesley estimated. Still slim, her grey-blond hair was cut in a page-boy style which gave her a youthful appearance.

'Yes. I'm on the village hall committee. Treasurer, actually.' The woman gave a brisk half-smile which disappeared rapidly.

'You'll know that Mr Shellmer was shot. Murdered.'

'Yes, of course. Terrible.'

Maggie Flowers arranged her features into an expression of polite sympathy, but Wesley sensed that she was a little wary. Then he realised that she had no idea he was a policeman and probably thought he was a reporter. But when he introduced himself her expression didn't change. Some of the middle classes, he thought, probably didn't have a glowing opinion of policemen either.

'I've been meaning to visit you to ask what you knew about the dead man.'

She smiled. Wesley sensed she was relieved. 'Then I'm afraid you'd have had a wasted journey. I hardly said two words to him. He just gave me the cheque and posed for the photograph. There was some small talk, of course, but I'm afraid that's all I can tell you.'

'Have you helped out at a dig before?' Wesley asked, making polite conversation.

'No. But I felt obliged to take some interest in this one. We used to own this field, my husband and I, and we sold it because it was the most suitable site for the new village hall. We live in that house next door, Derenham House.'

'Very nice place,' said Wesley appreciatively. 'My wife and I live in a modern house in Tradmouth and we'd like something with a bit more character eventually.'

'My husband's a surveyor for an estate agent's in Tradmouth so he saw it as soon as it came on the market. As I was saying to Neil Watson, it's wonderful to think we've got a bit of the old manor house buried in our garden.'

Wesley smiled. 'Neil and I were at university together. I studied archaeology, believe it or not.'

Maggie Flowers' expression grew a little warmer.

'Really? How on earth did you end up in the police force?'

'My grandfather was a chief superintendent in Trinidad, and when I stayed with him he used to tell me about his more interesting cases instead of a bedtime story. And I'd always been a great fan of Sherlock Holmes in my formative years.'

Maggie smiled. Then her expression suddenly became serious. 'Are you here about the bones they've just found?'

'Officially, yes. But if they're more than seventy years old – which I'm sure they are – they're not a police matter at all.' He hesitated for a moment, then decided that the question was worth asking. 'What did you think of Jonny Shellmer?'

She looked surprised by the question. 'I don't know what you mean,' she muttered quickly.

'What was your impression of him?'

'Well, he didn't say much but he seemed pleasant enough. I thanked him for his support on behalf of the village hall committee and we chatted for a few minutes about the village. He said he expected to move here as soon as he'd found a suitable property. He mentioned he was interested in the Old Vicarage. I was trying to make conversation and I told him about the famous people who already lived in the village. We've got Jeremy Sedley, the actor – he takes a lot of interest in the village; in fact he's doing a lot for the church history evening I'm organising. And there's Michael Burrows, the weatherman ... and Jack Cromer, the man who does that interview programme on TV. I can't really remember anything else. We just passed the time of day, I suppose.'

'One of our detective constables reckons Shellmer used to be one of the bad boys of rock; taking drugs, smashing up hotel rooms, that sort of thing.'

Maggie Flowers shook her head. 'Well, if he was, he showed no sign of it when I met him. He seemed quite ...' She searched for a suitable word. 'Quite ordinary, I suppose.'

'He must have mellowed with age,' Wesley observed with a smile.

He glanced over to where Neil and Laura Kruger were bending over the bones, newly lifted from the earth. He looked at his watch: he still had to visit the Hoxworthys. Then on to Neston to find out whether Angela Simms had any connection with Jonny Shellmer.

There was nothing more to be learned here for the moment. He'd leave Neil to it.

Fifteen minutes later Wesley was standing in the doorway of Lewis Hoxworthy's bedroom. Rachel Tracey stood by his side in silence. Jill Hoxworthy hovered behind them nervously, as though she didn't know quite what to do.

'I know it's a terrible mess,' she began apologetically. 'I've been meaning to tidy up but . . .'

Rachel turned to her. 'Don't worry, Jill. We've seen worse. Have you had a good look round to see if anything's missing? If he's taken things it might mean all this was planned.'

Jill shook her head. 'I'm going to have a go at it after supper. I know I should have done it already but I . . .' She sniffed and pulled a crumpled handkerchief from her sleeve. 'I don't seem to have had the time. I'm sorry.'

'That's okay. I understand.' Rachel put a comforting hand on the woman's shoulder. She was a good person to have around at times like these. Never intrusive, never insensitive, Rachel always knew the right thing to say.

Wesley turned to Jill and spoke gently. 'As Sergeant Tracey said, we've had a word with this Yossa and he says that Lewis sent him some e-mails.'

'Oh, I don't know anything about that. I'm not used to computers . . . not like Lewis,' she added quietly.

'What about your husband?'

Jill Hoxworthy shook her head again. 'No. He's no good on them neither. I said we should learn, go on a course, but what with the farm, we never seem to have the time.'

'Where's your husband now?' asked Rachel.

'He's gone down to the cow shed; one of the Jerseys has a touch of mastitis and he's meeting the vet down there. Terry's not been up here at the house much,' she said without resentment. 'It's his way of dealing with it.'

Jill Hoxworthy was a practical, independent woman; strong, some women's magazines would have called her. She would rather have her husband keeping busy to take his mind off his worry than hanging around in a futile attempt to comfort her.

'Would you mind if we had a look at Lewis's computer?'

'Help yourself.'

Rachel, who knew which end of a computer was which but who would never have claimed to be an expert, went downstairs with Jill, leaving Wesley to pick his way over the debris on Lewis's bedroom floor towards the cluttered computer desk. No wonder Jill hadn't had the heart to search through this lot, he thought. Excavating the stratified clothes, papers and rubbish was more a job for an archaeologist than a mother.

Before sitting himself down at the desk, he walked over to the window and looked out on the lush green landscape. He could see a solitary patrol car at the Old Vicarage, and he noticed a tiny distant figure entering the lodge, Gloria Treadly's son Alec perhaps. In a field he could just make out a Land Rover parked by what looked like a cow shed. Probably the vet.

But he didn't have time to waste gazing at the South Devon countryside, pleasant though it was. He sat down at Lewis's computer – the latest model with all mod cons as far as he could see – and switched it on.

But his efforts were fruitless. After ten minutes of fiddling around he came to the conclusion that Lewis Hoxworthy had deleted all his e-mails.

There had been something on that computer that Lewis hadn't wanted anyone to see and it would take more expert knowledge than Wesley's to retrieve it. He switched the machine off. There was nothing more he could do at Hoxworthy's Farm for the moment.

At 3.50 the call came through. A breathless female voice told the police to get over to Cawston Street in Neston as soon as possible. Something terrible had happened and an ambulance was needed.

The patrol car arrived to find a young woman dressed entirely in dusty black – with ears and nose pierced by an interesting variety of silver rings – waiting outside the small shop at 7 Cawston Street which bore the name Angela's Angels proudly above the door; she was pacing up and down, near to tears.

WPC Trish Walton climbed out of the car first and rushed over to her. PC Carl McInnery, all red hair and freckles, emerged from the driving seat and scratched his head. He was still coming to terms with the town of Neston.

'Did you call us?' asked Trish.

The young woman nodded, pressing a crumpled tissue to her cheek.

'I found her. She's inside,' said the girl, fighting back tears. 'There was no one in the shop when I went in but I heard a door slam in the back so after a bit I went to have a look. I saw the till was open. I think I disturbed a robber and he escaped through the back. Then I saw her lying on the floor.' The young woman was well spoken, dead posh, Chief Inspector Heffernan would have said.

'Show me.'

Trish allowed the young woman to lead the way. Carl trailed behind them, staring at his surroundings, at the rows of angels watching him from the shelves and posters in the dimly lit shop.

They were led through to the back of the building, to a small, shabby room which served as a kitchen.

'She's there,' the woman in black muttered, pointing downward.

A slightly built woman lay on her side on the brown linoleum floor, her eyes closed as though in sleep. Her long dark hair, streaked with grey, was matted with drying blood, and more blood had oozed onto the floor, creating a glistening red halo around her head.

'What's happened?' Carl asked.

'Head injury. I reckon somebody's had a go at the till and hit her,' said Trish urgently. 'Go and check if the ambulance is on its way, will you, Carl. She's still breathing – just. And get CID and the SOCOs over.' She nodded towards the young woman. 'And take this lady outside, will you.'

The woman who had made the call was standing next to a small gas stove, sobbing into a disintegrating tissue. Carl led her outside gently, holding her elbow. She would only get in the way.

Careful not to disturb the scene, Trish put the woman into the recovery position and felt the pulse in her neck, watching her anxiously, willing her to hold on to life. Lying on the floor near by she noticed a small but heavy-looking stone statue of an angel with smiling face and outstretched wings. She saw that the base was encrusted with dried brown blood, and she knew that she had found the weapon. The angel of death.

'Hold on,' she whispered to the unconscious woman. 'Just hold on. Please.' She watched the woman's grey-tinged face, listening for every shallow breath. 'Come on,' she whispered again. 'Just keep breathing.'

The three minutes it took for the ambulance to arrive seemed like three hours, and after the paramedics had worked with quiet efficiency the woman was rushed off, all sirens blazing, towards the hospital.

Trish felt washed out, exhausted by willing every breath from the unresponsive victim. She jumped when Carl McInnery touched her shoulder gently.

'I've had a word with the people in the shop next door – the one that sells all those crystal things – and they say they didn't see anything suspicious. And I've taken a statement from the woman who found her but she hasn't been able to tell us any more. She didn't know the victim – she said she just came in to buy a present for a friend. She's a bit shaken but I've asked her to wait in case CID want a word.'

'Yes, radio CID again and tell them to get a move on.' Trish stared down at the bloodstain on the floor. 'Tell them someone's tried to kill Angela Simms.'

Chapter Seven

Right worshipful husband,
I hear such tales in Tradmouth regarding the Queen's
fortunes. Some say she has won a great victory and King
Henry is restored to his rightful throne. Others that she
and her son are dead in some great battle. But chiefly I
am anxious regarding yourself and Edmund. Send word,
I beg you, that you are safe.

I pray most earnestly for your return for John has
fallen in with wicked men and I know not what to do. I
worry also for Elizabeth as she spends much time in his
company against my wishes. I seek a husband for her yet
there is no man here suitable. I have ordered Masses to
be said at All Saints church for your safe and speedy
return to Derenham.

Master Fletcher is travelling to Gloucester with cloth
and will endeavour to enquire for you and deliver this
into your hand.
Your most loving and anxious wife, Marjory

Written at Derenham this sixth day of May 1471

Gloria Treadly played with the key, passing it from hand to
hand, twisting it in her fingers, wondering what to do with
it. She comforted herself with the thought that it was
unlikely the police would search the cottage. From past

experience she knew that they had to have a good reason to obtain a search warrant. And they had no reason to search; no reason at all.

She heard one of the bare, polished floorboards creak behind her and she swung round. 'Alec, why do you have to creep around like that? You nearly gave me a heart attack.'

'Sorry, Ma. I was trying not to disturb you.'

She looked her son in the eye. 'You've been disturbing me ever since you were a nipper.' Her voice softened. 'Here, why don't you make yourself useful. Go up there and see that you've not left anything lying about. Make sure that there's no sign that you've been there. Understand?'

'Old Bill might still be up there.'

'If it's not safe you'll just have to come back here and we'll hope for the best, eh?' She stared at her son. Sometimes she didn't know why she bothered. But she knew in her heart of hearts she had no option. She would defend him to the last like a mother tigress defends her cubs. He was her Alec. He was all she had. Whatever he was. Whatever he might have done.

He took the key from her and put it in the pocket of his jeans. Then he left the room without a word and Gloria heard the front door of the cottage closing with a loud bang.

Rachel Tracey looked at the shop fascia of Angela's Angels, noting the ethereal beings flitting between bold Gothic letters. It reminded her of heavy-rock posters she had seen from times gone by.

She pushed the shop door open and bells tinkled – the early-warning system that must have alerted the robber who had made his escape when a customer crossed the threshold. She stood in the shop and looked around. Angels everywhere. Big angels, small angels, pictures, statues, books, key-rings, posters, mobiles. The place was dimly lit. It gave her the creeps.

She turned to Trish. 'I'll know where to come if I run out

of angels,' she said, trying to lighten the mood.

'My mum knows this woman who's into angels; she told me once that we've all got a guardian angel out there somewhere,' said Trish, looking around. 'I wonder if this Angela woman makes a living out of all this.'

Rachel, whose experience of angels had been limited to playing Gabriel once in a school nativity play, grunted with sceptical disapproval. 'The SOCOs have finished. Let's take a look around.'

She led the way into the back to a small kitchen which had a cheap utilitarian look; white melamine cupboards, a small Formica table and two bentwood chairs placed beneath a flaking sash window. A pile of clean white dishes was stacked on the stainless-steel draining board. The back door stood shut but unlocked. Whoever had robbed and attacked Angela Simms had left that way.

There was nothing to see now but a telltale bloodstain spreading across the grey lino floor. The angel of death had already flown off to the forensic lab in a plastic bag.

They walked through to the sitting room, a small, claustrophobic room with shabby rag rugs on the floorboards, faded Indian throws over the sofa and chairs, bright oriental hangings on the walls, and the debris of burned-out candles in the dusty iron fireplace. The aroma of incense hung in the air, and caterpillars of ash from burned-out joss-sticks crawled across a low pine coffee table.

'Bit of a time warp,' said Trish.

Rachel didn't answer. She crossed the room and opened a stripped-wood door. 'That leads upstairs,' Trish told her helpfully. 'I had a quick look around earlier, just to make sure there was nobody here.'

Rachel stood aside and let Trish lead the way. There was something about this part of the job, searching through the belongings of strangers, which fascinated yet repelled her. It was an irresistible imposition.

They made a perfunctory search of the two bedrooms; the first was piled with cardboard boxes – a storeroom for the shop's stock – and Angela's own was filled with heavy oak furniture, the kind unwillingly inherited from great-aunts. Rachel took the iron single bed as evidence that no lover had figured in Angela Simms's life.

She made a half-hearted search of the bed, finding nothing under the mattress and only a thin cotton nightdress and a key beneath the pillow. She found herself wondering about the injured woman's family and friends: they had found no address book and the only telephone was in the shop itself. A spartan existence – and a lonely one.

Trish searched the great dark wardrobe but found nothing but an assortment of clothes, mostly black and a few years old.

It was useless, Rachel thought. Angela was just another sad and lonely woman robbed while alone in her shop. Another crime statistic. She walked out onto the landing, her footsteps echoing on the bare floorboards. Then she stopped suddenly and Trish almost cannoned into her.

'That's it. Two bedrooms. Small bathroom. Did you find anything in the bedroom drawers?' Rachel asked.

'Nothing of any interest. But one of them was locked – the top drawer in the big chest.'

Rachel was holding the key she had found under Angela's pillow. She returned to Angela's bedroom and walked straight to a bulky dark oak chest of drawers, an ugly, overbearing piece that would be rejected by any discerning antique dealer. She turned the key and the top drawer opened smoothly.

The contents were illuminated by the weak shaft of light filtering in through the tiny window.

'I reckon we've found Jonny Shellmer's stalker,' said Rachel quietly.

Shellmer's face stared up at her from four framed photographs lying neatly to the left of the drawer. A pile of long-playing records, eight in all, was stacked up on the right. Rachel pulled the photographs out and examined them. Each one bore a handwritten message in the corner:

'to Angel with love from Jonny'.

'Looks like she was a fan,' said Rachel.

'More than a fan. She's been hanging around outside his house.'

'Bit old for that sort of thing, wasn't she?'

Trish shrugged.

Rachel reached into the drawer and pulled out a scrapbook. She carried it over to the bed and turned the pages carefully. It contained cuttings from newspapers and magazines, all about Jonny Shellmer's career, Rock Boat's tours, Jonny's divorce, his solo efforts. Loose at the back of the scrapbook was a photograph. She handed it to Trish. 'What do you make of this?'

Trish examined the photograph. 'It's just a group of kids. It's not very clear but you can tell it was taken round here – it looks like the waterfront at Derenham.'

She handed it back to Rachel, who peered at the image. 'The end's been cut off – look, you can just see someone's elbow. She's taken the scissors and cut someone out. Weird.'

Rachel placed the photograph back between the pages of the scrapbook. Then she put everything back in the drawer and locked it before putting the key under the pillow. 'Let's get out of here. This place really gives me the creeps.'

Trish followed Rachel downstairs and they walked out through the shop, past the ranks of angels, who watched them with knowing eyes.

PC Paul Johnson was just thinking that hanging around in the damp air outside Derenham's Old Vicarage was hardly the perfect way to spend a Saturday evening when he heard a noise. He froze and pressed himself against the stone wall of the house as a shape emerged from the late-afternoon gloom.

He stepped out of the shadows, his eyes on the man who was making purposefully for the front door, key at the ready.

'Can I help you, sir?' he said firmly, looking Alec Treadly in the eye.

But Treadly stopped in his tracks, balancing on tiptoe, prepared for flight. Johnson saw him shove the key into his pocket surreptitiously.

Treadly spoke quickly. 'It's the cat. It's been missing since last night. I wondered if it was ...'

'What type of cat is it, sir?' asked Johnson, humouring him. He didn't believe a word of it.

'Er ... a ginger one.'

'Name?'

'Er ... Ginger.'

'No. Your name, sir.' Johnson was beginning to enjoy this.

'Alec Treadly. I live at the lodge just down there. Ginger sometimes comes up here,' he added, trying to convince.

'Well, if I see Ginger I'll let you know.'

Alec Treadly sensed a finality in Johnson's last statement. There was nothing for it. He turned and walked back down the drive. He had no chance of getting into the Old Vicarage while the police were still around.

As soon as he was out of sight, Paul Johnson called the station on his radio.

At half past six Wesley returned to Tradmouth police station. He met Gerry Heffernan in the foyer and they walked together up the stairs to the CID office. After the first flight, Heffernan was lagging behind.

'Slow down, Wes, some of us aren't as young as we were.' The chief inspector sounded a little breathless.

Wesley slackened his pace, looking at his watch. Pam was planning takeaway pizzas that evening as she couldn't face cooking and she knew from bitter experience that when Wesley was on a murder case she couldn't rely on him to turn up on time, let alone help with matters domestic.

'Are you letting Heygarth go yet?' Wesley asked as they entered the office.

Heffernan glanced at him sulkily. 'Not yet.'

'But do you think keeping him here is going to do any good? He moved the body but he's not admitted to anything else.'

'It's a start. He'll talk eventually.'

Heffernan pressed his lips together stubbornly as he led the way into his office and slumped down in his executive leather swivel chair, which tilted back alarmingly under the weight. Wesley sat down in the grey upholstered chair on the other side of the cluttered desk.

'So what have we got?' said Wesley, thinking it was about time he arranged all their findings neatly in his brain. 'Jonny Shellmer's shot some time late on Wednesday afternoon. Then on Thursday morning Paul Heygarth arrives and moves the body with the help of Nicola Tarnley. There's no sign of a gun at the scene and Heygarth and Tarnley claim they never saw one. There's also evidence that the Old Vicarage was broken into by person or persons unknown, possibly the murderer ... or the victim ... or even somebody else altogether.' He paused, gathering his thoughts.

'And?' Heffernan prompted, looking at his companion intently.

'Then Lewis Hoxworthy, who may or may not have seen something suspicious from his bedroom window, disappears after boasting to his mates that he's found something that'll make him rich and that he's got a gun. I went to Hoxworthy's Farm and tried to look at the e-mails on his computer. It looks as if he's wiped them, but someone who knows what they're doing can retrieve them.'

Heffernan nodded. Another job to arrange. 'Are we any nearer tracing Shellmer's ex-wife?'

'Merseyside are still trying, but I don't suppose it's their main priority. Are we sending someone to have a word with that ex-member of Rock Boat who lives up in Gloucestershire? It might be worth checking up on his whereabouts.'

Heffernan grunted in agreement. 'What else?'

'We need to find Shellmer's car. But it could be miles away by now. I think it's time we notified other forces, don't you agree? And there's been a message from Rachel and Trish. They've been having a look around Angela Simms's flat and they say they've found pictures of Jonny Shellmer locked in a drawer. It looks as if we might have our crazed fan after all.'

'Do you think she could have shot him?'

'Not necessarily. But it's possible that she was following Shellmer and she witnessed the shooting. What do you think?'

But before the chief inspector could answer Steve Carstairs gave a perfunctory knock on the office door and walked in. 'A call's come through from Johnson at Derenham, sir. Thought you might be interested.' He placed a piece of paper on Heffernan's desk and made a rapid retreat without glancing in Wesley's direction.

Heffernan waited until Steve was out of earshot before he spoke. 'Alec Treadly has been caught up near the Old Vicarage. He claimed he was looking for his cat. Did you notice a cat when we were up at the lodge?'

Wesley smiled. 'No, but your average cat doesn't usually jump all over visitors when they arrive. It could have been out murdering a few mice or whatever it is cats do in their spare time.'

'Never mind the moggie, listen to this. Paul saw Treadly making for the front door with a key. When he spotted him he put it away quick.'

'The Treadlys told us they didn't have a key to the Old Vicarage.'

'Right. What do we know about them? Nothing. Look them up on our infernal machine, Wes. You're better with computers than I am. They always break down when they see me coming.'

Wesley glanced at his watch. It was coming up to seven. Pam wouldn't be pleased. 'Steve's sitting out there contemplating his overtime payments,' he said lightly. 'I'll ask him to do it, eh?'

Heffernan sat back and chuckled wickedly. 'There's nothing like a bit of delegation.'

Wesley's request was greeted by sullen silence. But ten minutes later Steve burst into Gerry Heffernan's office bearing a printed sheet aloft.

'Alec Treadly. Five years ago he was sent down for three years for offences against young boys. He's a bloody pervert, sir. Shall we bring him in?' His grin of triumph was even projected in Wesley's direction, all prejudices forgotten for the moment. Everybody hates a child abuser.

Heffernan and Wesley exchanged looks. Each thinking of Lewis Hoxworthy.

It was Wesley who spoke first. 'Get us details of his offences, will you, Steve.'

He watched Steve rush from the office, a feeling of sick dread welling up in his stomach.

Wesley arrived home at eight. Pam greeted him in the hall, the baby grinning happily in her arms, and announced that she was about to bath him. It was Wesley's job to phone up and order the pizzas.

Wesley hardly liked to mention that the news he had learned about Alec Treadly had taken away his appetite. 'Tell you what, I'll give Michael his bath and you phone the takeaway.'

Pam agreed. She had had her son all day, it was about time he and his father did a bit of male bonding. 'Your mum rang at lunch-time,' she said wearily. 'Don't forget we're meeting her in Morbay tomorrow for lunch.'

She saw Wesley hesitate on the stairs. 'Oh, Wesley, don't tell me you've forgotten.'

'No, I haven't forgotten,' he lied convincingly. 'It's just that we've got a murder, the possible abduction of a teenage boy and the attempted murder of a shopkeeper in Neston on our hands.'

'You can't let your mother down. We haven't seen your parents for months. I'm busy too but I make time for my family. In fact my mother said she was coming round tonight.'

'That's all we need,' Wesley muttered under his breath. Then he suddenly felt guilty. Pam looked exhausted, so perhaps her mother could be persuaded to make herself useful – for a change.

'I'll have to work tomorrow but I'll be there at lunch-time ... promise.' He assumed what he considered to be a sincere expression and hurried upstairs to get out of the firing line and prepare Michael's bath.

As he played with his baby son, a handsome child with a shock of straight black hair and golden-brown skin, making a yellow plastic whale squirt water from its mouth – some-thing which young Michael considered hilarious – Wesley shuddered as Lewis Hoxworthy leapt unbidden into his thoughts. Jill and Terry Hoxworthy had once bathed him and played with him like this. He was someone's beloved son. He thought of Alec Treadly living so near to the farm. He had four convictions for indecency against boys aged between ten and fifteen in the area of Kent where he had spent much of his life.

Wesley lifted Michael from the bath, wrapped him in a large fluffy towel, and held him close, cuddled against his chest, protected.

Just as Wesley and Pam were taking the last bites from the pizzas they had ordered, Pam's mother, Della Stannard, arrived bearing gifts. From her brightly coloured carrier bag, she pulled a bottle of wine, a carrot cake and a selection of CDs.

'You're looking tired, Pamela. Aren't you well?' Tact had never been Della's strongest virtue. She sat herself down on the settee and pulled down her short red skirt. She didn't wait for Pam to answer. 'Get some glasses, will you, Wesley. I've come to help you with your enquiries.'

'Turning yourself in, are you, Della?' he said with a straight face.

'Don't be cheeky. I've brought you these CDs – three Rock Boat albums and a couple of Jonny Shellmer's solo efforts. He wrote all the songs himself. I thought you might like to hear them.'

Wesley couldn't for the life of him think how Shellmer's albums could help to catch his killer but he thanked Della anyway. Perhaps they would provide some clue about Shellmer's nature – but he wasn't holding his breath.

Wesley and Pam tried their best to hide their relief when Della stood up and announced she was leaving at 9.30 to go for a drink with some of her students. She taught sociology at a local college and regarded drinking with the students as a perk of the job.

'I hope you're not drinking and driving,' Wesley said, semi-seriously.

'I've only had one glass of wine, Wesley. It's like living in a bloody police state.' She fished her car keys out of her bag. 'Enjoy Jonny Shellmer's songs. There's a lovely one called "Angel" on Rock Boat's first album.'

Wesley saw his mother-in-law out. Angel, he thought as he watched her drive away. The card in Jonny's drawer had been from an 'Angel'.

He returned to Pam in the living room and switched the CD player on.

As Wesley and Pam were settling down to spend what remained of their evening with a bottle of red wine, a patrol car prowling the Saturday night streets of the sprawling seaside resort of Morbay spotted a yellow sports car driving at considerable speed.

After a brief chase along the promenade the sports car crashed into a bollard, leaving its two occupants shaken but not seriously hurt. Young and unlicensed to drive they might have been, but at least they had had the foresight to wear their seat belts.

The patrol car driver confirmed that no ambulance was required and that the driver of the yellow car – who gave his name as Mickey Mouse – was not, in fact, the owner of the vehicle but had nicked it for a bit of excitement. He was about to take the young driver and his accomplice back to the station when he noticed the registration number of the stolen vehicle, which now sported a deep dent in its front bumper. It seemed familiar. He conferred with his partner, who consulted his notebook.

As the two lads, who looked not a day over sixteen, waited sulkily in the back of the patrol car, the driver spoke into his radio. 'That stolen vehicle involved in an RTA, it's a yellow Porsche and the registration number matches the one CID are looking for in connection with that murder in Derenham. Get a recovery vehicle here right away, will you, and get it taken back to the station so Forensics can give it a going over.'

Yossa Lang sat silently in the back of the patrol car with his mate, awaiting the inevitable.

Sunday morning dawned dull with fine drizzle blowing off the hills in gossamer sheets. Wesley Peterson hadn't slept well, and he arrived at the police station wet and tired. And Pam hadn't been in top form when Michael had woken them up. She had felt queasy – some sort of stomach bug, she thought.

Wesley found Gerry Heffernan in the CID office talking to Rachel, who looked surprisingly fresh and alert for first thing on a damp Sunday morning.

'Anything new?' Wesley asked.

It was Rachel who answered. 'Yossa Lang was picked up last night. Joy-riding. Driving Jonny Shellmer's missing sports car. It's at Morbay nick now and Forensics are giving it a good going over.'

Wesley raised his eyebrows. This was an unexpected development. 'Where did Yossa say he'd nicked it from?'

'A multistorey carpark in Morbay,' said Heffernan. 'The

bad news is that their security cameras weren't working when it was parked there. The wonders of modern technology, eh?'

'What did Yossa have to say for himself?'

'He said he'd found the car unlocked with the keys in and couldn't resist the temptation of a ride in a Porsche. He got quite offended at the suggestion that he might have had anything to do with Shellmer's shooting.'

'Do you believe him?'

'I'll know better when I've spoken to him but I suppose I do.'

'Could Yossa have broken into the Old Vicarage? Perhaps he was carrying a shooter to make himself feel big. What if Shellmer was looking around the place alone and he caught him breaking in. Then Yossa panicked and shot him.'

Wesley looked pleased with himself. It was a perfectly feasible theory.

Rachel nodded with approval. 'I think we should have Yossa brought over here so we can question him.'

Heffernan shrugged. 'Yeah. But I reckon we've already got the man who killed Jonny Shellmer. Heygarth's a vicious bugger. Nicola Tarnley told me he hit her, bashed her about and ...'

Wesley interrupted, surprised that his boss didn't seem to be keeping an open mind about this particular case. 'Is Paul Heygarth still in custody?'

'Charged and released on bail.' Wesley detected a hint of bitterness in his boss's voice. 'We'll need more evidence, Wes ... and we'll have to find that gun. Heygarth's got no alibi for the probable time of Shellmer's death, you know. He said he left Shellmer alone in the house just after five but he didn't arrive back in his office until six-thirty. I've checked.'

'What does he say he was doing?'

'He said he paid a call on an ex-ladyfriend who lives in Neston. But she was out. No witnesses.'

'So he could easily have shot Shellmer, driven his car to Morbay and dumped it in the multistorey carpark, then gone back for his own car at his leisure. Clever, hiding Shellmer's car in the multistorey, anonymous amongst all the other cars. A forest is always the best place to hide a tree.'

'There was another thing, sir,' said Rachel efficiently. 'Forensics have found an address book in the glove compartment of Shellmer's car. Someone's bringing it over.'

'Great. That's what we need. Merseyside haven't had much luck tracking down his ex-wife. But if she's married again, changed her name ... The murder's been in the news so you'd think she would have seen it and come forward ... or her son.'

But his train of thought was interrupted by a middle-aged uniformed constable from Morbay who had just arrived in the office, carrying a plastic evidence bag which contained a small book. He asked for Chief Inspector Heffernan and was directed towards the boss, who greeted the newcomer like an old friend.

'Pete, good to see you. How are you keeping?' Heffernan slapped the constable heartily on the back. 'What have you got for us, eh?'

'The address book found in the glove box of that yellow Porsche, Gerry. Belongs to that pop star who was shot at Derenham, so I've heard.'

'That's right. Let's hope it throws some light on the subject.'

There was an awkward pause, as though the constable were weighing up his next question. 'I hear you've pulled Paul Heygarth in for this murder. Is that right?'

Wesley, who by now was fingering the address book, impatient to read its contents, looked up. There was something in the constable's voice that told him this was no casual enquiry.

'Yeah.'

'Deserves all he bloody gets if you ask me.' The man touched Heffernan's arm, a gesture of support, before saying goodbye and wishing them luck with the case.

'Know him, do you?' Wesley asked casually once the constable had left.

'Yeah. We trained together, me and Pete. Go back a long way. And his wife used to work at the hospital with ... with Kathy.'

Something, a slight unsteadiness in Heffernan's voice, told Wesley that further questions would be unwelcome. He turned his attention to the book. 'Right, then, let's see who figured in Jonny Shellmer's life.'

As Wesley opened the small, leather-bound book, he saw that there was a distant look in his boss's eyes.

Jill Hoxworthy had begun to sort through the contents of Lewis's bedroom on Saturday night. But this Herculean task had progressed slowly. By ten o'clock she had managed to clear the floor, placing clothes in the linen basket, books and CDs on the desk and used tissues and other assorted rubbish in a bin-bag. She had even made the bed for the first time in weeks. But then, exhausted and miserable, she had abandoned the room for the night and joined her husband downstairs, where they had sat in a silent vigil, staring at moving images on a television screen which might just as well have been blank.

She hadn't slept. Neither had Terry. They lay awake listening. Listening for any sound that might herald Lewis's safe return. The next morning Jill – who had not cried since her son's disappearance – stood in Lewis's half-tidied bedroom and burst into tears.

She knew Terry was out working around the farm as usual and she was glad he wasn't there to witness the collapse of her stoical façade. She slumped down on the newly made bed and wept, only stopping when she heard Terry opening the back door. She didn't want him to find her like that. If she wasn't strong, they would both go under.

150

She blew her nose on her damp handkerchief and stood up, taking a deep breath. She would finish tidying Lewis's room; see whether anything was missing or whether there was anything that gave a clue to his whereabouts. The police officers had suggested it – Stella Tracey's daughter, Rachel, and that nice young dark inspector. They had been so kind. Everyone had been kind. But it didn't help to find her Lewis.

She began with his desk, and when she had finished it looked presentable; books neatly stacked and Lewis's beloved computer sitting in pride of place in the centre.

The wardrobe was next. She opened it and looked down. Clothes had fallen off hangers and lay in the bottom mixed with worn-out trainers and discarded school bags. Boxes of toys, untouched for years, lay stacked behind. They should have gone to a jumble sale, thought Jill, trying to be practical. Or been put in the loft for grandchildren. This last thought brought the tears back again. She saw the interior of the wardrobe mistily through the water welling up in her eyes. But there was work to be done. She told herself sternly to pull herself together.

She began to pull the clothes out, piling them onto the bed. Lewis had most likely grown out of half of them . . . or would have rejected them as too unfashionable. The bottom of the wardrobe was quickly dealt with and all good shoes that were outgrown were placed in bags to donate to a charity shop. Jill found the tidying therapeutic, and by the time she reached the wardrobe shelves she was feeling a little calmer.

She pulled twisted jumpers and heaped sweatshirts from the shelves, folding them tidily before replacing them. Then, right at the back of the third shelf down, her hand brushed against something that felt like a metal box. She reached into the dark recess and pulled it out, her heart beating a little faster.

She stared at the box for a few moments. It looked old, rusty and solid with flakes of black paint. She opened it carefully and saw that there was a layer of snowy-white tissue paper inside. Jill peeled it away.

There, lying in the bottom of the box, cold, hard and grey, was a small handgun. Jill dropped the box and screamed.

Chapter Eight

Right reverend and worshipful mother,
I write this with a heavy heart for my father was injured
in battle a sennight since. He lies with the good brothers
of Tewkesbury Abbey, who have him now in their care
and prayers, and the brother infirmarer of the Abbey
assures me of his swift recovery.

Our army hastened to the town of Tewkesbury, where
King Edward and his army came upon us on the fourth
day of May. My mind is filled still with the horrors of
the battlefield, and I dream nightly of the screams of
dying men and the cruelties I witnessed. Prince Edward,
son of our sovereign lord King Henry VI, was most
piteously slain, as was the Earl of Devon, the Duke of
Somerset and divers knights, squires and gentlemen. It
was a most grievous defeat for the noble house of
Lancaster.

If God spares my father we shall return to Derenham
when he is fit to travel on the rough and dangerous
roads. Convey my affectionate greetings to my sister
Elizabeth and tell her how I long to see her sweet face
once more. My father is most worried concerning my
stepbrother, John's, behaviour, and I pray, dear mother,
that he does not bring more trouble on our house at this
time.

My father speaks of making gifts to the church in

thanks for our deliverance from the perils of battle. But we will speak of this on our return to Derenham.

> *Written in haste at Tewkesbury this eleventh day of May 1471 by candlelight. By your loving son, Edmund*

At ten o'clock on Sunday morning Gerry Heffernan flicked through the pages of Jonny Shellmer's address book. There were a lot of entries, many in the London area, and to his surprise he saw Angela Simms's address and phone number written in bold black ink, which made the theory that she was an obsessed fan seem unlikely: if Jonny had her details in his private address book, the interest couldn't have been one sided.

Most of the addresses could be checked out by his team. But there was one he wanted to keep to himself. The name Liz, followed by an address in the Allerton district of Liverpool. Shellmer's ex-wife's name was Liz. And Allerton was his own territory, where he had been born and brought up. He knew the road – near Calderstones Park. Nice. Liz Shellmer – or whatever her surname was now – had done well for herself.

He smiled as he contemplated a quick trip up North. He might have time to drop in on his son, Sam, who was up at Liverpool University studying to become a vet. And he'd take Wesley up with him, show him the sights, take him for a trip on a Mersey ferry. It'd be a treat for him, a change of scene. And of course it was vitally important that they speak to Jonny Shellmer's ex-wife. That went without saying.

As Heffernan was formulating his plans, Wesley strolled into the office and sat down.

'I thought you'd like to know they're bringing Alec Treadly in for questioning.' Wesley looked solemn. Their discoveries about Treadly's past had opened a new dimension on the case, an evil dimension that the average police officer would rather never encounter. Wesley hoped that their assumptions were wrong.

'Check his movements over the past few days and all. If he's farted I want to know about it. Any news of Angela Simms?'

'Still unconscious. But I reckon she was lucky. If that woman hadn't gone into the shop when she did and disturbed the attacker, he might have been able to finish the job and we'd be looking at murder. I've arranged for an officer to stay at the hospital and let us know if she comes round or . . . We've not been able to track down any next of kin yet.'

'Better keep trying. There must be someone who cares about the poor woman. Do you think it was a robbery that went wrong?'

'It looks that way.' Wesley hesitated. 'Or perhaps that's what we were meant to think.'

'Who knows, Wes. Anything from Forensics yet?' Heffernan looked at his watch.

'They didn't find any prints on that stone angel, if that's what you mean.' It would have been too much to hope that the robber had been obliging enough to leave a clear set of prints.

Heffernan shifted in his seat. He'd have to be off to church soon – the choir couldn't function without him.

Wesley was about to leave the office when Heffernan called him back. 'We're off up North . . . probably Tuesday. Tell your Pam it's likely that we'll have to stay over. We're paying a call on a lady called Liz – Shellmer's ex-wife. Her address is in Shellmer's book.'

'Have you notified Merseyside?'

'Oh, aye. They're breaking the bad news, but I still want to talk to her. I want chapter and verse on Jonny Shellmer – who his friends were, what kind of man he was, whether he had any strange tastes or interests. Sherry Smyth's not known him that long and I get the feeling we're only getting the sanitised version. And I want a word with this Hal Lancaster character and all, but he's not back home yet. I spoke to his housekeeper again and she says he's gone off sailing. He's got a boat called the *Henry of Lancaster*.

How's that for modesty? Calling your boat after yourself.'

Wesley smiled. 'Sounds like something out of the Wars of the Roses to me. Henry of Lancaster – Henry VI, maybe ... a few chicken legs short of a banquet and married to Margaret of Anjou, the original domineering wife. Or Henry Tudor – Henry VII.'

Heffernan was starting to look bored. 'Like I've always said, Wes, you're a mine of useless information. Don't know where you get it all from.'

Wesley smiled. 'You should brush up on your history, Gerry. It's amazing what you can pick up.'

Before Heffernan could think of a witty reply, the door opened and Trish Walton hovered on the threshold of the office, a piece of paper clutched in her hand.

'There's been a call from Mrs Hoxworthy, sir.'

Wesley and Heffernan exchanged looks, each hoping that the call had been to say that Lewis had turned up safe and sound.

'She was tidying the missing boy's room and she's found something, sir. It's a gun. She says she found it in a box in the wardrobe.'

Having delivered her message, Trish made a swift exit, leaving the two men staring after her, open mouthed.

'I think we'd better get over there,' said Wesley after a few moments, picking up his jacket from the back of the chair. The choir would have to survive that morning without Gerry Heffernan's contribution.

To Neil Watson Sunday was just like any other day. And as archaeology was his passion as well as his livelihood, he was happy to work at it seven days a week. The novelty of the enterprise had lured a few of the volunteers to share in his labours. But others were off doing Sunday things; playing sport, visiting relatives or washing the car.

Neil squatted in one of the damp trenches uncovering what looked like the base of an oven in what had once been the manor house kitchen. When he heard the clinking of china, he looked up and saw Maggie Flowers holding a wooden tray filled with brightly coloured mugs.

'I'm sorry I couldn't help out today, Mr Watson,' she began apologetically. 'But we've got people coming over for Sunday dinner.'

'That's okay,' Neil replied, eyeing the steaming mugs.

'I thought you might be in need of some refreshment.'

Neil took the largest mug gratefully. 'Thanks. But you don't have to go to the trouble, you know. Most of us have brought our own.'

He saw disappointment on Maggie's face and guessed that she was the type of person who liked to have her finger in any available pie. He watched as she made for the other trench, where his colleagues were awaiting the arrival of the tea with undisguised enthusiasm.

As he rested his mug on a soil ledge at the side of the trench, he heard a female voice coming from somewhere above him.

'Hello, Neil.'

A dark-haired woman in her late twenties was standing at the edge of the trench. He stared at her for a few seconds before he spoke. 'Hello, Anne. Long time no see. What brings you here?'

It was almost a year since they'd last met at Wesley and Pam's house. Neil had thought her attractive then and, standing there, his eyes level with her shapely legs, he had no reason to revise his opinion. She was a friend of Pam's, a widow with two young children whose husband had died in a car crash: he remembered that much but little else.

'I'm meeting my sister at the Red Bull. They do good Sunday lunches. Pam rang me and mentioned you were looking for an edition of the Merrivale letters and I just came to tell you I've tracked a copy down. You're not the only person who's been after it. I had a phone call last week asking if we had a copy.' She toyed with a small book she was holding. It had been rebound recently in brown – a dull sparrow of a book.

157

'I've had a look at the letters – they seem quite interesting. There are only eleven of them so they shouldn't take you long to read.' She smiled shyly and handed him the book. 'What are you digging up here, then?' she asked, looking around.

'A house which might have belonged to the Merrivale family. That's why I've been trying to get hold of the letters.' He paused. 'Have you heard about that big painting that was found in a barn over on the other side of the village? The experts say it's a medieval Doom.'

Anne nodded. 'Pam mentioned something about it.'

Neil put his trowel down and brushed the soil off his hands in a futile attempt to look more presentable. 'They're moving it back to the church for this history evening they're organising in aid of the village hall fund – there are posters all around the place. Do you fancy coming?'

Anne blushed. 'When is it?'

Neil took a deep breath and wished the earth would swallow him up. It had never occurred to him to find out the date. He shrugged his shoulders. 'Don't know. Soon,' he added hopefully.

'Well, if you find out when it is, I might consider coming along.' She turned to go.

Neil watched her walk away and experienced an uneasy feeling that he hadn't made a very good impression.

Jill Hoxworthy opened the front door of the farmhouse. Wesley could see that her hands were shaking. She stood aside to let them in.

'It was in the back of the wardrobe in an old metal box,' she said as she started to climb the stairs ahead of them. 'I've put it back where I found it.'

She was trying to sound normal, practical. Trying to hide her gnawing anxiety. But it was too close to the surface to fool Wesley. One wrong look, one word out of place, and the façade would drop.

Wesley and Heffernan remained silent as they followed

158

her upstairs and into Lewis's bedroom, which, Wesley noted with approval, had been transformed. The carpet, which had been concealed beneath mounds of debris, was bright blue and newly vacuumed. The furniture was white melamine, wiped clean of finger marks. The bedding was decorated with fresh yellow checks. Wesley allowed himself the optimistic thought that, when Lewis returned, he'd be pleased with the transformation. Then he mentally substituted the word 'if' for 'when'. It was best to be prepared for the worst.

Jill Hoxworthy walked slowly over to the wardrobe in the corner of the room and opened the door. 'I didn't touch the gun. I didn't take it out of the box,' she said quietly. 'I thought you'd want to see ...'

'Thanks,' said Wesley. 'You did the right thing.'

Wesley could see the metal box on the shelf. After putting on a pair of plastic gloves, he pulled it out gently and took the lid off. There was a thin veil of tissue paper inside, which Wesley peeled away carefully to reveal a small handgun. It looked almost harmless lying there, like the toy guns he had used as a child to fight a thousand fantasy battles before his mother had read somewhere that such games fostered violence in growing boys. But this was the real thing: an instrument of death.

'Where the hell did the lad get it?' asked Gerry Heffernan rhetorically.

Wesley stood there asking himself the same question. He turned to Jill, who was hovering behind them, chewing her fingernails nervously. 'You'd no idea about this? He'd never spoken about it or hinted ...?'

The question, he knew, was naive. The last people Lewis Hoxworthy would have let in on his secret were his parents. Jill shook her head.

Wesley turned to Gerry Heffernan, who was staring down at the gun with his mouth slightly open. 'I really think we should have a go at reading all Lewis's e-mails. I'll ask Tom from Forensics to come over here first thing tomorrow.'

'Do you think this has something to do with his disappearance?' Jill asked quietly.

'I don't know.' Wesley was about to say that he hoped so in the light of what they had discovered about Alec Treadly, but he didn't want to add to the Hoxworthys' worries. The fact that a boy had gone missing and there was a convicted paedophile living virtually next door had caused the police to put two and two together, and Wesley was almost grateful for this glimmer of hope that their worst assumptions were wrong.

He glanced at his watch. Eleven-forty-five. He was meeting his mother and Pam in Morbay at one. 'We'll have to take the gun back for examination,' he said.

'Take it,' Jill Hoxworthy said, looking him in the eye. 'I just want it out of here.' She was near to tears.

Gerry Heffernan put a comforting hand on her shoulder. 'We'll do our best to find him, love, we really will.'

Heffernan took charge of the box containing the gun. As they left the house, they met Terry Hoxworthy coming in the front door.

'You've got it, then? She's told you?' The man looked exhausted. He couldn't have been more than fifty but he had the drained pallor of an old man. The dark shadows beneath his eyes told Wesley that he probably hadn't slept since his son left. He felt like assuring him that Lewis would turn up, that everything would be all right. But lies only postponed the pain.

They drove away from the farm, and when they reached the old barn they turned into the lane and drove past the Old Vicarage's tiny lodge. There was a police car parked outside. Alec Treadly was being brought in for questioning.

Wesley just hoped that when he returned from his lunch appointment he wouldn't be expected to take part.

Morbay's Royalty Hotel had an impressive façade. A great white wedding cake of a building, visible for miles around, it was a fine example of art deco architecture dating from the late 1920s, when Morbay had been the epitome of style, the place to be seen.

The wealthy had built their villas there, and the beautiful people of the time had taken their leisure in the shade of the resort's palm trees: a little piece of the Riviera on the south-west coast of England. Back in the 1930s famous crime writers had conjured murder mysteries, far more glamorous – and painless – than any Wesley Peterson had ever investigated, in the town's most sophisticated haunts. The pre-war age of titled ladies and vintage motor-cars had been Morbay's time in the sun.

Morbay's glory may have faded since those heady days but, like an ageing actress undergoing face-lift after face-lift, the old trooper kept on doing her best against the rising tide of foreign holidays, unemployment, outlying problem housing estates and rising drug addiction. And the Royalty Hotel remained a gracious landmark on the promenade – although the retired colonels and the titled ladies were long gone and it catered mostly for the conference trade.

Wesley stood outside the great revolving door with its framework of gleaming brass, and straightened his tie. He pushed at the door, which spun round and deposited him in the hotel foyer, a well-preserved art deco vision in marble and polished walnut.

He looked around. Seventy years ago someone of his racial origins would have felt out of place in such an establishment. But now there were many Asians, black and Chinese faces in the milling crowd of conference attendees. Wesley looked quite at home among the assembled doctors of Great Britain, and a few even nodded to him, thinking him one of their own, as he set off in search of his wife and mother.

They were to meet in the conservatory, which, being well signposted, was easy to find. It was an elegant room with windows on three sides giving a panoramic view of the hotel's extensive gardens. With the plants only in bud as yet, the grounds were a mere shadow of their future selves – the view in summer would be spectacular.

The furniture, in keeping with the conservatory theme, was well-upholstered wicker, with comfortable chairs arranged in clusters around low bamboo tables. It was Pam who spotted him first and waved. He hurried over and his mother stood up, arms outstretched to greet him.

Dr Cecilia Peterson had been a beauty when young and was still an attractive woman now she was in her mid-fifties. She was a little taller than her daughter-in-law, who sat beside her with her baby grandson on her knee. Not as slim as she once was, but dressed with elegant simplicity, she could have passed for twenty years younger. She smiled, a dazzling smile, took her son in her arms and kissed him firmly on both cheeks.

'Wesley, it's so good to see you.' She held him at arm's length. 'Let me have a look at you, son. You're looking well. And what about Michael? Look at the size of him. I can't believe how he's grown.' She leaned down and touched the baby's cheek and was rewarded with one of Michael's wide grins. 'Your father sends his love,' she continued. Her accent was soft Trinidadian, musical, redolent of sunnier climes. 'And did you know Maritia brought her boyfriend to meet us last weekend? He's curate at a church in Oxford. Such a nice, gentle young man. I told her she could do worse.'

'She told me. She e-mailed us last week,' said Wesley, not mentioning that his sister had said that, before taking her new love to meet their parents, she had felt a little apprehensive. They had pointed out the possible pitfalls of a mixed-race marriage when Wesley and Pam's relationship had become serious. Now Maritia too had chosen a white partner but, from Cecilia's reaction, it seemed that the curate had made a favourable impression – but then the Petersons were devout, churchgoing folk.

'She e-mailed you? Don't talk to me about computers, son. The ones in my surgery are always crashing or whatever it is they call it. Terrible things. More trouble than they're worth.'

'My boss says exactly the same,' said Wesley, laughing.

'How is he, this Gerry Heffernan? Still getting on all right with him, are you?'

'Oh, Gerry's like a big teddy bear,' said Pam. 'He growls a bit but he's soft underneath.'

Wesley smiled. He doubted whether Steve Carstairs would have agreed with Pam's description of the boss.

'Is he still seeing that American lady from Stokeworthy, Wes?' Pam asked.

'I think she's away at the moment.'

'That's a shame,' said Pam with genuine sympathy. 'I'm sure he gets lonely in that house all by himself.'

'He's a widower, isn't he? What happened to his wife?' Cecilia asked. She had always been interested in people: that was what made her a good GP. 'How did she die?'

Wesley hesitated. 'I think it was some sort of car accident but it's not something you like to ask about, is it? It might bring back painful memories.'

Cecilia nodded, happy with the answer; happy that she'd brought her boy up to consider other people's feelings. 'So what case are you working on at the moment, Wesley? Pamela tells me there's been a shooting.'

Wesley hadn't wanted to talk shop but his mother, head inclined slightly, was clearly awaiting an answer. 'Yes. A former rock star called Jonny Shellmer was shot in a small village near Tradmouth.'

'Oh, yes, I read about it in the paper. I remember Jonny Shellmer from years ago. He was in Rock Boat, wasn't he?' To Wesley's astonishment, she began to sing a snatch of a song, very softly, almost inaudibly. Then she started to laugh. 'Your father and I used to like that one when we were first married. It was on the radio all the time. "Angel", that was it.'

Wesley was lost for words at discovering a side of his parents' life he had never encountered before. He suddenly saw in his mind's eye a young couple, newly qualified as doctors, in love and far from their native land, setting up home together, decorating their first flat and singing along with the songs on the radio – singing along with Jonny Shellmer.

'There are some terrible things happening in this world,' Cecilia muttered, shaking her head.

'I expect you see some awful things in your job too,' said Wesley lightly, trying to change the subject.

Cecilia frowned. 'I had three cases of suspected child abuse last week, as well as the usual quota of women who'd "walked into a door" – or into their boyfriends' fists,' she added with disgust. 'And then there was a woman the week before who was raped by her own brother. Honestly, I see some things that make my blood run cold.' She saw that her son and daughter-in-law were listening intently.

'I suppose it's always gone on but now people are more willing to talk about it and get help,' said Pam thoughtfully.

'You're probably right, Pamela. But let's change the subject, eh? We're here for a nice lunch, so let's forget about the world's problems for a while.' She picked up a menu that was lying on the table. 'What do you fancy, then?'

Wesley and Cecilia studied the menu as Pam went off to obtain a highchair for Michael. Wesley made his choice, handed the large, shiny menu over to his mother and surreptitiously glanced at his watch. If he ate slowly he might avoid questioning Alec Treadly altogether.

'Where's the chief inspector?' Wesley asked as he made for his desk. The lunch had been good and he felt pleasantly full. It was a pity he had to return to the station instead of enjoying a leisurely Sunday in the bosom of his family.

It was Rachel who answered. 'He's down in the interview room questioning Alec Treadly, and he's left us to phone everyone in Jonny Shellmer's address book. Did you enjoy your lunch?'

'Yes, thank you. It was lovely.'

'How's your mum enjoying Morbay?'

'She's spent most of her time at the conference, so she hasn't had much time for sightseeing.'

'She's not missing much,' Rachel answered with a smile. 'The boss took Steve down with him to interview Treadly,' she went on, suddenly solemn. 'Do you fancy relieving one of them? Fresh face, fresh approach?'

Wesley shook his head. If possible he wanted to avoid spending any time cooped up with a paedophile. 'I'm sure Steve and the boss are managing okay,' he said quickly. 'I'll give you a hand with the phone calls. Have you come across anything interesting yet?'

'Angela Simms's number's in the book.' She looked at him expectantly but Wesley made no comment. He was thinking.

'I know. Anything else?'

'Most of the numbers are in London. Everyone seemed quite shocked and eager to help and there was nothing that rung any warning bells. The Met are going to have a word with the people who claimed to know him well.'

'What about the ex-member of Rock Boat who lives in Gloucestershire?'

'No reply. I've a feeling that one might be worth following up.' She opened Shellmer's address book. 'Then there's a number written in the front of the book with no name by it. I rang it and guess who answered. Jack Cromer – the TV presenter. It's his number.'

Wesley raised his eyebrows. Jack Cromer was a household name. He had started his TV career by presenting popular consumer watchdog programmes, but now he was famed for his aggressive interviewing technique. His rise in the BBC had been fairly meteoric. He habitually made mincemeat of the victims on his programme – it was rumoured that he had reduced some unfortunate spokeswoman for a holiday company to tears with interrogation techniques more brutal than anything permitted by the Police and Criminal Evidence Act. And now, along with several of his fellow celebrities, he had a second home in Derenham.

'Will you interview him or shall I?' Wesley asked nervously.

'Rather you than me. I said someone'd be round to have a word this afternoon. He's travelling back to London tonight. We can both go if you like. Moral support.'

'We'll need it. I've seen grown men turned into quivering jellies by Jack Cromer.'

Rachel smiled. 'But don't forget, it's us who'll be asking the questions this time. Shall we go over to Derenham and get it over with?'

As they were about to leave the office a young uniformed constable handed Wesley a sheet of paper.

'What is it?' asked Rachel, hoping it was nothing that would take Wesley away and oblige her to face Jack Cromer alone.

Wesley studied the paper for a few seconds. 'It's the report on Jonny Shellmer's car. The only fingerprints found on the driver's side belonged to Shellmer, the two lads who stole it and – surprise, surprise – Paul Heygarth. I think that lets Yossa and his mate out and puts Heygarth firmly back in the frame.'

'Unless the killer told them about the car – boasted where he'd dumped it. Unless ...'

Wesley was halfway out of the door. He stopped and turned to face her. 'Unless what?'

'Unless Jonny Shellmer was killed by Lewis Hoxworthy. He had the gun.'

'Go on,' said Wesley. She had his full attention now.

'I don't believe in coincidences, Wesley. Shellmer was killed in a house just next door to Hoxworthy's land. Lewis had a gun and his mates are found in possession of the dead man's car. Then Lewis disappears. Young as he is, I think he's got to be a suspect. Don't you?'

'Motive?'

'I don't know.' She hesitated for a few moments, turning possibilities over in her mind. 'What if Jonny Shellmer, Alec Treadly and Paul Heygarth were abusing Lewis? What if Shellmer was a paedophile too?'

'There's no evidence of that. And at the moment we've no evidence that Alec Treadly had ever had any contact with Lewis.'

'Paedophiles can be good at covering their tracks.'

'Have you mentioned this theory to anyone else yet?'

Rachel shrugged. 'I bounced the idea off a few of the DCs in the office. They didn't think it was too far fetched. Do you?'

Wesley hesitated before answering. He needed time to think it over. 'The boss and I will be having a word with Shellmer's ex-wife when Merseyside police track her down. If there's any dirt to be found on him she's bound to have chapter and verse, even if he's been on his best behaviour with Sherry Smyth. And I think we need to talk to Paul Heygarth again. The boss is convinced he's hiding something, and now it looks as if he's right.'

'He might be part of a paedophile ring too. They might all be involved.'

Wesley sighed. 'Come on. Let's go and have another word with Yossa Lang. Then we can give Jack Cromer a good grilling – let him have a taste of his own medicine.'

He left the station deep in thought. Things weren't getting any easier.

Gerry Heffernan had to get out of the interview room. Sitting facing Alec Treadly across the narrow table for two and a half hours, breathing in the sharp odour of his sweat, was not his ideal way of spending a Sunday lunch-time.

Treadly swore that he had never met Lewis Hoxworthy. He had been behaving himself, trying to mend his ways, he assured Heffernan and Steve, looking from one to the other in an attempt to convince. He would sometimes go over to Morbay and watch the kiddies playing in the park, he said with studied innocence. But it was a case of look and don't touch. And he certainly hadn't touched Lewis – he swore that on his mother's life. He'd never even seen the boy. He was trying to put the past behind him, he protested self-righteously, so why did the police keep harassing him?

But Gerry Heffernan had known that he was hiding something. Whether it was to do with his past inclinations or something entirely different he wasn't sure, but he wasn't going to let him go, even though Treadly's keen young solicitor, a young man with a lot of chunky gold jewellery and very little hair, was sitting there glowering at him, hostile and impatient.

Then came the confession. Alec Treadly admitted that before they had moved abroad Colonel and Mrs Porter had gone to visit their daughter in Scotland. They had left his mother with the key to the Old Vicarage and asked her to water their house plants. Alec had taken the key into Tradmouth to be copied, thinking that when they moved abroad it might come in useful.

Quietly, almost shamefaced, he admitted to the system-atic theft of small items from the house which he sold to local antique dealers. Nothing too big or valuable – just the odd silver spoon here, the odd Spode plate and silver photo frame there. Nothing they'd miss when their stuff was finally shipped over; nothing that couldn't be blamed on the removal men or the estate agent. Alec used the money for his little flutters on the gee-gees, as he put it.

When PC Johnson had caught him up at the house, he had been about to carry away a rather nice Crown Derby milk jug. He had known it was wrong, he assured the chief inspector. But the temptation of having what was in effect his own private cashpoint a hundred yards up the Old Vicarage drive was too much to resist. He had no sugges-tions to make about the break-in. All he could say was that he hadn't been responsible. He hadn't needed to break a pane of glass in the kitchen door: he had a key.

He had never seen a gun in his life, he assured them. Neither had he seen Lewis Hoxworthy – he wasn't even aware of the boy's existence. He had never met Jonny Shellmer although he had heard of him. He hadn't been up at the Old Vicarage at the time of the murder. The last time he had been inside the building was over a week ago.

Then he sat back in his plastic chair and announced that he had told them everything and he wasn't saying any more. At that point Heffernan charged him with the thefts and handed him over into the custody sergeant's tender care.

He couldn't stand one more minute in the company of the greasy-haired creep and his chippy solicitor. He needed to get out into the clean fresh air, blow the cobwebs out. He needed to spend a couple of hours on the river.

Yossa Lang's mother had sworn to the magistrate that she'd keep a better eye on her son in future. It was the first time her Joseph – as she called him in court – had ever crashed a stolen car and she wouldn't let it happen again. She would make sure he didn't get into more trouble.

But somehow Donna Lang didn't associate all her righteous protestations in the magistrates' court with the realities of everyday life. It would never have occurred to her to forgo an evening down at the Coach and Horses in order to stay in and 'keep an eye' on Yossa. He was fifteen, hardly a baby. Besides, there was a lorry driver who had taken to buying her drinks. Why shouldn't she have a bit of fun?

She had just left the house when the doorbell rang. Yossa, slumped in front of the television watching a horror video, let it ring twice more before he wiped his greasy, pizza-stained fingers on his jeans and bothered to answer it.

He opened the front door and looked Rachel and Wesley up and down. 'What is it?' he asked, mentally composing the complaint he was going to send in about police harassment.

'We'd just like to ask you a few questions, Joseph.' Rachel tried her best to sound friendly, but she was aware that she was failing miserably. 'It's nothing to do with the car – we just want you to help us find your friend, Lewis.'

He stood aside to let them in and watched warily as they

sat down. He didn't trust the police. They were trouble.

'Have you ever heard any of these names before, or have you heard Lewis mention them?' She recited the names of Paul Heygarth and Alec Treadly and received a blank stare in return. It was only when she mentioned Jonny Shellmer that there was a flicker of recognition in Yossa's eyes.

'That's the one who got shot near Lewis's place. My mum said she used to have some of his records a long time ago,' he added, as if Rock Boat's heyday was as distant to him as the age of the dinosaurs.

Rachel and Wesley left a few minutes later, none the wiser, and headed for Derenham.

Half an hour later they drew up outside Jack Cromer's house in the centre of Derenham village, just opposite the Red Bull. After the Winterham estate, the village of Derenham seemed like paradise itself.

'Nice place,' Rachel said with a touch of envy.

Shipwreck House was a substantial double-fronted structure painted pristine white, with spring flowers tumbling from window boxes and wooden tubs placed either side of the front door.

'How much do you reckon it's worth?' she asked. 'Half a million? Six hundred thousand? More?'

'More than a policeman can afford,' Wesley replied with a sad smile. 'Not an honest one, anyway. There was an inspector I knew at the Met who was done for taking bribes from drug dealers – he had a big place in Essex. I'd always thought he was a good bloke until it all came out ... you never can tell.'

'You always think too well of people,' said Rachel with a shy smile.

'After a few years in this job?' Wesley laughed. 'You must be joking. Come on, let's go and grill Jack Cromer. It'll be a new experience for him to be on the receiving end.'

'I think you're looking forward to this,' Rachel observed

mischievously as they got out of the car.

Wesley marched up to the front door of Shipwreck House, rang the polished brass doorbell and waited.

Jack Cromer himself answered the door, dressed for the river in white trousers and a Guernsey sweater. A pair of navy blue deck shoes completed the ensemble, but somehow Wesley had the impression that, unlike Gerry Heffernan, the man wouldn't know one end of a boat from the other.

He invited them in, his sharp, watchful eyes assessing their every move ... but paying particular attention to Rachel's legs. They were shepherded into the living room, which was large, low beamed and filled with antiques, many of a nautical nature. This was a retreat far from the stress and sophistication of London, but high on creature comforts.

Wesley and Rachel sank side by side into a soft leather sofa and were offered tea by a stunning blonde, at least twenty years Cromer's junior. The standard-issue second wife, Rachel thought; a trophy wife won by fame and money.

Jack Cromer sat down in an armchair facing them and looked Wesley in the eye. He was a tall man in his early fifties, his thick dark hair greying at the temples. He had keen, watchful eyes which, combined with an aquiline nose, gave him a hawkish quality.

'I'm always happy to help the police in any way I can, Inspector,' he began in the deep, smooth Scottish voice familiar to millions of television viewers. 'But I really don't see how I can be of much use to you.'

'Did you ever meet Mr Shellmer?' Wesley asked.

'Just the once. I was doing a programme on the negative influence of pop music on kids and we had some big rock star lined up to take part. He dropped out at the last minute so my researchers found a replacement which turned out to be Jonny Shellmer. Apart from that, our paths never crossed.'

171

'How did the interview go? Was it . . .' Wesley searched for the right word. 'Controversial? Did you part amicably?' Knowing Cromer's interviewing techniques, he'd have been surprised if there hadn't been a little metaphorical blood spilt.

Cromer shook his head. 'The original guy I'd lined up was someone who gave parents nightmares. That's what people watch my shows for, a bit of controversy, a few lost tempers. But Jonny Shellmer was rather tame by comparison and consequently it wasn't much of a show – in fact Shellmer came over as quite a reasonable guy,' he added with what sounded like disappointment.

'Did you know he was moving to Derenham?' Rachel asked.

'I saw an article in the local rag saying he'd made a donation to the village hall appeal fund.' He paused. 'I've, er, been considering making a donation myself, as a matter of fact – got to do what you can for the community, haven't you.'

Wesley nodded. He suspected any donation would be attended by the maximum publicity – Jack Cromer didn't strike him as a man who would do something for nothing.

'Can you tell us where you were last Wednesday, sir?' Wesley asked politely. He saw Rachel watching him.

'Wednesday? I was recording my show on Wednesday,' answered Cromer with easy confidence.

'And you came to Derenham on . . .?'

'Friday.'

Wesley tried again. 'How do you explain the fact that your telephone number is in the front of Jonny Shellmer's address book?' Wesley produced the small leather-bound book and passed it to Cromer. Cromer passed it back to him, apparently puzzled. He looked a little less sure of himself now.

'I really don't know, Inspector. It's a total mystery. Perhaps he intended to contact me about something in the future and somebody had given him my number. I really

172

don't know. I certainly didn't give him my number, and I can assure you that he hasn't called me. As I said, I've only met the man once, and then we hardly said a word to each other off the screen.'

It was Rachel who spoke next, tentatively, as though Cromer's overbearing presence had cowed her a little. 'How long have you lived here, Mr Cromer?'

He looked at her and smiled, a charming but predatory smile which disappeared as soon as his wife entered the room with a tray of bone-china cups and saucers. 'We've had the place eighteen months now, haven't we, darling?'

The wife nodded her blond head and set about distributing the drinks.

'We divide our time between here and London. You know how it is – busy, busy, busy. I wish we could spend all our time down here but ...'

'Was the telephone number changed when you moved in?'

Cromer shrugged. 'I don't think so. No.'

'Who owned the house before you?'

Wesley looked at her, impressed. Of course, the number in Shellmer's address book could have been a few years old. It was a good line of questioning and he wished he'd thought of it himself.

'A couple who were looking for something smaller. They moved to the other side of the village near the church. Why?'

'What were their names?' Wesley asked. He leaned forward, breath held, awaiting the answer.

Cromer looked at his wife. Wesley had seen that look before, when Cromer had been questioning some squirming politician or shifty businessman. He suddenly felt sorry for the woman.

'What was their name, Carla? Do you remember? It's on the tip of my tongue. In fact somebody rang up and asked for them last weekend – obviously hadn't been given their new number.'

'The person who rang – was it a man?' Wesley asked.

'Yes. Had a slight Liverpool accent. Come to think of it, it could have been Jonny Shellmer – certainly sounded like him; not that I made the connection at the time, of course. Oh, what was the name of those people? It was something to do with gardens. What was it, now? Come on, Carla. Think.'

Carla closed her eyes in concentration, showing a fine display of powder-blue eyeshadow above long mascaraed lashes.

'It was Flowers,' she announced suddenly after a few moments. 'Jim and Maggie Flowers.'

She opened her wide blue eyes and beamed first at her husband and then at Wesley and Rachel, as if she expected a round of applause.

'That's it,' said Cromer with a smile. 'I remember now. He asked for a Mr Flowers.'

The River Trad was a little choppy but this didn't bother Gerry Heffernan. He had never suffered from seasickness. He stood on the deck of the *Rosie May*, the twenty-seven-foot sloop he had bought and lovingly restored to her former glory just after Kathy's death, and altered course for home. The damp breeze swept through his unkempt hair and he breathed in deeply. There was nothing like the smell of seaweed and salt water. He loved it – that and the sound of the gulls overhead.

The sea had always been there, part of his life. He was raised in a seafaring city, in a family where going to sea was the norm. He had left his grammar school at the age of sixteen and joined the merchant navy, studying for his master's ticket.

He was serving as first officer aboard a cargo vessel awaiting his first command when he was struck down with appendicitis as his ship was passing the South Devon coast. He had been flown by helicopter to the nearest hospital – Tradmouth; a place he'd never visited before, a port in Devon with a rich seafaring history stretching back to

174

medieval times. In Tradmouth hospital he had been cared for by a pretty dark-haired staff nurse called Kathy, whose charms had been stronger than the call of the sea. He had stayed in Tradmouth and joined the police force at the suggestion of his uncle, who was a bridewell sergeant in Liverpool. He had, as they say in seafaring circles, swallowed the anchor and moored himself in Tradmouth for good.

He and Kathy had married and brought up two children in the pretty white house on Baynard's Quay. But then, when those children were in their teens, Kathy had died. He had been told the news by a nervous young constable, then he had identified her and cried over her broken body, wondering how he was going to tell Rosie and Sam that they would never see their mother again. He had been a churchgoer all his life, and he had prayed, prayed that the pain would ease, prayed that Kathy would have justice.

Even after four years the pain hadn't gone away. It returned when he was alone or when something reminded him. When he was sailing he often thought of her, heard her voice on the wind.

But now he tried to put her from his mind. He forced himself to think of the Jonny Shellmer case, of Alec Treadly. Talking to that man had made him feel unclean. He was a father. Most fathers, he was sure, would have felt the same having to sit so close to a man who had abused vulnerable youngsters.

He had received a message to say that Wesley and Rachel had gone to Derenham to visit some TV presenter whose phone number was in Shellmer's address book. There was also the welcome news that Paul Heygarth's prints had been found on Jonny Shellmer's car and that Heygarth was being brought in again for further questioning.

Not so welcome was Rachel's theory that some kind of paedophile ring was operating in the area. If so, surely he would have heard something. Surely there would have been some hint from schools and Social Services. But then such people were more skilled in subterfuge than the secret service. Gerry Heffernan shuddered and hoped with all his heart that Rachel's suspicions were groundless.

He sailed past the twin castles perched on the high headland, either side of the river entrance, and brought the boat around, heading for home. There was a stiff breeze now and the *Rosie May* raced across the waves. Soon he saw Baynard's Quay and the row of pastel-washed houses with his own set back at the end, snuggling against its larger neighbour. He was about to drop the anchor when he looked up and saw a brilliant white yacht sailing down the main channel out to sea. Flashy, he thought without envy. A gin palace, a rich man's toy. A beautiful craft but not his style at all.

Then he saw the name painted in bold black letters on the stern. *Henry of Lancaster*.

He made sure the *Rosie May* was properly moored before searching in his pocket for his mobile phone.

Chapter Nine

To my most beloved sister Lucy,
I have word that my husband was wounded in battle at
Tewkesbury but the Lord spared his life and he is well
cared for by the brothers of the Abbey there, and Edmund
is safe there also.

Have you spoken with the widow More of Tradmouth
concerning my stepson, John? If she is willing he should
call upon her. I make it no secret that I have had cause
to chastise him of late, but I pray that a good wife will be
a blessing to him as I assure you that he is but a little
wild. He is most gentle and loving with his sister, my true
daughter Elizabeth, and spends much time in her
company. It may be that the widow More will find him
agreeable.

My dear son Edmund returns with his father when he
is well enough to travel, and it will bring me much joy to
see him. Yet I grieve for King Henry and Queen
Margaret's defeat.
Your loving sister, Marjory

Written at Derenham this twenty-fifth day of May 1471

Monday dawned fine. As Wesley Peterson was eating his
cornflakes, the weatherman on breakfast television made
extravagant promises of sunshine in the south-west. He

used the word glorious – always a bad sign. Wesley picked up his waterproof coat as he left the house.

He kissed Pam goodbye as she set off to drop Michael at the childminder's before heading schoolward. She looked drawn and tired again that morning, and Wesley wondered whether the job was becoming too much for her. But they needed her salary, so she didn't have much choice in the matter – she had to carry on. As she drove off his thoughts turned to the case, to Jonny Shellmer.

Wesley felt that they still didn't know enough about Shellmer; they knew about Shellmer the rock star, Shellmer the songwriter, Shellmer the boyfriend of Sherry Smyth – but not Shellmer the man. Sherry Smyth hadn't known him for long ... and there was a part of his life that he had kept hidden from her, either by accident or design.

Gerry Heffernan had spotted Hal Lancaster's boat heading out to sea and he was contacting the harbourmaster, an old acquaintance of his, first thing to find out all he could. If Lancaster's boat had been in the area at the time of Shellmer's death, it opened up a whole new range of possibilities.

When Wesley reached the station, Heffernan was sitting in his glass-partitioned lair drinking coffee, while the workers in the outer office sorted through papers, spoke on telephones and punched information into computers. Officers drifted in and took their places wearily, taking up where they had left off the previous night.

Rachel looked up and smiled when Wesley walked in. 'I've got a print-out of all the numbers Jonny Shellmer rang from his phone in the cottage. He rang Jack Cromer's number on Sunday, which fits with Cromer's account of receiving a call asking for the Flowers, I suppose. I'm going over to Derenham to have a word with them,' she added, trying to hide her keenness under a cool veneer.

'But Maggie Flowers told me she didn't know Shellmer. She'd only met him briefly when he presented the cheque.'

'Perhaps she was lying,' Rachel replied with the hint of a

wink. 'Are you coming with me?'

She knew the proximity of Neil Watson's dig to the Flowers' house would prove too tempting for Wesley to resist, and she was glad. The alternative was to be teamed up with Steve Carstairs, and she could think of better travelling companions. And she enjoyed Wesley's company, enjoyed it too much perhaps. But she hardly dared to acknowledge this, even to herself, and certainly not to others. She didn't want to spark off the station's ever-efficient gossip machine which, unlike the business of catching criminals, required no solid evidence of wrongdoing for a conviction.

Wesley agreed to go over to Derenham later, and Rachel returned to her paperwork, satisfied that she'd won one small victory so early on a Monday morning.

Through the glass partition, Wesley could see Gerry Heffernan gesticulating wildly, beckoning him with extravagant arm movements like a constable on point duty. He opened the door and the boss stood up.

'Have you heard, Wes? Heygarth's been brought in again. I wanted to see how he explained away the fact that his fingerprints were all over Shellmer's car. He's made another statement.' He snorted. 'Another pack of lies.'

'Anything else new?'

'I've been on to Captain Shaw, the harbour-master. He told me that Hal Lancaster's sailed off to France – expects to be back in Tradmouth later in the week. If we travel up to Liverpool tomorrow then we should be back in good time to give him a warm welcome when he arrives.'

'If he arrives,' said Wesley realistically.

'Captain Shaw seemed pretty certain he'd be back. Lancaster told him he had some business in Tradmouth.' Gerry Heffernan was trying his best to sound optimistic, but a note of doubt had crept into his voice.

'Did he say if Lancaster was with anyone?'

Heffernan shook his head and ran his fingers through his unkempt hair. 'He said he was alone when he called at the harbour office and he never saw anyone else aboard the *Henry of Lancaster*. But there's nothing unusual about that. I usually sail alone. She's a lovely craft, that *Henry of Lancaster*,' he added appreciatively with a faraway look in his eye. 'But a bit flash for my taste.'

'What about the time Shellmer was killed? Was Lancaster's boat moored at Tradmouth then?'

'Apparently not. He arrived on Friday. But that doesn't mean he didn't head up the river and drop anchor near Derenham before that.'

'I suppose we'll have to wait until he comes back to find out,' Wesley consulted a sheet of paper – his list of things to do. 'Tom from Forensics is over at Hoxworthy's Farm now seeing what he can dig up on that computer of Lewis's. I spoke to him and he reckons he can resurrect any e-mails that have been deleted.'

'The ghosts in the machine, eh?' said Heffernan. 'Let's hope they tell us where Lewis has got to.'

Wesley sat down. He had some time to kill before his trip to Derenham to see the Flowers and he wanted to talk about the case, to put his thoughts into some sort of order. He took a plain piece of paper from a pile at the corner of Heffernan's cluttered desk and laid it neatly in front of him.

'Have we had confirmation yet that the gun found in Lewis's room was used to kill Shellmer?' he asked.

Heffernan held up the piece of paper his mug of tea had been standing on and waved it in Wesley's direction. 'Faxed to us by Forensics first thing. I told them it was urgent so they pulled their fingers out.'

Wesley played with his pen, a Christmas present from his parents. He began to speak slowly, thoughtfully, making notes on the blank sheet of paper in front of him to get things straight in his mind. 'So Shellmer was shot with a gun that was later found to be in the possession of Lewis Hoxworthy, who disappeared two days after the shooting. Shellmer was shot in the Old Vicarage some time on Wednesday, and there's evidence of a break-in.

Then his body was moved by Paul Heygarth, the estate agent, with the help of his lovely assistant Nicola, the day after. Heygarth claims he only moved Shellmer because he didn't want the sale of the house disrupted. He says he needed the money from the commission. Having met Heygarth, I'd say that was possible. What does this new statement of his say?'

'He says he moved the car for the same reason as he moved the body – so that nobody would associate the property with the murder. He kept on about how he was desperate for the commission from the sale.'

'Believe him?'

Heffernan grunted slightly and studied his knuckles.

Wesley continued. 'Then the day after Shellmer's body's found Lewis goes missing, having boasted to his friend – if you can call Yossa a friend – that he's found something that'll make him rich and that he has a gun. Shellmer's car's dumped by Heygarth and then it turns up in the possession of Lewis's mate Yossa. Is that coincidence – it's not unknown for the likes of Yossa to hang around carparks in the hope that something'll turn up – or did the lads have some sort of contact with Heygarth?'

'Then there's a convicted paedophile living near by who has free access to the Old Vicarage. And there's Angela Simms, who was seen at Shellmer's house. Her name was in Shellmer's address book so they must have known each other somehow. She's robbed and left for dead, which may or may not be connected with Shellmer's shooting. Then someone – a man with a slight Liverpool accent: possibly Jonny Shellmer – rings Jack Cromer's house asking for a Mr Flowers.'

Wesley examined the notes he had made and sat back. 'What the hell's this all about, Gerry? What's going on here?'

Gerry Heffernan looked across the chaos on his desktop, watching Wesley's face. His brow was furrowed in concentration, exasperation. If this had been a jigsaw puzzle he would have thrown the pieces to the floor in frustration by now.

'Don't worry, Wes. It might all get a bit clearer once we've read Lewis's e-mails and had a word with Shellmer's ex-missus. I always say if you find out about the victim's life and associates you're halfway there ... unless it's a random killing, of course, but I don't think for a moment that this one is. We'll get off to Liverpool as soon as we can, maybe tomorrow. And we can stop at Chris Pauling's on the way and have a word with him.'

'Chris Pauling?'

'Rock Boat's drummer. The one who lives in Gloucestershire ... just on our way.'

'So have you any pet theories?' asked Wesley, looking at his watch.

Heffernan drained his mug of lukewarm tea and pressed his lips together stubbornly. 'You don't move a body and get rid of evidence unless you've got something to hide. Perhaps Rachel's paedophile ring idea's not so far fetched. I want to find out everything there is to know about Paul Heygarth. If he's ever farted in public I want to know about it ... and I want to know everything he gets up to in private. If he's a pervert and Lewis was one of his victims then there might be evidence that Lewis has been in his flat. I want it searched, turned upside down; same goes for Treadly's place and Shellmer's cottage.'

He slammed the mug down. Wesley watched him, noted the bitter determination in his eyes. For such an easy-going man, Gerry Heffernan was giving a good display of behaviour that seemed to border on the obsessive. But then perhaps he had a point about Heygarth. Wesley hadn't taken to the man either.

'What about the theory that Lewis shot Shellmer?'

Heffernan shrugged. 'He had the gun in his possession. If Shellmer was a pervert too and they were in league with Alec Treadly, who let them use the Old Vicarage ... I want Forensics to give that place a really good going over in case there's evidence of anything untoward in the bedrooms.' He raised his eyebrows and Wesley looked away.

It was something he didn't like thinking about. But it had to be considered.

There was a phone call from Laura Kruger. She had Jonny Shellmer's post-mortem report typed up and ready for them. Wesley told her he'd pick it up on his way to Derenham, and Gerry Heffernan said he'd come along for the ride. When Wesley broke the news to Rachel she shrugged, resigned to the fact that the chief inspector had pulled rank.

When they reached the hospital they looked in on Angela Simms. She was still in intensive care and they could only stare at her through a glass partition. She lay sprouting tubes and wires which monitored her every breath and heartbeat, small and still on a stark white bed.

PC Wallace sat on a grey padded chair outside the room, sipping coffee from a plastic cup and watching a pretty Chinese staff nurse as she went about her duties. He stood up when Heffernan came into view.

'Anything to report, Wallace?'

'They took her down for a scan this morning but I don't know any more and ...'

'And what?'

Wallace's cheeks reddened. 'Nurse Chang said there's been a phone call asking how she was – a man, she said. When she asked if he was a relative he rang off.'

Heffernan and Wesley looked at each other. 'If there are any more calls, let us know, will you? I'm sure you can rely on Nurse Chang to keep you informed,' Heffernan added with a wink.

They left Wallace blushing and headed for the mortuary.

Shellmer's post-mortem report contained few surprises. Although Laura Kruger's social chitchat was hardly up to Colin Bowman's standard, Wesley did manage to discover that she had trained in Liverpool – a fact that raised her a few notches in Heffernan's estimation – and that she had a boyfriend who worked in the psychiatric department of Morbay General Hospital. A jocular comment from Gerry Heffernan about mad psychiatrists brought the conversation to an awkward halt, but Wesley retrieved the situation by changing the subject to his own family's medical careers. He mentioned his mother's visit to the Morbay conference, and the reputation of the CID was salvaged after ten minutes of cosy medical gossip. Gerry Heffernan's heart might be in the right place most of the time, thought Wesley, but he had been at the back of the queue when the tact was given out.

They were about to leave when Laura pointed out a postcard from Colin Bowman, bearing a coloured photograph of the medieval walled French town of Carcassonne on the front, pinned in pride of place on the office notice-board. Gerry Heffernan cheekily took the card down and read it. Colin was having a wonderful time, it said. Good food, good wine, good scenery. He passed the card to Wesley, who read it with a pang of envy. Some people had all the luck.

Laura was about to bid them farewell when a head appeared round the office door. Neil Watson looked genuinely surprised to see Wesley and his boss there and said as much.

'We can't keep away, Neil,' Heffernan said with inappropriate cheerfulness. 'What are you doing here? Looking for old bones?'

Neil chose to ignore him and addressed Laura. 'Have you anything for me on the Derenham skeleton yet?'

Laura nodded. 'I finished the report last night. Come and have a look.'

Neil turned to Wesley. 'Coming, Wes?' He grinned at Gerry Heffernan. 'Bring your friend.'

Wesley looked at his watch. He had time . . . just. He followed Neil and Laura through swing-doors into a bright white steel-furnished room. Gerry Heffernan walked, uncomplaining, by his side, glad of a little distraction from murder.

They crowded round a steel trolley on which lay a set of dirty-looking bones which formed what looked like the skeleton of a tallish adult. Most of the bones were there. Now that the skull had been cleaned up, Wesley saw a pair of deep cuts on it – more evidence that the poor wretch had suffered a vicious attack before he had been decapitated. During his archaeological training, Wesley had come across skeletons of those killed in ancient battles which bore similar wounds, and he wondered just what had happened at Derenham's old manor house all those centuries ago. The unfortunate victim had not met an easy end.

Laura picked the skull up carefully in both hands and stared at it for a few moments, holding it as though she were auditioning for the part of the prince in *Hamlet*. 'This is a male,' she began, 'probably in his mid to late teens. He was tallish and probably well nourished so he may have been from the wealthier classes ... but that's just speculation.

'I can give you a definite cause of death – decapitation,' she continued. 'And there's evidence of a fierce attack, probably with a sharp sword. The defensive wounds on his forearms indicate that he probably wasn't armed himself when he was hacked to death.'

'Hardly cricket, is it,' said Wesley. 'Killing an unarmed man like that.'

'And burying his head in what would have been the kitchen garden and the rest of him in the midden,' said Neil. 'They were very worried about being buried in consecrated ground in the Middle Ages. And let's face it, even today you don't go around burying people in your vegetable patch unless you've murdered them first. Am I right, Wes?'

Wesley nodded with appropriate solemnity. 'If someone starts digging up human bones with their carrots we usually start asking questions.' He thought for a moment. 'From the archaeological evidence, when would you say these bones had been buried?'

Neil shrugged. 'From coins and pottery found around

185

and above the remains, I'd date them to the late Middle Ages – 1460 to 1480 or thereabouts.'

'The Wars of the Roses. Any battles fought in Derenham?'

'No. Devon was full of Lancastrian supporters but there were no actual battles fought around here. The battles are all well documented – Towton, Barnet, Tewkesbury ...'

'Just a thought,' said Wesley.

Neil looked at his watch. 'I'd better get over to Derenham. The Doom's being moved to the church for the history evening next Saturday and I've arranged to meet one of the village celebrities.'

'Who?'

Neil frowned. 'Can't remember his name but he's a famous actor and he's been taking an interest in the history of the church. And I want to have a look at the Merrivale tombs while I'm at it.'

'I'm going to Derenham,' said Wesley. 'Want a lift?'

'In the back of a cop car? No thanks. I've got my reputation to think of. And my car's parked outside.'

'Our choir are singing at the history evening,' Heffernan chipped in.

But Neil either hadn't heard or chose to ignore him. 'Hey, Wes, did I tell you I found an old map of Derenham which confirms that the house we're digging up belonged to the Merrivales?' He didn't wait for an answer. 'Must be off. See you later. Thanks, Laura.'

He swept out of the room, humming a tune under his breath which seemed familiar to Wesley, yet unplaceable.

Laura looked at Gerry Heffernan speculatively. 'Is this Derenham history evening going to be any good?'

''Course it's going to be good. Nice spicy story ... a couple of naughty priests in thirteen something who were responsible for half the village babies, at least three vicars with a nice little sideline in smuggling, a highwayman who turned out to be the churchwarden and a couple of ghosts thrown in for good measure. You should come.'

Laura Kruger looked as though she might be tempted. 'Maybe I will if I can get the time off.'

Gerry Heffernan turned to Wesley. 'Where are we off to now? Derenham?'

'Derenham,' was the decisive reply. 'I'm going to ask the Flowers about that phone number in Shellmer's address book.'

But Heffernan was halfway out of the room. 'Thanks, Laura, love. See you,' he said as he disappeared out of the swing-doors.

Wesley turned to Laura and shrugged his shoulders apologetically.

But he saw that she was smiling. There were some battles that couldn't be won.

Jill Hoxworthy put the mug of steaming tea down by the young man's elbow. She was careful to place it on a mat. She didn't want to mark the top of Lewis's desk. When Lewis came back she wanted everything nice for him. Everything right.

She didn't even know whether she should be allowing this tall, fair-haired boy who looked little older than Lewis himself to intrude into the inner workings of his precious computer. Some instinct told her that she ought to defend her son's property.

But then the reality of the situation hit her like a punch from a heavyweight boxer and, with a sick lurch, her heart plummeted into an abyss of despair. Lewis was gone. Nobody knew where he was. The police came with their grave faces and asked their gentle questions. They muttered reassuring words, but she knew what they were thinking. She had seen the way Stella Tracey's daughter, Rachel, looked at her with eyes full of pity, the pity reserved for the bereaved. Stella herself had rung from Little Barton Farm to ask if there was anything she could do. Kind people, well-meaning people, people who couldn't have a clue what it was really like. Stella had three boys as well as Rachel.

Jill only had Lewis. And now he was gone.

She still made his meals; set three places at the kitchen table. As pagans made offerings to their gods to summon and appease them, so Jill Hoxworthy lovingly prepared her gifts of food for Lewis and laid them out on the checked table-cloth. He would be back, she told herself, believing it for a split second. Then came the grief of loss; the pain almost physical, eating at her. The seesaw – hope and despair.

Tom from Forensics looked up at Jill and thanked her for the tea with a nervous smile. He assured her that he wouldn't be long now. He had almost finished, and he was certain that he had found what he was looking for.

Jill didn't enquire further. She dreaded that Tom's discoveries would confirm what she most feared. She had read about it in the newspapers, seen it on the television. How they made contact with kids through the Internet. Kids who weren't streetwise. Lonely kids. Kids like Lewis. Then they arranged to meet them and . . .

She rushed out and made for her own room, where she flung herself on the old double bed she shared with Terry. Burying her face in the pillow so Tom in the next room couldn't hear, she wept angry, helpless tears.

Wesley and Heffernan parked their car by the field where Neil was excavating the remains of Derenham's old manor house, reduced now to a grid of stone walls that protruded barely a foot above the muddy earth. Wesley peered over the gate but Neil was nowhere in sight.

He followed Gerry Heffernan to the front door of Derenham House, thinking that the grand name hardly suited a building which wasn't much bigger than a cottage. Maggie answered the door and led them inside where Jim Flowers was seated on a large and well-worn chintz sofa in a tableau of connubial calm, two mugs of hot tea set before him on a polished oak coffee table. Maggie invited them to sit and hurried from the room in search of more mugs for the visitors.

When she was out of the room Flowers was quick to assure them that he had just called in for a cup of tea on his way to conduct a survey on a house in Neston. He worked for an estate agent in Tradmouth, he explained in an accent Wesley took to be Australian. He was a surveyor, he said, and a partner in the firm. Wesley watched him. He was a tall man whose flesh seemed too big for his frame, and he reminded Wesley of a large guard dog, watchful and restless.

'Which estate agent?' Wesley asked, making conversation to put the man at his ease before be began asking serious questions.

'Heygarth and Proudfoot in Tradmouth High Street.'

'You'll know Paul Heygarth, then?' Wesley asked, glancing at Gerry Heffernan, who had sunk into a worn armchair which looked as though it might be difficult to get out of. The chief inspector's expression gave nothing away.

'I know Paul, yes.' Jim Flowers' deep voice suddenly sounded wary, as though the subject of Paul Heygarth was one he would rather avoid. He glanced at Heffernan, and Wesley thought he detected a momentary flash of fear in his eyes.

'It seems that he found the body of Jonny Shellmer in the Old Vicarage at the other end of the village, and he claims that he moved it out of the house so that it wouldn't delay the house sale. Would you say that was the sort of thing he'd do?' Wesley knew the question was forthright but he considered it would do no harm to have someone else's view of Heygarth's story.

Flowers nodded solemnly. 'Paul's never been worried about cutting a few corners, and it's common knowledge that his ex-wife's bleeding him dry, so he wouldn't want anything to stand between him and a few thousand in commission. I've heard through the office grapevine that Nicola Tarnley helped him. Is that right?'

Wesley nodded.

'Silly girl,' was Flowers' only comment before picking

up his mug and taking a long drink.

Gerry Heffernan shifted his body forward in the chair and looked Flowers in the eye. 'Did Heygarth ever mention Shellmer? Did he say he knew him?'

'He said he was very interested in the Old Vicarage.' He pressed his lips together. That was all he was prepared to say.

Maggie floated into the room with a big wooden tray which she set down on the coffee table. Like the perfect hostess in a 1950s advert, she offered round tea, biscuits and home-made cake. Gerry Heffernan swooped on the latter as if he'd not seen food for weeks and bit ecstatically into a large wedge of fruitcake.

Wesley was glad of the interruption. Whenever Paul Heygarth's name was mentioned Gerry Heffernan seemed to acquire a zealous gleam in his eye. Perhaps he had a down on estate agents; perhaps he just didn't like the man. But whatever it was, Wesley hoped that he wasn't allowing his feelings to interfere with his judgement.

He decided that there had been enough small talk. Now that they were all sitting comfortably it was time to get to the point of their visit. He produced a small book from his pocket and turned to the front page.

'This is Jonny Shellmer's address book. We found a telephone number written in the front. Would you take a look at it and tell us if you recognise it.' He handed the book to Jim Flowers, who took it from him with nervous hands.

Flowers stared at it but said nothing. Maggie took it from him, glanced at the number, then handed it back to Wesley.

'I'm sorry, Inspector. We can't help you.'

'Look at it again, Mrs Flowers.'

He held the book out to her and sensed that she was about to object. Then she relented and took it from him.

'I'm sorry. I still don't ...' She passed it to her husband stiffly. 'Does it ring any bells, Jim?'

Jim Flowers shook his head and looked at his watch. 'I'm sorry, I really must be going.' He heaved himself out of the soft upholstery, handing the book back to Wesley quickly. Nobody had wanted to hold on to the thing for long – it was like a game of pass the parcel.

'It's the number of your old house. Shipwreck House. Is that right?'

Jim and Maggie glanced at one another.

'I'll take your word for it,' said Jim casually. 'We moved out about eighteen months ago. I'd ask the new people about it, if I were you. Jack Cromer, the TV presenter bought the place.'

Pass the parcel again. Jim Flowers was anxious to deny any connection.

'We've asked them already,' said Wesley. 'They say they didn't know Shellmer. They also said that they received a phone call last Sunday, three days before Shellmer died. We think the call was from Jonny Shellmer and, according to Mr Cromer, he was asking for you.'

Jim Flowers looked wary. 'I've never met Jonny Shellmer. Why should he want to talk to me? He was dealing with Paul, and why would he have my old number? I don't understand.' He frowned, turning over the possibilities in his mind. 'Unless he wanted to speak to Maggie about the cheque he gave for the village hall. Perhaps he'd looked in an out-of-date telephone directory and got our old number.' Jim Flowers looked pleased with himself. It was as good an explanation as any.

'So you've never spoken to Jonny Shellmer?'

Jim Flowers shook his head, avoiding Wesley's eyes.

Wesley watched him closely. 'By the way, sir, where were you last Wednesday?'

Flowers shifted awkwardly. 'Er, I was at work. I had a couple of surveys to do but I was in the office the rest of the time.'

'What time did you get home?'

Flowers hesitated, his brow furrowed in concentration. 'Around six o'clock. Maggie was in London visiting her sister. She stayed the night.'

Maggie Flowers nodded in confirmation and Wesley stood up. Unless he was going to start interrogating this pair – something he had no inclination to do at this point – he felt that there was nothing more to be said.

But Gerry Heffernan had just helped himself to another slice of fruitcake.

'Will you be helping out with the dig today, Mrs Flowers?' Wesley asked, killing time.

'I suppose so.' There was no enthusiasm in Maggie's voice. She wanted them gone.

Wesley tried again. 'How's the village hall appeal going?'

She forced herself to smile. 'Very well. We're just two thousand pounds off our target. Perhaps you and the chief inspector ...'

The doorbell rang and Maggie hurried out to answer it. If she hadn't, Wesley suspected he would have been shamed into making a donation. Gerry Heffernan finished his cake and stood up, shamelessly scattering crumbs onto the plain beige carpet.

'My wife makes a good cake,' Jim Flowers said pointedly as he made his way into the hall and picked up a dark grey anorak from the coatstand. The two policemen followed him.

'By the way, Mr Flowers,' said Heffernan. 'I can't quite place your accent. Australian, is it?'

Flowers shuffled his feet awkwardly. 'New Zealand, actually.'

'How long have you been over here?'

'About fifteen years now.'

'I believe it's nice, New Zealand.'

Flowers nodded and looked at his watch.

'We'll leave you to it, then, sir.'

Wesley noted the relief on Jim Flowers' face as they moved towards the front door. But their exit was blocked by Maggie Flowers, who stood with her back to them talking to a tall, middle-aged man with a shock of white

192

hair. Wesley was certain that he'd seen the man somewhere before, then he remembered. It was Jeremy Sedley, the actor who had so impressed Rachel on their drive through the village.

Maggie and Sedley stood aside to allow the policemen to pass, their expressions neutrally pleasant, giving nothing away. Jim Flowers, Wesley noticed, was still in the hallway, hovering, hesitating. Perhaps waiting for them to leave.

They walked to the car in silence, Wesley craning his neck to see into the field. Neil still wasn't there.

'What do you think?' Heffernan asked bluntly. 'Do you forget your old phone number that quickly?'

'Some people might,' said Wesley, turning the key in the ignition. 'But I thought they were definitely hiding something.'

'Then we'll just have to dig it out of them,' Gerry Heffernan replied, stretching out his legs. 'That bloke who called – his face looked familiar.'

'It was Jeremy Sedley, the actor. He's been in a lot of things on television.'

'That explains it. Seems the Flowers like to have friends in high places.' He sighed and patted his abdomen. 'All that cake's given me an appetite. Fancy an early lunch at the Red Bull?'

Wesley nodded. Perhaps he'd think better on a full stomach.

Wesley finished his frugal tuna sandwich, the cheapest thing on the Red Bull's lunch-time menu. Gerry Heffernan had consumed a fat sausage and an enormous quantity of chips. Not the best thing for a middle-aged man with a tendency to overweight – but then in all the time Wesley had known him Heffernan never had eaten healthily.

Perhaps he ought to suggest to the boss that he should go on a diet. But how could he say anything without sounding nanny like, and health obsessed? Perhaps women could

have a tactful word with each other about such things ...
but men were different creatures altogether. It was a pity,
he thought, that Gerry and Mrs Green hadn't become closer
in the time they'd known each other, or that Rosemary
Heffernan, away studying music in Manchester, couldn't
keep a better eye on her father. It was terrible that Kathy
Heffernan had died so young. Tragic.

Perhaps he'd mention the problem in passing to Pam to
see whether she had any tactful suggestions.

Heffernan's mobile phone rang and he answered it while
chewing a mouthful of the syrup sponge he'd ordered for
pudding. Wesley had done without.

'That was Tom. He wants us round at Hoxworthy's Farm
now. He says he's found something interesting on Lewis's
computer.'

Wesley waited while the syrup sponge was consumed
with an enthusiasm he considered a little unseemly in the
circumstances. Missing youngsters usually had the opposite
effect on Wesley's appetite. When they left the comfort of
the Red Bull there was a fine drizzle in the air again, the
kind that soaks by stealth, so they drove the three hundred
yards to Hoxworthy's Farm and emerged dry at the other
end.

Jill Hoxworthy opened the front door to them. Her face
was drawn, almost grey, and the flesh around her eyes was
puffy and reddened. She had been crying. Wesley had
thought her a good-looking woman when he had first seen
her, but now grief and worry had robbed her of her looks.

She stood aside to allow them to pass and mumbled
something about Tom being upstairs in Lewis's room.
Wesley looked around the hallway. There was no sign of
Terry Hoxworthy. But then a farmer's work, like a
woman's, is never done.

Tom was waiting for them, sitting on the typing chair
which he twisted from side to side with restless energy. His
bright young face, which still bore the faint scars of adoles-
cent acne, was alight with the triumph of discovery as he

gazed upon Lewis Hoxworthy's computer.

'I've managed to retrieve all his e-mails. I've printed them out for you.' He handed Wesley a sheaf of A4 paper and waited.

Wesley read in silence, then passed the sheets to Gerry Heffernan. 'Looks like we've got him. He arranged to meet an H. Lancaster aboard his boat, the *Henry of Lancaster*, the day he disappeared. That's Hal Lancaster. Jonny Shellmer's ex-manager. It's a connection.'

'Right, Wes, we'll have him brought in, never mind waiting until he turns up in Tradmouth again. I want him and I want him now.'

Wesley reread the e-mails, flicking through the boastful ones meant for teenage friends, the ones which made Lewis Hoxworthy sound as if he possessed a glamour and confidence that were far from reality. Some poor girl in the States was under the illusion that Lewis drove a Porsche and ran his own software business. Wesley smiled – at least the boy had had his dreams.

But it was the correspondence with H. Lancaster that interested them. The rest of the stuff seemed irrelevant. Lewis had advertised what he described as 'rare old letters' on the Internet and he had had a reply from a H. Lancaster asking for details. Lewis had replied that there were thirteen of them, they seemed to be extremely old and they mentioned the Wars of the Roses. He said he'd found them in an old box in a barn which someone had told his dad was medieval, and he reckoned the letters were medieval too. Lewis's literary style was rambling and immature. English probably wasn't his best subject.

'Hal Lancaster's housekeeper said he was a collector and we didn't think it was important at the time,' said Wesley. 'If it's old manuscripts he collects . . .'

'Look at this one,' Heffernan said, pointing to the last e-mail from Lancaster. 'He arranged to meet Lewis at the time he disappeared. He told him to come to his boat at the exact time Lewis said he was going to Yossa's.

He even sailed up from Tradmouth to Derenham to meet him.'

'It's not far,' Tom chipped in. Heffernan gave him a withering look. Computer experts should know their place. Tom fell silent again and pressed some keys.

'Do you still think Lewis's disappearance is linked to Shellmer's death?' Wesley asked.

'Well, Lewis had the gun. And if the theory about the paedophile ring stands up ...' He didn't finish the sentence.

'If it is a paedophile ring, it's likely they've done something like this before,' Wesley said, deep in thought. 'We should ask about Alec Treadly's associates, if he had any, and find out if he knew the others.' He looked at Lewis's computer. 'Mind you, with these things it's easy to make contact with like-minded people you may never have met before. Maybe Lewis was the first lad they've managed to lure away like this.'

Heffernan shuddered. 'Well, at least we know who to look for now,' he said quietly. 'If Lancaster tries to moor that floating Rolls-Royce of his in any harbour in Britain, I want to know about it. And we can get on to the French authorities and all.'

'Let's hope he makes life easy for us and comes back to Tradmouth like he said,' mumbled Wesley. 'We could do with some luck on this case.'

'You can say that again.'

Gerry Heffernan swept out of the room and Wesley looked at his watch. It was going to be a long day.

The Derenham Doom, as it was beginning to be called in museum circles, had been moved from the barn and now stood propped against the wall in the north aisle of All Saints church. A great wooden semicircle, it had once fitted into the arch above the rood screen, where the congregation couldn't have avoided its horrors.

But it held no terror for Neil Watson. He didn't believe

in such things as hellfire and the torment of the damned. He stood there staring at it, a curiosity, a relic of more colourful and desperate times perhaps. He had once seen a Doom in a church at Wenhaston in Suffolk which was of a similar size and subject matter. But the artist who had created Derenham's Doom had far outstripped his Suffolk contemporary. The suffering of the damned in Derenham's version was real, vivid; their faces contorted in agony. Whoever had painted this thing so long ago in a small Devon village had possessed a formidable talent.

'Death, judgement, heaven and hell. The four last things.'

The resonant voice, rather like the voice of the Almighty Himself, made Neil jump. He swung round to see a middle-aged man standing behind him, tall and tanned with a shock of white hair. He was staring at the Doom, mesmerised by its writhing images.

'If you want to know more about that thing,' the man began, as though making conversation, 'we're having a history evening here next Saturday. We've arranged music and drama and . . .'

'Yes, I know. I'm planning to be there.' Neil thought it was time he presented his credentials. 'I'm Neil Watson from the County Archaeological Unit and I'm in charge of the excavation down the road.'

The man looked faintly embarrassed at having taken Neil for a member of the public. He held out his hand. 'Pleased to meet you. I'm Jeremy Sedley. I've been reading up on the history of Derenham church – cribbing from the guide-book if the truth be known.' He looked down at the floor modestly. 'I'm speaking at the history evening. We all have to do our bit for the community, don't we. Are you taking part?'

'Maggie Flowers has asked me to say something about the dig.'

'Maggie's a hard woman to say no to.'

Neil grinned. 'You could say that.'

'Tell me about your dig. Have you found anything exciting? It must be wonderful to dig up all those treasures – I'm really quite envious.'

'It's not all Tutankhamun's tomb, you know,' said Neil, anxious to put the actor right. 'We've found the remains of an old manor house that we think belonged to a family called Merrivale in the fifteenth century. In fact I'm reading some letters written by them at the moment.'

'What do they say?'

'They're quite interesting – all about the mum trying to get the kids married off and having a problem stepson. There's a bit about the Battle of Tewkesbury as well – reading an account written by a man who was there brings it to life.'

Sedley nodded, seemingly fascinated. It never occurred to Neil that the man might be using his well-honed acting ability to feign interest. 'What about that skeleton you dug up? Any clues?'

Neil shook his head, disappointed that he couldn't answer. He was only halfway through the book and he had, as yet, found nothing to help him solve the mystery of his skeleton's gruesome death. 'Do you know much about the Merrivales?' he asked hopefully. 'I presume they had connections with this church.'

'There are some early brasses marking Merrivale tombs in the chancel and the guidebook says that some of them are buried in the family chapel over there.' Sedley pointed to a small chapel at the end of the aisle, partitioned off from the rest of the church by a richly carved oak screen.

Neil strolled over to the Merrivales' chapel and entered through the narrow doorway. A small altar stood at the east end, decorated with a vase of dying flowers. There was an aura of dust and death in the chapel, and somehow the dying flowers looked right. It wouldn't be the place for fresh, vibrant blooms.

In the centre of the chapel stood a large tomb chest upon which lay an alabaster effigy of a knight in armour beside a lady who was, presumably, his wife. They lay side by side as though resting on a great double bed, their hands pointing to heaven in a pious attitude of prayer.

'Rather magnificent, isn't it,' whispered Jeremy Sedley, who had followed him in. 'Richard and Marjory Merrivale.'

Neil recognised the names – the authors of the Merrivale letters. He stared at their effigies, studying the carved faces.

Sedley stood and watched while Neil circled the monument. Neil ran his fingers lightly over the lettering around the edge of the tomb. He translated from the Latin in his head. 'Pray for the souls of Richard and Marjory Merrivale and of their children.' All pretty standard stuff, he thought – until he saw the words beneath. 'And may the soul of the wicked one be cursed to everlasting damnation.'

He took a step back. 'Strange inscription,' he said, turning to Sedley, who was watching him intently, as though waiting for him to make a dramatic discovery.

'Yes. I read about it in the guidebook. Odd.'

'Who's the wicked one, then?'

'I don't think anybody knows. Have you seen the effigies on the other side? I presume they're the children. I take it they're buried here too.'

Neil walked slowly to the other side of the tomb, not taking his eyes off the carved alabaster couple who were staring serenely at the ceiling. Set into the body of the tomb on the north side were three niches. Neil had seen tombs like this before where figures of dutiful children knelt in line in order of age, all in attitudes of prayer, interceding for the immortal souls of their dead parents. He had always found them rather amusing – the pious, mealy-mouthed offspring who probably hated each other and gave their mum and dad a terrible time in life, posed stiffly on their tomb, looking as though butter wouldn't melt in their mouths and all dressed up in their Sunday best, in the medieval answer to a family snapshot.

The first two figures were conventional enough. A young man and a young woman, richly dressed, kneeling in devotion. But he wasn't prepared for the contents of the third niche. The third figure wasn't kneeling. It was writhing in agony, engulfed by what appeared to be flames – and it was headless. Neil took a step back and stared at it.

'Strange, isn't it,' said Jeremy Sedley conversationally.

Neil thought for a moment. 'I wonder if this Richard Merrivale guy made a will. It might mention something about . . .'

'I've really no idea,' Sedley said quickly.

'We found a skeleton buried near the Merrivales' manor house. It belonged to a young man who had been decapitated.'

'Well, there you are, then,' said Sedley. 'There's your explanation.'

'It still doesn't tell us why he was buried there and not in the church with the rest of his family. Unless he was the wicked one who was to be cursed to whatever it was.'

Sedley looked around the chapel as though seeing it for the first time. 'The guidebook says that there are no Merrivale tombs in this church later than this one.'

'None whatsoever?'

'It was as if the family ceased to exist.'

'If the kids had died before Richard and Marjory then there might have been no heirs. But their manor house was destroyed about that time as well. Funny.'

Sedley said nothing. He turned and walked out of the Merrivale chapel, leaving Neil staring at the fiery headless figure on the side of the tomb. He noticed some tiny letters painted in the bottom right-hand corner of the niche but he couldn't make them out, even when he squatted down and looked closely. The medieval paint had faded over the centuries: unlike the Doom the job had probably been done with cheap paint, he thought as he tried to make out the words in the dim light that filtered through a stained-glass window.

He could just make out a couple of the letters. T . . . Am. But the rest were indecipherable. He straightened himself up and marched quickly from the chapel, feeling a strong urge to get out of that place of death. The Merrivale chapel gave him the creeps.

*

It was a matter of waiting patiently for Hal Lancaster to turn up. But patience had never been Gerry Heffernan's strongest virtue.

Paul Heygarth was sticking to his story that he left Jonny Shellmer looking around the Old Vicarage on Wednesday afternoon, returning the next day to find him dead and then proceeding to cover up the fact that murder had been committed in such a lucrative property. The police had got no more out of him so they had no alternative but to release him – much to Gerry Heffernan's displeasure. He was sure of Heygarth's guilt.

He was restless, pacing up and down the CID office like a caged animal. Wesley felt it would be best if he was distracted, but he couldn't quite decide how to do it.

Rachel Tracey sat at her desk, working with quiet efficiency, talking on the telephone, calling up information on her computer. Wesley watched her, half admiring, half concerned. He suspected that she was burying herself in her work, trying to forget the events of six months ago which had left such deep emotional scars. Not that Rachel would admit that anything was wrong: she kept up an impressive façade. But Wesley knew the truth ... and he didn't know what to do about it.

She saw him watching her and smiled shyly. Steve Carstairs, at the next desk, noticed and smirked knowingly before bowing his head over a mountain of statement forms. Wesley looked away. This was how gossip began, and Steve wouldn't be averse to causing a bit of trouble.

Rachel stood up and walked over to Wesley's desk. She glanced warily at Steve before perching herself on the edge. He didn't look up.

'I've been on to Kent police about Alec Treadly and his known associates,' she began. Her voice was impersonal, professional. 'They reckon that Treadly was a loner. He didn't tend to associate with other paedophiles, at least not to their knowledge. But he might have branched out, of course.'

Wesley sensed there was more. 'Go on.'

'His cottage has been searched thoroughly ... much to Ma Treadly's annoyance. She didn't half give the officers a hard time.' She grinned. 'Nothing was found and there's certainly no computer on the premises, so if someone was surfing the Net looking for likely victims, it wasn't Alec Treadly. There was no computer in Jonny Shellmer's cottage either.'

'It doesn't mean he didn't contact them in other ways.'

'Treadly denies knowing Paul Heygarth, Jonny Shellmer or Hal Lancaster. And Paul Heygarth swears he's never heard of Alec Treadly.'

'Do you believe them?'

Rachel thought for a moment. 'I don't want to but ... yes, I do. And I've drawn a blank on any organised paedophile activity in the area. Nobody's heard a whisper.'

'So either they're good at covering their tracks or ...'

'Or Hal Lancaster's acting alone.'

'Or perhaps Lewis's disappearance has got nothing to do with paedophiles after all.' Wesley looked at his watch. Three-thirty. He felt he needed something that would set his thoughts on the right track.

When Steve Carstairs announced to the office that the chief inspector had ordered him to visit Shellmer's place and bring back any personal papers he could find, Wesley said he'd go with him. He didn't pretend to enjoy Steve's company but he wanted to pay another visit to the picture-postcard cottage that had been Shellmer's last home.

Steve was silent for the first part of the journey, which was much as Wesley had expected. So he was rather surprised when Steve began a conversation.

'What do you make of all this, sir? Do you think it's got something to do with perverts or what?' He sounded worried, as if the case was preying on his mind.

Wesley looked at him. This wasn't like Steve at all.

'I wish I knew,' he replied. 'I'd like to find out if Shellmer had any connection with this area.'

'There's nothing about Devon in his authorised biography,' said Steve with authority. 'I was reading it last night. My girlfriend lent it to me.'

A girlfriend. This was news Wesley hadn't heard. No wonder he seemed to have mellowed.

'It says he lived in Liverpool,' Steve continued, 'and he used to take his holidays in North Wales, but it never mentions Devon. I can bring it into the office tomorrow if you like,' he offered. There was an eagerness in his voice Wesley had rarely heard before. Things were looking up.

'Thanks, that might be useful,' Wesley said as they drew up outside Warwick Cottage. A biography was hardly evidence, but it might tell them something new about the dead man. And Steven's new-found enthusiasm was something to be encouraged.

'Is Sherry Smyth still here?' said Steve with a detectable leer.

'No. She went back to London yesterday.'

'She's fit. I wouldn't kick her out of bed, eh?'

Wesley suppressed a smile. The old Steve was back. They let themselves into the cottage with the key Heffernan had kept in his possession, watched by the two women next door, who stood at their window and gave a tentative wave when they knew they had been spotted. Wesley raised his hand in acknowledgement.

'Pair of old dykes them two – you can tell,' Steve commented knowingly as they stepped over the threshold.

Wesley didn't answer. Perhaps hopes of a new, reconstructed, caring, sharing Steve Carstairs were pie in the sky after all.

'Have a look around,' he said quietly. 'See what you can find.'

Steve began his search while Wesley went upstairs, in pursuit of inspiration. There was something he had seen upstairs, something that might be important. He entered the bedroom, remembering that Sherry Smyth had been in residence since his last visit. But she had left little trace of her presence behind. A pair of laddered tights and a few used tissues stained with make-up discarded in the wicker waste basket were the only indications that she had ever been there.

Wesley began to search through the drawers again, idly pushing underwear and clothes around, looking for anything hidden that he might have missed last time. But there was nothing. He picked up the card with the angel on the front – Angela Simms had stocked similar cards in her shop. The more he thought about it, the more he was convinced that the 'Angel' who had sent it was Angela herself.

Then he saw the photograph nestling in a cocoon of socks in the top drawer. He pulled it out and sat down on the bed, staring at it. He had only given it a cursory glance the last time he had visited the cottage but now he studied it carefully. There were four children, three boys and a girl. Wesley couldn't decide whether there was any resemblance between them, and he stared hard at their faces, searching for telltale signs of some genetic relationship. But the snap was small and unclear, as though it had been taken with a cheap camera some distance away from its subjects. After a while he thought he could detect a likeness around the eyes – but, he told himself, it could have been his imagination.

Sherry Smyth hadn't known whether Jonny Shellmer had had any brothers or sisters – it was something he never talked about. He had told her there was someone down in Devon he wanted her to meet – but that could have been anyone, Wesley thought, frustrated at his lack of progress, his inability to penetrate the mystery of Jonny Shellmer's last hours.

He kept staring at the photograph, willing it to give up its secret. Four young people sitting on the waterfront at Derenham on a hot summer day.

To the left of the group stood a tall, thin boy with dark hair who glared arrogantly at the camera. Next to him was a girl with huge dark eyes and curly dark hair. Then a

204

chubby boy who looked about fifteen. And to the right, slightly apart from the rest, was a boy in his late teens, more a man than a child. The dark-haired boy stood close to the girl, their arms touching. Brother and sister or just friends? Wesley couldn't tell. But he was almost certain that the dark-haired boy was Jonny Shellmer.

He put the photograph in an evidence bag. He would take it back to the station and show it to Gerry Heffernan. It was always worth getting a second opinion.

He was about to leave the bedroom when Steve appeared in the doorway. He held some papers that looked ominously like bills of some kind, the sort of post that arrives, unwelcome, on most doormats with monotonous regularity.

'I've found a piece of paper pushed under the phone. It's got a number on it. I'll check it out when we get back to the station.'

They drove back to Tradmouth. Wesley attempted to strike up a conversation, asking Steve what else he'd learned about Shellmer's early life from his authorised biography. But Steve hadn't progressed much further. All he knew was Shellmer's parents had broken up and Jonny had stayed with his mother in Liverpool.

Wesley asked if there was any mention of what had happened to Shellmer's father. But Steve shook his head: any painful or embarrassing facts had been glossed over. Not much dirty linen had been washed in *Jonny Shellmer – Rock Boat Legend*, published by Tring and Jarman, price £12.99, Steve told him with some regret.

Neil Watson pushed open the glass doors of Tradmouth library, strode towards the counter and asked whether Anne was about. A severe-looking woman in an inappropriately floral dress told him that Anne was in the back looking for something, and instructed Neil to wait. A queue of elderly ladies was building up behind him, all clutching thin romantic volumes to their tweed-clad chests. Neil shifted from foot to foot, hoping Anne wouldn't be long: he was already on the receiving end of some very dirty looks.

A few minutes later Anne emerged from a doorway marked 'staff only'. He took the book out of his coat pocket. It was not much thicker than the old ladies' romantic novels – but it lacked the regulation sensually enticing cover.

Anne approached him, smiling, and he held the book out. 'Here it is. I've brought it back.'

She took it from him and began to flick through the yellowed pages. 'Have you read it?'

He looked sheepish. 'Yes. It didn't take long. There are only eleven letters and the rest of the book's just some old Victorian vicar waffling on about the Wars of the Roses. There are one or two mentions of the house in the letters, and the bits about Richard being injured in the battle and getting mugged are interesting.'

Anne turned the book over in her hands. 'Do you want to keep it out a bit longer?'

'Yeah. If that's okay.'

'No problem,' she said with a shy smile. 'Have you found out the date of that history evening yet?'

'It's next Saturday. I'm doing a talk about the dig and Jeremy Sedley's taking part. Have you heard of him? He's an actor – been on the telly.'

Anne nodded, wishing he'd get to the point.

'Come along if you like. It should be good.'

He was about to turn and leave, but he hesitated. 'Er, thanks, Anne.' He looked down at his shoes, still muddy from the dig. 'Look, er ... if you're free one night why don't you come down to the Tradmouth Arms. We're down there most nights.'

Anne took a depth breath. Pam had warned her about Neil's vagueness. She had no intention of getting a babysitter and venturing into the pub on her own just on the off-chance that he'd be there.

She reached over to the counter and picked up a pen and a piece of paper. 'I'll give you my number. You can ring me when you're planning to be there. Okay?'

Neil took the paper and stuffed it into his pocket. Then he raised a hand in farewell and left.

Anne took her place behind the counter and an elderly lady handed her a book that bore a picture of two unrealistically attractive people in a passionate clinch below the words 'A Foolish Attraction'.

She smiled as she stamped it and handed it back. Probably an omen, she thought.

Steve Carstairs studied the list of numbers called from Jonny Shellmer's telephone. Angela Simms's Neston number featured several times. Perhaps Sherry Smyth had had a rival. But having seen both women, he couldn't imagine it somehow.

He placed the piece of paper he had found by Shellmer's phone on the desk in front of him and checked it against the list. Shellmer had called the number on the Wednesday morning; the day of his death.

Steve dialled and, after a brief conversation, replaced the receiver and scowled before walking slowly over to Wesley's desk.

Keeping the number of a provincial public library by the telephone was hardly the behaviour one would expect of a bad boy of rock.

Chapter Ten

Right reverend and worshipful mother,
We were on the road for Tradmouth on Monday last
when five or so persons, lying in wait on the highway,
did set upon us and rob us. Whereupon, knowing the
great power of the evil-doers and for fear of death, I fell
upon my knees before them and cried them mercy on my
father who is still weak of his wounds gained in battle. At
that they mocked us and beat me and robbed us of all we
possessed. It is said there is no country in the world
where there are so many thieves and robbers as in
England. A priest found us and took us to the magistrate
who took pity on us and clothed us and gave us shelter,
for the robbers had beaten me sorely. We set off for home
as soon as my father is strong enough to travel.

I beg you, good mother, to discover if my brother,
John, was abroad that night, for I am certain that he was
among them who robbed us, though they hid their faces. I
pray I am mistaken for my father's sake.
Convey my greetings to my sweet sister, Elizabeth.
Your loving son, Edmund

Written at Master Ralph Browne's house near Exeter
this twenty-eighth day of May 1471

When Wesley arrived home at a reasonable hour, Pam

suggested that he make the supper. He put some chips in the oven and began to prepare an omelette. It was about time he did something, he thought to himself, especially as he was deserting the nest the next day to travel up to Liverpool. And Pam still looked tired. If his waking thoughts hadn't been filled with Lewis Hoxworthy and the Shellmer case, he might have been worried about her health.

Gerry Heffernan, excited at the prospect of returning to his roots for a day or so, had made generous offers to guide Wesley around the city's attractions. Wesley hadn't the heart to tell him that he just wanted to get back to Devon as soon as possible.

On the way up the M5, they were to call on Chris Pauling, Rock Boat's former drummer, who had hit hard times in Gloucestershire. Steve had telephoned him and he was expecting them. Steve said he'd sounded friendly on the phone, but then commented cynically that he supposed it was to put them off the scent – nobody looked forward to a visit from the police. But the absence of a warm welcome had never put Tradmouth CID off before.

Wesley had found Steve's other bit of news that after-noon – the fact that Jonny Shellmer had telephoned Tradmouth library on the morning of his death – rather puzzling. The library had been contacted and nobody had remembered talking to him. But if it had been a general anonymous enquiry, that was to be expected. They had checked and confirmed that Jonny Shellmer did not hold a library ticket. But he might have been planning to take books out and had rung up to enquire about the procedure and the opening hours. Steve's discovery might mean some-thing – but, on the other hand, it might mean absolutely nothing.

When the meal was finished Wesley thought to himself modestly that his cooking skills were showing a slight but noticeable improvement. But Pam made no comment as she cleared the dishes away. You can't win 'em all, thought

Wesley philosophically as he got up to answer the front door.

Neil stood on the front step and grunted a greeting before walking in. Pam had just disappeared upstairs to bath Michael. Wesley could hear her singing to him – 'Frère Jacques' again; the child would be speaking French by the time he was five, thought the proud father. Wesley led Neil into a living room strewn with brightly coloured plastic toys.

'What brings you here?' he asked, suddenly feeling weary, hardly in the mood for socialising.

'I've been reading the Merrivale letters,' Neil announced, sitting himself down on the sofa.

'Interesting?'

'Mmm. The father, Richard Merrivale, has a son, John, by his first wife who's a bit of a lad and gets involved in all sorts. They try to get him married off to calm him down. Then Richard and his younger son, Edmund, go away to fight in the Wars of the Roses and the mum, Marjory, is left trying to find a wife for her wicked stepson, John, and a husband for her own daughter Elizabeth. You can imagine this poor woman tearing her hair out and desperate to get the kids off her hands.' He handed Wesley the book. 'The best bit is where Richard and Edmund, the younger son, are mugged on the way back from fighting in the Battle of Tewkesbury and the boy suspects that his stepbrother was one of the muggers.'

'Any clue to the headless skeleton's identity?'

Neil shrugged. 'Not really. I'm presuming the Merrivales who wrote the letters are the same ones who owned the place I'm digging up – they mention their manor house at Derenham but there's nothing about any beheadings or fires.' He gave a swift résumé of his visit to the Merrivale chapel and his discovery of the strange burning image on the tomb of Richard and Marjory – the pair who, he had discovered, featured so prominently in the letters. 'There is a brief mention of the Merrivale chapel in All

Saints church but that's about all,' he added with some regret.

'Nothing about the Doom, then?'

'Not a sausage. Talking of sausages, have you had your dinner?' Neil leaned forward hungrily. 'I'm starving.'

'We've already eaten.' In more leisured times, Wesley would have offered his friend some sustenance. But he was tired. And he had the long drive up North in the morning. 'The Tradmouth Arms do very good bar meals,' he said, hoping Neil would take the hint.

Neil stood up. 'Fancy a pint, then?'

There was a wailing sound from upstairs. Michael had been taken out of the bath he so enjoyed. 'Better not. Long day tomorrow.'

'I'm off to Exeter as soon as I can get away from the dig to see what else I can find about the Merrivales,' Neil said, making for the door. 'Sure you won't join me for a pint?'

Wesley shook his head. As Neil disappeared down the drive he found himself yawning. He turned and saw that Pam was standing at the bottom of the stairs watching him.

'Something wrong?' she asked gently.

He closed the front door and took his wife in his arms. 'It's this case,' he said, kissing the top of her head absent-mindedly. 'It's not certain but there's a chance that the missing lad was abducted. He'd arranged to meet a man he'd been in touch with on the Internet. I don't know if I'm getting soft but it makes me feel . . .'

'I know.' She gave his hand a sympathetic squeeze.

He nodded, glad that she understood. 'I've got a feeling we're not going to find that poor boy alive.'

Pam put her arms around him and they clung together until the sound of the baby's urgent cries wafted down the stairs.

Gerry Heffernan had begged a lift to All Saints church, Derenham, from one of his fellow choir members. An extra rehearsal for the history evening had been called for that

211

night. And Heffernan was only too glad to get out of his empty house, where he knew he would brood about Heygarth's release. It was better to be with people.

All Saints church was packed, and he meandered up towards the choirstalls, pushing past the assembled actors on the chancel steps. He mumbled a swift apology as he trod on the trailing hem of a woman's medieval gown and pressed on to where his fellow choir members were sorting through their music. He saw Nicola Tarnley sitting at the end of a group of large sopranos, her head bowed over a sheet of paper, and he felt a sudden desire to speak to her – but now wasn't the time.

As the choirmaster hadn't arrived, Heffernan wandered off down the church again. He didn't know much about the history of All Saints, but no doubt he would soon be enlightened by the motley throng of amateur actors who were milling about in costumes from various centuries. He recognised Maggie and Jim Flowers, who were dressed in rich medieval garb, their demeanour and hairstyles, however, proclaiming them to be firmly rooted in the present day. He was about to greet them but they looked away. Perhaps the prospect of socialising with a policeman who had called at their house to question them didn't appeal. Or perhaps they had something to hide.

He was about to wander back to the choirstalls when the lights in the side aisles flashed on and he saw the Doom, illuminated in all its lurid horror. Heaven and hell; vengeance and punishment. He stopped in his tracks and stared: it wasn't a thing that could be easily ignored. He hurried back up to the chancel. Five minutes later the first dress rehearsal began.

Heffernan recognised the man who took his place at the great brass eagle lectern. He had seen him at Jim and Maggie Flowers' house and in many other guises on his TV screen. The man introduced himself as Jeremy Sedley, actor and presenter of the church history evening, and Heffernan thought that it had been quite a coup for Maggie

Flowers to persuade him to undertake the task. His visit to the Flowers' had probably been about the rehearsal. But something made him uneasy.

Sedley gave a series of succinct talks, scripted by Maggie and enlivened by his masterful presentation, which were then illustrated by brief dramas featuring the main players in the church's past. Heffernan watched as a Saxon monk, a Norman baron and a collection of plague-ridden fourteenth-century peasants did their stuff, and after each section the choir sang something appropriate to the period being illustrated: plainchant and a couple of jolly medieval carols for starters.

Things hotted up a little when Sedley mentioned the Doom that had recently been discovered in a nearby barn and which was bound, by the laws of probability, to have belonged to Derenham church. A spotlight was trained on the object in question as he described it in salacious detail. He said that as the Merrivale family were lords of the manor around the time the Doom was painted, they were probably responsible for its creation. Then he took a step back, a smile playing on his lips.

Heffernan watched as Jim and Maggie Flowers did their bit, forgetting their lines at a crucial moment. They were Richard and Marjory Merrivale, who had endowed the chantry chapel where they were later to be buried. They were portrayed reading out some letters they had written to each other when he was away at some battle or other. At that point Gerry Heffernan's mind began to wander.

It seemed an age before they reached the modern day via the Civil War and an assortment of vicars, several involved in the smuggling trade, and the evening was rounded off by a vacuous modern hymn which lacked the melodious liveliness of its historical counterparts. When the whole thing was over, his mind strayed to more immediate matters. He had to talk to Nicola Tarnley.

His chance came when they were preparing to leave. He saw she was alone and moved swiftly over to the opposite choirstall, where she was taking her car keys from her bag.

'It went okay,' he commented as casually as he could, thinking that some small talk might be needed.

Nicola turned round. She looked tired, as though she hadn't slept for several nights. 'Yes. Not too bad.'

'Yeah. Let's hope some of those amateur actors have bucked their ideas up by Saturday. But that Jeremy Sedley's a marvel; the way he ...'

'Look, er, Chief Inspector. I've not heard anything from the police for a while and I was wondering if I was going to be charged ... about moving the body, I mean. It's been worrying me and ...' She gabbled the words out quickly. The prospect of further police involvement and the acquisition of a criminal record had obviously been giving her sleepless nights.

Heffernan tried to assume a reassuring expression. 'It's not really you we're interested in, love. Are you still working for Paul Heygarth?'

Nicola looked at him and shook her head. 'No. I've left Heygarth and Proudfoot. I didn't want anything more to do with him after ...'

He took her arm and gently shepherded her away from a pair of staring altos who were obviously suspecting that his intentions weren't honourable.

'Look, Nicola, it's important that I – we – know if there's any dirt on Heygarth. I mean, do you know anything about him that might help us nail him? You were close to him. Do you know if he was interested in ...' He hesitated. He had rehearsed this speech so many times in his head but the reality of saying it was quite different. 'In young boys, for instance.' He saw that Nicola was shaking her head.

'Young girls maybe, but I don't think boys are his thing, if you see what I mean.'

'Young girls? How young?' Perhaps he had struck lucky after all.

The truth dawned on Nicola. 'Old enough. He's not

some kind of pervert, if that's what you're thinking. He's nasty but he's not that nasty.'

Gerry Heffernan felt a little disappointed. That was one possibility disposed of. 'Is there anything you know about him that the vicar wouldn't approve of, then?' he asked lightly to put her at her ease.

Nicola gave a weak smile. 'Plenty, I should think. But mainly shady business dealing. Amoral maybe, but not strictly illegal.' She looked him in the eye. 'You still think he killed that pop star, don't you? I'm hardly Paul Heygarth's greatest fan but I'm certain he's innocent: I'm sure he just wanted the body out of the way. That's how he thinks – if anything gets in the way of him making a few quid, he removes it. And he's been even worse since his ex-wife has got her claws into his assets.'

Gerry Heffernan was about to make a risqué quip but he thought better of it. He produced a battered business card from his jacket pocket. 'Look, love, if you remember anything that might help us, anything at all, give us a ring, eh?'

'You really want to get him for something don't you?'

Heffernan didn't answer.

He looked round and saw that Jim Flowers was heading their way, his eyes on Nicola. Then he remembered that Flowers and Nicola were – or had been – colleagues, and it was obvious from Flowers' expression that he wanted to speak to Nicola in private. Heffernan decided to make a strategic retreat.

Jill Hoxworthy stared at the grainy black-and-white image on the inside page of the *Tradmouth Echo*.

She turned to her husband. 'Are you going to tell the police?'

'Leave it, Jill. Don't you think we've got enough on our plates with Lewis?'

'It says the police are looking for anyone who knows Angela Simms. And you know her, don't you, Terry?' She emphasised the word 'know'.

Terry winced and turned away. 'How many times have I got to tell you . . .?'

'You'd rather go and see her than stay with your own wife when . . .'

'Shut up,' he snapped. 'You don't know what you're talking about.'

'And where were you on Saturday when they say she was attacked? And where were you when that pop singer was shot?' An edge of hysteria had crept into her voice. 'Answer me, Terry. Where were you?'

Terry Hoxworthy rose from the settee stiffly and made for the door.

'Where are you going?'

'Out. Out for a drive. Anywhere.' He slammed the door behind him and Jill sat, perfectly still, staring into space.

She sat like that until Terry returned home two hours later.

The next morning Wesley and his boss made an early start. Five am. Wesley had left Pam asleep and tiptoed softly into Michael's room, just to watch him sleeping. He had touched the tiny hand and felt a sudden and overwhelming surge of love for the small, innocent human being in the cot. He could easily understand why a parent would kill to defend or avenge a child.

But was that what the killing of Jonny Shellmer was about? Was his death connected to Lewis Hoxworthy's disappearance? He had asked himself this question many times, and he hoped that the people they would question today, people who knew Jonny Shellmer of old, might provide the answer. He went over the case in his mind as he helped himself to a hurried bowl of cornflakes before driving down to the police station to pick up Gerry Heffernan. It was always Wesley's job to drive. Gerry never navigated on dry land.

The motorway up to Gloucestershire was mercifully free of traffic. The holiday season hadn't yet begun – when it did vehicles would be bumper to bumper most days and at a complete standstill on Saturdays. But today they sailed through to their first port of call, discussing the case on the way, each man offering speculation after speculation – but until Hal Lancaster was picked up and interviewed, they knew they would be going around in circles.

There was still no news of Rock Boat's former manager. European police forces had been alerted, but if he had scurried south to a small French or Spanish port he might be difficult to find. Neither voiced the fear that Lewis might not be with him – that the boy might already be dead, his body disposed of at sea.

When they came off the motorway Gerry Heffernan took charge of the map and navigated down the narrow country lanes. Wesley was becoming used to country driving, and these lanes were nothing like as fearsome as the narrow Devon tracks with their hedges that seemed as high as houses blocking the view either side. After fifteen minutes of driving they located Chris Pauling's place with ease.

On the gate hung a hand-painted sign which bore the name 'Windy Edge'. The countryside around was rolling and lush, and fat cream-coloured sheep grazed contentedly in the fields with their tiny white lambs by their sides. Even back in medieval times this was rich wool-producing country, prosperous and beautiful.

In contrast, 'Windy Edge' was a run-down cottage with a green flaking front door and grubby windows. A trio of scrawny hens clucked about in the yard, their beady eyes fixed firmly on the littered ground, and a thin goat, tethered to a drainpipe, showed little curiosity when the visitors emerged from the car.

'Not much of a place,' Gerry Heffernan commented under his breath.

Wesley didn't answer. He wanted to get the visit over with. There was no bell or functioning door knocker so he rapped on the wood with his knuckles. When there was no sound of movement in the cottage, he knocked again and waited. He knew they were expected.

Just as he was about to consult the chief inspector about their next move, a woman appeared around the far corner of the building. She was tall and slim with straight hair, blond peppered with grey, that swung down to her waist. Her face bore telltale signs of age, but she had weathered well and could have been anything between thirty-five and fifty-five. She saw them and smiled. When she smiled she was stunning.

'You'll be the coppers from Devon,' she began. Her voice was pleasant with a slight Essex twang. 'Chris won't be long. He's just seeing to the piglets.' She looked at them and smiled the dazzling smile again. 'Come along in, then. It's not much but it's home.' She spoke with a cheerfulness Wesley couldn't help but admire. There wouldn't be many stunningly beautiful women with the face and figure of a supermodel who would respond to such spartan living conditions with good cheer.

Wesley stepped forward and introduced himself and his boss. The woman said her name was Sandra and led them into the cottage. She walked ahead of them, her head held high and her hips swaying. Wesley and Heffernan followed, and were soon seated on an ancient moquette sofa with vicious springs, sipping tea from chipped mugs. The cottage was shabby but it was clean, and there was a vase of fresh spring flowers on the table.

Sandra sat with them and expressed what seemed like genuine sorrow at Jonny's death. She had known Jonny in the days of Rock Boat, she said. She and Chris had been together a long time, through thick and thin – mostly thin, she added without bitterness. She had been a model when they had met and had worked with all the top photographers of the day. It amazed Wesley that she didn't express resentment at her steep descent in wealth and lifestyle, and he found himself liking Sandra Pauling. He looked at Gerry Heffernan, who was sitting on the edge of his seat staring at her admiringly, and guessed that he shared his opinion of the woman.

Chris Pauling appeared fifteen minutes later, apologising and muttering about piglets. Sandra put a reassuring hand on his shoulder and disappeared into the tiny kitchen to fetch another cup of tea. He was a small, weather-beaten man with long, lank, greying hair which protruded beneath a threadbare woollen hat. He had the cheerful face of a slimmed-down garden gnome, and his manner was friendly but solemn as he expressed his shock about Jonny's death. He had the vestiges of a Liverpool accent, and soon he and Gerry Heffernan were comparing notes about what part of the city they came from and what schools they had attended. Chris Pauling chatted away openly with no sign that he had anything to hide.

Wesley and Heffernan hadn't expected such a warm welcome from the Paulings. But perhaps their isolation meant that they had few visitors. When Sandra had presented her husband with the tea she sat down again and leaned forward, listening intently.

'I can't believe it about Jonny, I really can't. I mean, who'd want to shoot him?'

'We were hoping you'd tell us,' said Heffernan bluntly.

Chris shook his head. 'We were a bit wild in the old days – all of us, me included.' He hesitated. 'Look, it's no secret. We downed a lot of booze, took a few illegal substances, got through a lot of women who were ready, willing and able. But we were young and the fame thing happened so quickly that it went to our heads. And we made a fortune – the others are still worth a packet. But me? I took some bad advice, made stupid investments, lost the lot.' He shrugged and gave Wesley a wide grin. 'But what the hell, it's only money. I've got my Sandra, a few animals to keep us going and a roof over my head. What more could a man ask for?'

'What indeed?' said Wesley. He had imagined that Chris Pauling would be full of bitterness about his straitened

219

circumstances and the reality – if it wasn't an act put on for their benefit – was unexpected. 'Tell us about Jonny,' he said. 'We know the version in the biography but what was he really like?'

'Jonny was an ordinary lad like the rest of us. He could play the guitar and sing, but apart from that ... Look, we were four lads up in Liverpool, living in the aftermath of the Beatles and the Merseybeat era. We were playing the clubs when this American manager saw us one night and signed us up. We couldn't believe our luck and the rest, as they say, is history.'

'The American manager, would that be Hal Lancaster?'

'Yeah. He's a good bloke, Hal. Always straight with us. He didn't rip us off like some you hear about.'

Wesley sat forward. 'Look, Mr Pauling, I won't beat about the bush. Did you ever have any inkling of either Jonny or Hal Lancaster having any ...' He felt the blood rush to his face as he searched for the most tactful way to put it. 'Did they have any unusual sexual tastes? Children, for instance?'

Chris Pauling stared at him for a few seconds with his mouth wide open. Then he turned to Sandra, who seemed equally amazed at the question. He shook his head. 'If you're asking me whether Jonny and Hal were child molesters, I can tell you categorically that they weren't – well, not to my knowledge anyway, and you get to know people pretty well when you're touring with them. Jonny was one for the girls, even when he was married with a kid. He always had a load of groupies around him.' He glanced at Sandra. 'As we all did before we settled down. But I can assure you that he wasn't into anything nasty. No way. The rest of us would have known. The same goes for Hal – he never went short of women. We lived so close in those days that I'm sure I'd have been aware of anything like that going on. Jonny had fourteen-year-old girls throwing themselves at him but he never took the bait – he always went for their big sisters, if you see what I mean ... even their mums sometimes.' He grinned.

'What about boys?' Wesley suggested. The question had to be asked.

Chris smiled and shook his head. 'No way. You think I wouldn't have known?'

Wesley and Heffernan looked at each other. That was it. Jonny Shellmer and Hal Lancaster were no paedophiles. In a way Wesley felt a tremendous relief. But on the other hand, it made the case more baffling.

'Had Jonny any enemies? Or any nutcases who used to follow him around? Can you think of anything, anything at all that might help us catch whoever did this?'

Chris Pauling shook his head again, looking genuinely regretful. 'Sorry. I always reckoned Jonny was a nice bloke underneath all the rock-star rubbish, and as far as I know, he didn't have any enemies. And as for nutcases, I can't think of any. There was the odd fan who went a bit over the top but . . .'

'Was there talk of Rock Boat getting together again?'

'Hal wanted us to do a reunion tour.' Pauling sighed. 'But I don't suppose it'll happen now Jonny's dead.' He looked around the shabby cottage. 'I could have done with it – a few quid to get this place on its feet.'

Wesley took Jonny's address book from his pocket. 'There were a couple of numbers in Jonny's address book we haven't traced yet. Did he know a Jim or Maggie Flowers?'

Pauling shrugged. 'They don't sound familiar.'

'What about Jack Cromer? Did he know him?'

Pauling grinned. 'Everyone knows that bastard. Jonny was on his show once.'

'But did he have any more contact with him?'

'Not that I know of. Sorry.'

'Where were you last Wednesday?' Heffernan asked bluntly.

Pauling looked at Sandra, who gave a slight nod. 'I went up to London.'

'Why?'

Pauling looked embarrassed. 'I went to see someone at an auction house. I thought they might be interested in selling my old drum kit and some other stuff I've got from the Rock Boat years. It's only cluttering up the outhouse.'

Sandra touched his arm. 'I didn't want Chris to sell his things but ...'

'They're no use to me now.' Chris Pauling smiled sadly.

Wesley looked down at his notebook. 'Has Jonny ever mentioned a woman called Angela?'

Pauling thought for a few moments. 'There were a lot of girls around in the old days. There might have been an Angela among them.'

Gerry Heffernan nudged Wesley's elbow. It was time to go. But there was one more question Wesley wanted to ask.

'Do you know if Jonny ever lived in Devon when he was young? Or did he ever mention spending his holidays there ... in a place called Derenham?'

Chris Pauling hesitated. 'I remember he had some connection with Devon ... or was it Dorset? I think he had some relatives there but he never talked about it. Before the group got going he used to go down to stay sometimes. Then one year, just before we hit the big time – he must have been about seventeen – he came back from a visit and he was acting a bit strange; quiet, like, subdued. He never talked about that holiday and as far as I know he never went there again. I reckoned he'd had some sort of row with someone, and when I asked him about his holiday he just told me to mind my own business. Funny, that ... it wasn't like Jonny at all.'

Wesley and Heffernan looked at each other. Wesley had always suspected that the answer lay somewhere close to home.

PC Wallace took his eyes off Nurse Chang for a moment and glanced at the newcomer, a big, awkward man in a shabby waxed jacket and flat cap who carried a bunch of flowers in front of him like a shield. He recognised him, and was surprised to see him there at the hospital, especially in view of the fact that his son was missing.

The man had a brief conversation with Nurse Chang, handed her the flowers and turned to go. When he had disappeared through the swing-doors, Wallace caught the nurse's eye and smiled.

'I know that man. What did he want?' he asked as casually as he could manage.

'I was just going to tell you. He wanted to see Angela Simms, but I told him it was relatives only.'

'Thanks,' Wallace said before asking whether he could use the phone in the sister's office.

As he neared the end of the M62 Wesley glanced at the man slumped in the passenger seat. There was a beatific smile on Gerry Heffernan's face that had appeared as soon as he saw the large sign welcoming him to Liverpool. The chief inspector had come home.

He directed Wesley straight to Liz Carty's – formerly Liz Shellmer – address: a large detached house with snowy-white pebbledashed walls and sparkling leaded windows, probably built in the early quarter of the twentieth century. It was near a set of magnificent park gates with proud liver birds strutting in their centres, flanked by a quartet of large statues representing the four seasons – a relic of Victorian municipal pride. Wesley, who had never visited Liverpool before, was pleasantly surprised.

'Nice area,' he commented, earning himself an approving look.

'I did a lot of my early courting in a rowing boat on Calderstones Park lake,' Heffernan announced as he unfastened his seat belt. 'Either there or in the back row of the Allerton Odeon down the road. Happy days, eh?'

Wesley said nothing, not wanting to trigger a stream of teenage reminiscences. He didn't think he could take it after such a long drive. He just wanted to be sitting on Liz Carty's sofa with a cup of tea in his hand.

He locked the car and marched up the path of Liz's budding and well-stocked front garden, noting the fine display of daffodils beneath the bay window. He lifted the polished brass lion's head on the shiny black front door. It landed with a resounding bang. Then he stepped back and waited, admiring the house. It was solid, boasting of prosperity without opulence or any overt show of wealth. Wesley approved. It was hardly what he'd expected of the ex-wife of a rock star. But then people often didn't conform to stereotypes.

Liz herself was no stereotypical ex-rock-chick. She was an attractive middle-aged woman who had taken care of herself. She wore a straight grey skirt and a floral blouse, and her hair was cut into a neat, sensible bob. Her clothes were good quality, expensive but not flash. The woman seemed to match her house. She invited them inside with impeccable good manners and offered them tea.

'Nice place this,' said Gerry Heffernan as he made himself comfortable on the sofa.

But before Wesley could reply Liz came back in with the tea and sat herself down in the armchair facing them.

'I still can't believe anyone would want to kill Jonny. I didn't hear about it until the police rang and said my address had been found in his address book and ...' She began to play with the thick gold band on her wedding finger.

'Didn't you hear about it on the news? It was on the telly. We were expecting you to get in touch with us,' said Gerry Heffernan bluntly.

Liz shook her head. 'We were away in Italy when it happened.' She gave a weak smile. 'Venice in the spring. Norman took me for our wedding anniversary. By the time we returned all the fuss had died down and there was nothing on the television about it – not that I watch much television,' she added righteously. In Wesley's experience people who made that claim always seemed to know in detail, perhaps by some form of telepathy, the plots of every soap opera.

Wesley looked her in the eye. 'Can you tell us about your relationship with Jonny?'

She shrugged and fluttered her hands, as if she had no idea where to begin. But after a few seconds' hesitation she soon got into her stride.

She launched into an account of how she had met Shellmer – funnily enough hanging around Calderstones Park lake at the age of fifteen. Gerry Heffernan grinned approvingly. Jonny had been three years older than her and, in a flurry of teenage rebellion, she had married him at the age of seventeen. Their only son, William, was born soon after. The marriage had lasted four years, most of which they spent apart as Jonny had shot to fame by then and most of his time was taken up with touring or recording in London.

They lived apart and grew apart. Liz stayed in Liverpool, eventually moving back to her family home so her parents could help with William's upbringing, and Jonny did his own thing. She had always had a soft spot for him and they had kept in fairly regular touch. Later she had married a chartered accountant called Norman, had two more children, worked part time for a local cancer charity and led a life of blameless domesticity a world away from any excesses of sex, drugs and rock and roll. Boring, perhaps, but Liz Carty seemed happy enough with her lot.

Wesley listened carefully. She was being completely honest with them, he could tell. When Gerry Heffernan asked her what Jonny had been like, a smile came to her lips as she remembered her first love. He had been fun, she said. Talented and exciting with a quick tongue and a temper to match. A good lover, she added with a blush. And he had been the sort of boy her strait-laced parents disapproved of, which had made him doubly attractive. But he wasn't a bad person – he could be kind in unexpected ways. Liz's soft spot was now on open display.

'But you still split up?' Wesley asked gently.

Liz nodded. 'After we'd been married a couple of years

I caught him in bed with a girl, one of Rock Boat's many groupies, I think. It was then I knew that it was hopeless. You might think it strange but I wasn't angry or anything – I just knew that the parting of the ways was inevitable. And I suppose that what my parents told me about children from broken homes never being able to keep their own marriages together must always have been at the back of my mind.'

Wesley sat forward. 'What do you mean?' This was something he hadn't heard before – something they hadn't considered.

'Jonny's mother wasn't actually married to his father,' Liz said, matter-of-factly. 'His dad had two families – Jonny and his mother and another family down South. Shellmer was his mother's maiden name. Jonny told me he used to go on holiday with his mum to Wales every summer, then he'd go off to stay with his dad and his family down South for a few weeks.'

'Whereabouts down South?' Gerry Heffernan shifted himself to the edge of his seat.

Liz thought for a moment. 'I think it was near where Jonny died. Devon. But I can't be sure. He never talked about it if he could help it.'

'Did he keep in touch with his father?'

'No. I think there'd been some sort of row before I met him because he didn't even invite his father to our wedding. And it wasn't until I'd known Jonny for a while that I discovered that he had a half-brother and sister. He'd got drunk one night and mentioned them, but when I asked him about them afterwards he wouldn't talk about them. I think there must have been some sort of argument, something he wanted to forget.'

Wesley looked at Gerry Heffernan. He could almost hear the cogs whirring in the older man's brain. 'His biography mentions the Welsh holidays but not Devon. Can you think why?'

'As I said, I'd got the impression there'd been some sort

of bad feeling between him and his father. Perhaps he didn't want reminding of it.'

This didn't square with the fact that Jonny Shellmer had intended to settle in Devon. But Wesley didn't voice his doubts. 'Did he ever mention a village called Derenham? It's near Tradmouth.'

'Isn't that where he was killed?' Wesley nodded. 'I'm sure he never mentioned it.'

'Is his mother still alive?'

Liz shook her head. 'No. She died about fifteen years ago. Jonny phoned me late one night to tell me. He was drunk and he was really upset about her death and, before you ask, I've no idea whether his father's alive or what became of the half-brother and sister he wouldn't talk about.'

'Did you know that he was hoping to move to Devon? He was looking for a property.'

'There you are, then,' said Liz sensibly. 'Whatever family he had down there have probably died or moved away by now, so he'd have no reason to avoid the place any more. Have you managed to trace them at all?'

Gerry Heffernan grunted. 'No, love. In fact it's the first we've heard that he had any family down there. We suspected there was some connection but we didn't know what.' He turned to Wesley. 'Have you brought that photo you found at Jonny's cottage?'

Wesley had left it in the car. He hurried outside to retrieve it. When he returned he found his boss getting his feet firmly under Liz Carty's table. He was slurping a second cup of tea and munching what looked like a home-made scone. It must be the unkempt, neglected widower look, he thought to himself – there was something about Gerry Heffernan that awakened some women's maternal instincts.

But Wesley wasn't to be neglected. When he had finished his own scone, he handed Liz the photograph he'd found in Jonny's drawer and asked her whether she recognised anybody. She studied it for a while with a frown of concentration. Then she spoke.

'It's not a good picture, is it? I recognise Jonny, of course, but I've no idea who the others are.'

'Did Jonny ever tell you his brother and sister's names, love?' asked Heffernan, helping himself to another scone.

Liz thought hard. 'After Jonny and I split up I was clearing out a drawer and I found an old Christmas card stuck at the back: it said "to Jonny with love from Dad" and a woman's name and ... I think the next name was Angela and there was a boy's name ...' She shook her head. 'It was something short but I can't think what. I only remembered Angela because it was the same as my best friend's.'

'Did you keep the card?'

'No. I'm sorry. I've not been much help, have I.'

Wesley stood up, triumphant. 'On the contrary, Mrs Carty, you've been very helpful. By the way, we'd like a word with your son. Could you let us have his address.'

She smiled. 'You'll have to get the Mounties to do the job for you. He's in Canada. He works as an accountant in Edmonton, Alberta. I'm afraid I haven't seen him for a year – or my two grandchildren. I've let him know about his father, of course, and he says he's coming over as soon as he can.'

'So Jonny was a grandfather?' said Wesley gently.

Liz nodded. 'Doesn't really fit with the rock-star image, does it? But he was delighted when he found out.' She looked Wesley in the eye. 'I hope you get whoever did this to Jonny.'

'We'll do our best, Mrs Carty,' he said, shaking her hand.

They left Liz alone. Wesley suspected that she would mourn Jonny Shellmer, that grief would creep up on her unexpectedly in quiet moments when she least expected it. He had been part of her life, dimly and in the background. And now he was gone for ever.

He walked faster to keep up with Gerry Heffernan, who

looked as though he knew where he was going. He was making for the park. Wesley felt mildly irritated. It was 2.15 and he had no desire to find himself in some strange hotel for the night. He wanted to get going, to get home to a hot bath. And he was worried about Pam. He didn't want to leave her on her own for too long.

But at least he knew the probable identity of Jonny Shellmer's long-lost half-sister. If it was Angela Simms, it explained a lot.

It was a long walk to the lake. It is always sad to return to the scene of childhood memories, for nothing is ever the same. Wesley watched as his boss stood at the railings of the lake and stared across to the boarded-up boathouse, long out of use owing to vandalism and municipal cutbacks.

'They've knocked the old Odeon down and all,' was Heffernan's only comment. Wesley stood by his side and bowed his head in a few seconds of silent remembrance for Gerry Heffernan's lost youth.

After a while the chief inspector spoke. 'Me and Kathy came here when I brought her up to meet my folks.'

Heffernan had never mentioned his parents before, or any brothers and sisters come to that. Wesley was curious.

'Are your parents still alive?'

'No. Both dead. I've got a brother who lives in Leeds and a few aunties and cousins dotted about around here. We send each other Christmas cards. It was Kathy who kept up with all the relatives, but after she died ...'

'How did Kathy die?'

As soon as the words were out, Wesley regretted them. He had no right to pry, to pick at old wounds. He had never enquired about Kathy's death before for that reason. At first he had supposed it was cancer or some other dread disease – then he had picked up hints that she had been killed in some sort of car accident, but he had been reluctant to ask anybody about the details.

'I'm sorry,' he muttered quickly. 'Forget I asked.' He

thrust his hands in his pockets and turned away. It was time they headed for home.

But Gerry Heffernan stood there, still staring at the abandoned boathouse across the murky lake. 'It's okay, Wes. It's about time you knew anyway. Kathy was murdered.'

Wesley's mouth dropped open. He hadn't expected this.

'When I say murdered, I don't mean it was treated as murder by our lot. But some bastard murdered her all the same – ran her down and left her to die.'

'I'm sorry.' Wesley whispered the words and realised how trite and inadequate they sounded. 'Did they get who did it?'

'Oh, they got him all right, 'cause a witness had taken the car number. Only he told the oldest story in the book. My car was stolen, Officer. I wasn't drinking. I've got a bloody great alibi. Bloody great alibi, my arse. He'd been drinking with a work colleague at a pub in Neston. He said he'd come out and found his car missing ... only it took him three hours to report it. Then he claimed he spent the rest of the evening with some girl who had big tits and the IQ of a goldfish. She backed up his story, and the car was found abandoned the next day. There was nothing we could do to prove he was driving.'

Heffernan clenched his fists with pent-up anger and Wesley touched his arm. 'I'm sorry.'

'It was Paul Heygarth.' Heffernan almost whispered the words.

Wesley nodded. He had always suspected that there was some history behind Heffernan's dislike of the man. 'I'm sorry we couldn't put him away for you,' he muttered, knowing that the words were inadequate.

'I wanted to get him for something but I reckon he's telling the truth about Jonny Shellmer.'

Wesley stared ahead of him, not meeting his boss's eyes. 'The murder charge would never have stuck. But we can charge him for moving the body and Shellmer's car.'

Wesley could think of nothing else to say. He leaned

against the railings and watched as a mother duck swam across the grey waters of the park lake with her brood of six fluffy ducklings following behind.

After a short silence, Heffernan slapped him on the back. 'Come on, Wes, let's get going. If we go down to the Pier Head I'll take you on a ferry trip across the Mersey. Then I'll give my Sam a ring and we can sample the exotic night life. We can book in at one of those new hotels near the Albert Dock.'

Wesley forced a weak smile and prepared to bow to the inevitable. 'I'll place myself in your capable hands, then.'

Heffernan marched on slightly ahead of him, making for the park gates. Wesley knew that he had seen more of the true Heffernan than anyone else had been permitted to see; he had glimpsed the pain behind the thick hide of jokes and bonhomie the man presented to the world. He wasn't looking forward to the evening, as he suspected that a cocktail of drink and home-town nostalgia might encourage more maudlin thoughts and revelations. He wanted to get home, back to Pam and Michael.

As though in answer to his thoughts, his mobile phone rang in his coat pocket. After a brief conversation he turned to Gerry Heffernan.

'We'll have to postpone the guided tour of Liverpool,' he said, trying to hide his relief. 'Hal Lancaster's just arrived back in Tradmouth and they've brought him in for questioning.'

Heffernan hesitated, his disappointment obvious. 'I suppose we should get back. We'll make it by this evening if you put your foot down.'

Wesley Peterson normally drove within the confines of the law, but on the return journey from Liverpool to Tradmouth he found himself exceeding the speed limit by at least twenty miles per hour.

Chapter Eleven

To my dear and most beloved sister Lucy,
Good sister, I rejoice that my husband and my Edmund are home with us in Derenham at last. My husband is to endow a chapel at the church of All Saints here in thanksgiving for his deliverance from the dangers of battle, and we shall make provision for our tombs there and those of our children and cause Masses to be said there for our souls.

We rejoice also because my husband's son, John, is to marry the widow More within the month. I pray that the wisdom of a sensible wife will be the making of the lad.

I see a great change in Edmund since his return from battle. He speaks harshly and his manner is rougher and he doth awake screaming in the night. How war doth change men. Yet he and Elizabeth are become close and when he was ill she spent much time caring for him in his chamber.

I hear tales that King Henry has been slain in the Tower of London on the orders of the usurper who now calls himself King Edward IV. If this is true it is grievous news, for King Henry was a simple and saintly man. Henry Tudor's supporters gather in France, yet I fear the cause of the House of Lancaster is lost.
I am, your loving sister
Marjory Merrivale

Written at Derenham this twentieth day of June 1471

Hal Lancaster was not a happy man. Just as he was mooring the *Henry of Lancaster* at a convenient berth on the River Trad, he received a visit from a DS Tracey and a DC Carstairs.

The young woman officer, DS Tracey, had explained politely that they wished to interview him concerning a serious matter. But Lancaster reckoned that the other officer, DC Carstairs, had some sort of problem. Hal Lancaster wasn't accustomed to being treated like the lowest form of common criminal – money and a flash yacht usually spoke volumes.

He was cautioned and taken to Tradmouth police station, where he received a rubbery cheese sandwich and a cup of weak tea in a plastic cup. He had been looking forward to a decent meal cooked by a well-known celebrity chef in the exclusive surroundings of the Carved Cherub on the waterfront, but he tried not to let his disappointment show.

His protestations that the police had made some sort of mistake cut no ice. A couple of senior detectives were on their way to talk to him about the murder of Jonny Shellmer and the disappearance of a boy called Lewis Hoxworthy. He expressed shock at Jonny's death – he had been out of touch with the news on his yacht and this was the first he'd heard of it – and explained that the singer's demise would hardly be good for his business interests.

Then Lancaster related how he'd met Lewis briefly when he'd bought some old manuscripts advertised over the Internet, but he knew nothing of his disappearance. There was nothing more to tell them, but he'd do anything in his power to help nail Jonny's killer.

As Rachel had anticipated, Lancaster demanded the services of a solicitor, the most expensive he could find, all the way from Exeter. She had taken the precaution of consulting the superintendent, just in case Wesley and Heffernan were held up, and he was willing to authorise Lancaster's detention once Rachel had convinced him that the man's ocean-going yacht could sail to anywhere in the world once the suspect set foot outside the police station. Rachel Tracey could be very persuasive when she wanted to be.

It was 8.15 when Wesley swung the car into the station carpark. As they hadn't stopped during their journey, he was hungry, and so was his passenger who was making a considerable fuss about the empty state of his stomach. They used their rank to send out for two Chinese takeaways from the Golden Dragon before they confronted Hal Lancaster and they were given the news that Terry Hoxworthy had paid a visit to the unconscious Angela Simms in hospital. Interesting though this last snippet of information was, they had no time to act on it now. Lancaster was awaiting them in Interview Room 2.

As they walked in, Rachel announced their arrival to the tape recorder. Then, at Heffernan's signal, Rachel and Steve left the room and Heffernan parked his expanding backside on the plastic chair. Wesley sat down beside him and studied Hal Lancaster. He was a big man with bright blue eyes and a mane of grey hair tied back in a ponytail. He had an air of authority, that of a man used to giving commands, not taking them. But then for several decades he had had the power to make or break fortunes in the perilous pop music industry. When Hal Lancaster had spoken, hundreds of would-be stars had obeyed.

It was Lancaster who spoke first. His voice was deep and smooth with a pleasant American twang; an easy voice to listen to. 'Your colleagues told me about Jonny and I can tell you it's come as one hell of a shock. I've been away so I haven't seen the papers or TV. Hell, I was hoping to get Rock Boat back together for a tour but ... Look, I'll help in any way I can.' He shook his head and stared down at the table's shabby laminate top as though he were fighting back tears.

Wesley glanced at his boss. Lancaster was playing the bereaved friend rather than the murder suspect. 'Where were you on the Wednesday afternoon Shellmer died?'

Lancaster told them and invited them to consult his

boat's log. Then produced a credit card slip from his wallet which bore the name of an exclusive restaurant at his port of call with the date and time in question clearly printed above it.

Gerry Heffernan tried to look unimpressed and started on another line of questioning. 'You've admitted that you met Lewis Hoxworthy on your floating gin palace.'

Lancaster nodded.

'After that meeting he disappeared and was never seen again. What have you got to say about that?'

'I collect old manuscripts, Chief Inspector. I saw an advert on the Internet; a private sale. I arranged to meet the seller, and nobody could have been more surprised than I was when this young kid turned up – I was expecting a dealer or a fellow collector.'

'So what happened?' asked Wesley.

'I met him in Tradmouth first and he showed me a sample of what he had to sell. I was interested so I arranged to sail up the river to a place called Derenham to complete the deal. He turned up, I examined the rest of the merchandise, handed over the money – he wanted cash – and then I sailed to France where I'd arranged to meet a dealer who said he had a sixteenth century book of hours I might be interested in.'

'Did you buy it?' asked Wesley.

'No. It was a fake.'

'But Lewis Hoxworthy's letters weren't?'

'As far as I could tell they were the genuine article. He'd found them in a box in some old barn: thirteen letters, all in remarkable condition, considering.'

'Where are they now?'

'In the safe on board my boat. You're welcome to see them if it helps get this mess sorted out.' He looked Wesley in the eye, all co-operation. The good and helpful citizen.

'And Lewis?'

'He left with the money straight away. He was a strange kid. I guess he was trying to act grown up.' He smiled. 'He

235

shook hands and said it was nice doing business with me and I thought to myself that he'd go far. He seemed keen on medieval history, and I was interested to hear what he had to say about the letters.'

'And what did he have to say?'

'That they were dated 1471 and concerned a family called Merrivale.'

Wesley edged forward and his plastic chair scraped nosily on the floor. 'And?'

'I haven't studied them properly yet. I've been busy with this and that, you understand.'

'Do you know a man called Alec Treadly?'

'Never heard of him.'

'Paul Heygarth?'

Lancaster shook his head. 'Should I know them?'

Wesley didn't answer. 'Do you have any objection to us searching your boat?'

Lancaster shrugged theatrically. 'None whatsoever.'

'You have a computer on board, I take it?'

'How else would I have contacted the kid by e-mail?'

Heffernan looked at him, eyes narrowed. Hal Lancaster was too smoothly confident for his taste. When a suspect was being so helpful, warning bells rang in his head. 'If you've nothing to hide, you won't mind if one of our computer experts has a rummage through your files?'

'Help yourself. I've nothing to hide. But there's confidential stuff in there – business, you understand.'

Heffernan nodded. He had the same faith in Tom from Forensics as ancient tribes used to have in their magic men. If Lancaster had anything dubious locked away in that computer of his, Tom would find it. He changed the subject. 'While you were in Tradmouth, did you contact Jonny Shellmer? Did you know his new address?'

'Sure, Jonny let me know he was moving down this way. I'd spoken to him a couple of times recently about this reunion I was planning. When I arrived in Tradmouth I rang his number – I was going to take him out for lunch –

236

but there was no reply so I thought he must be away or back in London.' He looked down at his empty plastic cup as though stifling tears. 'I guess he was dead by then. I can't think who'd want to do that to Jonny, I really can't.'

'What was Jonny like?' Wesley thought he might as well ask.

Lancaster smiled. 'Talented. Full of life. A bit wild when he was young but then which of us wasn't? He was married to his childhood sweetheart when Rock Boat first hit the big time – but it didn't last long.'

'We've met his ex-wife,' said Heffernan bluntly. 'He never married again, I take it?'

'No. But that doesn't mean he lived like some sort of monk. He was always popular with the chicks and I heard he was getting pretty serious with a lady named Sherry. I met her once – lovely girl. Jonny was a lucky guy.'

'Did he ever mention someone called Angela to you? Possibly his half-sister.'

Lancaster shook his head. 'No, I never knew about a half-sister. There was that song, "Angel" – great hit. He'd never say what that was about. Angel ... Angela?' He shrugged. 'Your guess is as good as mine.'

'To get back to Lewis. When was the last time you saw him?'

'Like I said, he made the delivery, I examined the goods, I paid him, he left. That's it. End of story. I never saw him again.'

'How much did you pay him?' Heffernan asked suspiciously.

'Fifteen hundred pounds. I reckon it's an important collection and I'd have paid a hell of a lot more at auction. Why?'

Heffernan and Wesley looked at each other. If young Lewis Hoxworthy was wandering around with fifteen hundred pounds in cash in his pocket, this changed things considerably. If Hal Lancaster was telling the truth.

*

Wesley arrived home just before midnight, opening the front door quietly, trying his best not to wake Pam. But his efforts were in vain. She was awake and standing at the top of the stairs as soon as she heard his key turning in the lock.

'You said you were staying the night in Liverpool,' she said accusingly.

'Sorry to disappoint you. You've not got a man up there, have you?'

'The only man I've seen today is Neil. He came round earlier to ask if I'd like to bring my class to his dig in Derenham. He's just after cheap labour, if you ask me.'

Wesley said nothing. His mind was still on Gerry Heffernan. They had parted in the High Street, stranded stone cold sober amidst the last stragglers ejected from the late-night pubs. Nothing more had been said about Kathy's death but, as Wesley had watched Heffernan walk away towards his empty house, it had filled his thoughts.

Paul Heygarth had probably been drunk when he had killed Kathy in a hit-and-run accident – and he had got away with it. No wonder Heffernan had wanted to get him for something serious like murder.

But however much Wesley sympathised, he knew it wouldn't work: the evidence would be torn to shreds and Heygarth would walk out of court laughing – as those more guilty than him often did. It had taken Wesley a long time to come to terms with this unpalatable fact when he had first joined the force.

They could do Heygarth for moving the body and stealing the car. It was something. But it wasn't enough. Then the image of the old painting he had seen in Terry Hoxworthy's barn flashed into his mind. The Last Judgement. Wesley smiled to himself. Perhaps one day in the distant future Paul Heygarth would get his just deserts.

'Do you want something to eat?' Pam interrupted his thoughts.

'No thanks. We had a Chinese at the station.'

238

'All right for some. How was Liverpool? Gerry show you the sights?'

Wesley mumbled a non-committal answer before walking into the living room, where he switched the television on and opened a can of beer. He wasn't in the mood for conversation and he didn't feel like sleeping just yet. There was too much on his mind.

'I nearly forgot,' said Pam, following behind. 'Anne rang. She said one of your colleagues had been round on her day off asking if Jonny Shellmer had rung the library. She said she spoke to a man with a Liverpool accent last Wednesday but they didn't get as far as names. He just wanted to know if the library had an edition of the Merrivale letters – the one Neil's got. Does that make sense?'

Wesley nodded. 'I think so. Thanks.'

'It seems a funny thing for a pop star to ask for,' was Pam's only comment before leaving the room.

Wesley sat there with his eyes shut. There was a Hollywood action movie on the television but the fast-moving sounds from the screen didn't register on his tired mind as he went over the day's events. Something had been pushed to the back of his mind in all the excitement of Lancaster being brought in. A name from Jonny Shellmer's past. Angela. Jonny Shellmer had a half-sister called Angela. And Jonny had been in contact with Angela Simms, who was now fighting for her life in hospital. And Angela Simms had been visited by Terry Hoxworthy.

It seemed that Terry Hoxworthy had a few questions to answer.

The next morning it was raining heavily as Wesley drove into Tradmouth. He ran from the carpark to the police station, his jacket shielding his head against the wet, and when he arrived in the CID office he found it buzzing with activity.

There was a message from Tom on Wesley's desk.

Nothing remotely suspicious had been found on the laptop computer Hal Lancaster used aboard his yacht, and his e-mails had concerned either business or the collecting of old manuscripts. Tom, whose turn of phrase lacked some originality, concluded that he was as clean as the driven snow. With the news of Lewis's fifteen-hundred-pound windfall, the paedophile theory seemed to be dead in the water, much to Wesley's relief.

Gerry Heffernan was nowhere to be found, and a reliable informant told Wesley that he had gone down to the canteen for one of his hearty breakfasts. The chief inspector didn't allow much to get in the way of his appetite.

Wesley strolled into Heffernan's empty office and saw that the file on Paul Heygarth was sitting in pride of place on the desk. He opened it and leafed through the papers, noticing that on one sheet the words 'released on bail' were underlined angrily in red Biro. He closed the file and put it back in its original position, hoping Heffernan wouldn't be tempted to join the ranks of coppers – good ones sometimes – who fabricated evidence to get some vicious toerag put away and then found themselves in trouble and the toerag in question laughing with the case against them dismissed. Wesley would make sure that any case against Heygarth was conducted strictly by the book – for Gerry's sake.

He was greeted at the office door by Rachel. 'Do you want me to come with you to see Terry Hoxworthy? I know the family and ...'

'Yes. Good idea.'

'Do you think Terry could be connected with all this? Could Lewis have witnessed something and run away?'

Wesley shrugged. It was as good a theory as any. He walked to his desk, followed by Rachel, and took Jonny Shellmer's photograph from his top drawer. Rachel watched, perched on the edge of the desk.

He pointed to the dark-haired boy in the picture. 'I think this one's Jonny Shellmer. I think this was taken when Jonny came down in the summer to stay with his father and his second family.' He pointed to the girl, who was staring wistfully at the camera lens. 'Could that be Angela Simms? Is she really Jonny's half-sister?'

Rachel stared at the picture in silence. Wesley turned to look at her. 'What is it?'

'When Trish and I had that look through Angela's things we found a very similar photograph there: probably the same children. Only that boy at the end was missing.' She pointed to the eldest boy. 'In fact the end had been cut off . . . perhaps with him on it.'

'Family quarrel?' Wesley suggested.

'Who knows. Or perhaps he was someone she didn't know well and she cut him off the end to make the picture smaller . . . to fit into a frame or something. If Angela comes round, hopefully she'll be able to tell us.'

Wesley studied the picture again. 'That boy there looks a bit like the photos we've seen of Lewis Hoxworthy. You don't think it could be Terry, do you? If he and Angela were childhood friends . . .'

'We won't know if we don't ask.'

Half an hour later they drew up outside Hoxworthy's Farm. Jill had heard the car and rushed out to meet them, anticipating news of Lewis. When Rachel told her gently that there was none, the spark of hope in Jill's eyes disappeared and the strain and worry returned. She told them Terry was in the new barn seeing to one of the tractors. He liked to keep busy.

They walked to the barn, a huge nineteenth-century edifice, more convenient for the farm but lacking the charm of its medieval counterpart some way away down the lane, and found the tractor parked just inside the great double doors. Terry, wearing an oil-stained boiler suit and a pre-occupied expression, was examining the engine. He looked up as they approached and grunted a wary greeting, on his guard.

'Any news?'

241

'Sorry. But no news is good news, eh?' said Wesley, wondering how to broach the subject of Angela. He paused for a few seconds while he arranged his thoughts. 'I believe you visited Tradmouth Hospital last night and enquired about a patient called Angela Simms.'

Terry examined an oily rod he had just pulled out of the tractor engine and said nothing.

'May I ask why you visited her?'

'Old friend, isn't she.'

'How did you know she was in hospital?'

'Read about it in the *Echo*, didn't I. There'd been a robbery at her shop. Not safe anywhere these days.' He shot Wesley a hostile glance, as though he were solely responsible for the police's lack of efficiency.

'How well do you know Ms Simms?'

'Like I said, she's an old friend. I've known her since we were kids.'

'So you'll know about her connection with Jonny Shellmer.'

'I might do.'

Wesley was growing impatient with the farmer's cagey answers. 'She was Jonny Shellmer's half-sister. Is that right?' He looked Terry in the eye, challenging him to offer another evasive answer.

Terry knew he couldn't stall any longer. 'Okay. I knew her dad had a woman and kid up North somewhere – things get round in a small community and folk like to gossip. Her dad used to bring the lad down every summer, bold as brass, and he used to tell his kids that they could all be one big happy family. But of course it didn't quite work out like that, and there was a lot of bad feeling, especially from Angela's mother. I was only young, but I could tell.'

'When you found Jonny Shellmer's body you said you didn't recognise him.'

'That was the truth. I'd not seen him for over thirty years. People change,' said Terry, shuffling his feet awkwardly.

Wesley decided to leave that question for the moment. 'What was Angela's relationship with Jonny?'

'I don't know.' Terry replaced the dipstick and began to undo a bolt.

Wesley glanced at Rachel. Terry wasn't making it easy for them.

'Have you seen much of Angela recently?' asked Rachel.

'Might have done.'

'We've evidence to suggest that she had seen Jonny on several occasions; that she even visited him at his cottage.'

No answer.

'Has Angela mentioned Jonny to you?'

Terry Hoxworthy shrugged his shoulders.

'When was the last time you saw Angela Simms?'

'I drop in on her from time to time just to see if she's all right.'

'Is there any reason why she shouldn't be?'

Terry looked up from the engine. 'Woman on her own and all that. Like I said, she's an old friend.'

Wesley realised this was going nowhere. Nonetheless there were a couple more questions he wanted to ask.

'I presume Angela's parents are both dead.'

'She died of cancer and he drank himself to death,' Terry said with relish.

'Angela had another brother. What happened to him?'

Terry shrugged. 'No idea. I heard he'd gone abroad and died. Went away and never came back. Not that he was missed.'

'What do you mean?'

'I don't mean nothing.'

'What was the brother's name?'

'James. Look, I've got to get on, so if there's no news of Lewis . . .'

Wesley and Rachel knew when they were being dismissed. But there wasn't much they could do about it. At least now they had a name for Jonny's half brother.

'I suppose he's got enough to think about with Lewis,'

said Rachel as they climbed into the car.

'Mm,' Wesley answered quietly. But he wasn't convinced by Rachel's suggestion. Terry Hoxworthy had been hiding something – and Wesley intended to find out what it was.

'I think we should check on the rest of Angela's family,' Rachel said as Wesley slowed the car. 'I'd like to see if there are any other Simms in the area: perhaps the brother didn't die; perhaps he's still living round here. And Terry Hoxworthy either doesn't know or isn't telling. I was thinking of looking through the electoral register.'

'Rather you than me,' said Wesley, bringing the car to a halt.

'Oh, I wasn't thinking of doing it myself,' she replied with a smug grin. 'Delegation's a wonderful thing.'

Wesley glanced in the direction of the church and saw Neil Watson disappearing into the porch.

'I've just spotted someone I want a word with,' he said casually. 'You get back to the station. I'll call when I want picking up.'

Rachel gave him a reproachful look. She knew exactly what he was up to. 'I'll come with you. It'll save time in the long run.'

Wesley nodded. She was probably right. He had a desk laden with paperwork but half an hour wouldn't make much difference.

When they entered the church they found Neil standing in front of the Doom, talking to another man; a man Wesley recognised from a number of TV dramas and films.

Neil swung round when he heard the church door open.

'Wes,' he called. 'Come and meet Jeremy Sedley. He's helping out with this history evening. Jeremy, this is a friend of mine, Wesley Peterson. He's a police inspector but don't hold it against him. Are you and Pam coming to this history evening next Saturday, by the way?'

'I haven't got much choice. Gerry's singing with the

244

choir. He's been handing out tickets all over the office.' He shook Jeremy Sedley's outstretched hand. 'Delighted to meet you, Mr Sedley.' He introduced Rachel, who greeted Sedley shyly, overawed for once by the man's fame.

'Jeremy's interested in local history and he's volunteered to narrate the history evening,' said Neil.

Wesley made a mental note to tell Pam: she would be impressed. 'Good,' was all he could think of to say.

Neil leaned towards him. 'I was planning to come round to your place to drop off that book Anne found for me – the Merrivale letters. I thought you'd like to see them.'

'Thanks.' Wesley hoped he'd have time to read it. Then he remembered that Jonny Shellmer had enquired about that very book. Perhaps he'd make time.

Neil turned to the Doom. 'I was just looking at this writing above the heads of a couple of these figures on the painting. It's very faint but you can just make it out. I think it's names. Tamar seems to be one as far as I can make out – the river east of here. The other one begins with A but it's very faint. But so would you be if you were hidden away for five centuries.' Neil chuckled at his own joke. Rachel watched him stony faced.

But Wesley had his notebook out and was copying what he could make out of the mysterious inscription while Rachel looked on disapprovingly.

'So you live in Derenham now, Mr Sedley?' Wesley said pleasantly when he had put his notebook away.

'Yes. I've been here two years now and I'm becoming quite attached to the place. I still have a little pied-à-terre in London, of course, for when I'm working there. But there's a lot of location work nowadays – I was filming up near Tavistock the other day.'

'It's good of you to give up your time to help the village hall appeal,' said Rachel meekly.

'Least I could do, dear lady,' he replied with charm. For a moment Wesley though he was going to take hold of Rachel's hand and kiss it.

Wesley asked him, 'Did you know Jonny Shellmer?'

'Er, no. Our paths never crossed,' he answered quickly. 'Look, I really must be off. It was nice to meet you, Inspector Peterson, Sergeant Tracey. I do hope we meet again soon.' He turned and marched quickly out of the church.

'He's in a bit of a hurry,' observed Neil.

Wesley smiled innocently. 'Was it something I said?'

Hal Lancaster loved old manuscripts. The feel of parchment against his fingers excited him as he thought of all the hands they had passed through and the eyes that had read them. He loved the link they provided with flesh-and-blood people from centuries ago. He often wondered what they would have said if they could see where their writings had ended up: being held by an ageing, overweight man, born in a land not even discovered when they were written, sitting in a well-appointed, centrally heated hotel room, with luxuries way beyond the imagination of anyone living in the Middle Ages. It seemed the police had cleared him for the moment: they had asked him to stay in Tradmouth and, as he fancied a change, he had checked into the best hotel in town.

But there was one drawback to Lancaster's hobby, something he never liked to admit to fellow collectors. He loved to possess the precious documents but he had terrible trouble deciphering what they actually said. He had tried many times to sit down and read the things, but the archaic handwriting usually defeated him and he'd run out of patience. And if they were in Latin he stood no chance.

He managed to bluff and sound knowledgeable to other collectors. And he'd managed to fool the police by repeating what the boy had told him about the Merrivale letters. His image as a connoisseur of old manuscripts had been maintained. If you spoke about anything with enough confidence, people would always believe you were an expert.

But he still had no idea of exactly what the Merrivale

letters contained, and he had been too proud to ask the boy for the transcription he said he had made.

Now he was sitting in his room with some time on his hands, so he put on the white cotton gloves he always wore when handling such things and took the pile of letters from their resting place.

For the first time in his collecting career, Hal Lancaster persevered, and two hours later had managed to decipher the Merrivale letters. And the story they were telling – especially the last ones – was turning out to be as interesting as any Hollywood movie.

Chapter Twelve

My well beloved wife,
I rejoice at the news of John's betrothal to the widow
More, although I worry at what you tell me of his behav-
iour of late.

I have a good price for our wool from a Bristol
merchant, better than the price in Tradmouth, and all the
talk is of the peace and good trade the new King Edward
hath brought to our land. I hear news that the old King's
supporters are in France with the Earl of Richmond, but
I feel it is best that we tend our lands and look to our
prosperity.

Do not concern yourself overmuch with young
Edmund's affection for his sister and the strangeness in
his manner. It is good that he should feel so protective
toward her. It may be that he is concerned lest her half-
brother John distress her in any way. Do not fret about
what you saw between them. It was only mere foolishness
between two young people. Elizabeth was ever a girl of
good sense and she knows right from wrong.

I return in a week and I pray God to keep you in His
care.
Your affectionate husband
Richard

Written at Bristol this nineteenth day of August 1471

Wesley Peterson emerged from his bath, just as the water was beginning to lose its heat. He hadn't arrived home until eight o'clock, and he and Pam had sent out for a Chinese takeaway: sometimes he felt that he was keeping the Golden Dragon in business single handed.

He donned his dressing gown and went downstairs, thinking it was time he and Pam spent some time together. He went into the kitchen and took a bottle of red wine from the rack, not forgetting the corkscrew and two glasses.

But when he walked into the living room, he saw that Pam was stretched out on the sofa with her eyes closed. Wesley smiled to himself: so much for an evening of conjugal bliss.

He picked up his notebook from the sideboard, then sat down in the armchair and began to study the page on which he'd copied down the faint writing he'd seen painted on the Doom. He sipped his wine as he tried to rearrange the letters. But nothing worked. Wesley had always considered himself quite good at crosswords and puzzles, but this one defeated him.

He closed his eyes and began to think, setting his mind running on different lines. Perhaps it wasn't a puzzle. Perhaps it was something that would have been obvious to the villagers of Derenham in the Middle Ages. The Doom was intended to be displayed in a church, after all, and its message must have been meant for everyone. Then a possibility struck him and he stood up and headed for the bookcase.

But before he could reach his destination the telephone began to ring. He picked it up and heard his mother-in-law's giggling voice on the other end. He looked across at Pam; the telephone had disturbed her and she was sitting up, rubbing her eyes. Wesley felt annoyed with Della for waking her, and all thoughts of the mysterious code fled from his head. The Doom would keep its secret for a while longer.

*

Carys Pugh, receptionist at the Ty Mawr Hotel, Harlech, North Wales, which nestled in the shadow of the town's great medieval castle, picked up the telephone and dialled the number of her local police station.

If that nice elderly couple from Liverpool hadn't left that day's copy of a national newspaper in the residents' lounge, and if she hadn't picked it up and carried it back to her desk with the intention of reading it when she had a quiet moment, Carys would never have seen the photograph. She would never have known that one of the guests staying in the opulent luxury of the Ty Mawr – an ideal base from which to explore the beauties of Gwynedd – was not all he seemed to be.

If what the paper said was true, the police needed to be told as soon as possible. She had just explained her predicament to the policewoman on the other end of the line when the visitor in question walked into reception and Cary's conversation switched effortlessly into Welsh while she smiled at the visitor as she handed over the room key. There was no way the visitor had understood what she was saying. And the police said they'd send someone round within the hour. No problem.

The next morning, as Gerry Heffernan was complaining loudly about the lack of a decent cup of tea, Wesley trawled through the files to see if there was anything he'd missed. Angela Simms, according to a message on his desk from PC Wallace at the hospital, was stable but still hadn't come round. Wesley wondered whether Steve had discovered anything about Angela's brother, James, yet. But Steve wasn't known for his dynamic powers of deduction, so he wasn't holding his breath.

Wesley's telephone began to ring. He picked up the receiver, hoping it wasn't more bad news. A crazed gunman opening fire in the Red Bull perhaps. Anything seemed possible in the village of Derenham these days.

'This is Sergeant Emrys Jones of North Wales police,

Harlech, here. Is that the officer dealing with the Lewis Hoxworthy investigation?' The voice was deep, male and decidedly Welsh.

Wesley answered in the affirmative.

'I've got a nice surprise for you. The missing lad has turned up on our patch. Staying in a posh hotel near the castle, he was; one of the staff recognised him from a newspaper picture. He told everyone he was one of those young Internet millionaires; took the best room and everything. Got to hand it to the lad, he had 'em all fooled. We've got him here at the station now and he tells us that he's been doing a tour of Welsh castles. Got a thing about castles, he has.'

Heffernan emerged from his office and noticed the smile spreading across Wesley's face as he covered the mouthpiece and shouted across the office. 'Lewis Hoxworthy's turned up alive and well. He's in North Wales.'

A cheer went up in the CID office. Happy faces for a change, and an excuse for a few celebratory drinks in the Fisherman's Arms later on. But Lewis Hoxworthy wasn't out of the woods yet. He had some questions to answer about the gun found in his bedroom.

As Wesley put the phone down, Steve strolled into the office, perplexed by the general mood of merriment. 'What's up?' he whispered to a grinning WPC Trish Walton. She told him, and he allowed the corners of his mouth to twitch upward.

Steve was just about to make for his desk when Gerry Heffernan spotted him and beckoned him over. 'Oi, Poirot. I want a word.'

Steve resisted the temptation to brush against Trish's ample chest and slouched over to the chief inspector's office. Wesley was standing by his boss, waiting.

'Don't suppose you managed to find out anything about this James Simms.' Gerry Heffernan had known Steve for too long to expect miracles.

Steve's face flushed red as he took out his notebook. 'As

251

a matter of fact I haven't, sir. Or rather I have found out something, but I don't know if it's important.'

Heffernan looked at Wesley and rolled his eyes to heaven. 'What's that supposed to mean?'

'It means I've not found anything about anyone called James Simms. Nothing at all.'

Heffernan grunted. This wasn't what he had hoped for.

But Steve hadn't finished. 'Then I went along to the *Tradmouth Echo* and looked through their back copies to see if there was any mention of anyone involved in this case. I reckoned it'd probably be back in the mid–1960s so I started with 1964 and when I reached 1966 ...' He hesitated, a smug smile playing around his lips. 'I found something interesting. There was no mention of Jonny Shellmer or anyone called James, but there was a report on the third of August 1966 of a girl nearly drowning in the River Trad at Derenham. The girl's name was Angela Simms and the boy who jumped in and rescued her was none other than Terry Hoxworthy.'

Heffernan was listening with interest. 'So the teenage Terry Hoxworthy was a hero. That's a turn-up for the books. Funny he didn't mention it – or maybe he was just being modest. Did the paper say anything else?'

'Terry was commended for his bravery, but from the report it wasn't too clear how the girl came to be in the water. It doesn't say she fell in or got into difficulties while swimming. Papers usually tell you that sort of thing, but this report seemed a bit ... I don't know, cagey.'

Wesley saw that his boss was standing there open mouthed. Steve had never displayed such initiative or insight in all the time he'd known him. In fact he'd never seen much evidence of any sort of activity going on in the space between Steve's left and right ears before. But there had to be a first time for everything.

Some inner voice told Wesley that Steve's discovery was important: they were definitely on to something. And yet, on the face of it, it seemed unlikely that Terry Hoxworthy's moment of heroism all those years ago could be connected with the discovery of Jonny Shellmer's body in his field thirty-five years later. But it would explain his friendship with Angela Simms, the girl he rescued: owing your life to someone would create a considerable bond. They would be visiting Terry soon to break the good news about Lewis, so there would be no harm in asking about the incident while they were there.

Wesley sat down at his desk and opened the drawer. Jonny Shellmer's photograph was still there, and he stared down at it. It was so clear now, that he knew who the children were. Terry Hoxworthy, Angela Simms, Jonny Shellmer and, presumably, James Simms. He studied the small blurred image of the unknown face: it was familiar but elusive. He closed the drawer and looked at his watch.

Steve left the office after a dose of appropriate praise – all the psychology books Wesley had ever come across had said it was important to reinforce good behaviour.

Gerry Heffernan had emerged from his lair and was waiting to get off to Hoxworthy's Farm, almost bubbling over with glee, anticipating the joy and relief on Jill's face when she heard the news that Lewis was safe and unharmed. They left the station and were soon driving down the narrow lanes to Hoxworthy's Farm. It was good to be the bearers of happy news for a change, even though Terry now had a few more questions to answer.

The manor house was emerging from the soil nicely and Neil Watson wondered, as he strolled to Derenham church, whether he could persuade the builders of the new village hall to give him a few more weeks' grace before the trenches had to be backfilled and built upon.

He felt restless and unsatisfied. There were still too many questions that remained unanswered. Who did the decapitated skeleton belong to? Why did the family suddenly disappear from the village when, judging by the letters he had read so far, there were two healthy sons and a daughter to carry on the Merrivale line? Why was the house destroyed and the site never built on again? And what was the meaning of the peculiar image on the Merrivales' tomb?

There would be some simple explanation, of course. The whole family might have been wiped out in a house fire – it happened even today. The 'wicked one' might have been some peasant with a grudge who started the fire and was murdered and decapitated by an angry mob of righteous villagers. It was a good theory, and Neil felt quite pleased with himself as he walked into the gloom of the church.

The rest of the team were enjoying their coffee break, but Neil wanted to have another look at the Doom, to see whether it held anything that might confirm his theory. He stood there staring at it and shuddered. Fire featured prominently, but apart from that he couldn't see much connection. Then something made his heart beat faster and he hurried to the chapel to take a look at the Merrivales' grand tomb. He was right; the rather smug-looking pair being ushered into heaven by an angel who wore the obsequious expression of a maître d' showing favoured diners into an exclusive restaurant were the spitting images of the pious figures on the Merrivale tomb. Richard and Marjory were strolling through the pearly gates unchallenged while the lower orders were thrown to the mercy of a battalion of devils who were clearly happy in their eternal work of torment and torture.

Typical, thought Neil. Nothing ever changes. But his musings on social justice were interrupted by the sound of someone clearing their throat a few feet behind him. He turned and was surprised to see Jeremy Sedley standing there.

'Can't keep away from it, can we.'

'Speak for yourself,' answered Neil, glancing at the Doom with distaste. 'Have you ever noticed that those two smug bastards being shown politely into heaven don't half look like those effigies of Richard and Marjory Merrivale on that tomb in their chapel?'

'I have indeed,' said Sedley, looking rather smug himself. 'And did you notice that a couple of people in the queue waiting for judgement resemble the portraits of the Merrivale children on the side of the tomb, and that one of the damned is almost definitely the one in the flames on the tomb – the "wicked one". Which stands to reason, I suppose.'

Neil said nothing. That was one theory down the drain. Some murderous medieval peasant with a grudge would hardly have featured on a posh, state-of-the-art tomb. The wicked one must have been closer to home: a maladjusted kid with a taste for arson? John Merrivale, the delinquent son, perhaps!

'I've spent a lot of time looking at this thing since it arrived here,' Sedley said with unseemly enthusiasm. 'It's going to make rather a dramatic backdrop to our history evening, don't you think? But perhaps in my profession a love of the dramatic is an occupational hazard.'

Neil nodded. He couldn't argue with that.

Gerry Heffernan had been looking forward to breaking the news about Lewis, and he entered the Hoxworthys' farm-house beaming like Santa Claus. In Wesley's experience most police officers felt like this when any missing child was found unharmed, but in this case his own feeling of elation was tempered by the knowledge that there was still a ruthless killer at large somewhere in or near the village of Derenham.

Heffernan announced the good news to Terry and Jill like a quiz-show host awarding a million-pound prize to a pair of bemused contestants. Jill burst into tears and clung onto her husband's hand, sobbing with relief. The Gwynedd police were bringing Lewis back and he would be home late that afternoon.

Jill murmured her thanks through her tears, and

Heffernan grinned back at her benignly. Now wasn't really the time to mention that they wanted to ask Lewis a few questions themselves about how the gun came to be in his possession. The bad news could wait.

As soon as Jill had left the room to prepare for the prodigal's homecoming, Wesley and his boss faced Terry Hoxworthy.

'We'd like to ask you some questions,' Wesley began.

'About Lewis?'

'No. About something that happened thirty-five years ago. You rescued a girl from drowning.'

Instead of looking proud of his moment of bravery, Terry Hoxworthy swallowed hard. 'So?' he said after a few seconds.

'You rescued Angela Simms.'

Terry nodded, still looking uncomfortable.

'Can you tell us what happened?'

'I'd rather not.' He glanced over his shoulder, as though afraid Jill would overhear.

'Why hide it? The reports in the paper said you were a hero.'

There was no response.

'Whatever you tell us won't go any farther if it's not relevant to our enquiries.' Wesley was trying to sound reassuring.

Terry thought for a few moments. 'Okay. But I wouldn't like this to be common knowledge. We tried to keep it quiet at the time for Angela's sake and ...' His voice trailed off. 'I've sort of been ... keeping an eye on Angela. Sometimes Jill doesn't understand. Angela's not a strong person. She's very vulnerable.'

Wesley detected the first signs of exasperation on his boss's face. 'Go on,' he coaxed. 'I can assure you that anything you tell us will be treated as confidential.'

Terry hesitated. He studied a scar on the palm of his right hand and touched it absent-mindedly, running his finger across the shining streak of flesh.

'It was in the summer of 1966. I was about the same age as Lewis is now, and a group of us used to hang around together on Derenham waterfront. There was Angela Simms, her brother James and her half-brother, Jonny, who came down from Liverpool every year for a few weeks in the summer. Jonny was different from the rest of us, the odd one out. He seemed more worldly wise, more glamorous. He'd formed a pop group with his mates at school and Angela adored him: she used to follow him around like a faithful puppy.'

'Why didn't you say you knew Jonny Shellmer when you found his body?'

Terry Hoxworthy shrugged. 'I don't know. I didn't realise who he was at first, and then I panicked when I found out: I didn't want to get involved. And he was on my land, so if I'd admitted I'd known him once ...' His voice trailed off. 'Then Lewis went missing and I had more reason not to want to get involved. That's all.'

'You are involved,' Gerry Heffernan said, a hint of threat in his voice. 'He was found on your land and the gun that killed him was found in your house. And on top of that you kept quiet about knowing him.'

'And if I'd killed him don't you think I'd have dumped him and the gun as far away as possible?' Hoxworthy said quickly.

Wesley nodded. He had a point. 'So what happened to Angela?'

It was a few seconds before Terry spoke. 'One day I went down to the waterfront where we used to meet. There was nobody there and I was about to go home. Then I saw Angela thrashing about in the water. I was a good swimmer so I waded in and rescued her. When my dad found out what I'd done he told the local paper I was a hero. I could have killed him.'

'Why?' The vehemence of his words surprised Wesley – but then parents can be a terrible embarrassment to a teenage lad.

'Because I thought Angela had tried to kill herself and I didn't want it splashed all over the papers.'

Gerry Heffernan looked surprised. 'What made you think that?'

Terry swallowed hard. 'Angela was very pretty ... everyone called her Angel. I didn't know why she'd done it until ...'

'Go on,' Heffernan prompted impatiently.

'I overheard my mother telling my dad that Angela had been taken to Tradmouth Hospital. She said she'd heard from someone who worked there that ...' He hesitated. 'I shouldn't be telling you this. If Angela knew I'd been talking about ...'

'Please, Mr Hoxworthy, it might be important.' Wesley spoke firmly. This was no time for scruples.

'I heard – and I don't know if it was true – that Angela threw herself into the river because she'd just been raped.'

'Did you ever ask Angela what happened?'

Terry shook his head. 'Of course I didn't.'

There was a long silence.

'Do you know who raped her?' Wesley said gently.

Terry Hoxworthy looked down, studying the scar again. 'I was at the top of the stairs listening to my parents talking. I couldn't hear clearly but I'm sure they mentioned Jonny's name. It must have been Jonny – her own bloody half-brother. He could be an arrogant so-and-so, always getting his leg over with the local girls when he was down here. And Angela used to spend a lot of time with him, always following him around.' He paused before delivering his final verdict. 'I think Jonny raped her.'

At Tradmouth Hospital Nurse Jenny Chang noted the patient's blood pressure and recorded her observations on a clipboard in small neat letters.

She looked down at the small figure on the bed. 'You're doing well, Angela. Doctor will be pleased with you.' She had felt awkward speaking to unconscious patients when she had first begun nursing, feeling that she was talking to herself. But now she always made the assumption that they could hear and told them what was going on around them. Her instinct told her that it helped: a world of silence would be a terrifying place.

'I'm just going to check your drip, Angela. Okay? And can I just have a look at your dressings while I'm at it? Make sure you're comfortable.'

As Jenny Chang touched the bandage on Angela's head, the patient's right arm made a sudden movement. She looked at her face. The eyelids were flickering.

'Angela.' Jenny bent over and touched the woman's face. 'Angela, can you hear me?'

Nurse Jenny Chang's question was answered this time by a whispered gasp as Angela Simms's brown eyes slowly opened.

The news was good for a change. Just as Wesley and Heffernan were contemplating Terry Hoxworthy's revelations, an excited PC Wallace rang from the hospital with the news that Angela Simms had regained consciousness. Wesley suggested that it would be best if Rachel Tracey paid her a visit. A rape victim, even after so many years, would need the gentle touch.

Rachel didn't seem surprised at Terry's revelation. 'There you are, then,' she said brusquely. 'Arrogant pop star thinks he can get his leg over with anything in a skirt, even his own half-sister. Then he turns up in Derenham again and tries to get all pally and act as though nothing had happened.'

'Could she have killed him?' asked Wesley.

'It's possible. And I can't say I'd blame her if she did.'

'We can rely on you to provide a sympathetic ear, then,' said Wesley. 'What about the attack on Angela?'

'It might have been a bungled robbery . . . no connection with the Shellmer case.'

Wesley thought about this for a few seconds and nodded.

'Do you want me to come with you to the hospital?' he asked.

Rachel turned away and picked up her coat. 'No thanks. I'll take Trish with me. I'm sure she'd rather talk to women.'

Wesley, as a mere man, felt he had no option but to agree. He left Rachel briefing Trish and headed for Heffernan's lair, where he found his boss leaning back dangerously in his swivel chair, feet on the desk.

'Rachel and Trish are going to see if Angela Simms is up to answering a few questions. She has to be a suspect, don't you think?'

'The wronged woman getting her revenge and all that.' Heffernan looked sceptical. 'It's possible. But where did she get the gun from?'

'And what about Terry Hoxworthy? He was friendly with Angela and he saw what Jonny did to her and the gun was found in his house. It might not have been Lewis who hid it there. Terry could have killed Jonny.'

'Again it's possible. But was Angela's attacker really after the money in her till? Let's face it, there couldn't have been much.' Gerry Heffernan put his head in his hands.

'We're missing something here,' Wesley said quietly. 'Has Steve managed to find out what happened to Angela's brother, James Simms?'

'He said he drew a blank. But that doesn't mean James Simms isn't abroad somewhere. It doesn't even mean he's still alive.'

'But if he is ...' Wesley didn't finish the sentence. 'I want to do a bit more digging.'

An hour later Wesley Peterson was still looking through his files. The answer had to be somewhere.

PC Wallace greeted Rachel and Trish at the door of the ward and told them that the doctor had given strict instructions that the patient was only to be subjected to the gentlest of questioning, which must stop the moment she showed any signs of fatigue.

Rachel didn't comment on this piece of what she considered to be medical bossiness. She strode, tight lipped, towards Angela's bed in a private room near the nurses' desk, Trish following in her wake.

Angela's dark eyes flicked open as the two policewomen approached. Rachel drew up a chair, introduced herself and smiled.

'How are you feeling?'

'Not too bad,' the patient muttered weakly, almost in a whisper.

'Are you up to answering a few questions?'

Angela tried to nod, but it wasn't a good idea. She winced with pain. 'Did you see who did this to you?'

'No ... I mean, I can't remember ...' Her voice was weak, husky.

Rachel came straight to the point. 'Jonny Shellmer was your brother, wasn't he?'

Angela stared at the ceiling. 'Half-brother. We had the same father.'

She paused and Rachel remained silent, waiting for her to elaborate in her own time.

'My father used to go to Liverpool on business and he had a girlfriend there and she had Jonny. Dad used to bring Jonny down to stay with us in the summer 'cause he wanted us all to be one big happy family. But my mum resented Jonny, although Dad never saw that – he looked at life through rose-tinted glasses, did Dad.'

'Did you have any other brothers or sisters?'

She hesitated. 'A brother.'

'What was his name?'

Another hesitation. 'James,' she whispered. 'Jim.'

'Are you still in touch with him?'

Angela closed her eyes. 'He went away.'

'Where is he now?'

'Dead,' she said quickly.

'I believe you were friendly with Terry Hoxworthy when you were young.'

'Yes.'

'We've just heard that his son, Lewis, has been found safe and well.'

Angela made weak noises of relief, but Rachel knew there was still fear there, skulking in the background like a beast in the undergrowth. But whatever Angela might be feeling, Rachel knew it was her job to uncover the truth. 'Terry rescued you from drowning.'

No reply.

'He told us what happened – about Jonny.' Rachel spoke quietly, almost in a whisper.

A spasm of pain passed over Angela's face.

'You had a very good reason to kill Jonny Shellmer,' said Rachel, watching Angela's face.

'No.'

'Then if you didn't kill him, you're protecting whoever did.'

'No.'

'You've met Jonny several times recently. You visited his house.' Normally Rachel would have been all gentle understanding and sisterly solidarity with a rape victim, but something about Angela Simms didn't quite ring true. 'Why did you stay in contact with him? Why did you keep his pictures in your bedroom drawer?'

Angela was silent. Rachel saw the fear in her eyes as her hand crept over the sheet, searching for the buzzer that would call the nurse. She pressed it and a few seconds later Rachel heard bustling footsteps approaching.

But Rachel had one parting shot. 'What happened to your brother James? How did he die?'

A tall, fair-haired nurse appeared like a pantomime fairy godmother. 'That's enough for today,' she said firmly, giving Rachel a hostile stare. 'She needs to rest.'

Rachel knew she was on to something so she pretended she hadn't heard. 'What happened to James?' she repeated.

262

'He went abroad. He died,' Angela mumbled quickly as the nurse frowned down at them.

Rachel knew then that Angela Simms was a very frightened woman – and it couldn't be the dead Jonny Shellmer she was afraid of.

Chapter Thirteen

My most dear wife,
I return tomorrow but I send this ahead by a carrier
bound for Tradmouth. I was greatly distressed by your
news. Are you certain of the truth of it, for I cannot
believe that he would defile his own kinswoman, his own
sister. Yet would Elizabeth lie to you about such a thing?

I do not think him capable of such evil against his own
blood, but if it is true he shall pay for this dishonour with
his life, and I swear I shall destroy him with my own
hand.

As for Elizabeth, she must go to the holy sisters at
Stokeworthy, for no man would have her as his wife so
defiled by her own kin. She must bear the child you say
she carries in deepest shame, and I pray God to have
mercy on her.

See the priest and ask his counsel. I shall be in
Derenham within two days.
Your husband Richard Merrivale
Written at Bristol this twenty-fifth day of August 1471

Wesley could tell Gerry Heffernan was restless. He wanted
something, anything, to happen. Rachel's report of her interview with Angela Simms had whetted his appetite. Was there
something about Jonny Shellmer's half-brother, James, that
they should be investigating. His life? His death?

Rachel's encounter with Angela had been discussed and analysed. It was possible that she had killed Jonny. But she had kept his pictures and it seemed they had been in regular contact since Jonny moved to the area. She might even have been the person Jonny wanted Sherry Smyth to meet.

And there was the old snapshot Rachel said she'd found in Angela's flat; the photograph with somebody's image carefully cut out, a memory obliterated. He took the photograph he had found at Jonny's cottage out of his drawer and stared. Was the missing boy Jonny? Or was it the older boy, the one he had assumed was James? In the fuzzy snaps it would probably be hard to tell.

Wesley sat back with a sigh; perhaps things weren't as straightforward as they thought. He wanted to speak to Angela himself but, after all she had been through, he didn't want to make things worse for her than they already were. He knew it would have to wait.

It was half past four when he received a call saying that Lewis Hoxworthy was back in the bosom of his family. Wesley, deep in paperwork and witness statements, looked at his watch: it would be another late night; another night when he wouldn't get home until after Michael's bedtime. He was becoming an absent father, he thought bitterly – and that was something he had never intended to be.

He followed Gerry Heffernan out of the office in silence. Rachel Tracey looked up from her desk and gave him a coy smile which he returned, wondering why life had to be so complicated.

On the way to Hoxworthy's Farm they passed the old barn. Wesley thought fleetingly about the huge semicircular painted vision of heaven and hell that had been found there. But there was no time for such thoughts now. They had to discover what Lewis Hoxworthy knew about the gun found in his wardrobe, and about the death of Jonny Shellmer.

They found Lewis seated at the dining table, tucking into what looked like a home-made apple pie. Wesley suddenly felt hungry. Terry was out, seeing to the business of the farm, but Jill hovered around the table like an over-zealous waitress, anticipating the prodigal's every desire. Lewis wore a self-satisfied grin. And why shouldn't he? He was being treated like visiting royalty. But Wesley and Heffernan, seeing the ecstatic relief on the mother's face, understood why. They were both familiar with the phenomenon of an errant child being greeted by joyful, tearful hugs rather than a scolding for all the trouble they'd caused.

Gerry Heffernan sat himself down next to Lewis without being asked. 'We'll have to ask you some questions, Lewis. You know that?'

The smug look disappeared and Lewis nodded warily.

'Your mum found a gun in your bedroom – the gun that killed a man at the Old Vicarage. Want to tell us about it?'

Lewis, whose mother had always instructed him not to speak with his mouth full, swallowed the piece of apple pie he'd been chewing. 'I just found him there ... with this gun by him as if he'd killed himself. I took the gun.' He hung his head and had the good grace to look ashamed.

'Why did you take it?'

Lewis swallowed hard. 'Yossa and all the others were always doing things, pinching things. They always said I was soft ... that I wouldn't have the bottle. I knew the Old Vicarage was empty so I broke in the back and looked round for something to take; something to prove to them that I had the bottle. Then I saw him lying there with this gun by him and ...'

'Lewis,' said Jill, shocked. Gerry Heffernan gave her a warning look. This was no time for parental admonishments to get in the way of the investigation.

'So you took it to look big in front of Yossa and his mates?' said Wesley gently. He looked at the boy and understood. Lewis had never been one of the chosen ones – breaking into the Old Vicarage and taking the gun was his passport to acceptance. 'Can you draw, Lewis?'

Lewis looked surprised at this unexpected question and nodded his head.

'He's very good at art,' Jill Hoxworthy chimed in proudly.

'Can you draw us a rough sketch of how you found the body, showing exactly where the gun was?'

Heffernan looked on approvingly but stayed silent.

'Did you see a yellow sports car outside the Old Vicarage when you broke in?'

'Yeah. It was parked at the front. Porsche. Nice.'

'Is there anything else you can remember, anything you can tell us?'

Lewis shook his head.

'How about telling us why you went off without a word to anyone and worried your mum and dad sick?' Heffernan said. 'And then you can tell us all about the letters you sold to an American gentleman on a yacht for a considerable sum of money. Well?'

Lewis hung his head again, the naughty schoolboy found behind the bike shed by the headmaster. The sullen teenager had metamorphosed into a little boy.

'I don't know why I went off. That bloke on the posh yacht gave me all this money and I thought why don't I have a bit of an adventure for a change, so I went up to Wales to look at the castles – I've never been there before and I stayed in nice hotels, the lot. We never get to go on holiday 'cause of the farm. I've only ever stayed with my aunty in Cornwall and that doesn't count.'

'And you never thought to let your mum and dad know you were safe?'

Lewis glanced at his mother. 'I never thought. They're always busy with the farm and that – I never thought they'd be worried.'

'Of course we were worried.' Jill was close to tears. 'We were worried sick.'

There was an awkward pause, and Lewis pushed what remained of his apple pie around his plate.

'How much money have you got left, Lewis?' Wesley asked.

Lewis shrugged his shoulders. 'Not much. I didn't know hotels were so dear,' he mumbled, avoiding Wesley's eyes.

'Where did you find the letters you sold?'

'In the old barn – in a tin box behind that horrible painting propped up in the hayloft. There were thirteen old letters – fifteenth-century. I copied them out before I sold them. I reckon they were written by those people who've got that big grave in the church. The Merrivales. They're digging up their old house near the church, you know.'

Wesley leaned forward. 'And what did the letters say?'

Lewis delved into his trouser pocket and produced a few crumpled sheets of paper. He handed them to Wesley. 'Keep those, if you like. I've got another copy.' The bravado was gradually seeping back into his voice.

'If you're so interested in history, why don't you go and help out at the dig?' said Wesley helpfully. 'A friend of mine's in charge, so I could put in a word ...'

Lewis looked tempted for a few seconds, then shook his head.

Wesley put the copies of the letters in his pocket and looked at Lewis, who was stuffing a chocolate bar into his mouth, watched by his doting mother. He took a deep breath. There was another question he wanted to ask.

'On the Wednesday afternoon, before you broke into the Old Vicarage, did you see anyone around? Your dad says you were helping to clear out the old barn. Did you see anyone passing in a car ... or perhaps someone on foot taking a short cut back to the village? Anyone at all?'

'No.'

Wesley looked him in the eye and he looked away. Lewis Hoxworthy was not a very good liar.

Wesley wanted to talk to Terry Hoxworthy again while the questions were fresh in his mind. He hadn't told them everything at their last meeting, he was certain of that. There was more he could reveal about that distant August thirty-five years ago.

Gerry Heffernan walked silently by his side away from the farmhouse. Lewis had confirmed Paul Heygarth's account of exactly how the body was found, and it looked more and more as if Heygarth had been telling the truth. They would have to look elsewhere for Jonny Shellmer's killer.

They found Terry outside the new barn. He looked up nervously as they approached, as though he had other things on his mind than Lewis's homecoming.

'Can we have a word, Mr Hoxworthy?' Heffernan began.

Terry nodded. He could hardly refuse.

'How well did you know Jonny Shellmer?' There was no more time for the niceties.

'I told you, he was Angela's half-brother. He used to come down to stay during the summer when we were kids. I hardly knew him at all.'

'Is there anything else you can tell us? Anything at all?' said Wesley gently. 'What about Angela Simms's family? How did they react to her suicide attempt?'

Terry hesitated. 'All families have their secrets and I suppose the Simms were just a bit worse than most. They swept the whole thing under the carpet, I reckon, and hoped it'd go away. Only things like that never go away, do they? Look, I don't know anything for definite. I can only guess what really went on.'

'What happened when Jonny left that summer?'

'I don't remember much about it. I only remember going round to the Simms's house one day and overhearing Angela's mother saying Jonny was a liar and that Angela was covering up for him. Of course, I didn't know what it meant at the time, but I put two and two together later on. Then Jonny left and never came back.'

'And what about Angela? What happened to her after that?'

'Angela's always been a bit ... I think odd's the only word I can think of ... or fey, sort of not quite with us, if you know what I mean. She started her angel shop with the money her dad left her when he died, and she's never had a boyfriend or anything like that, even though she isn't bad looking.' He blushed. 'I've always kept an eye on her. I don't know why, but I've always felt a bit responsible. I'd go round to her place every so often and meet her for a drink sometimes. Not that Jill understands. I don't always tell her if I'm seeing Angela – she'd get the wrong idea.'

'Did Angela mention Jonny coming back to the area? Did she say she'd seen him?'

'Before he died I hadn't seen her for a month or so and it wasn't until he was shot that she got in touch with me again. She was really upset, but she didn't confide in me or anything like that. She never even mentioned Jonny's name.' He thought for a moment. 'Something in the local paper upset her. There was a picture of that ugly great painting they found in my old barn, and when she saw that she asked me to meet her in the Red Bull ... said she needed to see me. We had a drink and then we went for a walk. She began to cry, and then she told me that ... whatever had happened had happened in the hayloft and she'd seen the picture then ... all the devils and that. She said it brought it all back.'

'And she didn't mention calling on Jonny?'

Terry shook his head.

'What about Angela's brother James?'

Terry thought for a moment. 'He went away soon after Jonny left and we never heard from him again, so I've no idea what became of him. I was fifteen when he went and he'd have been about eighteen, so I doubt if we'd recognise each other even if he stood right in front of me.'

'Didn't you think that was strange, him going off like that?' Heffernan asked.

'Not really. The Simmses were a strange family – not like our conventional set-up. The father had another woman up in Liverpool and, as far as I can see, the mum was expected to accept that – and Jonny coming down and reminding her every summer. I think Angela's dad considered himself a bit of a bohemian, a free spirit. The trouble was that her mum didn't see things in quite the same way. I'm sure she resented Jonny.'

'What was James like?'

'He was a big-headed, arrogant sod. He used to go to some drama group in Tradmouth and word had it that he was a very good actor, but I don't know. I don't remember that much about him.'

'What do you think happened to Angela the day you rescued her?'

Terry thought for a while. 'I think she was probably messing around with Jonny in our barn and he did something . . . perhaps he attacked her. Or perhaps it was just a bit of horseplay that got out of hand.'

'Maybe we should ask her outright instead of pussyfooting around,' said Heffernan bluntly.

'No. I think you should leave her alone. I tried to ask her years ago and she just clammed up . . . went all withdrawn. You don't know what harm you might be doing if you rake it all up again.' He looked at the chief inspector pleadingly. But Gerry Heffernan wasn't going to promise anything.

'Jonny became pretty famous. Didn't you follow his career at all?' Wesley asked innocently.

'Knowing what I did about him, I was never exactly a fan.'

'So how did you feel when you heard Jonny was moving back to Derenham and giving money bold as brass to the village hall fund?'

'I was worried for Angela. It was strange – she'd always followed his career and even kept pictures of him. I couldn't understand it.'

'Angela says her brother James is dead. Could Jonny have had anything to do with his death?' Wesley decided on the blunt approach.

Terry pressed his lips together. 'What did Angela say exactly?'

Wesley didn't answer.

'I don't know what happened to James, honestly.'

'Is there anything else you can tell us about Jonny?'

Terry shook his head. 'I've told you everything I know.'

'And about James Simms?'

Another shake of the head. 'For all I know Angela could be right. James might be dead.'

'What if Jonny was responsible for James's death?' asked Heffernan.

'It's possible.'

'I'll get someone to do some more checking on James Simms – see if there's any record of his death,' said the chief inspector, watching Terry's face carefully.

Wesley said nothing. The more he thought about this case, the more confused he was.

Pam Peterson greeted her husband at the front door, holding the wriggling baby in her arms.

'My mum's been,' she said, handing him the baby. 'You've just missed her.'

Wesley attempted to look disappointed but failed miserably. 'Have you given her her Rock Boat albums back?'

'She says we can keep them a bit longer if we like.'

'Good. I want to listen to that song again – "Angel".'

'Getting to be a fan, are you? There's a programme about Rock Boat on telly tonight – a tribute to Jonny Shellmer. I suppose you'll want to watch it.'

Wesley shrugged. He supposed watching the programme would be in the line of duty – but he couldn't say he was looking forward to it.

'Neil called in too. He dropped off a book – said it was some letters he'd promised to let you see.'

'He's a bit late. I've already got copies from someone else.'

Pam smiled. 'I wouldn't tell him that if I were you. He said he'd come out of his way to deliver them.'

She disappeared into the kitchen, leaving him to entertain Michael. But after the seventh game of peek-a-boo, the devoted father's mind was beginning to wander back to the puzzling code painted on the Derenham Doom. He had been rudely interrupted by a phone call the last time he had tried to crack it, but now he was determined to put his theory to the test. He carried Michael over to the bookcase and took out the Bible his parents had given him on his marriage, a gift for his new home.

Tamar. A local river or something else? He could hear Pam humming a familiar tune in the kitchen – 'Frère Jacques' again. He wished she'd choose something else; the repetitive melody was beginning to get on his nerves.

But he tried to block out the sound as he began flicking through the pages – and just as Pam called to say the dinner was ready, he found what he was looking for. He had cracked the code.

He remembered the copies of the ancient letters that Lewis Hoxworthy had given him, and he put Michael in his playpen while he retrieved them from his coat pocket in the hall. As he read through the letters, copied carefully in Lewis's neat handwriting, and compared them with the ones in the book Neil had left, he knew he was on the right track.

If only he could say the same about the investigation into Jonny Shellmer's murder.

Yossa Lang sat on a bench by the river at Tradmouth, flanked by his two cronies, Daz and Mick, who raised Coca-Cola cans to their lips in the fading light.

There wasn't room for Lewis Hoxworthy on the bench so he stood, shifting from foot to foot, hands in pockets.

Yossa kicked out at a curious seagull that had landed near his feet, then he glanced up at Lewis, an expression of studied boredom on his face. 'Hey, Lew. Got much cash left?'

Lewis shivered. It was getting cold now that the weak sun had gone. 'Not much. Blew it all, didn't I. Had champagne most nights.'

The three boys on the bench looked at him, unimpressed, and exchanged knowing smirks.

'Bet you didn't. Bet you spent all your time looking round old castles.'

'I didn't,' said Lewis quickly. 'I never went anywhere like that.'

'Meet any birds?' asked Daz, a gangling youth whose pasty face was decorated with a fine array of pimples.

'Loads,' came the answer. 'They're all over you if you've got money.'

Yossa took a long swig from his Coke can. 'Were you bullshitting about the shooter?'

'Nah. I found it by the dead body when I did that big house.'

'Still got it?'

'The filth took it away.'

'Shame,' mumbled Yossa.

'What does a dead body look like? I never seen one,' Daz said with what sounded like genuine curiosity.

Lewis shrugged. 'It wasn't scary or nothing.'

'What did that Yank pay you for them old letters, then?' asked Yossa.

'Two grand,' Lewis answered. A bit of exaggeration wouldn't do his image any harm.

'And you spent it all?'

'Yeah, easy.'

There was a long silence as Yossa stared at a swan floating past on the water.

'Did you see the murderer, then?' asked Mick, tall, swarthy and the best looking of the quartet.

'Yeah. I got a good look at him but he didn't see me.'

Daz nudged Yossa. 'Bet he didn't. Bet he's bullshitting again.'

'I did. I saw him.'

'Do you know him? Do you know the murderer?'

Lewis hesitated. 'Sort of. I know where he lives.'

'He's making it all up,' Yossa said dismissively.

274

'I'm not. I saw him. Honest.'

Daz stood up. 'Let's go. Coming, Yossa ... Mick?' He avoided Lewis's eyes.

But Yossa was staring at Lewis, an unpleasant smirk on his face.

'Want to earn yourself another couple of grand, Lew?'

There was something in Yossa's voice that made Lewis uneasy, but he answered in the affirmative, knowing that any hesitation would make them leave without him.

'Yeah. How?'

'If you're telling us the truth, it'll only take a note through the murderer's letterbox. Dead easy. Don't be too greedy. Just ask for another couple of grand.'

Lewis latched on quick. 'No way.'

'You're scared. Little Lewis is scared.'

Daz and Mick began to make clucking noises. 'He's chicken,' they chorused. 'Chicken. Chicken. Chicken.'

Lewis's chest began to tighten. He felt in his pocket for his inhaler.

Yossa grinned, enjoying his victim's discomfort. 'Just keep the note simple,' he said before draining his can. 'Just put something like ... "I saw you".'

He saw the fear in Lewis's eyes.

'And if you don't get the money we'll know you're chicken, won't we, lads?'

The other two nodded and resumed their soft clucking.

'And you know what happens to chickens,' Yossa said before striding away, the hint of a threat in his voice.

The next morning Neil Watson's Mini chugged and spluttered its way to the City of Exeter. Neil was constantly amazed that the faithful old thing kept going. He managed to find a space in a municipal carpark, just outside the Roman city walls, from where he marched briskly through the drizzle to the county records office.

Half an hour later he was gazing at the will of Richard Merrivale. He had read quite a number of medieval wills in his time, and he had always found their hypocritical piety and their desperate last-minute scramble for spiritual merit points faintly amusing. But he didn't feel like smiling as he read this one.

He made a copy of it before he left and walked back to his car feeling mildly depressed. But he told himself he had to look on the bright side. At least the Derenham Doom made sense at last.

He pulled his mobile phone from his pocket and dialled the number of Tradmouth police station.

'According to your friend Dr Kruger, Shellmer couldn't have fired the gun and killed himself, but what if she was wrong? The gun was fired at close range.' Gerry Heffernan leaned over the sketch that Lewis had made of the position of the body and the gun.

Wesley didn't answer. He was thinking. He had watched the tribute to Jonny Shellmer on the television the night before. They had all been there – the great, the good and the bad of the rock music scene in Jonny's time. Liz Carty gave a brief interview and expressed what seemed like genuine affection for her ex-husband. Even Chris Pauling had been enticed out of his rural hideaway to give his own simple and moving tribute. He had been a good bloke, the best. A bit wild, perhaps, but good hearted. And a man who'd rape his own sister? Wesley was beginning to have his doubts.

'Suicide,' Heffernan repeated. 'Could Jonny have killed himself after all?'

'I'm sure that's what we were meant to think,' Wesley answered decisively. 'Until Paul Heygarth went in and messed up the murderer's carefully staged tableau. Jonny was buying a new house, starting a new life. And anyway, why would he do it in a strange house, a house he was thinking of buying? And what about the angle of the bullet hole ... and the forensic evidence that Shellmer hadn't fired a gun. And he didn't leave a note. I think we can rule out suicide.'

Heffernan looked disappointed. 'Shame. It would have saved us a lot of time and effort. So if we rule out suicide have you had any more ideas about who shot him?'

'The paedophile theory has come to nothing,' said Wesley, watching his boss's face carefully. 'And I think we can eliminate Paul Heygarth – no motive. And Hal Lancaster was trying to get the group together again – it would hardly have been in his interests to get rid of the lead singer, and Lancaster strikes me as a man who puts his financial interests first. Also I can't really see Alec Treadly carrying a gun when he went to help himself to the knick-knacks up at the Old Vicarage – and shooting someone who walked in on his little scam would hardly be his style.'

Heffernan nodded. Reluctantly, he had to admit that he couldn't prove Paul Heygarth's guilt – but he had still been charged with moving the body, so that was some small consolation.

'That leaves Jonny's newly discovered sister. Angela Simms.'

'Not forgetting the mysterious James, who may or may not still be alive.'

'I haven't forgotten him, Gerry. I'm just wondering how he can be around here without us knowing about it. Surely, if he is, Angela would know, and possibly Terry Hoxworthy. I suppose they could be covering up for him.'

'Unless he's changed over the years. I've got a cousin who's about three years older than me and I used to hang round with him a lot when we were kids. Then he went to Australia when I was about sixteen and I didn't see him again until five years ago. I'd never have known him. His appearance had changed along with his accent and, unless I'd been told who he was, I could have been speaking to him for hours and I'd never have recognised him.'

'So James could be living around Derenham now and Terry might not know him. But Angela was his sister.'

'And I reckon Angela's bloody terrified.' Heffernan

grinned triumphantly. 'I think we're on to something here, Wes. Let's go and have another word with Angela.'

Wesley looked uneasy. Angela was recovering well but she was still fragile and he didn't want to be responsible for a relapse in her condition. Sometimes he thought Gerry Heffernan had no sensitivity. 'We'll take Rachel, shall we?'

'No need.'

'I think a woman officer should be present while we're interviewing her in view of . . .'

Heffernan looked exasperated. 'Okay. The more the merrier, I suppose. But I don't want any of this namby-pamby pussyfooting around. I want to get the bloody truth out of her this time. I want to get to the bottom of all this.'

Wesley didn't reply. He hurried off to find Rachel, telling her it was important, and soon the three of them were heading off to have a word with Angela.

As Wesley walked the short distance to the hospital he allowed his mind to wander back to the letters he had read last night.

Lewis had discovered the originals of the letters that had been published in the book Anne had found for Neil. The Merrivale letters. Once Wesley had begun to read them, he had had difficulty putting them down. Michael had been yelling and his supper had been congealing on the plate when Pam had finally found him sitting in an armchair, his mind completely absorbed, letters in one hand and book in the other.

For those few minutes he had been back in the fifteenth century at the time of the Wars of the Roses, with a family of local gentry who supported the House of Lancaster. He had read how Richard Merrivale had been injured in the Battle of Tewkesbury when the Lancastrians had been defeated; he had learned of the Merrivales' domestic problems and smiled at the unfolding tale of the obedient son and daughter, Edmund and Elizabeth, and their wayward half-brother John, a fifteenth-century young offender who so exasperated his stepmother that she was desperate to get him married and off her hands.

Then Neil's edition had come to an abrupt halt and he had turned his attention to Lewis's copies. There were two extra letters that weren't in Neil's book: something was wrong, and Marjory was worried about her daughter. Then it had happened: Elizabeth had been defiled, which could only mean one thing in medieval parlance. And by her own kin. He thought of the words on the Doom he had deciphered last night. It fitted so perfectly. And the people of fifteenth-century Derenham, staring up at the Doom, the terrifying depiction of hell dominating the front of their parish church, must have understood. This is what John Merrivale had coming to him for what he did to his sister, Elizabeth.

But was it a coincidence that history had repeated itself in Derenham? Or perhaps the letters themselves had provided the idea. The rape had taken place in the old barn near the Doom: the sight of it in a newspaper photograph had stirred up raw and painful memories for Angela Simms. Lewis Hoxworthy had found the letters there, so wasn't it likely that Jonny had read them and the idea had festered in his head?'

Wesley shuddered, and it suddenly occurred to him that if he had a half-brother who had done that to his own sister, he would feel like killing him. An urge for vengeance was natural. The wayward John had raped his own half-sister all those centuries ago, bringing disgrace on his family. And Jonny Shellmer had raped the fragile Angela, who had been so besotted with him. And someone, possibly the mysterious James, had avenged her.

No wonder Jonny had died, shot through the head as though he had been executed. The Jonny Shellmer thought of with affection by his own ex-wife and the whole pop music establishment was a sham. He was a vicious rapist, an arrogant bully who had enjoyed his power over someone weaker – and worse: he had attacked his own half-sister. Even the great taboo of incest had meant nothing to him.

'You're very quiet, Wes,' Heffernan observed.

'I'm sure those letters Lewis Hoxworthy sold to Hal Lancaster are significant somehow.'

'Why?'

Wesley shrugged. A hunch is hard to put into words. 'I've read Lewis's copies of the originals and there are two more letters than there are in the Victorian edition Neil had from the library. I think the local vicar who had them published left them out because he didn't consider them fit for public consumption.'

'Not much was in them days ... nothing juicy anyway,' was Heffernan's only comment, earning him a censorious look from Rachel.

Wesley continued. 'The last, unpublished ones are about a brother who defiled his sister, which can only mean one thing. Lewis found them up in the hayloft of the old barn, which means Jonny could have had access to them when he was here as a teenager.'

Gerry Heffernan didn't join in Wesley's speculations. He too was thinking, considering the implications of Wesley's words. The trio reached the hospital and made straight for Angela's ward, where they found PC Wallace chatting to an attractive nurse. He stood to attention when he saw Heffernan approaching and relayed the information that Angela had managed to eat something and the doctors were pleased with her progress.

Angela was lying against a heap of snowy hospital pillows, looking stronger than when Rachel had last seen her. Heffernan placed his large frame in the chair by her bed and asked her how she was.

Angela managed a weak smile. 'A bit better.'

'Look, love, I'll come straight to the point,' he began, avoiding Rachel's gaze. 'I'm sorry to bring this up, but we've heard that you were, er, attacked when you were young by the man who was found murdered. You appreciate, love, that we have to ask some questions.' This was Gerry Heffernan at his most tactful, but Rachel, mindful of the official procedure for dealing with rape victims, felt she had to step in.

'It's all right, Angela, just take your time. If you'd prefer just to speak to women officers we can arrange ...'

Wesley saw Gerry Heffernan give her a withering look.

'We just want to know what dealings you had with Jonny Shellmer before his death. We know you were in touch with him.'

Angel's answer was quiet and unexpected. 'He came back. He came to see me ...' She stared into space, a smile playing on her lips. Whatever memories Jonny Shellmer's name evoked, they seemed to be pleasant ones.

Wesley looked at Rachel and noted the surprise on her face. This wasn't what she had expected. He preferred to keep a more open mind.

'You were glad to see him?' asked Rachel with incredulity.

'He used to make up songs for me when we were kids.' Tears began to well in her eyes.

'You were pleased to see him ... even after what happened?' said Rachel bluntly.

'What?' Angela sounded puzzled.

'Jonny. He attacked you when you were fifteen.'

Angela closed her eyes and shook her head. Then she winced with pain at the movement.

'Well, if we're wrong, are you going to put us right, love?' Gerry Heffernan was beginning to lose patience.

'Why did Jonny leave Derenham suddenly and never come back?' Wesley tried.

Angela didn't answer. She turned her head away.

Wesley looked at Rachel. He had to ask the next question. 'So why did you throw yourself in the river? What happened that day, Angela?'

But Angela was staring at the wall opposite, lost in her own world. 'Will you go now, please,' she whispered. 'I'm tired.' She closed her eyes.

Rachel sprang from her seat and Wesley reluctantly

followed. Gerry Heffernan remained seated, looking like a man with unfinished business. But even he realised that it was hopeless. Angela wasn't going to talk.

'What do you reckon?' Wesley asked as they headed back to the station. 'If Jonny didn't rape her, who did? Who's she trying to protect?'

'Or who's she scared of? Poor little cow's frightened out of her wits,' Heffernan observed.

'From the way she was talking, she seemed fond of Jonny,' said Wesley.

'Some women can seem devoted to their abusers,' said Rachel with what sounded like authority. 'It's a known fact. It's all about control. And Jonny had control over her. Jonny Shellmer had come back into her life and was manipulating her so someone put him out of the way to stop him doing any more damage.' Rachel looked satisfied with herself.

'What about this missing brother, James? According to Terry Hoxworthy, he left Derenham shortly after whatever it was happened and never came back. Perhaps he could have been involved somehow.'

'It was Jonny who was accused by Angela's mother, Jonny who was sent away and presumably never contacted his own father again. He didn't talk about the Simms family to Liz when he met her a couple of years later, only mentioning them in an unguarded moment when he'd had too much to drink. His connection with this area wasn't even mentioned in his biography – it actually emphasises the fact that he spent his holidays in Wales. There must be a reason behind all the secrecy. Anyway, the other brother, James, was older – maybe he was due to leave home anyway and never thought it worth keeping in touch with such a dysfunctional family. He probably had his own life to lead.'

Wesley wasn't convinced by Rachel's conclusions. He was thinking along different lines, but he wasn't willing to put his thoughts into words yet.

He began to hum to himself. 'Angel' was an infectious tune.

Neil Watson put his mobile phone back in his pocket. Wesley wasn't there. His news would have to wait.

He strolled out of the wooden shed where the more mundane finds were being processed and stored and looked around the site. The dig was progressing well. They had just opened another trench near what was, in the house's heyday, the great hall. They had another six weeks, but that was no problem, thought Neil with a smile. In spite of the weather they were on schedule: the remains of Derenham's old manor house would be excavated and recorded before the foundations of the new village hall were laid.

He took the copy of Richard Merrivale's will out of his pocket and began to stroll out of the field towards the church. He had to look at the Doom. He had to see whether the final pieces of the jigsaw fitted. When he was certain that they did, he thought to himself, he would try Wesley's number again.

Wesley sat in the CID office going through witness statements. Jonny Shellmer stayed at the Old Vicarage after telling Paul Heygarth he wanted to look round on his own. Had he arranged to meet someone there? He had been shot and his yellow sports car had been left there, only to be driven to Morbay the next day by Heygarth to cover the fact that murder had been committed in the house. It had been dumped in an anonymous multistorey carpark in Morbay – and left unlocked with the key in, providing Yossa with irresistible temptation later on.

The gun was of a type easily obtainable by anyone who was criminally inclined. The car had been left outside and the gun had been left beside the body. If Paul Heygarth hadn't meddled with the evidence, Jonny's death might have been taken for suicide at first glance.

Wesley frowned. The back door had been firmly locked

when Lewis broke in, and Heygarth had said he'd closed the front door behind him. Jonny must have trusted his murderer if he had admitted him – or her – to a deserted house. But how did the killer get there? Did they drive up undetected by Gloria Treadly? Or did they live in Derenham, so near to the Old Vicarage that they could walk there and slip into the grounds unseen?

Jonny could have met Angela there to show her the house he intended to buy. Or Terry, who lived near by. Or his long-lost half-brother ... whoever he was.

He began to finger the photograph that lay on his desk, swathed in a plastic evidence bag; the photograph he had found in the bedroom of Jonny Shellmer's cottage. He hesitated, then he pulled it from the bag and stared at it again, thinking of something Gerry Heffernan had said. Thirty-five years playing havoc with facial features; middle-aged spread giving a chunkier body shape; all added to a change of accent. What resemblance would a seventeen-year-old boy have to a man in his fifties? What ravages and indignities did time inflict on human flesh?

It was understandable that Terry Hoxworthy might not have known him. But Angela had more reason to have his image burned on her memory. The tune Pam had been singing around the house echoed in his head. Frère Jacques – Brother James. But where was brother James?

The telephone rang again and Wesley picked it up. It was Neil, boasting excitedly that he had found something on his visit to Exeter that had brought him near to cracking the Merrivale puzzle. Wesley smiled. Neil wasn't the only one. He knew the truth about Angela and he knew who had killed Jonny Shellmer. He put through a call to London and waited.

Chapter Fourteen

Found in archives relating to the Parish of Derenham:
To all true Christian people of Derenham. Sir Richard
Merrivale, knight, and Lady Marjory his wife, send
greeting in Our Lord Everlasting. Know ye that we have
promised and granted and be fully purposed to find an
honest and discreet priest to sing and say Mass within the
Parish Church of Derenham in the County of Devonshire
during our life and to pray for our souls after our death.
For this purpose we will cause a chapel to be made in the
said Parish Church where our bodies shall be buried
also.

Know ye also that we have caused a great Last
Judgement to be painted for the said Parish Church for
the instruction of all parishioners and to serve as
reminder of the vile sin of our most wicked kinsman who
violated the laws of God and man and who burns now in
everlasting fire, and to the memory of our daughter,
Elizabeth, who died in child bed a month since.

In witness we have set our seals, the twentieth day of
May 1472.

Wesley and a pair of uniformed officers had already visited
the suspect's house but they had found it empty, as Wesley
had known it would be. The telephone call he had made to

London earlier had confirmed that the suspect's alibi was false. He had lied to the police, and the more Wesley thought about it, and the more he stared at Jonny Shellmer's childhood photograph, the more convinced he was that he was on the right track.

He would try the house again later. But in the meantime he would seize the opportunity to meet Neil at All Saints church. He had to return the book of Merrivale letters, and Neil had said that he had found something of importance during his visit to Exeter, the last piece of the jigsaw. And Wesley could never resist a puzzle.

He hurried up the church path, holding his coat tightly around him against the fine drizzle blowing in from the river. There were no lights shining behind the stained-glass windows, and the ancient building looked deserted. He pushed the great oak door and it opened stiffly with a loud creak, as effective as any intruder alarm. He stepped inside the darkened church, and for a few seconds his eyes could make out only shapes and shadows. Then, as they adjusted, he spotted a familiar figure in the chapel on the far side, standing by the Merrivales' impressive tomb.

Neil turned as he heard Wesley's footsteps approaching up the north aisle. 'Thought you wouldn't be able to stay away,' he said.

Wesley thrust his hands into his pockets. There was a chill in the church which he hadn't noticed before. 'What have you found?' He drew the small brown book from his pocket and handed it to Neil, who gave him a sheet of paper, a photocopy, in return.

'I found this in the diocesan archives – it's about the Merrivales having this chapel built and donating the Doom to the church. Interesting, the bit about the vile sin of our most wicked kinsman. I reckoned it must have been something more than parking his horse on a double yellow line so I investigated further.'

'Go on,' said Wesley.

'Have you read the Merrivale letters?'

Wesley nodded. 'And I've tracked down the originals and they include a couple of extra letters that our upright Victorian clergyman didn't think were fit for . . .'

But Neil wasn't listening. He was carried away with his own theories. 'Well, putting two and two together, I reckoned that the most wicked kinsman must have been Richard Merrivale's son, John, and the dreadful thing he did was to rape his own half-sister, Elizabeth.'

'That fits with the names on the painting,' said Wesley, looking at the faded letters. 'Tamar and the other word worn away which seems to begin with A? Having been sent to Sunday school every week as a child I thought it might be a Bible reference. I thought Tamar sounded familiar so I looked it up in the Old Testament: King David's son, Amnon, raped his half-sister, Tamar.'

As one who had never attended Sunday school in his life, Neil tried not to look impressed. Then a grin spread across his face. 'But I'm one step ahead of you this time. I've found Richard Merrivale's will and I know the whole story – about the headless skeleton, the lot – and I can tell you that you're very warm indeed but not red hot.'

Wesley could see that Neil was enjoying dangling the solution tantalisingly out of his reach. 'Aren't you going to tell me?'

Neil hesitated, then relented. He delved in his pocket and pulled out another sheet of paper, crumpled and warm. Wesley took it from him and straightened it out.

'Read that, Wes. I'm going to give a copy to Maggie Flowers so it can be read out at the history evening tomorrow night. It should liven the proceedings up a bit. Will you be there?'

Wesley, who had only just got around to considering their Saturday night arrangements, read the words on the paper and nodded. 'I'll be there,' he said quietly.

The suspect's public-spirited neighbours informed PC Johnson that the person in question might not be back until later that night or even early the next morning. Wesley told Johnson it would wait. The main thing was to be discreet; they didn't want to show their hand too soon.

As there was nothing much he could do until their quarry appeared, Wesley arrived home at a reasonable time. Pam rushed into the hall when she heard his key in the lock and stood in the hall, clutching the radiator, as if warming her hands. Wesley kissed her, then he looked her in the eye. There was a suppressed excitement there: she had some news.

'I'll make the supper,' he offered, surprised at his own recklessness. 'Give you a break. How was school?'

'As okay as school ever is. I'm taking my class down to Neil's dig next week.'

Wesley raised his eyebrows.

'Well, he did offer, so he's only got himself to blame if the little darlings trample all over his precious trenches.' She smiled, a secret smile that Wesley suspected had nothing to do with the prospect of thirty eleven-year-olds frolicking in the Derenham mud.

'Anything wrong?'

Pam shook her head. 'Nothing. Nothing at all. In fact ...' She reached for his hand and placed it on her stomach. 'I went to see the doctor today.' He hesitated, suddenly coy. 'I'm having another baby.' She looked into his eyes hopefully, watching for signs of delight or disappointment.

Wesley stood frozen for a moment. They had had such trouble conceiving Michael that this news was unexpected. He had only just got used to being a father, and he didn't know how he felt about starting the whole process again. But he couldn't let Pam see that he had any misgivings. He put his arms around her and held her, his mind racing.

'Aren't you pleased?' she asked anxiously.

'Of course I am,' was the automatic reply. He forced himself to smile. He'd get used to the idea. He'd have to.

'I know Michael's only one, but they say small age gaps are best,' she assured him.

He'd take her word for it. 'It's great news,' he said,

trying to sound enthusiastic but with half his mind on his workload. Police work being what it was, he was afraid he wouldn't be much help to a wife with one small baby, another on the way and a full-time career. The thought depressed him for a few moments, but then he tried to put on a brave face.

He reckoned they could both do with an evening out. 'Can we get a baby-sitter for tomorrow night? It's that history evening in Derenham. Gerry's singing in the choir.' A couple of hours away from home listening to Gerry's vocal efforts was better than nothing.

'Then how can we miss it? I'll ask Lisa down the road. It shouldn't be a problem.'

'I'll make the supper, then. You go and put your feet up.'

He watched as Pam disappeared into the living room and suddenly felt very helpless against the forces of nature.

Saturday morning was like any other in the CID office. Weekends seemed like an ancient custom from some idealised, slower past, peopled with rosy-cheeked milk-maids and labourers trudging behind horse ploughs.

It was 2.30 when PC Johnson reported in. The suspect had arrived home at 11.30. Alone. The only visitors had been the postman and a red-headed teenage lad who looked very like the boy who'd gone missing – Lewis Hoxworthy. The boy had left his bike at the gate and had pushed something through the letterbox, but Johnson couldn't see what: perhaps it was just an outlying part of the lad's paper round.

Wesley said that Steve Carstairs was coming out to Derenham to relieve him and Johnson sounded happy at the news.

The sound of singing wafted from Gerry Heffernan's office. He was getting some practice in before the big night. The tune sounded cheerful; a bouncy ditty in medieval Latin.

'*Verbum caro factum est . . .*' boomed out Heffernan's baritone.

'What's he on about?' Steve Carstairs mumbled as he swept from the office to take over Johnson's vigil. There was no pleasing some people.

Wesley abandoned his reports and ambled into the singer's lair. Heffernan stopped in mid-phrase and gave a devilish grin. 'All ready for tonight, Wes?'

'Pam's got a baby-sitter so we'll both be there.' He paused, wondering whether he should mention Pam's revelation. He felt he had to tell somebody – and he regarded Gerry as a friend as well as his boss. 'Pam's having another baby.'

A wide smile spread over Gerry Heffernan's chubby face and he grabbed Wesley's hand and shook it heartily. 'Congratulations. Shows you're not working hard enough here if you've got the strength left for that sort of thing.' He emitted a cheeky chuckle. 'Pam okay, is she?'

Wesley nodded. At least someone was pleased. But maybe he'd feel more enthusiastic himself once he got used to the idea.

Heffernan made a quick search of his desk and produced a couple of sheets of paper stapled together at the left-hand corner. 'Look at item seven.' He pushed the papers towards Wesley, who picked them up. They were a copy of the running order for the performance, beginning with monastic plainchant in the bell-tower. Each piece of music sung by the choir followed a reading or a dramatised account of some aspect of the church's history.

'We had a rehearsal last night and your mate Neil was there. He told Maggie Flowers about this old will he'd found and she agreed it should be read out after the piece of drama about the Merrivales. Some people from the village have volunteered to do readings, and look whose name's down against the new one.'

Wesley stared, then he smiled. 'You mean he'll actually be reading out Richard Merrivale's will?'

'Why is that so funny? I was just pointing out that he's

down to do a reading. Does it matter what reading? Anyway, he might not be doing it. I'm going to have him picked up and questioned this afternoon.'

'I think we should let him do the reading. I want to see his face when he sees we're watching him, when he realises that we know.'

Heffernan shrugged. 'Okay. So we arrest him after the history evening if you think it might give us some more evidence against him.'

'It's not that,' said Wesley, almost to himself. 'I just want to see how he reacts when he reads that will – whether he gives himself away.'

'What's in the will anyway?'

'You'll find out tonight.'

'Any news on Angela Simms?'

'She's improving steadily. If she goes on like this she should be out of hospital in a week or so.'

'I think we should still keep an eye on her.'

'Yes. There's always the chance the killer'll try and finish what he started.'

'So you don't think it was a robbery?'

Wesley shook his head. 'That's what we were meant to think, but there's someone around here who's got a very good reason for wanting Angela Simms out of the way.'

Wesley went off in search of Rachel, who told him she'd visit the hospital after she'd caught up on her paperwork to see how Angela was progressing. She would, hopefully, have another word: if she could gain the woman's trust she would be bound to confide in her eventually.

As they talked, Wesley wondered whether he should tell Rachel his news about Pam. But something made him stay silent. As he noted the wisps of fair hair escaping from her ponytail against the slenderness of her neck, somehow he didn't feel like sharing the news with Rachel.

He walked slowly back to his desk with a feeling of deep regret that shocked him.

*

Derenham was a boring place, thought Steve Carstairs as he sat in his car, keeping watch outside the suspect's house. Nothing ever happened there. True, there was a fair smattering of well-known faces who used the village as a retreat from the hurly-burly of the metropolis – and there had been a murder. But now nothing was happening, and if anyone was to ask his opinion he'd tell them that his vigil was a waste of time.

The suspect hadn't moved from the comfort of his own home. He hadn't been spotted through his front-room window strangling someone in full view of passers-by; he hadn't disposed of any dismembered corpses by burying them in the front garden or stuffing them into his dustbins; and he hadn't run amok with a shotgun and massacred the entire population of Derenham.

Sometimes Steve didn't know why he did this job.

He closed his eyes. He had had a heavy night last night, out with Melissa sampling a new club in Morbay; too much booze and a bit of the other. He knew that if he wasn't careful he would fall asleep. But what did it matter? The suspect wasn't going anywhere on this damp, grey day. Steve sank down in the driver's seat and began to drift off into oblivion.

It was only when he heard a car engine revving then fading into the distance that he opened his eyes. He stared at the empty space where the suspect's car had been parked and uttered a string of oaths that would have made Gerry Heffernan blush.

Gerry Heffernan punched his desk, making Rachel Tracey jump. 'I'll swing for that bloody Steve. I'll have him handing out parking tickets in Tradmouth High Street – that's about all he's good for. I only asked him to watch the house and follow the suspect if he went out. Surely that's not hard for someone of normal intelligence.'

Rachel thought it best not to comment on her colleague's shortcomings. 'I've been to the hospital, sir. I tried to have another word with Angela but she still won't say anything about what happened. 'It's funny, she still seems upset about Jonny Shellmer – I don't understand it. And she can't or won't say who attacked her in the shop. She just says she can't remember.'

'It could have been some robber after her angels. On second thoughts ...' Heffernan sighed. 'We'll just have to wait. There's always a chance that our man's cocky enough to think we don't suspect him. In which case he'll turn up to do his bit at the church history evening tonight as arranged. And if he does we'll all be there and we'll pick him up afterwards and bring him in for questioning.'

'Is that an order, sir?' Rachel didn't share Wesley's enthusiasm for things historical.

Heffernan stroked his chin and thought for a while. 'Yes, it is. It's about time you were made to hear me sing.'

Rachel thought it best to say nothing.

It was 5.45 when Lewis Hoxworthy returned from Tradmouth, where he had met up with Yossa.

As he cycled back through Derenham, he stopped for a few moments to stare at the house, wondering whether its occupant had received his note. It wouldn't be long now, he thought, a wave of fear rising in his stomach. He'd soon have his hands on two thousand pounds.

Yossa and his mates had egged him on, saying that it was just a matter of business; buying silence like any other commodity. Easy money was easy money.

Lewis had been careful not to let them know he was scared: one hint of weakness and he knew the torments and mockery would start again.

As he cycled uphill he had the sudden, unsettling thought that the man he had sent the note to had killed once, and that thought brought on a fresh wave of cowardice. But Yossa had pointed out that the murderer wouldn't know who the note was from and would be gone by the time Lewis picked up the money. He couldn't lose. So why did he feel so frightened?

He'd asked for the cash to be left at the old barn at midnight. He had liked that touch. It reminded him of the adventure stories he used to read long ago ... when he was a kid.

Lewis heard a car engine behind him and steered his bicycle to one side to allow the vehicle to pass him on the narrow lane. But it stayed there at his back. He dismounted and pressed his body against the hedgerow. But the car remained there, a great black bulk, creeping after him like a stalking cat.

He felt uneasy and quickened his pace. But as he speeded up, so did the vehicle behind him. He glanced round and saw that the windows were tinted black. It was like a car without a driver. A ghost car.

He wasn't far from the farm gate now. But the engine suddenly revved and a second later a door was flung open.

Then the car turned into the gate and set off down the drive at a sedate pace.

Gerry Heffernan arrived at Derenham church at 6.30, having begged a lift from one of his fellow singers.

A final rehearsal of the more difficult pieces, then they would put on their robes and assemble in the room beneath the bell-tower, ready for their big entrance at eight.

As they straggled up the aisle from the choirstalls after the rehearsal, Heffernan found himself walking next to Nicola Tarnley. She smiled at him shyly.

'How are you, love? Got another job yet?'

'I'm still working for Heygarth and Proudfoot. Jim Flowers asked me to come back. He said that in view of the situation they needed someone experienced to run the office.'

'What situation?' Gerry Heffernan had been talking for the sake of politeness and only half listening to Nicola's answers. But now he gave her his full attention.

'Paul and Jim have had a big row. They used to be friends as well as partners, but Jim found out that Paul's been doing some crooked deals behind his back; one of Jim's friends lost a house because Paul had someone else lined up for it who gave him a backhander. They had a big falling out and Paul's moved over to our Neston branch, so I don't see much of him now. In fact I've been made assistant branch manager at Tradmouth,' she added with a modest blush.

'Congratulations.'

Nicola hesitated, wondering whether it was the right time to say what was really on her mind, to ask the question that had been causing her sleepless nights. 'Look, er, Gerry, I've been really worried about whether I'm going to be prosecuted about helping Paul . . .'

'Not up to me, I'm afraid, love. Heygarth will definitely get done for it but . . .' He looked at the young woman's face and felt sorry for her. She'd done something really stupid for a man she was besotted with; made a daft mistake. But it was out of his hands now, and it wasn't impossible that Nicola Tarnley would be the owner of a criminal record. There was nothing he could say that would make her feel better. 'Sorry love,' he muttered.

To Heffernan's relief they became separated in the tower-room crush and he had far too much to occupy him to think about what Nicola had told him. But he filed it away at the back of his mind for future reference.

The church was in darkness when the plainchant, redolent of ancient cloisters, drifted through the tower-room door. Wesley shuddered. He hadn't expected Derenham's history evening to be quite so atmospheric. Pam reached for his hand and squeezed it. He hadn't told her that he was on duty, and didn't intend to until it was absolutely necessary.

A sudden shaft of light illuminated the lectern at the front of the church. Jeremy Sedley was standing there looking over the audience, glasses perched on the end of his nose: Sedley was playing a new role, that of the learned historian, and the performance was every bit as convincing as his numerous TV roles.

He began, reading from the script but sounding as though he were an expert on church history, outlining how the church had been built in the eleventh century on the site of an earlier Saxon structure of which nothing remained. There was no record of the date of the tower, he said regretfully, but the majority of the towers in Devon churches were built as strongholds and places of safety in the reigns of Richard the Lionheart and his weaselly brother, King John. Then the church had been reconstructed in the fourteenth century – bigger and better and a real status symbol for the village of Derenham.

Wesley listened, impressed, and craned his neck to look at the front pew, where various readers were sitting, ready to do their bit. A fair smattering of celebrities had volunteered. Another actor whose face was familiar from the television, a tall, thin weatherman and a well-known author whose face Wesley recognised from TV arts programmes. All doing their bit for the village hall. Wesley wondered whether Jonny Shellmer would have been among their number if he had lived. Probably not, he thought.

The lights dimmed again and the tower-room doors swung open. Two lines of flickering candles emerged, heading slowly for the church's east end. Sedley announced that at Candlemas each year the medieval villagers of Derenham would have processed around the church, carrying candles and singing. Taking their cue, the choir burst into the catchy little medieval number Gerry Heffernan had been singing around the office. Pam started tapping her feet. The tune was infectious, and Wesley suspected that it would be going around their heads that night, keeping them awake.

Then, as the choir shuffled to their seats in the chancel, a figure flitted down the aisle, scurrying to the front of the church and sitting down in the front pew, where the other readers shifted up to make room for him. Wesley turned round. Steve was seated in a pew near the main door; Rachel, Trish and Paul Johnson sat beside him. Rachel caught Wesley's eye. They were ready as soon as he gave the signal.

The story of the Merrivales was next on the agenda. To Wesley's surprise, it was Neil Watson, dressed in clean sweatshirt and jeans, who replaced Sedley at the front of the church. Pam gave Wesley a hefty nudge and both leaned forward, fascinated to see how Neil would tackle the job. As far as Wesley was aware, he didn't know one end of a church from the other – unless he was digging it up.

Neil took a deep breath and began. 'At the time of the Wars of the Roses in the fifteenth century, when England was split by civil war between the supporters of the House of York and those of the House of Lancaster, the Merrivales were lords of the manor of Derenham. A family of minor Devon gentry, they were supporters of the powerful Courtenays, the Earls of Devon, who in turn were great supporters of the House of Lancaster.' He paused, looking at his audience. 'My team have discovered what we believe to be the Merrivales' manor house in a field just two hundred yards from this very spot. The new village hall is to be built on the site as soon as we have finished our excavation.'

'Get on with it,' thought Wesley, watching his quarry. Interesting though he found Neil's musings on medieval life, he wanted to get this over with.

All of a sudden a spotlight flashed on in the north aisle, bathing the Doom, which up to now had been in darkness, in brilliant light. There was a shuffling in the pews as the audience craned to see it. Some gasped. Most just stared.

'This Doom, discovered in a nearby barn, was painted for the church on the orders of Richard Merrivale, who is buried in his family's chapel. When I first investigated the story behind this strange commission, and its link to a grisly find we made during our dig, I concluded that the decapitated skeleton we found was none other than John,

Richard's elder son, who was accused of raping his half-sister, Elizabeth.'

There were a few mutters from the older members of the audience, who thought that incest and rape were hardly suitable topics to be discussed at such an event.

But Neil had no such inhibitions. He carried on regardless. 'The skeleton we found had been beheaded and buried in what was probably the manor house garden. When Richard died without heirs, he ordered that his house be destroyed, and indeed we found evidence that it had been burned to the ground. According to Richard's letters, Elizabeth was sent to a convent, where she died giving birth to John's child. Or at least, that is what I thought until I found the last piece of the jigsaw puzzle that completed our picture of the fall of the house of Merrivale.'

Wesley glanced at Pam, who was watching Neil with admiration. He was doing a good job. But he focused his eyes on the great eagle lectern, where the appointed readers, famous and not so famous, were taking it in turns to read out various interesting snippets and documents concerning the church's history.

The next reader approached the lectern, climbed the single step then looked down at the sheet of paper set out by the previous reader. His performance would be unrehearsed, but the reader hadn't anticipated that this would be a problem.

'The Last Will and Testament of Richard Merrivale.' The reader spoke confidently at first, then began to hesitate. Then, obviously deciding it was better to get the thing over and done with, he rushed to the end, as if he hoped that nobody would be listening very carefully to what was being read.

But Wesley Peterson was listening. He watched the reader's face, noting every nuance, every stumble, every mumble of the painful words. Then he turned round and caught Rachel's eye. She gave him an imperceptible smile which said it all. Guilt confronted by guilt. The oldest trick in the book.

He looked at Pam and felt a sudden pang of conscience. He'd have to leave her to drive home alone. He would be otherwise engaged after the history evening was ended.

Wesley sat quite still as the story of Derenham church moved on through the centuries, but he was only half listening to the narrative and the accompanying music. He was watching and waiting, impatient to get the arrest over with and haul his quarry off to Tradmouth for questioning.

The choir sang their last piece and the audience burst into polite applause, which was only interrupted when Maggie Flowers stood up to thank all those involved and to say that the evening had raised over five hundred pounds for the village hall fund. Neil Watson lurked near the pulpit, looking as if he would be first off the starting blocks in any dash down the aisle and into the Red Bull.

Wesley noticed that Maggie Flowers had gravitated to the front pews to chat with the assembled readers, but Jim Flowers was pointedly ignoring his wife while she sucked up to the village celebrities. He was a man with other things on his mind.

Gerry Heffernan lumbered down the chancel steps to join the rest of his team, who were standing near the door, watching as people began to drift out of the church towards home or the inviting open fires of the Red Bull.

Wesley noticed that Jim Flowers was staring at Heffernan and he nudged his boss, who turned round. 'Leave him.' Heffernan mumbled, turning back. 'Is that door the only way out?'

'There's another door in the bell-tower but I think it's locked.'

'He's started to move.'

They heard a new piece of music, a jaunty electronic rendition of the 'Ride of the Valkyries' – Gerry Heffernan's mobile phone. He flushed red and answered it. After a brief conversation he turned to Wesley.

'Lewis Hoxworthy's gone walkabout again. He promised his parents he'd be back home by six, and when he hadn't got back at eight-thirty they reported him missing. They've spoken to Yossa, who said he left him in Tradmouth at five – Lewis said he was going straight home.'

'So what shall we do about it?' Wesley asked. With their suspect on the move, they hardly had time to concern themselves with wayward teenagers.

'The lad's probably got a taste for travel – he'll have taken off again. We'll catch up with him. But first things first, eh?'

They turned and watched as their quarry began to stroll down the aisle. The will had unsettled him for a while, but now he had regained his composure. His eyes were on the doorway as he walked.

Heffernan nodded to Rachel, who began to move from her seat. Steve and the others followed. They would head him off discreetly and ask him to go with them to the station to answer a few questions. Rachel had rehearsed it in her head a thousand times during the evening – as history wasn't really her thing, she had thought of little else.

But the suspect didn't turn left towards the main door as they had expected. He was heading for the tower room.

It was Steve who moved first, hustling Rachel out of the way, and soon he was half walking, half running towards the back of the church, like a hunting-dog with the fox in its sights. He pushed past restless children and elderly matrons in his single-minded pursuit of his man. His quarry disappeared through the door leading to the room below the church tower, but when he reached the spot a few seconds later Steve found that the room was empty.

He turned round and saw that the others were closing in on him. But this one would be his. He'd show them all he could do the job as well as Rachel Tracey. He fought with billowing red velvet curtains and discovered that they concealed a great oak door which led outside. He tried it and found it unlocked.

He hurried out and heard a voice behind him shouting for

him to wait. But there was no way he was going to let Rachel take the credit this time: this was his collar. He ran out into the churchyard just in time to see the lights of a large vehicle disappearing down the lane.

He could hear footsteps behind him and DCI Heffernan's booming voice calling his name. They were gaining on him.

The worn stone path seemed longer now, and it was littered with people who seemed determined to impede his progress. As Steve ran he could hear his own heart beating in his ears as he panted for breath, and his legs felt as if they were weighed down with lead, heavier with each step. He was unfit, out of condition. He could hear footsteps behind him, but he would be the one to make the arrest. He had to make it to the car. He had to follow.

He made for the lychgate standing open ahead of him. This was his chance to be a hero for the first time in his life. This was why he had joined the police force – not to attend racism and sexism awareness seminars and fill in forms. This was dangerous and real.

He leapt into his car and took off at speed, leaving his colleagues staring at his disappearing exhaust pipe. He could see them in his rear-view mirror, climbing into Johnson's patrol car. But he would be there first . . . wherever 'there' was.

Steve rounded a bend and saw the red tail-lights of a large car ahead of him. He smiled as it turned into the long track which he knew led to Hoxworthy's Farm. He stopped his car and got out, closing the door carefully so as not to be heard. Then he scurried up the track, flattening himself against the hedgerow.

As he reached the dark bulk of the old barn, he saw a large four-wheel-drive vehicle parked in front of the building. A shadowy figure was leaning into the boot, reaching inside and pulling out an object. A box? Steve strained to see but couldn't quite make it out. The barn door opened and closed again quickly. The figure had disappeared.

Steve heard a car approaching slowly with purring

engine and creeping tyres. He darted over to the barn door and pushed at it gently until it was open just wide enough for him to see inside.

A man's voice was speaking softly. 'They'll think you were in here messing about. Lads your age can be careless with matches ... they do something stupid then ...'

Steve held his breath, standing quite still. The suspect had someone in there with him. Lads your age ... Lewis Hoxworthy? It was time he showed himself, caught his quarry off his guard ... made his arrest. He pushed the door open farther but the hinges creaked angrily. Steve froze.

The voice again. 'What was that?'

'It'll be my dad. He'll be looking for me. Dad!' a young voice called out in panic. 'Dad!'

The boy's cry stopped suddenly, as though he had somehow been gagged.

Steve heard the noise of a car door slamming behind him. He turned round. The patrol car was there, the DCI and Rachel had just climbed out of the back and DI Peterson was still in the front with Johnson. The track was blocked. There was nowhere to escape to now.

Steve could hear a shuffling sound in the barn and a smell reached his nostrils; the smell of petrol. It was time to go in. The others were moving silently towards him. He glanced round at Gerry Heffernan, who gave him a nod.

'Go, go, go!' Steve shouted, just like he'd seen on the telly. He barged in and looked around the barn. He couldn't see anybody there at first, then he raised his eyes to the hayloft.

'Bloody hell,' Heffernan growled behind him. He sniffed the air.

'Petrol,' said Wesley quietly. 'He's going to burn this place to the ground.'

'Lewis Hoxworthy's up there,' said Steve, taking off his jacket.

He looked up. A big figure, tall with the profile of a

hawk, stood above him in the hayloft, silhouetted against the light of an electric lantern. Steve tried to sound authoritative. 'If I were you I'd come quietly, sir.'

The figure froze.

'You were talking to someone. Who's up there with you?'

Silence. Steve began to walk towards the hayloft ladder, reciting the familiar words of the caution. 'You do not have to say anything. But it may harm your defence if you do not mention, when questioned, something which you later rely on in court. Anything you do say may be given in . . .'

Wesley caught his arm. 'Be careful.'

But Steve shook him off and began to climb the ladder. Wesley followed; he could see the outline of the man standing at the top, looking round for an escape route that didn't have police officers crawling all over it.

As Steve reached the top of the ladder, a leather-soled shoe made violent contact with his hand. But in spite of the sudden pain, he knew he couldn't let go. He made a grab at the ankles but they evaded his grasp.

Then the figure sprang forward like a lion leaping on its prey. Steve, unprepared, made another feeble grab at the feet and ankles, but the legs kicked him off. He began to lose his balance. He had underestimated his opponent's strength and was paying for his mistake.

Steve's hands grasped at air as they searched for something solid. He knew he had to fight back.

And when he lost his footing he let out a scream and hung on for dear life.

The figure crouched against the back wall of the barn like a hunted animal. Wesley took Steve's place on the ladder, reaching the top unchallenged and glad to get his feet onto the solid hayloft floor. He saw his quarry in the torchlight. The man who had put fear into the hearts of the great and good of the public world was watching him, cunning and defiant.

He glanced down at his colleagues, his back-up. Steve was standing next to Rachel, examining his hands and groaning. The others were looking on anxiously, ready to spring to his aid. He turned his attention to the scene in front of him.

Lewis Hoxworthy was sitting on the floor a few feet away, trussed with rope, a rag stuffed into his mouth. The smell of petrol was stronger now, and Wesley's chest tightened. A can stood next to Lewis, its cap missing and its contents scattered on the dusty, hay-strewn floor.

Jack Cromer straightened himself up, looked Wesley in the eye and smiled, taking a silver cigarette lighter from his pocket.

Wesley reached his hand out to Cromer. 'Give me the lighter,' he said softly.

Gerry Heffernan had made it to the top of the ladder. He moved forward to Wesley's side and both men held their breath and waited. Jack Cromer had a choice. Life or death.

Chapter Fifteen

23rd May in the eleventh year of the reign of King Henry VII (1496)

I, Richard Merrivale, being sick in body but of good mind and perfect memory, do ordain and make this my last will and testament.

First I bequeath my soul to Almighty God my Maker and my body to be buried in the church at Derenham next to my late wife, Marjory, our daughter, Elizabeth, and my son, John, died of the fever in his twenty-third year, in our chapel there, and I leave ten pounds for Masses to be said for my soul and for the souls of my wife and the said children.

After my death my house is to be destroyed and the land never built upon. I confess now before my Maker that when I discovered my son, Edmund, had violated his sweet sister, I struck his head from his body with my sword and buried his remains in the garden of my said house. For this sin I beg the Lord's forgiveness and mercy, trusting through the merit of His Son to have my wrongdoings pardoned and my soul saved. But I ask that the said Edmund's bones may never lie in hallowed earth and that the great Last Judgement I caused to be painted for the church remain for ever as a reminder to all of the consequences of lust and evil.

My other goods and monies I give in equal portions

to the church at Derenham and the poor of the parish.

In witness thereof I set to my hand and seal the day and year above written.

Wesley watched as Jack Cromer was pushed unceremoniously into the police car, handcuffed and humiliated in front of the assembled police officers and the fire-fighters who had been called out just in case.

Terry and Jill Hoxworthy had arrived, pushing forward to take Lewis in their arms as soon as he emerged from the barn. They stood close to each other for warmth and support as they watched anxiously for their first glimpse of their son. He was safe and that was all that mattered.

Wesley spoke to Terry after the car containing Jack Cromer had driven away and Jill and Rachel had taken a shaken Lewis back to the farmhouse.

'Did you know he was James Simms?' Wesley asked.

Terry shook his head, puzzled. 'I never thought. I'd seen him on the telly enough times but ... Of course, I never had much to do with James. He was older than me and ...'

'And Angela never hinted?'

'It was something she never talked about. I think she'd tried to block the whole thing from her mind. When her mother sent Jonny away and he never came back I just assumed ... Everyone assumed ...'

'Why do you think he killed Jonny?'

Terry Hoxworthy shrugged his shoulders. 'Maybe Jonny recognised him and guessed the truth. I really don't know. And I don't understand why he'd want to harm Lewis. What's Lewis got to do with all this?'

'I assume Lewis must have seen him the day Jonny Shellmer was killed and he found out somehow.'

'How could the bastard harm a kid like that?' said the farmer innocently.

'How is Lewis?' Wesley asked.

'He's young. He'll get over it,' said Terry with brittle confidence. 'It'll be something to boast to his mates about.'

Wesley said nothing, but he feared that the Hoxworthys' problems weren't over just yet.

Terry Hoxworthy paused for a few seconds. 'I used to like Jonny when we were kids. He was a bit wild, a bit unconventional, a real city lad, but he made the effort to fit in around here. I liked him.'

Wesley nodded. He supposed there was no better epitaph for Jonny Shellmer.

He looked at his watch. Pam had driven off from Derenham church at speed with Neil following behind in his Mini. His powers of detection told him that she wasn't happy that her Saturday evening out had been turned into a full-scale police operation.

But he had no time to think of that now. He had to get back to the station and question Jack Cromer. He climbed into the car beside Heffernan, feeling rather pleased with himself. It was Pam's class's venture into learning French that had given him the final clue.

Jack in England is usually thought of as a diminutive of John. But in France Jacques is James: Frère Jacques – Brother James. And the real James Simms had been sleeping, all right.

Later that evening Cromer sat across the table from them in the interview room, his eyes bright and defiant. The man's arrogance shone out, and Wesley found himself resisting an urge to wipe the self-satisfied smirk off his face. But the fact that Cromer's expensive solicitor was sitting beside him was enough to make the police watch their ps and qs.

Ignoring the solicitor's advice to stay silent, Cromer recited the history of his crimes with something approaching pride; not a hint of remorse. After a heavy lunch-time drinking session in the Red Bull one sultry summer back in the 1960s, he had found himself alone in the Hoxworthys' old barn, where they used to play, with his sister Angela, a pretty girl of fifteen with a budding, innocent beauty. A few weeks earlier, he'd found some letters in the barn – very old ones on fragile parchment housed in an old tin box: part of a job lot of supposed junk bought by Terry Hoxworthy's father when the contents of the Old Vicarage were auctioned off. He had taken them away to his room and read them in private. A couple of them had spoken of a young man having sex with his sister, and James read them over and over again; read them while he drank the bottle of whisky he'd filched from his father's downstairs cupboard; read them until his imagination was excited – until he was imagining himself with Angela.

To James Simms everything had been an experiment, an experience: taboos were there to be broken. And what James had wanted, James had always got. Including Angela. The contents of the strange old letters in the barn stayed in the back of his mind, tantalising and arousing. And, unfortunately for Angela, the drink stripped him of any inhibitions he might have had.

It had never occurred to James that his action was wrong, or that Angela might suffer. Nothing and nobody got in the way of the desires of James Simms. This ruthless streak was later to get Jack Cromer to the top of his chosen profession, because to him every other person was an insect under his microscope, an object to be used for his own ends.

After his hasty departure from Derenham, having told his mother that Jonny, the stepson she so resented, was responsible for the state of his traumatised sister, he had decided to remove himself from the confined society of the village permanently and take on a whole new identity, that of a little Scottish boy who had died at the age of eighteen months. It is easy to change your past with a new birth certificate if you know what you're doing. And he had always been so good at acting and mimicking accents.

There followed a career as an investigative journalist on a Scottish newspaper, then his breakthrough into television, where his single-minded disregard for the feelings of others had made him a force to be reckoned with. Then came the day when his researcher introduced him to a has-been rock star called Jonny Shellmer. If he'd known about the meeting he would have avoided it. But it was thrust upon him suddenly, Shellmer being a last-minute replacement for another ageing pop singer.

He had seen Jonny watching him, his brain working overtime. Then Jonny had uttered the fateful words – 'you remind me of someone'. But Jack had bluffed it out, said that it was impossible. They had never met before. But Jonny had an excellent memory for faces and, as the months passed, he had become more and more certain of the truth.

Jack had bought his retreat in Derenham from Jim and Maggie Flowers. He didn't know why he chose Derenham. Of course, it was the up-and-coming place for those in the media to have their weekend places, and the semi-resident actors, author and weatherman had spoken of it in glowing terms. Jeremy Sedley had come on his show to publicise his new TV series, and he had talked fondly of his new home in Derenham: a heaven on earth on the banks of the River Trad.

The people Jack had known from his childhood years might still be there. But it never occurred to him that his new identity wasn't impenetrable. Such was his supreme self-confidence that he thought his return would present no problems. In fact he found it rather amusing to see people he had known; people like Terry Hoxworthy, whose father's farm and barn he had used as a summer playground. It gave Jack great pleasure to nurse his secret; to pass them in the village street and watch their faces as they recognised Jack Cromer off the television – but not James Simms, who had left them far behind all those years ago.

But there was one ghost from the past he couldn't ignore. Local gossip had it that Jonny Shellmer, ex-lead-singer of Rock Boat, was moving to the village: he had decided to leave the bustle of London and settle in the countryside.

Then came the telephone call; the one he'd lied to the police about. It had been no wrong number; the caller hadn't asked for Jim Flowers. It had been Jonny Shellmer and he wanted to arrange a meeting. Jonny was staying in Whitely and said that he would meet him at a property in Derenham he was interested in buying: it was somewhere private where they wouldn't be disturbed. He'd rung on the Sunday and Jack had told him that Wednesday would be convenient. He needed time to think.

For the first time in years James Simms – or Jack Cromer – was afraid. If his past were revealed to the media, if Angela came back into his life like an avenging angel, he'd be finished.

When he met Jonny, his worst fears were realised. Jonny said he'd been uneasy when they had met for the interview; his mannerisms, the way he scratched his nose, his habit of brushing imaginary fluff off his trousers, had seemed familiar. Jonny had a phenomenally good memory and these things were etched on his brain. How could he not remember the boy who'd violated Angela and left him to take the blame and be sent away? Since their meeting for the TV interview, Jonny had made enquiries into Jack's background. He had studied old photographs, and he had become more and more convinced that Jack Cromer wasn't who he claimed to be.

Jonny had told him that he had been fond of Angela and had never forgotten her. He had looked for her and had found her living in Neston. They had been seeing each other, getting on well, although it was early days and Angela was still vulnerable.

She'd kept apologising, Jonny said, for the fact that she had been so traumatised that she hadn't spoken up, that she had let Jonny be blamed. But now she was beginning to feel that, with Jonny's encouragement and support, she might be able to reveal the truth about what happened.

She'd spoken of some old letters that had put the idea

310

into James's head all those years ago – medieval letters written by a family called Merrivale that he had spoken of that afternoon up in the hayloft. Jonny was trying to get hold of them to see if they held any useful evidence. He was determined that eventually justice would be done. This had sealed Jonny Shellmer's death warrant.

Jack had taken a gun he had obtained on some foreign journalist mission with him – just in case. If Jonny were seen to have committed suicide then, even if Angela's story did come out, everyone would assume he had been responsible – just another nasty abuser. It would hit the tabloids for a few days, then Jonny Shellmer would be forgotten under a blanket of public distaste – the pop star who had raped his own sister before his days of fame. Just another degenerate old has-been. He shot Jonny at close range and put the gun beside his body. His car was left parked outside the Old Vicarage: suicide in an empty house. Simple.

Jack had been concerned when the police appeared to be treating it as murder. But he'd kept his head down and stayed away from Derenham as much as possible without arousing the suspicions of his wife, which hadn't been difficult, he said, as she wasn't the brightest of women.

The history evening, of course, had been a long-standing engagement, and it would hardly have been good public relations to have let the village hall appeal down.

And he had had to ensure that Angela didn't cause him any trouble – who knew what ideas Jonny had put into her empty little head? He had visited her at her pathetic little shop, he said with a sneer. He had waited until she was alone and then walked in, like any other customer. The look of fear on her face when she saw him said it all. Jonny had been talking to her.

He persuaded her he wanted to talk, and once they were out of sight of any passing member of the public, he hit her with a stone angel he'd picked up from the shop display. Then he opened the till and took all the money so that the police would assume that robbery was the motive. The blow hadn't killed her, and he was about to finish the job when he was disturbed by someone entering the shop: he made his escape through the back. He should have kept his head and killed her, he said with regret: leaving her alive had been a big mistake. He'd have done Angela a favour really, he assured Wesley, looking him in the eye. She had turned out very strange, very strange indeed. A sad woman.

Wesley looked at his boss and saw the look of disbelief on his face. Jack Cromer had long since ceased to consider those not in his élite circle as human beings. There was no regret, apart from the obvious one that he'd been caught.

'What about the young lad you were going to burn alive in the barn?' Gerry Heffernan snapped.

Cromer shrugged his shoulders. 'I'd seen him push a note through my door. It said he'd seen me coming away from the Old Vicarage the day I shot Jonny. I took a short cut I knew over the Hoxworthys' land. The stupid kid had the bare-faced cheek to say that two thousand pounds left in the old barn would ensure that he kept his mouth shut. I found him and took him to the barn, where I planned to teach him a lesson he wouldn't forget. Boys play in barns and barns have been known to burn down. Problem solved.'

'You'd have burned down a barn with a fifteen-year-old kid in it?' Wesley leaned forward, looking Cromer in the eye, searching for some feeling, some emotion, some regret. But he saw none.

'It would be taken for an unfortunate accident.' He turned to his solicitor and smiled. 'Besides, the boy was blackmailing me. I was doing your job for you, Inspector – ridding the world of a criminal.'

'He's fifteen.' Wesley was struggling to keep his temper.

Cromer shrugged his shoulders and his cashmere jacket fell to the floor.

Wesley looked at Gerry Heffernan, who was sitting beside him, seething. It was time for a break.

Wesley had returned home at three in the morning. He was

due to resume questioning Cromer at 9.30. It was Sunday, so he crept out of bed, leaving Pam snuggled beneath the duvet, dozing until Michael demanded her attention.

They hadn't spoken since last night. Not surprisingly she had been asleep when he had finally made it home. Wesley made his way to the kitchen and poured some cornflakes into a bowl. He took it through to the living room and ate on the sofa. On the coffee table in front of him were two empty beer cans: Pam had had a visitor last night in his absence. Neil probably. He felt a momentary pang of envy which he quickly dismissed as being a product of exhaustion. Then he looked at his watch. It was time to return to the police station.

Bob Naseby, standing behind the reception desk holding a Sunday morning cup of tea, greeted him with a wide grin.

Wesley was about to climb the stairs to the CID office when Bob called him back. 'Nearly forgot, there's a gentleman to see you. He's waiting in Interview Room One. He asked to see DCI Heffernan but I told him he's busy. I expect you'll do,' he added with a wink.

Wesley made for the interview room, wondering who the visitor could be, and he was surprised when he saw Jim Flowers sitting there, clutching a plastic cup which had recently contained the liquid that passed for tea in Tradmouth police station.

Flowers stood up. 'I've come to make a statement.'

'If you could give me some idea of what this is about, sir . . .'

'Four years ago I, er, made a statement to the police.' He hesitated. 'And I've found out since that I, er, made a mistake.'

'You want to change your story?'

'Yes . . . no. I want to add something to it.'

Wesley prepared to write. 'Very well, sir, let's start at the beginning.'

'It's about a man called Heygarth. I was having a drink with him one night and . . .'

Wesley looked up. 'Would this be the night a Mrs Kathy Heffernan was killed in a hit-and-run accident?'

Flowers swallowed hard and looked guilty. Then he nodded. 'Paul was driving. The car was never stolen. I never actually lied. I just said that I was in the pub with him and he left.' He looked down, studying his hands, avoiding Wesley's eyes. 'But what I didn't say is that Paul came back an hour later and said that he'd had an accident and that he was going to report that his car had been stolen and get one of his girlfriends to back up his story. He'd had a bit of drink and he was panicking. I didn't think I was doing anything wrong at the time.'

'Except not telling the police the whole story,' said Wesley, looking Flowers in the eye.

'I didn't want to get involved . . . you know how it is. And I had to work with him – we're business partners.'

'Go on. What happened next?'

'He was going to dump the car and he asked me to follow in mine and give him a lift to this girl's place in Morbay.'

'And did you?'

Flowers nodded, shamefaced. 'I didn't like to say no. And at that time I didn't know anyone had been hurt. I just thought it was to avoid a drink-driving charge. I know it was a stupid thing to do but . . .'

'What has made you come forward now?'

Flowers sat up straight in his plastic chair. 'I've never been comfortable about it, especially when I heard that a woman had been killed. It's been on my conscience, but sometimes it's easier to keep your head down and do nothing, know what I mean?'

Wesley nodded. He knew what he meant, all right. 'But why tell us now?'

'It was Nicola, who I work with – she told me that she knows the dead woman's husband, sings in a choir with him. She said he was a good bloke and that got me thinking how I'd feel if some bastard did that to Maggie. It makes one hell of a difference when you know someone, doesn't it

314

– they're like ... a real person, not just a name in a newspaper.' He hesitated. 'And besides, Paul's just let me down big time and I don't reckon I owe him anything any more.'

Wesley nodded and began to write. It looked as if Kathy Heffernan was going to get justice after all.

It was finished. James Simms, also known as Jack Cromer, was charged with the murder of Jonny Shellmer and with the attempted murders of Angela Simms and Lewis Hoxworthy. Angela's condition continued to improve, and the doctors expected her to make a full recovery. It seemed that she would be all right physically – but Wesley feared what the future held for her. Jonny had made a difference to her life; he had put her on the long, steep road to recovery. But Jonny was gone.

Paul Heygarth had been picked up and charged with causing Kathy Heffernan's death. Gerry hadn't seen him and had said nothing since Wesley had broken the news to him. He had scurried into his office and hadn't emerged since. Wesley guessed that he wanted to be on his own.

He walked to Rachel's desk. 'I'm off to Derenham now to see Terry Hoxworthy. Are you coming?'

Rachel shook her head. Wesley wasn't disappointed. If he went alone he could visit the dig; talk to Neil and find out about his nocturnal visit.

He arrived at Hoxworthy's Farm just in time to meet Terry emerging from the doorway of the old barn.

'How's Lewis?'

'Quiet. I think he's had a bit of a shock ... hasn't moved out of his bedroom since it happened. I asked him before if he was off out to meet his mates and he just said no.'

Wesley didn't comment. Presumably Terry didn't know about his son's feeble attempt at blackmail, and he didn't intend to be the one to tell him. 'I expect he'll be giving you a hand with the farm work,' he said, making conversation.

Terry rolled his eyes heavenward. 'You never know your

luck.' He hesitated. 'What's happened to Simms?'

Wesley took a deep breath and told him about James Simms's confession. When he had finished Terry said nothing for a few seconds. He was still taking it in.

'I can't believe that I never recognised him, that no one realised who he was. Mind you, he was always a nasty bit of work, was James.' Terry held out his right hand to Wesley. He turned it over to reveal a shiny scar running across the flesh. 'When we were kids he held my hand over an electric fire. He would have kept it there only Jonny stopped him.'

'Didn't you tell your parents?'

'Jim wasn't the sort you told tales about, if you see what I mean. There was something about him ... something ... evil sounds a bit dramatic, but I suppose that's what it was. I told my mum and dad it was an accident. If you were wise you learned to keep your head down and avoid Jim Simms.' He thought for a moment. 'And there were other incidents that people talked about. I think most folk round here were glad when he left.'

Somehow this didn't surprise Wesley. That kind of psychopathic behaviour fitted his assessment of James Simms to a tee. It was a pity that nobody had picked up on it earlier.

'Why didn't you tell us about all this, Mr Hoxworthy?'

'I thought he was probably dead. He just looked so different on telly, and the Scottish accent – there's just no way I could have guessed ... Anyway, I hope you lock the bastard up for life after what he did.'

Wesley thought it was time he changed the subject. 'Are you selling the old barn?'

Terry shook his head. 'It's being listed, so there'd be too much red tape and it could take years to get round it. My other barn near the house is nothing special so I've decided to convert that instead. It means we'll have the folk who buy it living that bit nearer, but we need the money and, with any luck, they might only be here at weekends and

holidays. Let's just hope they don't object to a few farm-
yard smells. I'm not going around putting deodorant under
my pigs' armpits and providing nappies for my cows.'

Wesley laughed. At least, against the odds, Terry had
managed to retain a sense of humour.

An hour later, Wesley left and drove the short distance to
the other end of Derenham. Neil would be working: he had
never been one to observe the Sabbath during a dig – or at
any other time, come to that.

Sure enough he was there, squatting by a trench, sketch-
ing its contents. He looked up when Wesley approached,
raised a hand in greeting and carried on drawing.

'I believe congratulations are in order,' he said, grinning
widely. 'Pam told me last night. Good news, eh? Especially
after all the problems you had before.'

Wesley raised his eyebrows. It wasn't like Neil to discuss
such things. He and Pam must have had a real heart-to-
heart over the beer cans.

'You were out half the night so I kept her company for a
while. You ought to watch it, Wes. Women don't like to
feel neglected.'

Coming from Neil's lips this was totally unexpected.
Neil branching out into relationship counselling was like a
bishop singing bawdy rugby songs from the pulpit –
amazing and somewhat bizarre. He couldn't think of a
reply.

'Nearly finished here?' he asked after a few seconds.

'Yeah. Won't be long now. Then we'll fill in the
trenches and the contractors can move in to start the new
village hall.'

'It said in Richard Merrivale's will that he didn't want it
built on.'

Neil shrugged. 'That was a long time ago. His Doom's
going back in the church, so what more could he want?
Mind you, I wouldn't fancy having to sit there looking at
that thing.' He paused. 'I believe you got your man last
night.'

317

'Jack Cromer. He'd raped his sister then tried to murder her, shot Jonny Shellmer, and he was about to set fire to that old barn you're having listed with a fifteen-year-old lad inside.'

'Charming.' Neil smirked. 'I've always thought he was a nasty bastard.' He put his sketch down and stood up, stretching his limbs.

'You got your man too. Edmund Merrivale – the wicked one. What'll happen to his skeleton?'

Neil shrugged. 'It'll be decently reburied, I expect.'

Wesley nodded. He wondered whether to tell Neil about the discovery of Kathy Heffernan's killer. But somehow he didn't fancy talking about it. He'd had enough.

He walked away, the words of Merrivale's will ringing in his head. Richard's last wishes were to be disregarded; the village hall would be built on the site of his house and the son he had obliterated from the earth would have a decent burial instead of being thrown into the ground like the animal Richard considered him to be.

But the Doom would remain. A terrible warning. Wesley drew some comfort from this as he drove back to Tradmouth to visit Angela Simms.

Epilogue

Jonny Shellmer's funeral was a big affair, and the media were there in force, capturing the assembled grandees of pop music on film and video.

Liz Carty had come down from Liverpool, swathed in black. Her son – Jonny's son – was with her, holding her arm protectively. He was a tall, dark-haired young man who bore a strong resemblance to his father. Liz spotted Wesley and Heffernan in the throng outside Derenham church and approached them shyly.

'You got the man who killed Jonny, then,' she said, her eyes beginning to brim with unshed tears. She reached out her hand. Wesley took it and shook it gently. 'I'm glad, I'm really so glad.'

'All in a day's work, love,' said Gerry Heffernan cheerfully.

'You've not met Jonny's son. He's just come back from Canada for the funeral. This is William.'

Handshakes again. William looked solemn in dark suit that he seemed quite comfortable wearing.

'You're not into music like your dad, are you?' said Heffernan.

'No. Actually I'm an accountant like my stepfather.' The young man smiled as though he could see humour in the situation.

'It's probably for the best,' said Heffernan sympathetically.

'I heard that Jonny had found his long-lost half-sister.'

'Yes. The murderer tried to kill her too.'

'I'm sorry. I hope ... I hope she's okay,' said Liz as though she meant it.

'I believe she's making a good recovery,' said Wesley. He liked Liz Carty. Perhaps Jonny Shellmer had been foolish to let her slip through his fingers. There was a lot to be said for the devil – or the angel – you knew.

As Jonny's ex-wife and son disappeared into the church porch, Wesley scanned the crowd for familiar faces. Terry and Jill Hoxworthy had come to pay their last respects to Terry's childhood friend. Lewis was with them, sticking close to his mother's side and staring sulkily about him, as though he had expected a celebrity's funeral to be more fun. Other familiar Derenham faces were there: whether from respect or curiosity, Wesley didn't know.

He could see Hal Lancaster near the churchyard gate talking to some TV reporters, a furry microphone held over his head like a flying rat. Chris Pauling and his wife were with him, along with two other long-haired middle-aged men who were accompanied by preternaturally attractive female partners. Standing at the edge of the group was Sherry Smyth, beautiful in black. They were giving Jonny Shellmer a good send-off.

Wesley craned his neck to look round. Pam had said she'd be there with her mother, who had been a great Rock Boat fan in her day. The atmosphere in the crowded churchyard was somewhere between that of a medieval village fair and that of a public execution. They were there for a solemn reason, but they were determined to enjoy themselves while they were at it.

Gerry Heffernan gave Wesley a hefty nudge. She had arrived. The crowd parted as she walked slowly up the church path. Angela's head was still bandaged but she had made a brave attempt to conceal her wounds with a large-brimmed black hat. He watched as Liz approached her and, after a brief exchange of words, embraced her new-found

320

sister-in-law and linked her arm through hers.

There was silence, then a ripple of conversation. A reporter, followed by a man with a flying rat and a video camera, pushed his way through, followed by others. The whisper went up 'the sister . . .'

Wesley and Heffernan caught each other's eyes and moved as one man towards Angela. Wesley reached her first and shepherded her and Liz into the church porch while Gerry Heffernan gave the assembled media representatives the benefit of his wisdom.

'Come on, you lot. This isn't the time or the place. Leave her alone, eh?' he said, holding up his warrant card like a magic wand to dismiss the powers of darkness, who melted back into the shelter of the churchyard wall.

The sun came out from behind a cloud the second that Pam Peterson appeared. She was walking close to her mother, Della, whose skirt, black to match her jacket, was too short as usual. Heffernan spotted Pam and waved, thinking how radiant she looked: pregnancy suited her. He looked round for Wesley to tell him of his wife's arrival, but he had already disappeared into the church with Angela.

The hearse arrived, laden with flowers fit for the last journey of an East End gangster. Then came an unseemly rush to enter the church. Things hadn't been this lively in Derenham for a long time.

Inside, the organ played, something suitably solemn, and when it stopped there was a moment of eerie silence before the song began and Jonny Shellmer's voice drifted over the congregation. Music from the grave.

'Angel, sweet angel, how good it was before the devil came. Angel, my angel, you were just part of his game.'

Wesley heard a loud sob to his left. He turned to see that tears were streaming down Angela's face. The song had been written for her and she knew it.

Liz Carty put a comforting arm around her sister-in-law's shoulder and Wesley looked to the front, watching the undertakers place Jonny's coffin on its bier.

Then his eyes travelled up to the Doom, which now hung over the chancel arch. He stared at it for a while, and as he stared he was sure that he saw the mouth of one of the angels twitch upward in a smile.

Historical Note

Depictions of the Last Judgement (or 'Dooms' as they were called) were a common sight in medieval parish churches, and were particularly popular in the fifteenth century, which perhaps tells us something about the preoccupations of that society.

The famous Doom at Wenhaston in Suffolk (mentioned by Neil Watson in this book) was painted on wooden boards joined together and hung over the chancel arch at the front of the church. It was whitewashed over in 1549 at the time of the Reformation, as it was considered to be a symbol of superstition, and then forgotten for over three hundred years until it was taken from the church in 1892 to be burned as rubbish. Fortunately, a shower of rain washed off the white paint, revealing the medieval painting beneath, and it was returned to its original place in the church, where it can be seen to this day. However, my Derenham Doom is purely fictitious: I know of no surviving Dooms in Devon.

Devon society in the Middle Ages was dominated by the Courtenay family, the powerful Earls of Devon who owned estates all over the county. The Courtenays were ardent supporters of the House of Lancaster during the Wars of the Roses. Through their influence, Devon became loyal Lancastrian country, and many of the lesser gentry (like my fictional Merrivales) would have fought on the Lancastrian side.

My Merrivale letters were loosely influenced by a collection of fifteenth-century letters written by a Norfolk family called Paston. The Paston Letters give a fascinating insight into medieval life and are recommended reading for anybody interesting in the period.

The years between 1455 and 1485 marked the climax of the long struggle between various branches of the English royal house, commonly known now as the Wars of the Roses. Fighting wasn't continuous and it wasn't a 'war' as we would think of it today, rather a series of battles fought as a result of the dynastic squabbles of the nobility, barely touching those who weren't directly involved.

However, the battles themselves were extremely brutal, not the chivalric affairs of the storybooks. A recently excavated mass grave of those killed at the Battle of Towton in Yorkshire (1461) contained skeletons which had suffered appalling multiple injuries. The Battle of Tewkesbury (Gloucestershire) mentioned in this book was fought on 3 May 1471, and many of the defeated Lancastrians were pursued into Tewkesbury Abbey, where they had sought sanctuary, and slaughtered. King Henry VI's seventeen-year-old son, Edward, died in the battle and was buried in the Abbey's choir, the hopes of the Lancastrian nobility temporarily buried with him.

Even off the battlefield, fifteenth-century England was a dangerous place. Nobody, even the clergy, was safe from criminals. And it wasn't only outlaws and the desperate who spread fear among the peaceable citizens; those in the households of great nobles often abused their position to terrorise their local neighbourhood.

Travel was a perilous business. Margaret Paston wrote, 'I never heard say of so much robbery and manslaughter in this country as is now,' and the Italian envoy reported that 'There is no country in the world where there are so many thieves and robbers as in England, insomuch as few venture to go alone into the country, excepting in the middle of the day and fewer still in the towns at night, and least of all in

London.' However, the Lord Chief Justice, Sir John Fortescue, actually boasted of the number of robbers England harboured, taking it as a sign of the country's great spirit.

Fourteen years after the Battle of Tewkesbury, Henry Tudor, the last hope of the Lancastrians, who was exiled in France, returned to England and defeated the Yorkist King Richard III at the Battle of Bosworth in 1485. Henry became King Henry VII and united the houses of York and Lancaster by marrying Richard's niece, Elizabeth of York. Their son became King Henry VIII ... and their granddaughter was to become one of England's greatest rulers, Queen Elizabeth I.

THE PLAGUE MAIDEN

When a letter arrives at Tradmouth police station, addressed to a DCI Norbert it causes quite a stir. For though DCI Norbert has long since moved on, the letter claims to have evidence that the man convicted of murdering the Rev. Shipbourne, Vicar of Belsham, during the course of a robbery in 1991, is innocent. Despite having a full case load, including investigating a series of vicious attacks on a local supermarket chain, DI Wesley Peterson is forced to at least follow up on the letter writer's claims.

Meanwhile archaeologist Neil Watson is excavating a site in Pest Field near Belsham church. He discovers a mass grave that leads him to conclude that the site – earmarked for development – is one of an ancient medieval plague pit. But, more disturbing, is the discovery that the grave is home to a more recent resident . . .

978-0-7499-3461-3

'Detective fiction with a historical twist – fans will love it'
Scotland on Sunday

A CURSED INHERITANCE

The brutal massacre of the Harford family at Potwoolstan Hall in Devon in 1985 shocked the country and passed into local folklore. And when a journalist researching the case is murdered twenty years later, the horror is reawakened. Sixteenth century Potwoolstan Hall, now a New Age healing centre, is reputed to be cursed because of the crimes of its builder, and it seems that inheritance of evil lives on as DI Wesley Peterson is faced with his most disturbing case yet.

As more people die violently, Wesley needs to discover why a young woman has transformed a dolls house into a miniature reconstruction of the massacre scene. And could the solution to his case lie across the Atlantic Ocean, in the ruined remains of an early English settlement in Virginia USA?

When the truth is finally revealed, it turns out to be as horrifying as it is dangerous.

978-0-7499-3606-8

'A beguiling author' *The Times*